SHE HAD NEVER FELT SO INTENSELY DRAWN TO A MAN BEFORE...

When Tobias leaned his head back against the cushions and closed his eyes, Genevieve had experienced the most dreadful urge to touch him, to stroke him—like some kind of pet.

She frowned, knowing that her feelings about Tobias Rakes were about as far from her feelings for a pet as they could get.

"Good heavens, this is awful."

As if it weren't bad enough having a family ghost trying to frighten Tobias Rakes to death, now she had to worry about her own shocking attraction to him...

Bittersweet Summer

BITTERSWEET SUMMER

RACHEL WILSON

JOVE BOOKS, NEW YORK

HAUNTING HEARTS is a registered trademark of
Penguin Putnam Inc.

BITTERSWEET SUMMER

A Jove Book / published by arrangement with
the author

PRINTING HISTORY
Jove edition / June 1999

The Penguin Putnam Inc. World Wide Web site address is
http://www.penguinputnam.com

ISBN: 0-515-12523-7

A JOVE BOOK®
Jove Books are published by The Berkley Publishing Group,
a division of Penguin Putnam Inc.,
375 Hudson Street, New York, New York 10014.
JOVE and the "J" design
are trademarks belonging to Penguin Putnam Inc.

PRINTED IN THE UNITED STATES OF AMERICA

10 9 8 7 6 5 4 3 2 1

Chapter One

The black surrey bumped along the uncared-for road, through thick woods that Tobias hadn't seen for almost twenty years. He looked around with interest, trying to suppress the twinge of nostalgia threatening to attack him. It was foolish to be sentimental about something that held nothing but painful memories, and Tobias knew it. Still, those memories were all that remained of Tobias's childhood, and he was hard-pressed to keep the faint longing at bay.

"I don't know why you're interested in this old heap, Mr. Rakes. There are much better properties for sale in Bittersweet. Properties that would require less work than this decaying pile of stones."

"I told you, call me Tobias."

"Tobias," Wesley Armitage said obediently.

Tobias Rakes glanced at Armitage, who was Tobias's attorney, and took cynical satisfaction from the fact that Armitage seemed to be valiantly trying to hide his true feelings. What the lawyer really wanted to say was that he considered Tobias a damned fool for exhibiting an interest in purchasing Crowfoot Castle.

1

It amazed Tobias that so trivial a thing as money could influence how one was treated in this world. As little as a year ago, when Tobias was one of the hundreds of penniless soldiers in the Army of the West who were attempting to rid the Dakota Territory of its so-called Indian problem, Armitage probably wouldn't have spoken to Tobias at all had they chanced to meet. That was before Tobias's tibia was fractured by a Sioux's arrow, and before his maternal grandmother died and left him a fortune. He was also sure Armitage couldn't care less about Tobias's near-fatal wound. It was the money that held Armitage back from speaking his mind.

Armitage wasn't alone. Now that Tobias was known to be a rich man, everyone seemed determined to call him a hero and curry his favor. He imagined he could shoot off his army revolver in the Bittersweet public square without incurring anything more serious by way of retribution than lifted eyebrows and behind-his-back gossip.

Which was all right with him. Thanks to that arrow, his military career was over, and it was just as well to be rich if one were crippled. A familiar wash of bitterness made him frown.

"For one thing," he said, resuming the conversation while bracing himself on the buggy seat and trying not to jar his leg, "it will annoy the very life out of my father. The Crowfoots and the Rakeses have hated each other for generations, you know."

"Yes," said Armitage, his tone indicating he was repressing another lump of bile, "I know. Everyone in Bittersweet knows about the feud."

"I'm sure they do." They didn't know, perhaps, that Tobias Rakes and his own father, Ernest, had been carrying on their own personal feud since Tobias's seventeenth year, half of Tobias's life. At least, they would have been feuding had Tobias remained in Bittersweet after the eruption. Instead, he'd spent the past decade and more roaming half the world over in an effort to escape his heritage and his own idiocy.

Armitage sighed deeply. "Well, take a good look, because

if you do aim to buy it, I don't want you blaming me if you have to sink a fortune into restoring it."

"I won't blame you, Wes."

Armitage drove his buggy as far up the overgrown drive as he could, but a fallen tree blocked their passage before they were even halfway there. Armitage glanced at Tobias with some concern. "I fear we'll have to walk from here. Will you be—all right?"

"Diplomatic of you," Tobias said dryly. "Yes, I'll be all right. I can't run and skip any longer, but I can walk." With the aid of his cane and a good deal of physical agony. Tobias felt his lips thin and made an effort to relax them. He didn't want anyone to know how galling he found his disabled state. To keep his mind from his plight, he forced himself to take stock of his surroundings.

Crowfoot Castle loomed up from the encroaching vegetation like something out of an Arthurian legend. Turrets soared and spires pierced the sky. Vines crawled up chimneys that undoubtedly housed the nests of generations of birds. Tobias wondered if the chimneys would smoke once they'd been swept free of debris. Probably. He'd have gas lines run into the old place, and install electrical wiring. No sense living in the dark ages, even if one did plan to live in a castle.

A crenelated wall surrounded the castle and from where the buggy waited, Tobias could barely see the huge stone porch and the enormous double doors to the castle. One could imagine knights saluting lovely ladies. The ladies, of course, would be standing on the castle leads, waving their men off to war.

Theirs would be a noble, chivalrous war. Not the kind of war Tobias had been engaged in, prompted by the white men's greed and the Indians' struggle to survive against a more powerful invading civilization. In Tobias's mind, there was nothing noble about chasing down starving Indians. He also considered that the Indians had been offered precious little justice by way of treaties and payments—which the whites had never yet honored—although he knew he'd never be able to make anyone else understand that. A fellow had to be there in order to understand it, and even then the whole situation had made little sense.

Annoyed with himself for allowing his mind to wander, he studied the castle. Wes was right about it, Tobias owned. But, while it had obviously been neglected in recent years, it could be a stunning building if someone poured enough money and heart into it. Tobias didn't have the heart, but he had heaps of money. That would have to do.

Created from honey-colored stone, quarried locally before the American Revolution, Crowfoot Castle seemed to absorb the summer sunshine and glow at him. The old place appeared almost friendly, for a castle. The word came to Tobias out of the blue, and he smiled because the image was so incongruous.

Contentious old Charles Crowfoot, the money-grubbing Yankee businessman who'd built the castle a hundred and twenty-five years ago, had, according to all accounts, been anything but friendly. Not that Tobias held Charles's lack of congeniality against him. According to those same accounts, Tobias's great-great-great-grandfather, Gerald Rakes, Charles's business partner, had been every ounce as mean-spirited and disputatious as Charles. In fact, they'd deserved each other.

Trying not to grunt with pain, Tobias lowered himself from Wes's surrey, being careful not to jostle his wounded leg any more than he had to. After the arrow had shattered his tibia, his femur had broken when he'd fallen from his horse. Tobias had barely managed to convince the field doctor—and then only at gunpoint—not to amputate the leg. He wasn't positive yet that sparing the damaged limb had been a good idea. Still, as long as it was attached to the rest of him, there was a chance it would heal eventually and allow Tobias to resume some of his former pursuits.

"The grounds haven't been kept in anything like order, as you can see," Wes said, sounding crabby about it.

When Tobias glanced at him, the lawyer was poking at an overgrown lilac bush whose blossoms scented the warm spring air. Trilliums and buttercups and dame's rockets rioted behind what looked like it might have been a privet hedge once upon a time.

Tobias remembered the names of all the flowers and was surprised at himself. His mother had taught him about flowers when he'd worked beside her in her well-loved garden. She'd died when he was ten, leaving him to the questionable mercies of his father, but Tobias still remembered the names of the flowers.

He shook his head and gazed beyond the flower beds to what had once been a rose garden. Unpruned rose branches reached for the sky through overgrown bushes and weeds, and hooked the leaves of unpruned bushes on their thorns. These were pleasure gardens run amok, and Tobias felt somehow akin to them.

He breathed deeply. Yes. Although he knew better than to hope for happiness in this life, he was beginning to get the feeling that, with luck and liberal applications of his maternal grandmother's money, he might find peace here. Even if his leg never healed enough for him to ride again, he could clear out the shrubbery and take long rambling walks on his estate. He'd get himself a couple of hounds to romp at his heels. Hounds were faithful, unlike people. Besides, merely knowing that his father would be home, hunched over his desk in the Rakes's estate and gnashing his teeth with fury, made the prospect a pleasant one.

They walked slowly through the brambles, bushes, and weeds, Armitage moderating his pace to suit Tobias's halting steps. A host of bees busied themselves among the flowers, a regiment of birds chirped from the trees, and Tobias saw a hummingbird dip its long beak into a bell-shaped purple flower on a straggly morning-glory vine. He'd forgotten how pretty the bluebirds were. By the time he and Armitage had walked through the wall's arched *porte cochère*, which reminded Tobias of the entrance to a cathedral he'd seen in France, and approached the stone porch, Armitage had a key out.

"I'm sure all the hinges in this place screech like banshees. Don't worry. The villagers claim the castle is haunted, but I'm sure it's only rusty hinges." Armitage set down the lantern he'd been carrying and worked on the lock.

Tobias laughed. "I'm not afraid of ghosts." He'd encountered much worse than ghosts in his life.

"Glad to hear it." Armitage pushed on the door. Sure enough, it groaned like a choir of off-key ghosts as it swung open to reveal the huge flagged entryway. Armitage stood aside and allowed Tobias to enter before him.

Tobias glanced around with interest. The castle was built on a grand scale. Faded tapestries that looked as though they hadn't been cleaned or dusted for decades covered the walls, and a tattered runner spanned the flags from the front door to the enormous oaken staircase, which divided halfway up into two arching stairways. "Charles Crowfoot didn't spare any expense when he built this place, did he?"

"No, he didn't. And his descendants haven't spared any to keep it up, either. Here, let me light this lamp. It's dark as a tomb in here."

Even after Armitage lit the lamp, the room seemed murky. "It's because all the curtains are drawn," muttered Tobias. He walked to a long window and pulled aside thick velvet draperies, dislodging a cloud of dust and exposing tall, leaded, and very dirty stained-glass windows. In spite of the impediments in its way, sunlight poured into the room. "There. That's better."

"If you say so."

Tobias chuckled at Armitage's tone, which was stuffed to the brim with disapproval. "Lead on, Wes. Show me the many wonders of Crowfoot Castle."

"I don't think there are any."

"Show it to me anyway. I want to know what I'll have to do to make the place livable if I decide to buy it."

"Tear it down and rebuild a decent house with modern conveniences in its place, would be my suggestion," Armitage posited acidly.

"Tut, tut. I think Crowfoot Castle will be the perfect home for me."

With a heavy sigh, Armitage shook his head. "All right, if you say so. Follow me."

So Tobias did.

Genevieve Crowfoot peered around with distaste and thrust
the enormous key to the front door of Crowfoot Castle into
her apron pocket. "Uncle Hubert didn't believe in wasting
money on servants, did he?"

Genevieve's aunt, Delilah Crowfoot, her nose wrinkled
and her brow furrowed, said tartly, "No, he didn't. He didn't
believe in spending money on anything except his precious
books."

"I've never seen so much dust."

"Nor have I. Not that it surprises me. Hubert always was
a mean, tight-fisted boy."

"Boy?" Genevieve laughed. "He was eighty-three when
he died, Aunt Delilah."

"You know very well what I mean, Genevieve Crowfoot."

"Of course I do, Aunt." Genevieve bent and deposited a
quick kiss on her much-shorter aunt's plump cheek. Then
she sighed. "I suppose we ought to get started. The sooner
we begin, the sooner we'll be through."

"I'll be glad to be rid of this old pile of stones."

"Oh, I don't know." Genevieve led the way through her
deceased uncle's dusty, gloomy entrance hall, carrying a
bucket and a mop and an armful of rags and other cleaning
implements. Her aunt carried a lantern. "I've always rather
liked knowing the castle belonged in my family. It's a nice
old place."

"Nice? Humph. It's ridiculous, if you ask me. Your great-
great-great-grandfather must have been awfully full of himself to want to build such a place in America. A castle, my
foot."

"Now, now, Aunt Delilah. The Revolution hadn't been
fought when he built it. New York was a British colony in
those days. I suspect Charles Crowfoot was merely being
traditional, and spent his money creating a grand estate, the
way he might have done if he'd remained in England."

Delilah uttered another *humph*, and Genevieve laughed.
"All right, perhaps he was being more extravagant than traditional."

The two ladies set to work with vigor, scrubbing and dusting and mopping. Genevieve had seldom been inside the castle, her uncle's eccentricity and misanthropy having successfully kept his family, as well as the rest of the world, at bay for twenty years and more. She would be sorry to see the old place sold, and she hoped whoever bought it wouldn't rip it down and build a new house, but would live in the castle. She'd hate to see it destroyed even if a castle was, as her aunt believed, somewhat out of place in the state of New York.

Genevieve herself had always lived in the much smaller cottage on the castle grounds. Originally built for the castle steward, the place had been plenty big enough for Genevieve, her parents, and her aunt Delilah. An only child, sometimes lonely, Genevieve had frequently thought how nice it would be to have swarms of children romping up and down the castle steps and playing in the expansive grounds. The grounds, which contained not only lawns and gardens, but a good-sized forest, were large enough to hold an army of children. She and Benton, her late cousin, used to play Robin Hood and his merry men for hours and hours during the long summers of their childhood.

Not that Uncle Hubert had maintained the grounds any better than he'd kept up the inside of the castle. Cocklebur bushes, nettles, weeds, and brambles choked pathways that had once been raked and graveled and that had twisted through several beautiful gardens. Genevieve, who enjoyed horticulture, would love to get her hands on some pruning shears and have her way with what used to be the rose garden.

She stood up, wiped her forearm across her dripping brow, and stretched the kinks out of her back. "I'll have to tackle those windows later. I'm sure we won't even get the hallway and the library finished today."

Delilah, red-faced with bending and mopping, straightened too. "I'm sure you're right." She frowned. "I don't know if it's worthwhile to spend a lot of time in here. Whoever buys it will probably only tear it down."

Genevieve snorted. "I'd be embarrassed to have anyone

even look at the place in its present condition.''

"Well, there is that."

"And if we can get it looking fairly decent, perhaps a buyer will see its worth and want to restore it."

Delilah said nothing, but Genevieve could tell her aunt didn't believe it, so she detoured to another tack. "Besides, this will give us a chance to go through Uncle Hubert's things and decide what to keep, what to sell, what to take to the poor box at church, and what to burn."

"I'm sure Hubert never had anything *I'd* want to keep."

"You didn't like your older brother much, did you, Aunt Delilah?"

Genevieve wasn't surprised to see a guilty expression settle over her aunt's gentle features.

"I'm sure that as a Christian woman I loved my brother, but you must admit he was a hard, tight-fisted man."

"You're right, Aunt. It's difficult to imagine the two of you coming from the same family."

A noise from the oak stairway made both ladies spin around, startled. Genevieve didn't put any stock whatsoever in rumors about the castle being haunted. Still, it was a huge, gloomy old place, made more gloomy by what seemed like centuries' worth of dust and decrepitude, grime, and cobwebs clinging to its walls, floors, and furnishings. She pressed a hand to her pounding heart. "My goodness, I do believe the spooky atmosphere in here is getting to me."

"It got to me before we even opened the door," Delilah said darkly. "Although, it's probably only remnants of Hubert's personality cleaving to the stones. He never wanted to part with anything at all, much less his life."

Genevieve gazed at her aunt with real appreciation. "You have a poetic streak a mile wide in you, Aunt Delilah. Did you know that?"

Delilah blushed. "Nonsense!" But Genevieve could tell she was pleased.

The noise came again, this time louder. Then Genevieve heard a voice.

"I don't know, Wes. I think the place has charm."

"Charm! Rats I'm sure it has. But charm?"

Genevieve almost dropped her mop when two men appeared at the top of the landing where the stairway divided. Delilah gasped and clutched Genevieve's arm, her fingers digging in like pincers. Genevieve recovered first.

"Who are you?" she inquired sharply. Then she recognized Wesley Armitage and let out a huge gust of breath. "Oh, Mr. Armitage! I didn't know you were planning to drive out here today. You gave us such a start."

"Miss Crowfoot." Armitage smiled broadly and ran down the massive oak staircase. He held out a hand as he approached the two ladies. "Yes, indeed, we have a possible buyer for the castle. Tobias and I came out today to look the place over."

At this news, Genevieve looked up quickly, and she saw the other man. With a small gasp, she drew herself up straight. Good heavens, what an unpleasant-looking fellow he was. He was tall and broad-shouldered, and he eyed her and her aunt as if he wished them to perdition. Dressed all in black, leaning on an ebony cane, and with an expression sharp enough to chop wood, he looked like he'd stepped out of one of Washington Irving's old tales about puritanical pilgrims.

Noticing her expression, Armitage turned. He maintained his own smile with no apparent trouble, obviously enjoying the situation. "Miss Delilah Crowfoot and Miss Genevieve Crowfoot, allow me to introduce you to Mr. Tobias Rakes."

Delilah let out a little squeak and a breathy, "Rakes?"

Tobias Rakes, a corrosive smile twisting his harsh features, came forward. He didn't carry that cane for looks, Genevieve noticed; he had a distinct—and, she suspected, painful—limp. "Indeed, ma'am." He removed his black hat and bowed. The gesture appeared supercilious to Genevieve. "Tobias Rakes, at your service."

It was not for nothing that Genevieve Crowfoot was well known in the small village of Bittersweet for possessing a sunny disposition. At once, the humor of the situation struck her and she laughed out loud, drawing a sour squint from Tobias Rakes. "It's rather daring of you to venture into enemy territory, Mr. Rakes." She held out her hand for him to shake. She had ages ago decided that a hundred years was long enough for any family feud, and she wasn't about to perpetuate it.

Tobias Rakes eyed her hand for a moment before he took it in his own black-gloved and much-larger one. "Miss Crowfoot." He made no comment about her reference to the Crowfoot-Rakes unpleasantness.

She refused to allow his dour manner to intimidate her, and hence, looked him square in the eye. Nor did she flinch at the frigidity she saw reflected in the ice-blue gaze staring back at her. Good heavens, the man was as cold as Bittersweet Pond in the dead of winter. "Are you looking the castle over for some fell purpose, Mr. Rakes?"

He left off glaring knives and daggers at her and glanced around the entry hall. Genevieve did likewise, taking pleasure in viewing the newly cleaned and shiny flags. The room would look quite nice with a few colorful rugs scattered around and perhaps some bright paintings on the walls.

"Yes, Miss Crowfoot. I'm thinking of buying it."

His words jolted her. "*You're* thinking of buying it? A Rakes?" Genevieve burst out laughing again, but, feeling foolish, slapped a hand over her mouth.

For the first time since she'd first seen him, Tobias smiled. His smile was so glacial, she wished he hadn't.

"Indeed, madam. I am seriously considering it."

"Mercy," Delilah whispered at Genevieve's back.

Genevieve choked back her laughter. Because the answer was important to her, she asked bluntly, "If you do buy it, will you tear it down, Mr. Rakes?"

"Tear it down?" He turned, pierced her with another blue stare that felt like tiny icicles stabbing into her, and lifted a sardonic black eyebrow.

"Mr. Rakes has taken it into his head to fix the place up if he offers for it, ma'am," Wesley Armitage said with a distinct lack of enthusiasm, his smile gone.

"Fix it up?" Delilah repeated blankly.

"Oh, Mr. Rakes, how wonderful!"

From his frigid mien, Genevieve guessed she should have contained her enthusiasm. Then she decided she didn't care if this cold, hard man considered her silly. His avowed intention thrilled her. "I do hope that you will buy it then, Mr. Rakes, and that you'll be kinder to the old pile than Uncle Hubert was. As you can see, he let it fall into dreadful disrepair. Aunt Delilah and I were trying to tidy it up before Mr. Armitage began showing it, although it will probably take an army of housemaids to make it respectable again."

"I should have told you we'd be coming out here today, Miss Crowfoot. I apologize."

Armitage looked contrite. Genevieve, as notorious for her soft heart as she was for her sunny disposition, laid a hand on his arm. "Oh, no. It's perfectly all right, Mr. Armitage. As long as you warned Mr. Rakes beforehand—"

"He warned me." Tobias sounded bored.

Nettled by his attitude, Genevieve said, "Fine. Then Aunt Delilah and I will continue our work." She inclined her head and turned away from him.

Poor Delilah, who never quite knew what to do in uncomfortable situations, nodded as well, and peered with some surprise at her niece. Genevieve imagined her aunt was shocked by her shabby behavior, but honestly! One should be expected to take only so much. If that man wanted to be aloof and unfriendly, so be it. Genevieve had better things to do than try to lure him into behaving nicely.

"Ahem. Yes. Well then, good day to you, Miss Crowfoot." That was Wesley Armitage, who had a manner or two to rub together.

Ignoring Tobias Rakes, Genevieve turned again, shook Armitage's hand, and smiled at him. "Good day to you, Mr. Armitage." And, without acknowledging Tobias Rakes's presence by so much as another glance in his direction, she resumed plying her mop.

She heard the two men talking as they headed to the front door, and she heard the front door open and bang shut as it closed behind them, echoing in the front hall like a vault door slamming. A shudder rippled through her. To dispel the eerie mood engendered by the unsettling sound, she snorted. "Well! If that man buys the castle, I suppose I'll be glad of it because he said he won't tear it down, but I've never met such a reserved, unpleasant man in my life."

"He's a Rakes, dear. You know what they say about the Rakes men."

"I don't believe being a member of any particular family gives one the privilege of being uncivil."

"No, I suppose not. But you must recall your uncle Hubert. If ever there was an uncivil man, it was he."

That drew a chuckle from Genevieve. "You're right, of course."

"And don't forget, dear, that poor Mr. Rakes has an exceptionally sad tale behind him."

"Ah, yes." Genevieve remembered. "Something about a failed love affair, wasn't it? And his father disapproving?"

"Disapproving? I suppose he did disapprove!"

"Hmm. I was only eight years old at the time, and no one would talk about it in front of me for fear the lurid tale might lead me into wickedness." She grinned at her aunt. "Why don't you tell me the story, Delilah? I'm past being corrupted."

"Corrupted?" Delilah clucked her tongue at her niece. "The things you say, Genevieve. Oh, it was awful, though. The beastly man disowned his son. Cut him off without a dollar to his name. And all because the poor boy had fallen in love with a female the old man considered unsuitable."

"The way I heard it, she was married. That sounds rather unsuitable to me."

Delilah sniffed. "Well, perhaps she was. But the dear boy was only seventeen years old at the time. He was only a baby, really, and she was ever so much older than he was."

"Hmm. So you believe the affair was her fault?"

"I'm sure of it. I knew Madeline Riley, my dear, and I can tell you that she was no better than she ought to be."

The expression tickled Genevieve, and she smiled as she dipped her mop in the bucket.

Delilah continued, her sense of injustice giving impetus to her broom. "And even if the poor boy did exhibit faulty judgment, I can't imagine casting off my only child, whatever the provocation. I knew his mother before she married

Ernest Rakes, you know, and she was a lovely person. I'm sure that if she'd lived, she could have steered her son in a more suitable direction. But that father of his was as hard and cold as an iceberg. He was totally unsuited to the rearing of a spirited young lad.''

Genevieve mulled over her aunt's words. ''Perhaps you're right, Aunt Delilah. It's hard for me to imagine disowning a child.''

''I should hope so. You, my dear, have a heart, unlike *some* people I could mention.''

Amused by her aunt's vehemence, Genevieve laughed as she carried her bucket of filthy water to one of the low panels of tall stained-glass windows in the hall. With some effort, she pried up the latch, then pushed the window open and lifted the bucket to empty the water.

When she glanced outside, she saw Tobias Rakes and Wesley Armitage standing in what had previously been a flower garden. Tobias had a hand resting on a stone dolphin protruding from what might have been a pretty fountain once upon a time. It looked to Genevieve as if he were attempting to take some of the weight off of his damaged leg, and she took herself to task for judging him without knowing his full story.

With a sigh, she dumped the dirty water onto the weeds choking the ground below and turned away from the window. ''He sustained a terrible injury in the army, too, if I recall correctly.''

''My goodness, yes. Why, he was attacked by Indians, Genevieve!'' Delilah's voice throbbed with excitement, and she gave an eloquent shudder. ''Can you imagine such a thing? Attacked by wild Indians. I believe it was in some outlandish place like the Dakotas or something.''

''Hmm. Yes, I think you're right.'' Genevieve contemplated the entryway and considered what to do next. They had determined to tackle one room at a time, but Genevieve rather thought she'd had enough of mopping for one day. ''Do you suppose we should start on the library now, Aunt? I'm tired of bending over and scrubbing floors.''

Delilah sighed. ''I suppose that's a good idea. I'm not

looking forward to dusting all those old, musty books, though.''

"Nor am I, but it must be done. I suppose some of them might be valuable.''

"You're right, of course.''

"There might be some treasures in the library. First editions and whatnot.''

"Humph.''

Genevieve grinned. She loved her aunt very much. Aunt Delilah's presence in her life did much to assuage the pain her parents' death had caused. "I think I'll leave the window open. Maybe the place will air out some.''

Delilah made a noise that clearly conveyed her doubt, and Genevieve's grin broadened. "Well, it can't hurt.''

"I suppose not.''

So the two ladies, armed with feather dusters, rags, and tins of furniture wax, entered a room at the end of the entry hall that used to serve as Hubert Crowfoot's library. Genevieve's heart fell when she pushed the door open and surveyed the room. "Oh, my. I had no idea he had so many books.''

"I told you he never relinquished anything, Genevieve. He was particularly greedy about his books.'' Delilah sounded as discouraged as Genevieve felt.

"Well, there's no help for it. The sooner we start, the sooner we'll finish.''

"Yes. Perhaps if you begin at that end''—Delilah pointed toward the west wall—"and I begin at this one, we'll meet in the middle someday.''

Because she was so fond of her sweet aunt, Genevieve kissed her cheek again. "Good idea, Aunt Delilah. And perhaps we should sing as we work. When Benton and I were made to do things we didn't want to do, we often found that singing helped us along.''

"Dear Benton.'' Delilah sighed, for Benton had been everyone's favorite. He'd died of a lung ailment when he was twenty and Genevieve but eighteen, and the family, such as was left of it, still missed him.

Because she knew her aunt had a strong religious streak,

Genevieve cast about in her mind for a hymn, leaving aside those that referred to the Holy Ghost, since she didn't want Delilah's fanciful mind to begin churning over old ghost stories. After a moment, she started singing "All Hail the Power of Jesus' Name," one of Delilah's favorite hymns. It also had a perky, if somewhat martial, tune to it, which added to its charm in this instance. Delilah joined in, and soon the library rang with music. Genevieve was sure the old castle had seldom been filled with song. It seemed a pity to her that it should be so. If she had her way, the whole world would sing, the sun would always shine, and people like Tobias Rakes would open their hearts to life's beauties and not dwell on past injuries and injustices.

They'd been working for an hour or more, pulling out the books one by one, clapping pages together, and dusting off cracked leather bindings, when a thick, yellowed paper fell from the book Genevieve held. She watched it flutter to the floor and sighed. She'd stood and squatted so much today, she was sure her muscles would scream at her tomorrow. Nevertheless, she squatted once more and retrieved the piece of paper. Its condition and the old-fashioned writing on it drew her attention, and she glanced more closely at the words written on it. Her cursory glance transformed into an astonished stare. "Aunt Delilah!"

Delilah sneezed, then turned, wiping her nose with a handkerchief retrieved from an apron pocket. "What is it, dear?"

Genevieve looked up from the paper. "Have you ever heard rumors about a treasure hidden somewhere in the castle?"

"A treasure?" Delilah blinked, her placid face expressionless. "I've heard about the ghost, but never anything about a treasure."

Nodding, Genevieve reread the words written on the paper. Maybe she'd read them incorrectly the first time. No. No matter how often she read the words, they remained the same.

"My goodness," she whispered. "My goodness gracious sakes alive."

"What is it, dear?"

"I do believe there may be more in this castle than dust and old books, Aunt."

"You do?"

"I do. According to this"—she held the paper out, being careful not to damage it, because it was very old and brittle—"Great-great-great-grandfather Charles Crowfoot was hiding a vast fortune in here somewhere." She smiled at her aunt. "And I aim to find it before that awful man does."

Her aunt's mouth fell open and her eyes widened. "Well, bless my soul!"

Chapter
Two

By the time Wesley Armitage called upon Genevieve Crowfoot to let her know that Tobias Rakes intended to make an offer for Crowfoot Castle, three weeks had passed. Genevieve and Delilah had almost finished cleaning up what Genevieve had begun to think of as the old dump. The treasure, if it existed, remained undiscovered, and she was peeved about it.

Feeling uncharacteristically grumpy, she stomped up the stone steps that led to the castle's attic. "Blast it, Aunt Delilah, I want to find that treasure."

Huffing after her niece, Delilah barely had breath enough to answer her. "It probably no longer exists, dear. If it ever did, which it probably didn't. It's probably nothing at all, really."

"Nothing, my foot. It's got to be something. It may not be diamonds and gold, but that paper mentioned 'a vast fortune.' " Genevieve stood in the cobwebby attic and glared around. "Tobias Rakes already has a vast fortune, Aunt Delilah. He doesn't need another one. We, on the other hand, do. Anyway, by rights, it's ours."

This was true. The Crowfoot family circumstances had declined considerably since Charles Crowfoot's day, before the Revolution. He'd been a successful merchant, trading in tea and furs. His descendants had done their best to keep the Crowfoot assets prospering, with varying results. Genevieve's father had not possessed much of a head for business, being intellectually inclined. He'd been more interested in teaching than in making money. While he'd managed to support his family, his teaching salary had been nowhere near vast.

Since her parents' death in a carriage accident a year and a half earlier, a calamity that devastated Delilah and still grieved Genevieve, she and Delilah had been existing on the income from Genevieve's small inheritance. It was sufficient, but not lavish, and Genevieve could think of many things she'd like to do if she were suddenly to find herself wealthy.

Not that wealth was the main reason she was still searching for the treasure. She mostly wanted to satisfy her curiosity. She and Benton used to spin lavish fantasies about pirate treasure and skeletons chained to the castle's dungeon walls—not that there was a dungeon in Crowfoot Castle. In a way, Genevieve thought that finding a hidden cache of anything at all would be a grand way of remembering Benton, whom she still missed terribly, and the castle itself, which soon would no longer be a Crowfoot family possession.

Besides all that, she'd taken an extreme dislike to the chilly and imperious Tobias Rakes, and she didn't want him to profit from a treasure that rightfully belonged to her and Delilah, if it existed. She knew her petty attitude did her no credit, but she couldn't help it.

She huffed indignantly. "At any rate, this is the only place we haven't searched, so let us begin."

Delilah sighed as she scanned the attic. "I don't expect there's much of anything up here. Some people use attics to store things in, but from the looks of the rest of the castle, I doubt that anyone ever got rid of anything at all, much less stored it in an attic."

"It does look rather empty in here, doesn't it?" Genevieve frowned at the cavernous room. Except for a trunk or two shoved up against a wall, it was mighty bare. "I suppose we ought to sweep it out, even if there's nothing here.''

So they set about with a vengeance, sweeping and dusting and sneezing. Since Genevieve was going to meet Tobias Rakes on the following day to sign the sale papers, he was on her mind today. ''I wish that man were a little more friendly,'' she muttered as she emptied the contents of a dustpan into a small barrel she'd lugged upstairs.

''Perhaps he will be when you know each other better, dear. He's a very handsome man.''

''Handsome!'' Genevieve looked over to find her aunt smiling sweetly at her. She knew what that meant. ''Don't even think about it, Aunt Delilah. I've refused perfectly pleasant men before now because I don't crave the married life. I'm certainly not going to fall in love with a hardhearted, bad-tempered man like Tobias Rakes, even if he *is* going to buy the castle.''

All at once a blast of frigid air shot through the castle attic. Genevieve looked around in alarm. ''Good heavens, where did that come from?''

Delilah rubbed her arms and squinted at the grimy attic window. ''I don't know. My rheumatism didn't predict rain for today.''

''It's not raining,'' Genevieve muttered. She rebuttoned her collar, which she'd unbuttoned only minutes earlier because she was warm. ''I don't know what it is.''

A piercing shriek sliced through the air.

Delilah gave a short, sharp scream.

Genevieve cried, ''Good Lord!''

Another shriek, longer, more shrill, reminding Genevieve of tales she'd heard of Irish banshees and fog-shrouded moors, pierced their ears. She dropped her broom, clapped her hands over her ears, and hurried to Delilah, who threw her arms around her.

''It's the ghost!'' Delilah whimpered.

''It's not a ghost!'' Genevieve pitched her voice to sound scornful, although it was an effort. She'd never been so frightened.

Sudden, horrible, echoing laughter filled the room. It swelled and swelled until Genevieve was trembling almost

as furiously as Delilah. She said, "It must be the wind." It
was feeble, and she didn't believe it—but what else could it
be? "You know, these old houses always have lots of odd
noises."

"It's the g-g-ghost."

Genevieve peered down at her aunt. Delilah's eyes were
squeezed shut, and she was shaking so hard Genevieve
feared she'd bite her tongue. Because she was alarmed herself, she wanted to step boldly forward and investigate the
awful noise, but it would have been cruel to desert Delilah.
"Nonsense!" she said stoutly. "There's some other—logi-
cal—explanation."

Another blast of arctic air, several loud groans, one more
shriek, and the sound of chains rattling made both ladies
jump and sent Delilah into a string of incoherent protests.
The phenomenon was beginning to irritate Genevieve, who
took strong exception to anything frightening her aunt.

She said, "Stop it!" although she suspected the words
would bear no fruit. How could mere words stop a natural
phenomenon? She had no doubt the cause of this odd dis-
turbance would turn out to be natural. Why, the very thought
of a ghost making all this racket was absurd. Laughable.

To prove it to herself, Genevieve laughed. Her first attempt
sounded strained, but she made a valiant effort to correct it,
and tried again with more success. Delilah subsided into silent paroxysms of shivers. When Genevieve glanced at her,
she saw Delilah darting terrified glances around the attic. It
made her angry to see Delilah thus.

"This is ridiculous," she declared.

"It's the ghost," whispered Delilah.

"Fiddlesticks!"

"*Fiddlesticks, is it?*" echoed from the rafters. "*Fiddlesticks?*"

Delilah began to moan softly at Genevieve's side. Genevieve, wrapping her aunt more snugly in her arms, was feeling a trifle moany herself by this time.

"*I'll show you fiddlesticks!*"

And with that, the ghost appeared.

Delilah fainted dead away into the pile of dust she'd just swept.

Genevieve was so startled that she could only stare for several seconds at the phantasm before her. Garbed in a gown that would have been fashionable a hundred years before, and with her hair powdered, coiffed high upon her head, and sparkling with jewels, the ghost hovered at the far end of the attic, her form wavering and shifting in the air. Genevieve blinked several times, sure it was a figment and would vanish shortly.

It didn't.

Then Genevieve realized her aunt had fainted. At once her anger boiled over. Genevieve had a very long fuse and seldom got angry, but at this moment she'd gladly have plunged a knife into the breast of that— that— that *thing* staring at her so very smugly from across the room.

"How dare you?" Her voice pulsed with wrath. "How *dare* you frighten poor Aunt Delilah this way? Who do you think you are, anyway, to make horrid noises and scare delicate old ladies? If you've done any harm to my aunt, I'll call the law down on you for malicious mischief!"

And with that, Genevieve knelt beside Delilah, pointedly ignoring whatever that thing was at the far end of the attic. Furious, she chafed Delilah's hands and spoke gently to her. When another cold blast shot past her, she whirled around and glared at the phenomenon, which was now hovering right overhead.

"Stop that this instant! If you have a quarrel with us, take it up with me, for heaven's sake. All you've succeeded in doing so far is making my aunt faint, and that's no very great feat. The poor dear has a heart condition, you know, and I won't have you bothering her!"

"Do you have any idea who I am, girl?" the thing asked, its voice strange and echoey.

"I don't care who you are! Or what! You're a vicious, mean thing, whatever you are, and I want nothing to do with you!"

"Is that so?" The thing sounded rather put out.

Genevieve didn't care. She lifted her aunt's head onto her

lap. Poor Delilah looked terribly pale. Genevieve wished she had some water to sprinkle on her forehead, but she wasn't about to leave Delilah alone in the attic with that *thing* while she went to fetch some. Her indignation was so great, it conquered her fear entirely. She glared fiercely up at the phantasm.

"Of all the nasty, spiteful things to do, I think frightening helpless old ladies is perhaps the most childish and mean-spirited of them all. What did you expect to accomplish by it, anyway? All we were trying to do was clean up this old run-down pile of stones."

"Run-down pile of stones?" Evidently, whatever the entity was, it didn't appreciate Genevieve's description of Crowfoot Castle. It puffed itself up like a balloon until it seemed to take up the entire ceiling. It was an interesting phenomenon, but Genevieve wasn't about to tell it so.

"Yes! It's a run-down pile of stones, and it's about to be sold. Aunt Delilah and I were trying to make it at least partially presentable, until *you* interfered. What did you mean by it?"

The being tried one more echoing cry and a louder rattle of chains. This time Genevieve even heard bells, sounding ancient and sepulchral in the background. They were effective in creating a spooky atmosphere, but she was in no mood to appreciate it. "Oh, stop that! Stop it this instant! You've made your point. You're able to frighten people. So what?" She gave the thing her hottest, most indignant scowl. It was the expression she saved for important occasions, and she seldom had to use it.

"Bother." The phantasm seemed to deflate, and it floated slowly over to rest on a trunk set against the attic wall.

Genevieve felt a lick of triumph for having quelled it, at least momentarily, whatever it was. Because she was still irked, she snapped, "What are you?"

"I'm not a what," the thing said. Its voice sounded hollow, as though it were speaking in a cavern. *"I'm a who. I'm Charles Crowfoot's daughter. People in Bittersweet had taken to calling me Granny Crowfoot by the time I died, even though I never married."* She sounded dejected.

Still rubbing her aunt's hands, Genevieve said, "I don't believe you. Ghosts don't exist."

Granny Crowfoot frowned at her. The expression appeared quite natural, as if frowning came easily to her. *"They do too."*

"Fiddlesticks." Genevieve chose not to look at the phenomenon calling itself Granny Crowfoot because, in spite of her bold words, she was unsettled by it. "Don't be ridiculous."

"Ridiculous?" Granny Crowfoot made a huffing noise that sounded like a sneeze in the big empty attic. *"What do you know about ghosts, girl?"*

She knew very little about them, actually, but Genevieve decided it would be prudent not to let on. She gave an indignant harrumph and continued ignoring the ghost, concentrating on Aunt Delilah, whose temporal form comforted her, even if it was unconscious at the moment.

Granny Crowfoot, if that was she, fluffed her skirts, drawing Genevieve's attention. Those skirts appeared as though they were sewn out of brocade, but they couldn't be because brocade was heavy. These skirts were so light as to be transparent. Genevieve looked away again, not wanting to dwell on it.

"I heard the two of you talking in here." Granny Crowfoot waved her hand to indicate the attic. *"I'm sure you were joking when you said a Rakes was going to buy the castle, although it's not a very funny joke if you ask me."* Her lips pursed. *"Young people today. You have no respect for anything."*

Frowning heavily, Genevieve dared look at Granny Crowfoot again. "I don't know about that, but I, for one, certainly have no respect for family feuds, if that's what you're talking about. Nonsensical things, feuds."

That set Granny Crowfoot off again. With a shrill whistle that seemed to stab through Genevieve's head like an arrow, she blew herself up until she'd spread out across the entire ceiling. Really, this was too much to bear. Genevieve said sharply, "Stop it! My aunt will never recover if you keep doing that!"

"Gerald Rakes murdered my father, you insolent girl!"

"So what? It happened more than a hundred years ago. Anyway, he was tried, convicted, and hanged for it. That should be the end of it."

"The end of it? The end of it?" Granny Crowfoot's incredulity was so great, her voice broke. *"My father was a gallant gentleman and a patriot, you insolent girl! He was one of the leaders of the Revolution!"*

"I'm happy to know I have such an illustrious ancestor, ma'am, but I still don't see why that justifies the perpetuation of a family feud and injury to my poor Aunt Delilah."

"Oh? Oh? And just how do you think you'd like it if someone murdered your father, you saucy baggage?"

"Stop calling me names. And I wouldn't like it at all, of course, but I can't understand blaming the grandchildren for the sins of their grandparents." To Genevieve, who had been devastated by her parents' deaths, the ghost seemed to be trying to trivialize them, and she resented it.

"Ha!"

To Genevieve, *ha* was insufficient justification for a hundred-year-old family feud, and she told the ghost so. "Besides," she continued, feeling smug, "it's going to end now whether you like it or not, because a Rakes man *is* going to buy the castle."

A long, drawn-out shriek met Genevieve's audacious declaration. Granny Crowfoot swooped and whished around the attic like a demented skyrocket, making Genevieve wish she hadn't been quite so forward. It was disconcerting watching a specter bounce through the walls and zoom here and there. Genevieve tried to duck every time it shot anywhere near her, but she felt an odd sensation of something cold going through her at least thrice. The sensation was most unpleasant, and really quite painful. "Stop it," she cried, not for the first time since she'd met the pesky thing.

At last Granny Crowfoot did stop. She sank down on the trunk again and appeared to be pouting. Too bad. There wasn't anything anyone could do to stop Tobias Rakes from buying the castle, because Genevieve was going to accept his offer. Tomorrow. And Granny Crowfoot could lump it if she didn't like it.

"You can't allow such a thing to happen."

Granny Crowfoot sounded breathless, a phenomenon almost more surprising than she herself was, to Genevieve's mind. "I can so. How can you stop the wheels of business from turning?" She thought better of telling Granny Crowfoot that she, herself, Genevieve Crowfoot, was going to be the one to sign the papers deeding Crowfoot Castle to Tobias Rakes. She had no idea how vast a ghost's powers might be—she rather doubted they were that great—but she didn't want to court catastrophe. Her life had too much catastrophe in recent years as it was.

Granny Crowfoot began pulling at her powdered hair. Genevieve watched, fascinated, and wondered if ghosts had to dress their hair, the way corporeal beings did. She didn't ask.

"Listen, Miss Crowfoot," she said, striving for a reasonable tone. "I honestly believe there's no need to keep the Crowfoot-Rakes feud active any longer. I'm sure no one alive today can even recall the facts of the case, and I'm even more sure that no one cares."

"Ooooooh!" Granny Crowfoot cried, sounding really quite pitiful. *"Aaaagh."*

Delilah stirred on Genevieve's lap. Genevieve didn't want her to catch sight of the ghost and faint again, so she said, "Will you please leave now? The castle will be sold to Mr. Tobias Rakes on the morrow, and that's that. Now go away before my aunt awakens. You've done enough damage for one day."

Granny Crowfoot rose from the trunk, looking like she wanted to kill something. Although Genevieve was quaking inside, she refused to show her fear, sensing that the old ghost would have won if she did.

"Noooooooo! Noooooooo! If a Rakes sets foot in this castle, I shall give him no rest! I shall haunt him until he begs for mercy!"

"Don't be silly. I'm sure you can keep him awake nights, but I'm just as sure you can't hurt anything," declared Genevieve, who was sure of no such thing. "For heaven's sake, you're a *ghost!* You can't even pick up anything that weighs more than an ounce or two, much less do anything with it. And flying through people only makes them feel cold and prickly. Mr. Rakes was a soldier on the frontier, and I'm sure he's endured much worse than cold spells in his life."

"Aaaaaaaaaaaah! Eeeeeeeeeeek! Aaaaaaaargh!"

Genevieve chuffed indignantly. "Oh, will you stop that! You've made your point. Now go away."

"You think I can't haunt that man? You think that, do you? Well, I'll show you who can haunt and who can't!"

And with that, Granny Crowfoot commenced flinging herself around the attic again. Genevieve sighed gustily, wishing her deceased ancestor didn't make so very virulent a spirit. She was alarmed when one or two loose objects—a nail and a dust ball—hurtled through the air. So the old bat could throw things around, could she? Well, Genevieve was still almost sure she couldn't do any more than that, or she'd have done it already.

"Wonderful," she said, making her tone as caustic as possible. "You can fling dust balls around. That will impress Mr. Rakes, I'm sure."

With one last string of ooooohs and aaaaaahs, the ghost vanished. And none too soon, by Genevieve's way of thinking, for Delilah's eyes were fluttering open.

By the time she'd helped her aunt out of the castle and done her best to soothe Delilah's shattered nerves, Genevieve was on the verge of consigning all ghosts to the pit, and particularly cantankerous Crowfoot ghosts. She didn't blame the Rakeses for steering clear of the Crowfoots for more than a hundred years, if all of Genevieve's predecessors were like Granny Crowfoot. She didn't even blame Gerald Rakes for murdering Charles Crowfoot, if Charles had been anything like his daughter.

"I shall never set foot in that place again as long as I live," Delilah said in a voice that shook pathetically.

Genevieve sighed. "I don't suppose you'll have any reason to after tomorrow, Aunt. I'm going to meet Mr. Rakes in Mr. Armitage's office at ten o'clock, and we're going to sign the sale papers. After that, whatever exists in Crowfoot Castle will be Mr. Rakes's problem.''

Genevieve awoke the next morning in an undecided mood. Should she tell Tobias Rakes about Granny Crowfoot or not?

She brooded about it all through breakfast. "I don't know," she said after swallowing a bite of toast smeared with blackberry jam. "What do you think, Aunt Delilah?"

Delilah, who was still pale and shaken, peered at her with wide eyes. "I think it's only fair to warn him, dear. No one should enter that place unprepared." She shuddered and could barely lift her teacup for the trembling in her limbs.

"I'm sorry you were so frightened, Aunt. That awful ghost has a lot to answer for." Genevieve wished she could return to the castle today and give Granny Crowfoot a good, hot lecture and a lesson in manners. Imagine, scaring poor Delilah so. Genevieve, whose sense of right and wrong was well-developed and unshakable, felt great indignation on her sweet aunt's behalf.

Poor Delilah glanced around the bright, sunny cottage kitchen as if she expected the ghost of Granny Crowfoot to materialize there. Genevieve expelled a breath. "I'm sure old Granny Crowfoot can't leave the castle, Aunt. I don't know much about ghosts, but I don't think they can haunt more than one or two places. Besides, I've never felt the atmospheric phenomena that accompanied her in this house. I think the castle's stuck with her."

"Oh, I do hope so!"

Immediately after the words popped out, Delilah realized her hope, if true, would make Tobias Rakes's life uncomfortable, and had the grace to blush. Genevieve smiled as she rose from her place at the table and picked up the jam pot. "I think you have nothing to fear in that regard. And don't feel guilty about Mr. Rakes, either. He's a grown man who's been through worse than being haunted by that miserable old ghost. Besides, he's been told by Mr. Armitage what to expect. Mr. Armitage told me he even warned Mr. Rakes that the castle is rumored to be haunted. He's buying the place knowing what he's in for.''

''I'll warrant he doesn't,'' Delilah said glumly. ''It's one thing to chat idly about a haunted castle. It's another matter entirely to be haunted in the flesh.''

Genevieve couldn't fault her aunt's reasoning, but she didn't want Delilah to worry. Delilah's sensibilities were fine, and she was apt to brood. She kissed the top of Delilah's head as she headed out of the kitchen to fetch her bonnet and shawl. Delilah stood in the doorway, framed by the red roses climbing over the trellis Genevieve had had Mr. Pickstaff build, and waved her off, still looking apprehensive.

The day was splendid, however, and Genevieve couldn't find it in herself to worry unduly about Tobias Rakes. He looked to her like a man who could take care of himself. Besides, maybe a good haunting would snap him out of his perpetually gloomy mood.

She glanced around with satisfaction as she walked down the road toward town. Buttercups bloomed beside the road, larkspurs and forget-me-nots bumped up against blooming hawthorn bushes, and Genevieve felt splendid—even if she was on her way to sell her family's castle.

In a way, though, while she was sorry to see the castle slip out of Crowfoot hands, she also felt as though this might be the first step in ending the entirely too-old Crowfoot-Rakes feud once and for all. It was true that members of the two families no longer took potshots at one another from behind hedges and so forth—and hadn't for a good fifty years or more—but it was also true that relations between the families had rarely been cordial at any time during the past century and more. The whole notion of a feud seemed preposterous to Genevieve, who found it difficult to hold a grudge for longer than ten minutes at a stretch.

Her sunny mood lasted until, having reached Bittersweet and paid a visit to Pickstaff's Dry Goods Store, where she bought a bottle of lavender toilet water for Aunt Delilah, which she hoped would make Delilah feel more the thing, she walked briskly up the steps to Wesley Armitage's law offices.

As soon as she opened the door, she saw Tobias Rakes. He rose stiffly from the chair in which he'd been sitting, turned to look at her, and she suddenly felt almost as cold as she'd felt when she'd encountered Granny Crowfoot the day before.

However, the fact that a Crowfoot and a Rakes could have the same unsettling effect on her buoyed her spirits almost immediately, and Genevieve gave him one of her friendlier smiles. No sense in allowing grouchy people to affect her own mood, after all.

"Good day, Mr. Rakes."

He nodded. "How do you do, Miss Crowfoot?"

They shook hands. "I'm very well, thank you, Mr. Rakes." Genevieve felt a tingly sensation when he took her hand, but she endeavored to ignore it and turned at once to Wesley Armitage, who had also risen upon her entrance. "And good day to you, too, Mr. Armitage."

Mr. Armitage smiled. His smile seemed to Genevieve a little tight. "Good morning, Miss Crowfoot."

She removed her wrap briskly and sat in the chair next to that from which Mr. Rakes had risen. "Well, shall we get on with it?" She kept her tone cordial but businesslike. "Are you ready to take possession of a haunted castle, Mr. Rakes?" Again she wondered if she should mention her encounter with Granny Crowfoot. She decided she'd take her cue from him.

"Yes."

He said only the one word, but from the look he gave her, which seemed cold and jaded, she saw Mr. Rakes didn't appreciate her little attempt at humor. Genevieve sniffed. Too bad for him. She wasn't going to subdue her good nature for him or anyone else. She also decided on the spot that she'd just keep her information about the castle's ghost to herself. He'd probably not believe her, and anyway she wasn't sure she liked him well enough to warn him. Let him meet Granny Crowfoot for himself and see how he liked it. Her. Whatever.

Armitage said, "He won't be swayed by anything anyone

says about it, Miss Crowfoot. He's set on buying the place and fixing it up."

Genevieve arched her brows. "From what I saw of it, it will take an army of carpenters and masons to put it in order again, Mr. Rakes."

"I'm prepared to deal with it," Tobias said shortly.

"He'll need a housekeeper, a groundskeeper, a cook, and who knows how many maids and gardeners." Armitage sounded both disapproving and discouraged.

"And someone to keep the stables, don't forget, Wes. I aim to stock it with fine horseflesh."

Genevieve glanced sharply at Tobias, whose tone had been dry. His words astonished her. "Oh, are you able—that is, can you—Oh, dear." She felt like a fool when her cheeks heated up.

"No, Miss Crowfoot, I cannot ride at the moment. That doesn't mean I'll never be able to ride again, however. And regardless of whether I can or not, I still aim to have horses."

If his tone had been dry before, it was positively desiccated now. Genevieve could have kicked herself for her maladroitness. "I beg your pardon, Mr. Rakes. I didn't mean to be rude."

"Of course not." He made a show of picking invisible lint from his immaculate black coat sleeve. He dressed very well. Genevieve felt like a chastened schoolgirl.

"I'm not sure where we'll get a decent staff for the old place," said Armitage, evidently trying to smooth over the moment.

"There must be people in Bittersweet who need work."

If Tobias Rakes could make himself sound more bored than he did then, Genevieve would be surprised.

"Yes, but, you see, Tobias, so many of the Bittersweet folks fear the ghost in the castle."

Tobias took this news the way Genevieve expected him to—he looked pained and said nothing.

"They wouldn't have to sleep in the castle," she said.

Armitage nodded. "I suppose that's true."

Suddenly a brilliant idea occurred to her, and she sat up straight in her chair. She'd been furious with Granny Crowfoot for haunting her and Delilah yesterday, thus preventing them from searching the attic thoroughly. If a treasure existed, they hadn't found it yet, and Genevieve had until this minute believed their chances for doing so were over. But perhaps she was wrong about that. She cleared her throat, and both Tobias and Armitage glanced at her, Armitage with interest, Tobias with palpable ennui.

"Perhaps I can help you with your staffing needs, Mr. Rakes." In spite of his grim aspect, Genevieve kept up her show of good humor. "I'm used to keeping house for my aunt and me. And I know everyone in Bittersweet, including those people who need employment. I think I could assume the role of housekeeper admirably." She knew her cheeks were pink. Indeed, they felt as if they were glowing with heat, but she didn't care. If she could get herself hired by this dreadful man, at least she could keep searching the castle for the treasure. Besides, there *were* folks in Bittersweet who needed work, and Genevieve was one of them. The profits from the sale of the castle would pay her father's last, lingering debts with little left over.

"You?" Wesley Armitage was clearly astonished by her offer. "But, Miss Crowfoot—you? A young lady? Why, I've never heard of ladies in your family taking employment before."

Genevieve's gaze thinned. "No, I'm sure you haven't. If they had, the family would probably be better off today than it is, Mr. Armitage." She regretted her tartness immediately, although she'd spoken only the truth. She turned to Tobias. "In all honesty, Mr. Rakes, I could use the employment, and I'm sure I'd be a good housekeeper for you. I'm familiar with the castle and with the people in the village. I'm sure I could help you staff the castle appropriately. And I need the income." There. She'd said it boldly, and didn't even regret it. Why should one regret speaking the truth?

Tobias stared at her—rudely, in Genevieve's opinion—for several seconds. She lifted her chin and refused to allow him to intimidate her. After what seemed like hours, he said two words.

"Very well."

Genevieve's heart soared.

Chapter Three

Tobias wondered if he'd made a mistake by hiring the amiable Miss Genevieve Crowfoot. He himself was about as amiable as a wounded grizzly bear—which was an apt comparison, if he did say so himself. He wasn't even sure he liked her. She was bright and bubbly and got on his nerves.

Still, she had a way about her. However, it was a way he didn't entirely appreciate. It was too damned cheerful, for one thing. For months now, Tobias had felt as though he were carrying his own personal storm cloud around with him everywhere he went.

She was probably right in her assumption that she could help him staff the castle though, and that was the important thing. There was certainly work aplenty to be done there, and he no longer knew anyone in Bittersweet. Hell, he hadn't even seen the place for seventeen years. It hadn't changed a bit, but that didn't negate the fact that he no longer had any contacts here. Let Miss Crowfoot do the work for him. He needed what little energy he possessed to heal.

He watched from the window of his hotel room as Genevieve Crowfoot hurried from shop to shop on Bittersweet's main street. He wondered if she was doing all that bustling on his behalf. The notion pleased him. While he didn't like her any better than he liked anyone, which wasn't much, there was something about her that struck him like a breath of fresh air. She seemed unspoiled. Unlike Tobias himself, who was so badly spoiled he was virtually worthless.

That gloomy thought kept him company as he turned away from the window and stretched out on the bed, careful not to jostle his leg too much. The doctor had told him he needed to rest as much as possible. Thirty-four years old, and he had to live like an old man, his body ruined. He and the effervescent Miss Crowfoot, whose body had appeared deliciously sound to Tobias, were polar opposites in that regard, as well as in their different dispositions.

He was surprised when he heard a knock at his door. He struggled to his feet, cursing under his breath because his leg throbbed like a sore tooth, and limped to the door. His surprise trebled when he opened it.

"Wes! What are you doing here? Come in." Tobias stood aside so the lawyer could enter his featureless hotel room.

"I hope you don't mind, Tobias. I wanted to chat with you about hiring Miss Crowfoot."

Tobias lifted an eyebrow in a manner he knew to be intimidating. The good Lord knew, he'd intimidated plenty of buck privates with that eyebrow. Armitage seemed to wither under it, and Tobias was ashamed of himself. To make up for it, he waved Armitage to a chair. "Sit down, Wes. Tell me why I shouldn't hire Miss Crowfoot. She sounded to me as though she needed the job."

Armitage frowned and sat. "Yes, it did sound like it. Still, I don't like it, Tobias. You can't forget the feud."

"The hell I can't." Tobias, taking much more time than Armitage, sat, too. His leg hurt like a son of a bitch and he really, really had to rest, but he wouldn't let on. Damn it, if he had nothing else left to him, he had some pride, for all the good it did him.

Armitage pursed his lips, propped his elbows on the arms of his chair, steepled his hands, pressed his fingers to his chin, and continued to frown.

"Why are you so set against Miss Crowfoot? She seems

like a sensible female. I'm sure she won't do anything to damage the place.''

A short laugh was startled out of Armitage. "No, I'm sure she couldn't. No one could do anything that might damage it any more than it's already damaged.''

"Besides, she's right, you know. She knows everyone in Bittersweet. I don't know anyone any longer. She's much more apt to find appropriate people than I am. Is there some reason you aren't telling me that I should avoid hiring her?''

After a brief hesitation, Armitage said, "No. Not really, I guess.''

Tobias shrugged. "She seems sharp enough, if a bit flighty.''

"Flighty?'' Armitage's eyes popped open. "You're the first person I've ever heard call Genevieve Crowfoot flighty.''

"Really?'' Tobias turned and looked toward the window. "Perhaps flighty isn't the right word.''

"I should say not. She's a fine woman. Gracious. Smart, too. Definitely not flighty.'' Armitage shook his head.

"Are you fond of her, Wes? Is that why you don't want her to work for me? I'm not fit to court a woman at the moment, you know, and won't be any time soon.'' And even though courting had been about as far from Tobias's mind in recent months as the North Pole, the truth of his statement galled him.

"Fond of her?'' Armitage seemed perturbed. "Of course I'm fond of her. Not in that way, though. I've known her ever since I came to Bittersweet.''

"Hmm.'' Tobias wondered suddenly if his life might have taken a different turn had he met Genevieve Crowfoot in his seventeenth year instead of the sultry Madeline Riley. Foolish thought. The Crowfoot girl would still have been in her single-digit years when Tobias had made such an ass of himself. He didn't want to think about it. "I didn't know length of association made much difference in matters of the heart.''

"Matters of the heart? Don't be ridiculous, Tobias. It's just—oh, I don't know.'' Armitage stood up. "I'm sorry I brought it up. I'm sure she'll do a fine job.'' His frown deepened. "That aunt of hers might be a problem."

"A problem? She seemed like a nice, old dear to me. A little dithery, perhaps, but I can't imagine her causing problems." Tobias had an odd feeling that there was more to Wes's visit today than met the eye. There had to be, in truth, because from what Tobias could see, there was no reason for it at all. "Is there something you're not telling me, Wes? Is the elder Miss Crowfoot prone to hysterical fits or something?"

"Hysterical fits? Good heavens, no." Armitage made a turn around the room, then stood at the door, holding his hat and glowering at nothing in particular. "I beg your pardon, Tobias. It was foolish of me to bother you when all I have is a vague sense of unease about the matter."

"Unease? I'm uneasy most of my waking hours, if it comes to that. If she fails to perform her duties well, I'll get rid of her and hire someone else. Is that all right with you?"

Armitage smiled at him. "Of course. Please forget I even bothered you with my idle fancies, Tobias. I'll get some men up to the castle to clear the drive, and you can move in whenever you wish."

"I'll have to get some furnishings first, and clean the place up some. I'm sure the chimneys are full of birds' nests and leaves."

"I'm sure you're right. I'll help you with that, too."

"Thanks, Wes. I appreciate your help more than I've said, I'm sure."

"You've paid me. That's all the thanks I need."

And with that, Wesley Armitage left Tobias Rakes to his pain, his bitter memories, and his bed. Tobias groaned heavily when he settled himself on the bed, and he drifted off to sleep thinking about Genevieve Crowfoot.

Genevieve moved into the castle a full two weeks before Tobias. She did so in spite of stiff opposition from her aunt, who pestered the very life out of her for agreeing to be Tobias Rakes's housekeeper.

"You *know* that awful ghost lives there, Genevieve," Delilah cried, wringing her hands. "How can you even think about living there with her? *And* with a Rakes!"

"To talk about a ghost living anywhere is foolish, Aunt Delilah. If she were capable of living, she wouldn't be a ghost."

Delilah didn't think it was funny. Not that Genevieve had imagined she would. She pondered the list in her hands. "I'm sure William Pickstaff is almost as unpleasant as Mr. Rakes, but he knows everything there is to know about horses."

"William Pickstaff?" Startled by Genevieve's seemingly out-of-the-blue comment, Delilah lost track of her argument, which was exactly what Genevieve had hoped would happen. "He's as sour as a crabapple. What does he have to do with anything?"

"He's the best horse person in Bittersweet, and he needs a job. His poor wife is doing her best at his father's dry-goods store, but it's an uphill battle with all those children to support and Mr. Pickstaff having lost his job at the stables."

The Bittersweet Stables had been on shaky ground for decades, and had finally lost the battle to stay open. William Pickstaff and his son, Small William, had worked at the stables and been only two of many men who'd lost their jobs when the millionaire who'd bought the stables lost his fortune on the New York Stock Exchange and had to sell out.

"Then there's the matter of a cook." Genevieve looked up from her list slowly, her most mischievous smile on her face. "You're a wonderful cook, Aunt Delilah."

Delilah's eyes went as round as pie plates, and she began slowly backing away from Genevieve as if she feared her niece might try to drag her to the castle by force. "I told you I'll never set foot in that beastly castle again, Genevieve Crowfoot, and I meant it. You can't make me."

Genevieve laughed. It was so easy to get Delilah flustered that it almost wasn't any fun to try. "I'm only joking, Aunt Delilah. I'd never ask you to cook for Mr. Rakes—and I'm sure I couldn't make you do anything you didn't want to do."

Delilah did her best to look stern. "You have a very forceful personality, Genevieve."

Tapping her chin with her pencil, Genevieve didn't bother replying. "Molly," she said musingly. "Molly Gratchett needs a job now that her engagement to Mr. Foster has gone belly-up."

Delilah sniffed. "That's a remarkably unladylike expression, Genevieve Crowfoot."

"I'm sure it is, Aunt." She turned and plucked her flowered hat from the hat rack beside the door. "Do you know if Molly can cook?"

"I have no idea, but I suspect not. Her mother was the worst cook in Bittersweet."

"Well, no matter. If Molly wants the job, I'll hire her. I'm sure she can read, and I'll just lend her a couple of the cookbooks from our kitchen until she gets the hang of it."

With her aunt's muttered protests following her down the walkway, Genevieve set out with her wicker suitcase in hand, ready to install herself in the castle. She was eager to recommence looking for whatever treasure lay hidden there, and she'd rather do it before Tobias Rakes took up residence.

When Tobias moved into Crowfoot Castle in June, the trilliums and flag lilies had given way to larkspur and hollyhocks, and the delphiniums and snapdragons were fighting for room with the skunk cabbages and thistles in the castle's still-overgrown gardens. Genevieve had set a regiment of children, out of school for the summer, to work pulling out the skunk cabbages and digging up the flag lilies. She aimed to separate the tubers and replant them so that next spring some sort of order might be achieved in the castle gardens for Mr. Rakes's delectation. She wanted him to appreciate her, because she aimed to keep her job until she'd uncovered the treasure, a prospect that had become almost an obsession with her.

Unfortunately, her duties as housekeeper had kept her from investigating the old building as much as she wanted in the weeks before Tobias's arrival. There was so much work to do to make the place habitable, that she sometimes despaired of ever having a moment to herself.

Nevertheless, when she heard Tobias Rakes's carriage barrel down the drive toward the entrance to the castle grounds, Genevieve was proud of the work she and her minions had accomplished. The whole place had been scrubbed within in an inch of its life, most of the rooms had been painted, the wall hangings had been cleaned and rehung—those that survived the cleaning—and she'd arranged quite artistically the furniture Tobias had bought.

The bedrooms had been aired, the bed curtains had been replaced, and all the bedding was new. She'd even had the elaborately carved maple bedstead in the master bedroom stripped and waxed twice. It now gleamed invitingly even if it was a very high bed. Genevieve hoped Mr. Rakes wouldn't hurt his wounded leg climbing into it at night. She'd had an oaken stair step crafted, polished, and set discreetly beside the bedstead for his use.

She was a little nervous about the advent of the master of the house. The staff she'd hired, while all desperately in need of work, collectively had little experience as servants in a grand household. Genevieve had tried her best to impress upon them the importance of assuring Mr. Rakes's comfort, but she was dubious about some of them.

"Stand up straight, Godfrey," she admonished the new butler sharply. "Never forget that you and your family need for you to keep this job."

Godfrey Watkins snapped to attention. "Sorry, Miss Genevieve. I forgot."

Genevieve heaved a big sigh. Perhaps she'd miscalculated with Godfrey. He did need the work, but he wasn't the brightest candle in the box. Still, his heart was in the right place. If Mr. Rakes could be persuaded into patience, Genevieve was sure Godfrey could be trained. She eyed him slantways and amended her assessment. She was *almost* sure he could be trained. Because she knew he'd never notice it himself, she darted over and straightened his tie.

In truth, she was more troubled about Molly, the cook, than about Godfrey. Genevieve imagined Mr. Rakes had as little experience with butlers as she had herself, but he was accustomed to eating three times a day, and there was no disguising the mediocrity of Molly's efforts. And that was on a good day, when she didn't burn anything. Mrs. Watkins, Godfrey's powerful mother, who had whipped the house-maids into order, had occasionally remarked that she believed Molly could burn water without half trying. Genevieve had contemplated having Molly and Mrs. Watkins trade places, but she didn't think Molly would be any better at supervising housemaids than she was in the kitchen.

Well, she'd just have to take things as they came. If she had to make some staffing changes, so be it.

At least William Pickstaff and Small William seemed to be competent in the stables. Mr. Rakes had bought five gorgeous horses and had them sent to the castle. Old William and Small William brushed and curried and exercised them diligently, even if the elder Pickstaff was as grouchy as a boiled owl most days.

She'd had no further intercourse with Granny Crowfoot during her tenure in the castle. She hoped this meant the ghost had given up her threat to haunt Tobias Rakes, but Genevieve knew better than to hope too hard. She didn't trust that ghost.

Genevieve had made the gardening staff prune all the shrubbery away from the main drive, and she'd had a ton of new gravel spread. Now, when she saw Tobias Rakes's elegant black traveling coach trundling down the way, she felt really quite pleased with her efforts. True, the weedy forest lining the drive hadn't been landscaped yet, but there would be time for that later. At least branches no longer reached out to whip the horses' flanks as they galloped by.

She nudged Godfrey when the coach pulled up. "Go open the carriage door, Godfrey. You know what we talked about."

Godfrey jerked out of what looked to Genevieve like a trance and stumbled on the first step. She grabbed him before he could tumble down the rest of the stairs and decided to accompany him to the door of the coach.

In order to cover Godfrey's embarrassment, she said

brightly, "Welcome to your new home, Mr. Rakes. I hope you'll like what we've done. There's lots more that needs doing, of course, but we've been working like beavers."

She might as well have saved her breath, she thought sourly, when she saw Tobias's glowering countenance. He didn't even acknowledge her comment, but concentrated on easing himself out of the coach. At once, Genevieve felt a smidgen of contrition. She really should try to remember that the poor man had been grievously wounded. Small wonder he was crabby. She hurried to his side, determined to make herself useful.

"May I help you, Mr. Rakes?" she asked solicitously.

"I can manage."

His tone was so sharp, Genevieve stepped aside immediately and was embarrassed. Suppressing the snappish rejoinder that leaped to her mind, she hoped he wasn't going to be short-tempered and sullen forever. Plastering a serene expression on her face, she folded her hands in front of her and watched, reminding herself that he was in pain. And, what's more, he was her boss. Blast it.

Then he looked up and smiled at her. "I beg your pardon, Miss Crowfoot. I fear I've not taken well to being crippled."

His smile was so unexpected, and so breathtaking, and transformed his harsh features so remarkably, that Genevieve's heart lurched. Oh, dear. Until that moment, she hadn't realized how exceptionally appealing Tobias Rakes could be. Since she couldn't think of a thing to say, she only smiled. He continued to gaze at her, however, and she scrambled for the social inanities that usually came to her with ease.

"Er, would you like for me to introduce the staff, Mr. Rakes? Or would you prefer to go inside first and see what we've done to the castle's rooms?"

Tobias straightened and glanced around. Genevieve held her breath.

"The place looks better already, Miss Crowfoot. I believe Wesley Armitage was right when he told me you were bright and competent."

Bright and competent? Well, Genevieve guessed she appreciated Mr. Armitage's assessment, although she wasn't

sure she liked knowing that he had talked about her behind
her back. She said "Thank you," because she couldn't think
of anything better to say. Then she said, "I'm eager to get
the gardens set to rights, because we only have about three
months of decent weather to work with here in New York."

He smiled again. Genevieve tried hard not to goggle.
When he smiled, he was an extremely attractive man. She
knew very well that, while she'd never been tempted by any
of the young men of her acquaintance in the small town of
Bittersweet, her innermost nature was ardent. Tobias Rakes,
unfortunately, stirred that hidden nature. She hadn't anticipated such a thing happening, and was annoyed when it did.

"Ah, yes, I remember the short summers here in New
York. My mother used to spend all summer outdoors in her
garden. She used to say she only had three months, and she
was going to make the most of them."

His smile gave way to a frown, and Genevieve felt great
relief. She really had to fortify herself against his smiles.

"May I take your hat and coat, sir?"

Both Genevieve and Tobias turned to stare at Godfrey,
whose cheeks blossomed bright red. Genevieve huffed with
annoyance. "Not now, Godfrey. Please allow Mr. Rakes to
enter his home before you relieve him of his outer gar-
ments."

"Of course, ma'am. I beg your pardon, sir." Godfrey's
lips barely moved, and beads of sweat broke out on his brow.

Genevieve shook her head. "I do hope you're a patient
man, Mr. Rakes. The staff is learning, but none of them have
been household servants before."

His grin might have made Genevieve swoon if her character was as flighty as that of her aunt. "It's perfectly all
right, Miss Crowfoot. I've never had house servants myself.
I'm sure we'll all learn together."

"Thank you, Mr. Rakes." Genevieve smiled at Godfrey
to let him know he was forgiven. He snatched a handkerchief
from his pocket and mopped his forehead with it. She jerked
her head toward the front door.

"Oh," Godfrey said. "Right." He stuffed his handkerchief back into his pocket and ran like a rabbit up the stairs

to the front door, where he skidded to a halt, grabbed the door handle, and jerked the massive door open. Then he stood like a statue, holding the door, while Tobias Rakes and Genevieve walked up to it. Only with an effort did Genevieve refrain from shaking her head in aggravation.

Mr. Rakes didn't seem to be limping as badly as he had been several weeks ago. She wondered if his leg were getting better. It must have been ghastly to be shot with an arrow. Genevieve couldn't really even imagine such a thing. The West was so far away. It might belong to another age, so distant did it seem to her. She'd love to hear any stories Mr. Rakes had to tell, although he didn't appear to be the type who'd relish regaling folks with yarns about his many adventures.

He stopped short as soon as he entered the hallway. Mrs. Watkins and her army of housemaids, black dresses and white aprons starched and ironed, formed a line spanning the front door to the parlor.

"My goodness," he said, startled.

Genevieve beamed at Mrs. Watkins, who didn't smile back. Mrs. Watkins took her duties seriously, and seldom found anything worth smiling about in her day-to-day activities. She dropped a stiff curtsy. "Good day, Mr. Rakes."

"Good day to you, er—" He looked helplessly at Genevieve.

"Mr. Rakes, may I introduce you to Mrs. Watkins. Mrs. Watkins has supervised the cleaning of the castle, and she's done a wonderful job."

"It wasn't easy," Mrs. Watkins announced grimly.

Tobias blinked at her. "No. I'm sure it wasn't. The place was a wreck when I saw it last." He took the time to glance around the entryway. Genevieve saw his gaze rest on the polished glass of the windows and the now-bright tapestries hanging on the walls. She was quite pleased when he nodded his approval.

"Yes, indeed, Mrs. Watkins, you've done very well. Thank you for your efforts on my behalf."

Mrs. Watkins didn't crack so much as a grin, but Genevieve could tell she was pleased when she gave Tobias another curtsy. There was an unmistakable air of triumph in her demeanor. At least it was unmistakable to Genevieve, who'd known her for eons.

Godfrey, on the other hand, seemed to have frozen solid with the door handle in his hand. Genevieve turned and grimaced at him, but he wasn't looking at her. She muttered, "Pardon me for a moment, Mr. Rakes," and hurried back to the front door. When she touched Godfrey's arm, he jumped like a frightened deer. "Shut the door, Godfrey, or you'll let all the black flies in," she murmured under her breath. "And you can take Mr. Rakes's hat and coat now as well."

"Oh! Oh, of course."

Godfrey raced over to Tobias, the door slamming behind him, rattling the stained-glass windows, and sounding like a cannon going off in the entryway. Genevieve cringed inside, and was relieved when Tobias only smiled again, as if he were rather enjoying all this fluttering and nervousness in his staff. He handed Godfrey his top hat and shrugged himself out of his coat.

Godfrey, as anxious as a cat, juggled Tobias's outerwear and eyed his cane. "Er, do you want me to take that, sir?"

Genevieve wanted to smack him, and Mrs. Watkins glowered furiously.

"No," said Tobias evenly. "I'm afraid I need my cane."

Godfrey, after shooting an apprehensive glance at his mother, bobbed his head up and down. "Oh. All right then. I'll just, ah, put these things up." He stood there for another second or two, looking uncertain. Then he glanced at Genevieve, who made a horrible face at him, and he rushed to the coat closet, his face as red as a ripe plum.

"I do apologize for Godfrey, Mr. Rakes," Genevieve felt compelled to say. "I keep hoping he'll learn, but he's awfully nervous today."

"He's probably heard what an ogre I am."

"Perhaps," Genevieve said before she realized it. Then she blushed, too.

She was relieved when Tobias threw his head back and laughed.

Her relief lasted through the rest of that day, as she showed

Tobias around his new castle. He complimented her and the staff on a job well done, and he even managed to wrest a grim smile out of William Pickstaff.

"Good job, Pickstaff," he said, watching Small William ride a huge black gelding in the meadow. "The horses look better than I expected they would."

"Aye," the taciturn Pickstaff said. "My boy and me, we know horses."

Tobias had folded his arms over the top board of the fence and was leaning on it to take the weight off of his leg. "I can see you do."

That's when Pickstaff smiled—sort of. Genevieve was relieved, though.

In fact, there wasn't anything about Tobias's first day in the castle that went really wrong. Godfrey remained edgy, but Tobias seemed to find his clumsiness merely amusing. And, while Molly's dinner wasn't superb by any means, at least she didn't burn the green beans or overcook the fish.

Genevieve was more pleased than not when she went to bed that night. She dropped right off to sleep, in fact, with visions of a smiling Tobias Rakes keeping her company.

Her pleasure remained undiminished until approximately three o'clock in the morning, when a hideous scream shattered the peace of the night.

Before her heart had stopped thundering from the scream, the chains began to rattle, the cellar doors slammed shut, and the moanings began.

Genevieve sighed gloomily and shook her head.

Granny Crowfoot.

Genevieve ought to have expected it.

Chapter
Four

"Er, did you sleep well last night, Mr. Rakes?" Genevieve eyed Tobias nervously after she served him his breakfast, hoping he wouldn't desert the castle immediately. She wanted him to stay here at least long enough for her to accomplish her purpose. If he abandoned the place, it would probably be torn down, and then who knew what might happen to any treasure hidden there?

He looked up from the rubber eggs Molly had prepared this morning. She hadn't got the hang of poaching yet. Genevieve planned to give her a lesson as soon as she'd talked to Tobias.

"Yes, I slept fairly well. Until about three. Then the old place started creaking and rattling like nobody's business. Does it do that often?"

His tone was mild, and Genevieve felt a wash of relief. As long as he didn't start to believe in ghosts, perhaps all would be well. She offered an airy wave of her hand. "Oh, yes. I understand many old houses are full of strange noises."

He grunted and eyed his eggs again. "It's probably the ghost," he said, sending Genevieve's heart plummeting to her feet.

She gave a tentative laugh, hoping he was joshing. He didn't seem like the type who would joke, but she didn't really know him.

He looked up again and smiled, and she took heart. "Armitage told me the stories about the old place being haunted. I can understand why folks think so if that sort of racket goes on all the time. Do most of the staff live here, or do they go home at night?"

"They mostly live in their own homes."

"Good thing. Otherwise, they'd probably all quit."

Oh, Lord, he was right. Genevieve spared a moment to be grateful Bittersweet was a small enough community that few of the staff had to sleep in the castle. "I'll, er, have Mrs. Watkins send a girl around to oil all the hinges. Again."

"Good idea." Tobias frowned. "You don't suppose the place has rats, do you? I can't seem to find the cuff links I wore yesterday."

Blast that wretched ghost! Genevieve was positive it had been Granny Crowfoot who'd filched Tobias's cuff links. If the beastly old girl could handle nails and dust balls, she could surely handle something as light as cuff links.

"Perhaps we should get a couple of cats," she said through clenched teeth. "In the meantime, I believe any marauding rodents might be dissuaded from pilferage if you locked your cuff links and any other lightweight personal items in a drawer." Could ghosts open drawers? The mean old coot had managed the cellar door last night—must have slammed it a dozen times or more, in fact. Genevieve wished she knew more about haunting.

"You're right, of course, Miss Crowfoot. I must try to be more tidy."

"Oh, dear, Mr. Rakes, I didn't mean to imply that you're not tidy. I'm sure, as a military man, you're neat as a pin."

He laughed. Genevieve went weak in the knees and had to sit down. Good grief, she almost hoped his attitude wouldn't cheer up if this was how she was going to react to his levity.

Tobias carved a piece of leathery egg and popped it into his mouth. Genevieve, who didn't care for hard eggs herself, shuddered. "I'm hoping Molly's cooking will improve, Mr. Rakes. I fear she's not the most experienced cook in the world. Please be assured that I'm working with her."

"I'm used to worse chow than this, Miss Crowfoot."

"It's kind of you to say so, Mr. Rakes, but you shouldn't have to put up with it in your own home."

He glanced up and smiled again. Genevieve's heart fluttered as if a battalion of butterflies had taken up residence in it. This was terrible.

"It's true that I wouldn't mind eating well, I must admit. But I'm more interested in my horses than my dinner, and the Pickstaffs seem to be doing a fine job with the stable."

Thank heavens he'd stopped smiling at her. "Yes. Yes, they're both excellent horsemen."

Tobias tilted his head and looked thoughtful. "Pickstaff. Pickstaff. Wasn't there someone named Pickstaff involved in the origins of our families' problems, Miss Crowfoot? I should remember. Lord knows, my father drilled his grievances into my head until I thought I'd never forget a single one of them." His expression turned sour. "Thank God for the Indian wars, or I might still recall every little detail about the feud."

That was an interesting way of putting things, Genevieve thought. She understood matters between Tobias and Ernest Rakes had never been smoothed over, and she felt rather sorry for the both of them. She'd hate to be on the outs with her own family, whom she loved with all her heart.

"I believe there was an Ivor Pickstaff who had entered into business with Charles Crowfoot and Gerald Rakes, actually," she said. "After the death of Charles and the hanging of Gerald, I understand Ivor lost all of his money. I'm sure the original Pickstaffs hated both of our families for causing the ruination of theirs." She sighed, wishing her ancestors had devoted themselves to something more useful than shady business practices and a family feud.

Tobias gave up on his eggs and placed his fork on his plate. "Hmmm. That's right. I'd forgotten. I hope the present Pickstaffs aren't as eager to hold a grudge as our families

have been over the past century and a quarter, Miss Crowfoot, or I fear for the health of my horses.''

"You needn't worry about that, Mr. Rakes. If William
Pickstaff has a bone to pick, it won't be with your horses.
He treats horses ever so much better than he treats human
beings."

He nodded his agreement with her blunt assessment. "The
man sounds about horses the way my father was about the
great feud. My old man loved our families' feud so much,
he had no affection left over to spare for his wife and son."

Saddened by the picture her employer painted, Genevieve
blurted out, "Oh, dear. I'm sorry, Mr. Rakes."

Blast! He laughed again. Well, no matter. She had duties
to perform, and she would not cross paths with Tobias Rakes
for the rest of the day. She devoutly hoped she wouldn't, at
any rate.

Tobias pushed himself away from the table and stretched.
Genevieve wasn't pleased to note that he'd come to the
breakfast table in his shirtsleeves. Not that she was a stickler
for formal dining apparel, but without his coat on, she could
clearly detect that he was built upon impressive lines. Broad-
shouldered and deep-chested, with biceps the size of tree
trunks, he fairly took her breath away. She'd wager any
amount of money that his musculature was well developed
from having lived such a strenuous life for so long. She
hoped he wouldn't allow himself to run to flab now that he
was no longer soldiering. Which reminded her of something.

"Didn't you do some adventuring before you joined the
army, Mr. Rakes?"

His eyebrow rose ironically, and Genevieve cursed herself
for forgetting she was in his employ. She'd spoken to him
as if they were conversing socially. "I beg your pardon,"
she mumbled. She hoped she wasn't turning red. She blushed
much too easily.

"Yes, Miss Crowfoot. After I ceased running off with
married ladies, I hired myself out to several expeditionary
groups. I've traveled extensively in the western territories,
and even went on a big-game hunting expedition in Africa
once."

"Africa," Genevieve said in an awed voice. "How exciting."

"My adventures in Africa were a shade more exciting than my adventures with the wicked damsel. Don't tell my father that. I'd hate to give him credit for being right."

His tone was so bitter, it sparked Genevieve's temper. Although she knew she should learn to mind her tongue, she yet said with something of a bite, "I asked your pardon, Mr. Rakes. I didn't mean to pry into your business, but I'm sure the entire community of Bittersweet is intrigued by your adventures. And I'm also sure most of us are infinitely more disposed to approve of you than of your father. He's not well liked in town."

Egad, she wished she'd held her tongue. Then she wished he wouldn't burst into laughter at the drop of a hat the way he was doing now. The sudden change in his demeanor from dour to amused was likely to be the death of her unless she managed somehow to get her reaction to him under control.

"Touché, Miss Crowfoot. And I'm very happy to learn about the sentiments of my hometown."

With her heart pounding like a drum, she watched him walk out of the room. He didn't have to lean so heavily on his cane now as when she'd first met him, she noticed. Perhaps one day he'd be able to throw it away.

One of Mrs. Watkins's housemaids entered the room to clear the dishes from the table, and Genevieve stood up and smoothed her apron. She smiled at the girl, who bobbed a curtsy—Mrs. Watkins had done a *very* good job with her crew—and decided she'd better visit the kitchen for a chat with Molly.

Then she was going to see if she could discover the whereabouts of a most mischievous ghost and try to talk some sense into her. She wasn't awfully optimistic.

Tobias felt pretty good when he left the breakfast table, in spite of having endured a difficult night and a less-than-spectacular first breakfast in his new home. In fact, he'd been feeling a lot better ever since he had arrived yesterday.

Maybe being around the sunny Miss Crowfoot was better for him than he had imagined. The fact that his leg didn't hurt as much as it used to helped his disposition, too—as did the notion of owning a castle. He'd told Genevieve Crowfoot the truth, though; he really didn't care much about food. He'd been eating camp fare for so many years, he could choke down damned near anything at this point and consider himself lucky to have it.

Genevieve Crowfoot. Now *there* was a palatable item. Tobias smiled to himself. He liked the way she piled her ash blond hair on top of her head and let it poof out to frame her face. She had pretty eyes, too, big and brown. They sparkled with good humor, which was a commodity that had been sadly lacking in his life. His father had been about as humorous as a funeral dirge.

Tobias could remember his mother laughing. And singing. He wondered if Genevieve Crowfoot liked to sing. He'd wager she did.

Yes, indeed. A very appealing female, Genevieve Crowfoot. She wasn't precisely gorgeous, but there was such animation in her features, and her figure was so delicious, that he wouldn't mind looking at her forever. Preferably naked.

He sighed. As if. It would be a long time before he was able to appreciate a lush, naked woman in the way she ought to be appreciated. In his present condition, his leg would give out if he even tried to mount a female. With a grin, he reminded himself that he wouldn't mind if Genevieve Crowfoot cared to mount him. He was sure he could handle that. She, on the other hand, as a properly bred gentlewoman, would probably faint dead away at the notion.

Ah, well. It didn't hurt to dream. Especially if dreams were about all that were left to one.

A horse, however, might be another matter entirely. It was his right leg that had taken the arrow, and he'd been exercising it rigorously for months now. If he could manage to swing it over a horse's back, perhaps he could ride again soon. His left leg would be supporting his weight in the stirrup, after all. He might even unbend enough to accept help from Small William, who seemed like an amenable lad.

Unlike his father, who was as dry as toast and about as interesting.

A group of schoolchildren seemed to be swarming in his garden, and Tobias walked over to investigate. A little blond girl and a dark-haired boy noticed him and stood to attention. Since he was feeling fairly mellow, he waved at them and smiled. He assumed they were doing something preordained by someone in authority and, therefore, on his behalf. The little girl curtsied, and the boy saluted.

"Good morning," Tobias called. "Finding worms, are you?"

They stared at him blankly, and he guessed his attempt at humor had flown right over their heads. He wished Genevieve were here to translate for him.

"Miss Genevieve told us to clean out them skunk cabbages," the boy said, gesturing at some tall, ungainly plants.

"And to put the flag lily roots in a sack so's she can separate them and make pretty gardens for next year," the little girl added.

Ah. Good for Miss Genevieve. Tobias wouldn't mind having well-tended grounds and gardens to look out on from his drawing-room window. He waved at the children again. "Keep up the good work!"

He moseyed on toward the stables, contemplating the extensive gardens. It was nice to know that someone was taking care of everything for him, including the gardens. He paused in his meanderings and turned to gaze at the castle.

It was quite a place, Crowfoot Castle. Old Charlie Crowfoot must have been really full of himself. Tobias felt a wave of contentment, as strange as it was powerful, fill him as he stared at his new home. He'd be even more content once he knew for a fact that his father knew he was here, living in enemy territory. The old man probably knew already. Maybe he'd write Tobias another letter, this time chastising his son for disgracing his heritage. Some heritage. A century-and-a-quarter-old family feud. All in all, Tobias would sooner have inherited some affection. Something at the castle caught his eye.

What in the world was that? Tobias squinted at the attic

window, where he was sure he'd just seen a flash like a small bolt of lightning issue forth. Shaking his head, he muttered, "Nonsense. You're taking these ghost stories too much to heart." So he turned around again, thereby missing the second flash of light Granny Crowfoot produced for his delectation and enjoyment. She glared after him, but he missed that too, her glare wasted.

Genevieve, however, had ample time to watch Granny Crowfoot do her evil deed, as she had reached the attic room where she and Delilah had first seen the ghost. Her temper reacted hotly to it, too.

"Stop that this instant," she shouted. She even grabbed at her, but her hand went right through whatever semisolid emanation Granny Crowfoot's form took. "I will *not* have you frightening Mr. Rakes."

The ghost flung herself down on the floor and looked about as sulky as a bear to have been found out. Genevieve wouldn't have been surprised if the old ghost had started drumming her heels and throwing a temper tantrum.

Genevieve didn't give a rap about Granny Crowfoot's moods; she was truly angry with the ill-mannered spirit, who crossed its arms over its buckrammed chest and glared at the wall, pretending to ignore Genevieve. Genevieve wasn't about to let her get away with it. She stood over the ghost and glowered down at her, tapping her foot.

"And you can tell me right here and now what you did with Mr. Rakes's cuff links, too. Of all the rude, impertinent things to do, I think stealing is one of the rudest and most impertinent—and downright illegal. You ought to be ashamed of yourself, a grown woman, snitching a pair of cuff links! A grown, *dead* woman!"

"*I didn't steal anything.*" Granny Crowfoot sounded disgruntled. "*I tidied them up. He threw them on the bureau like the boorish toad he is, so I decided to teach him a lesson.*"

"You have no business teaching the owner of this castle any lessons, Miss Crowfoot. Talk about boorish!"

Granny levitated up from the floor without standing, a feat Genevieve tried not to admire. "*It's a crime against nature that a foul Rakes spawn should own my father's castle!"*

"Nonsense." Genevieve kept her voice firm, although Granny Crowfoot had stirred up the atmosphere with her anger so that tiny flashes of lightning now darted around her head. The effect was quite disturbing, really, although Genevieve sensed she'd better not indicate her nervousness by so much as a bat of her eyelashes. She didn't trust the miserable old woman not to use any small show of uneasiness on Genevieve's part to her own advantage.

"It's not nonsense! That fellow doesn't belong here. This is Crowfoot land. It's been Crowfoot land for more than two hundred years, and he's an encroaching interloper and a trespasser onto my family's property."

"He *bought* the place, Granny Crowfoot, because none of the Crowfoots—the few who are left—have any money. *That's* what your precious family has come to. We're a raggedy nest of paupers."

Granny Crowfoot let out with such a screech of dismay that Genevieve clapped her hands over her ears in spite of her recent vow not to react to anything the old ghost did. "Stop that!"

"That awful man killed my father!" the ghost shrieked.

"He did not kill your father! His great-great-great-grandfather killed your father. And he was hanged for it."

"Mere quibbling."

"It's not quibbling! He was tried and convicted, and he paid for his crime with his own life, over a hundred years ago. That should have been an end to it, for heaven's sake. The law had its revenge. What more do you want?"

"I want that man gone from this place." Granny Crowfoot began rocketing around the castle turret.

Genevieve shook her head, wishing her ancestor weren't quite so volatile. "For heaven's sake, will you quit making a spectacle of yourself? Why don't you curl up in the bell tower and go to sleep or something."

The ghost came to a sudden halt in what looked like a puff of smoke that settled almost immediately into the form of Granny Crowfoot. Genevieve wondered what phenomenon of physics might account for that effect. Did all the plasma bunch up in a heap or something? She shook her head and told herself to think about it later. Right now she needed her wits about her to carry on this silly argument.

"*Ghosts,*" Granny Crowfoot announced in an awful voice, "*do not sleep.*"

"Well, that's a great pity, because the rest of us could certainly use some rest from your ridiculous haunting."

"*Ridiculous? I'll tell you what's ridiculous, young lady, and that's having a Rakes living in Crowfoot Castle!*"

Genevieve shook her head, feeling helpless. "You're like a bulldog with a bone, aren't you? You just won't give up once you've taken it into your head that you don't like something, will you?"

"*I shall never cease haunting that ghastly man until he leaves this place.*"

"Oh? From all I know about him, you aren't going to be able to scare him away. Not only is he not a man easily frightened, but living here will infuriate his father, and that seems to be an important issue with him."

Granny Crowfoot cocked her head. "*Oh? Doesn't like his father, eh? I suppose that shows some sense.*"

"Oh, you're impossible!"

"*Impossible, am I? At least I have some respect for my elders, you impudent whippersnapper!*"

"I have a great deal of respect for my Aunt Delilah. And for others of my elders who don't go around trying to make other people miserable. Isn't there some useful purpose you can put your life—your afterlife—to? I mean, don't you think it's rather wasteful to put all of your energies into so paltry a thing as haunting an innocent young man who's had a hard life and has been wounded into the bargain?"

"*Paltry! Innocent! Wasteful! I'll show you wasteful, you insolent girl!*"

And with that, Granny Crowfoot was off and hurtling again. Genevieve watched her and sighed. It was probably useless to argue with the stubborn old girl, yet she really did feel a good deal of sympathy for Tobias Rakes. She thought it sad that he'd bought the castle for no better reason than that his doing so would upset his father. What kind of relationship was that? Genevieve couldn't imagine it. Tobias Rakes was, in his own way, as foolish as Granny Crowfoot.

Which, now that she thought about it, might work to her advantage. A brilliant notion occurred to her.

"I know a way to get back at him."

Granny stopped hurtling in a rush. Again her spirit—or whatever it was—piled up in a heap of smokelike substance that almost immediately settled into the old lady's form. *"How?"* She looked skeptical, as if she didn't believe Genevieve had suddenly altered her position on the matter of making Tobias Rakes's life miserable.

"I found a paper in an old book that indicated there might be a treasure hidden somewhere in the castle. Do you know anything about it?"

The ghost squinted at her balefully. *"I don't believe you. I've never heard about any treasure."*

"I'll show you the note. I have the paper in my room. Come with me."

"I'll meet you there."

And with that, the ghost vanished through the stone walls and shot down through the ceiling. Genevieve wished she could get around so easily. As it was, after she had climbed down all the attic stairs, Genevieve discovered Granny Crowfoot sitting on her bed, her legs crossed and her feet dangling. Her pose reminded her of a mischievous five-year-old.

"That black looks good, Pickstaff. Your son rides like he was born to the saddle."

"Aye. The boy's good."

That was as long a sentence as Tobias had dragged out of William Pickstaff yet. He was encouraged. "I'm going to try to ride one of these days soon."

"Aye?" Pickstaff glanced pointedly at Tobias's ebony cane. Not a diplomat, his stable man. He told himself not to react.

"Don't let this fool you. Until that arrow got me, I rode all the time. Cavalry, you know."

The old man grunted.

"And I expect I'll ride again one of these days."

Another grunt.

"But I think I'll start on a smaller horse than the black. That little sorrel mare, probably."

Pickstaff squinched his eyes up, and Tobias remembered that they called sorrels chestnuts back here. He pointed with his cane. "That chestnut lady over there."

"Oh. Aye. She's a good 'un."

"In fact—why don't you go saddle that lady up for me, Pickstaff. Maybe I'll just give her a try this morning."

What the hell. It was early in the day. If he hurt himself too badly, he could always take a dose of laudanum and rest for the remainder of the day. Maybe he could have Miss Crowfoot send for the local bonesetter. The notion held no appeal, but he really ought to establish a relationship with the village doctor. Unfortunately, Tobias knew he'd need medical services. Besides, it would feel so good to get on a horse again that any resulting pain would be worth it. Tobias wondered if Genevieve Crowfoot rode. Probably not. He didn't think her family had enough money to keep a stable.

Pickstaff didn't answer with words. Tobias cringed when the taciturn man let out with a piercing whistle, drawing his son's attention. The boy rode the black gelding to the fence where Tobias stood with William Pickstaff.

"You're looking good, Small William. You like that big boy?"

The boy nodded and almost smiled. Thank God at least one of the Pickstaffs seemed to have an amiable personality, however minimal. "Yes, sir. He's a good 'un." The lad stroked the gelding's glossy neck.

"Will you saddle up that chestnut mare, Small William? Then maybe you can help me to mount her."

"You're gonna try to ride? With your leg like that?" The boy stared, big-eyed, at Tobias, who frowned back at him. Big William let out with a sour grunt.

"I'm hoping not to remain a cripple forever, William."

Small William's cheeks went rosy. He mumbled, "Beg pardon, sir."

Gruffly, because he didn't aim to encourage insolence, Tobias said, "No need. Just saddle the mare, and we'll see how it goes."

The boy didn't say a word, but dismounted, handed the gelding's reins to his father, and loped off to saddle the mare. By the time they'd struggled together to heave Tobias into the small mare's saddle, Tobias and Small William had established quite a rapport, which was a good thing, since Tobias's leg was throbbing so badly he could hardly talk.

"Here, sir, let me fix the stirrup."

Tobias could only hiss his consent. The boy carefully slid Tobias's right boot into the stirrup and arranged it so that some of the pressure was eased from the leg. Tobias thought he might survive, although he wasn't sure. Since he feared he'd embarrass himself if he tried to talk, he didn't, but he was very grateful when Small William seemed to understand.

"Why don't I walk next to you, sir. That way if you need—well, anything—I'll be right here."

Bless the boy for a saint. Tobias wondered where he'd inherited his tact. Couldn't have been from his father, who'd been watching and glowering at the two of them, chewing on his pipe and looking as if he considered both his son and his employer no better than a pair of fools.

Nodding at the boy, Tobias managed a short, painful, "Fine." Then he decided he'd save his breath for the ordeal ahead of him, and clicked to the horse, whose gait had seemed much smoother when he'd been watching her from a distance. Now, with every step she took, his leg felt like a hundred Indians were taking turns shooting arrows into him.

"If you can get through walls that easily, I'm surprised you haven't found the treasure yet," Genevieve muttered as she watched the ghost swinging her feet and looking smug.

Granny Crowfoot sniffed imperiously. *"I have no need for treasure,"* she announced in a voice that as much as told Genevieve she ought to have figured that one out on her own. *"We don't need anything so vulgar as base coin on this plane, you know."*

"No, I didn't know. How could I? I'd never met a ghost before you. Thank God." Feeling out of sorts, Genevieve crossed to her desk. She'd stashed the note in a box in the drawer, and she looked at it every now and then, trying to determine if it held any clues. Thus far, she'd found none. "Here. Let me read this to you."

"I can read it for myself." Granny Crowfoot was up and had snatched the note from Genevieve's hand before Genevieve had drawn breath. She glowered at the old ghost, who paid her no mind. Not that Genevieve had expected her to.

" 'All is in readiness. The war will come, and I am prepared for it. No one suspects that I have a vast fortune hidden here in the castle.' " Granny Crowfoot turned the torn page over and frowned. *"This is all?"*

"That's all I found, and I searched through the whole book. The paper looks like it was torn in half a million years ago."

"More than a hundred years ago, at any rate. Hmmm. This is my father's handwriting."

"Is it?" Genevieve considered snatching the note back from the old bat, but feared she wouldn't be quick enough and Granny Crowfoot would merely laugh at her and vanish with the paper. "What do you suppose it means?"

Granny Crowfoot drew herself up in a regal manner. *"It means that my father was a noble man and a patriot. If he was talking about a cache of money, I'm sure he was going to use it to help finance the Revolution.* He, *unlike some people I could mention, was a gentleman, a patriot, and a gallant man."*

"I'm sure he was." Genevieve cast a glance heavenward.

"I don't know where any treasure could be if it's here. I've never noticed anything out of the ordinary lying about. You've checked those trunks in the attic, haven't you?"

"Oh, yes. I looked at those the second day I came here to clean. That was the day after the morning we met you— and after my poor aunt revived and I saw her home." Because she was still peeved at the ghost for frightening Aunt Delilah so badly, Genevieve scowled at her. Granny Crowfoot, needless to say, didn't appear to care a jot.

"I have no idea where it could be. And, since you seem determined to condone that beastly Rakes man living here, I don't believe I'll help you to find it, either."

Genevieve wouldn't have been surprised if Granny Crowfoot had stuck her tongue out at her, she was such a childish old thing. "Fine. Don't help me. I don't want your help anyway. What I *do* want is for you to keep quiet at night so that poor Mr. Rakes can sleep. He needs plenty of rest or that leg of his will never heal."

"Good!"

Genevieve wished she'd kept her mouth shut about Mr. Rakes needing his sleep. Feeling aggrieved, she grabbed the note back from the miserable old ghost and put it away. Her desk sat beside the window in her room, and she was glad to see that the group of children she'd set to work in the garden were still hard at it. She'd asked Molly to prepare some sandwiches and apples for the children's lunches. Not even Molly could ruin a sandwich.

And there was Small William walking next to that pretty little chestnut horse, holding the stirrup—

"Merciful heavens!"

"What is it?" Granny Crowfoot wafted over and hovered beside Genevieve's shoulder. *"Oh,"* she said balefully. *The ghastly man is riding, is he? Well, I shall have something to say about that."*

And she was gone. Genevieve whirled around, but she only got out a sharp "What—" before she realized asking a question would be useless. The ghost was nowhere in sight. She'd undoubtedly left to pull some awful stunt on poor Mr. Rakes.

Well, Genevieve would just see about that. She dashed out of her room, ran down the castle stairs, raced across the flagged entryway, and tore out the front door in time to see a small flurry of leaves drop from a huge maple tree onto Tobias Rakes's hat.

Chapter
Five

"Good Lord, where did all that stuff come from?" Tobias batted leaves from his hat and shoulders and sneezed. He was actually grateful for the deluge, because it took his attention away from his leg for a moment or two.

Small William looked up into the tree, frowning. "I ain't sure, sir. I ain't never seen leaves just fall like that, with no wind or nothing." The boy sneezed, too, and wiped the back of his hand under his nose. "Might be the ghost." He made his pronouncement ominously, as if he suspected it was the truth.

Tobias eyed the boy curiously. "Do you believe in the ghost, William?"

"Aye."

No elaboration. To keep himself occupied with something other than pain, Tobias said, "Why? Have you seen it? Does it go on haunting sprees in Bittersweet?"

"No, sir, but I heard things."

"Ah."

The sound of someone running caught Tobias's attention, and he turned to see pretty Genevieve Crowfoot barreling past the working children, straight at his horse. He thanked his stars that the sorrel mare was a placid creature and showed no inclination to bolt. Sure that his seat wouldn't gallop off, he gazed at Genevieve, enjoying the sight of her pink cheeks and flying hair.

Tobias realized he hadn't seen a grown woman actually pick up her skirts and run since he'd left the Dakota Territory. Western females were less apt to place much store in proper decorum than their eastern sisters. This was, of course, because their lives were so much more precarious in the western territories than they were in the more civilized East. Corseting might also have something to do with it, although Tobias had never investigated that theory.

It did his heart good to realize Genevieve wasn't as stuffy as most of the women he'd been introduced to since he'd come home to Bittersweet, even if she did look mighty worried at the moment. She was close enough now for him to salute her. "Is anything the matter, Miss Crowfoot? The castle on fire or something?"

His attempt at humor appeared to sail right over her head. "Are you all right?" She sounded as worried as she looked when she skidded to a halt a few feet away from Small William, who backed up and gave her a disapproving frown even as he tipped his cap to her. She slammed her hand over her heart and panted like a winded hound.

Although smiles hadn't come easily to Tobias in recent months, there was something about Genevieve Crowfoot that made him want to smile, so he did. "I'm fine, thank you. Did you think I wasn't?"

She heaved a sigh of unmistakable relief. "I beg your pardon, Mr. Rakes. You'll probably think I've lost my mind—"

Small William nodded, and Genevieve shot him a look.

"—but when I saw all those leaves fall down on you, I feared you might have been—" She stopped speaking abruptly and swallowed. "That is, I feared a branch might have broken from the tree and landed on top of you."

"I'm fine," Tobias repeated. "I imagine a bird or a squirrel dislodged some of the leaves."

She was staring up into the tree as if she saw something there that shouldn't be. In spite of the pain it caused him,

Tobias turned to look as well, bracing himself with a hand on the mare's rump. He saw nothing but the tree, standing there, looking green and leafy and like a tree was supposed to look. He didn't even see a bird or a squirrel in it.

"It's nothing, really, Miss Crowfoot," he said when he turned to gaze at her again. For the first time, he wondered if Miss Crowfoot might be the least bit nervous of disposition. He hadn't noticed any particular tendency in that direction before, but he didn't know her well, and he could perceive no reason for her to be in such a lather.

"Thank God." She released another huge breath.

She sounded so grateful that Tobias began to suspect she knew something he didn't. "Er, is there anything going on here that I should know about, Miss Crowfoot? You appear to be concerned about something in particular."

"Concerned?" She opened her brown eyes wide and gave him a forced, false laugh. "Heavens no! I merely feared for you. The leaves, you know. And branches. Possible falling branches. And so forth. I mean, you know how badly my uncle kept up the castle grounds. There might be any number of tree branches just waiting to fall on one."

After a moment, when he was sure she was through blathering, Tobias said, "Of course."

Small William said, "You sick, Miss Genevieve?"

Tobias choked back a laugh.

Genevieve looked peeved. "Of course I'm not sick, Small William. I was merely concerned for Mr. Rakes's health."

Small William glanced up at Tobias, his brows knitted. "He ain't sick, neither."

"I didn't mean that."

Small William rolled his eyes, and Tobias could no longer stifle his laugh. Lord on high, he couldn't recall the last time he'd laughed so much. He discovered a reason to be glad he'd bought the castle—other than that his possession of a Crowfoot asset would give his father an ulcer. He was actually enjoying himself among these strange people. He hadn't enjoyed himself for so long he'd forgotten what it felt like.

He wanted to walk back to the castle with Genevieve, but

he didn't want to dismount in front of her because he feared his leg wouldn't hold him. He didn't want her to see him make a fool of himself.

"Are you sure you're well enough to ride, Mr. Rakes?"

Tobias realized Genevieve was staring at his leg, and his good humor fled. "I'm riding this minute, am I not?"

His tone was so sharp it made her straighten in surprise. For the briefest moment, Tobias thought he saw anger flash in her lovely eyes. The next instant brought compassion, however, and her expression softened. All in all, he believed he'd prefer to inspire anger than pity in a pretty woman's bosom, but he decided then and there that he'd take what he could get.

"Actually, this ride might not have been the best idea in the world, Miss Crowfoot. My leg was badly broken, you know, and it's pounding like a Sioux war drum at the moment. Perhaps, if you wouldn't mind assisting a poor injured soldier, you might wait there until Small William helps me to dismount. Then you can lend me an arm and help me back home."

"Of course, Mr. Rakes. You probably shouldn't have tried such exercise so soon after your arrival."

"I was wounded ten months ago, Miss Crowfoot. I can't remain bed-bound forever."

"Ten months is nowhere near forever, Mr. Rakes." She gazed at him sternly, provoking another grin out of him.

"You're right, of course," he said meekly. "Stand back. If I scream in pain, think nothing of it."

He expected her to laugh, but she only looked more concerned than she had before, and began wringing her hands. Small William ran to the chestnut's left side and held the stirrup steady. Preparing himself with a stiff breath and clamped teeth, Tobias managed to lift his right leg and heave himself off the chestnut's back without bellowing or otherwise humiliating himself.

He was awkward, and his leg hurt like crazy and he wasn't sure he'd live—but he'd done it. He'd ridden a horse, something the doctors had told him he'd never do again. Of course, most of the doctors hadn't believed he'd ever walk again, either. Or live. They all expected him to die from gangrene. One of them had even seemed to resent it when he didn't.

He only realized he was standing with his eyes squeezed shut and his teeth clenched when he felt Genevieve's small warm hands on his arm.

"Oh, Mr. Rakes, are you all right?"

She sounded like she expected him to faint dead away from suffering. He knew he was foolish to resent her tone, but he did. Striving to relax at least the muscles in his face— he was fairly certain the muscles in his leg wouldn't relax for another year or two—he opened an eye and squinted down at her. She wasn't very tall. Only came up to his shoulder. And her cheeks were flushed with concern and her eyes were wide and soft and pansy-brown, and she had the most kissable mouth he'd ever seen in his life.

He shook his head hard. "I'm fine."

She stepped back, shocked by his acerbic tone. "Good." Her own tone was acerbic too, and his humor returned in a rush.

He opened his other eye. "I beg your pardon, Miss Crowfoot. We cripples aren't the easiest of men to get along with, I'll warrant."

"Stop calling yourself a cripple," she said, more sharply still.

He lifted his left eyebrow, but made no comment. She muttered, "I beg your pardon, Mr. Rakes. I have no business giving you orders."

"True, but I do appreciate your concern."

She didn't answer because something in the tree behind him seemed to have distracted her. Tobias turned. Yet again, he saw nothing but leaves. Some wood. Even when he squinted, he couldn't discern so much as a bird's nest up there. He turned back to Genevieve. "What is it, Miss Crowfoot?"

"Nothing."

She flung both arms out in a warding-off gesture. Tobias had no idea what she thought she was doing, but he glanced over his shoulder at the tree again. Nothing. When he peered at Genevieve, she looked embarrassed.

"Fly," she said. "A fly was buzzing around my face. They're so bothersome, you know. And the black flies have quite a painful sting."

He knew she was lying, and he had no idea why. Her strange behavior had again taken his attention from his leg, however, and he was grateful to her for it. He thought he might survive until he made it back to the house.

"Shall we go on to the castle, Mr. Rakes?"

She was being deliberately cheerful, and he decided to contemplate her obsession with trees later. "Thank you, Miss Crowfoot."

They walked slowly up the path to the castle, pausing to chat with the children on their way. Tobias could see, now that the herd of young folks had been busy all morning, that the pleasure gardens in Crowfoot Castle were taking shape quite nicely.

"Do you have any particular flowers you'd like planted here, Mr. Rakes? William Pickstaff has agreed to double as chief gardener until Mr. Armitage finds a suitable replacement."

"Does he like gardening?"

She gave a short laugh. "I fear Mr. Pickstaff doesn't care much for plants, no, Mr. Rakes. He's competent, though, even if he isn't awfully cheerful about his work."

"I hope Wes comes up with a replacement soon, then. Pickstaff is good with the horses, and I'd hate to have him driven off because I'm having him do work he hates."

"Oh, don't worry about that, Mr. Rakes. William Pickstaff hates everything. And he needs the job, so he won't be driven off any time soon."

"I'm not sure I find that awfully comforting, Miss Crowfoot."

"No?"

Another of her tinkling laughs decorated the summer air. In spite of his aches and pains, Tobias felt grand. His good mood only increased as he leaned more heavily than he needed to on her arm and she braced him with a hand on his back. He probably should have felt a bit of penitence for having lured her into putting her arm around him, but he didn't. He even winked rakishly at the little dark-haired boy who goggled at the two of them as they made their way up the path and onto the great stone porch.

His sense of well-being lasted, in fact, until Genevieve pushed the huge door open; a blast of cold air ripped the door out of her hand, and a pennon with the Crowfoot crest embroidered on it sailed across the room and slapped him in the face.

"Grmph!" It was all he could say with a piece of cloth in his mouth. He yanked it out and glared at it. The griffin affixed to the cloth, rampant on what looked like a bale of hay, seemed to glare back. Tobias transferred his glare to the empty hallway. "Where in the devil did this come from?"

Miss Crowfoot was not amused. "This," she announced with seeming irrelevance, "is the last straw."

And to Tobias's dismay, she left off holding him closely, snatched the pennon out of his hand, and stormed away. She didn't even close the door behind him. Nor did she stop to give Godfrey Watkins, who was standing in the entryway staring at them, a lecture on how it was his job to open the castle door for the master. Tobias and Godfrey were left to gape after her as she took the grand staircase two steps at a time in the highest dudgeon Tobias could recollect ever seeing except when his father was in a snit.

"All right, you vicious ghost!" Genevieve didn't stop stomping until she'd made her way to the attic in which she'd located Granny Crowfoot that morning. "Where are you? You can't hide forever, you know. I'll find you someday, and when I do, I'll—"

"You'll what?" Granny Crowfoot materialized in a puff of plasma. She had the most conceited expression on her ghostly face that Genevieve had ever beheld.

"I'll have you exorcised!"

"Hogwash."

"It's not hogwash. I'm sure there are ministers or priests

who perform such rites. I'll have you ejected from this house, never to darken its doors again, if I have to send all the way to New York City for a clergyman!''

''I do not darken doors. In case you hadn't noticed, I can't even cast a shadow.''

''Don't bandy words with me!'' Genevieve was so angry, she'd begun to shriek and didn't even care. ''You caused a flurry of leaves to drop onto that poor man's head, and then you threw the Crowfoot pennon at him. He might have choked to death on it, you horrid old ghost!''

''It would have served him right. He doesn't belong here, and you know it.''

''I do *not* know it.'' Her fury rising by the second, Genevieve stormed around the attic. Every time she got close to a wall she pounded on it with her fist. Although she'd seldom experienced violent urges, today she wished she could pound on Granny Crowfoot's face so easily. But the ghost was translucent and, therefore, beyond physical punishment. Which made Genevieve think of something. She stopped stomping, planted her fists on her hips, and scowled at the ghost. ''Did your father ever paddle your rump when you were a little girl?''

''Good heavens, no. My father wasn't such a beast as that. I keep telling you so.''

''I didn't think so. You obviously were never given any lessons whatever in deportment and manners. Your parents were much at fault for it, too.''

''How dare you?'' Granny Crowfoot swelled, as she was wont to do when peeved. Genevieve cared not.

''I dare because it's the truth! Your manners are abominable.''

''At least I'd never speak in such tones to my elders, young woman. Talk about manners!'' The ghost crossed her arms over her chest and turned toward the wall, her nose in the air.

Genevieve walked right up to her and pointed a finger in her face. ''You leave that man alone, Granny Crowfoot. If you don't, I swear to you that I'll have your spirit exorcised from this castle!''

"Idle threats."

Perhaps they were, but Genevieve was so mad at the moment she was shaking. "Try me."

"You're a saucy girl, Genevieve Crowfoot, and you ought to have more respect for your elders."

Nevertheless, before she vanished through the wall, Granny Crowfoot dropped a pair of silver cuff links at Genevieve's feet. Genevieve would have liked to scold the old ghost some more, for her ire was far from satisfied, but, as she could no longer see her, the effort would have been for naught. With a snort, she stooped, grabbed the cuff links, and departed.

Just in case the ghost was somewhere nearby, she gave a parting shot before she descended the stairs to search for Mr. Rakes. "Just you be quiet tonight, Granny Crowfoot. I don't want you disturbing that poor man's rest another night."

Tobias blinked at the cuff links Genevieve held in her hand. When she'd finally come downstairs again, she'd hunted him down and made him go into his library. There she'd made him sit in a huge overstuffed chair and prop his legs up on an ottoman. She wouldn't take no for an answer, and she didn't seem to be a bit affected by his grouchy protests. He even redoubled them to see if he could provoke a snappish retort from her. He couldn't. She merely told him to stop being childish.

"My cousin would never do anything that was good for him, either, Mr. Rakes. It's all masculine pride and foolishness, and your foul temper won't deter me from seeing to your health, even if *you* won't."

"Shrew," Tobias muttered.

"You may call me any names you like, sir. I shan't be deterred."

She meant it, too. She wouldn't stop fussing over him until she had him settled in the chair, his feet up, a sheepskin rug settled over his legs, a dose of laudanum-and-water drizzled down his gullet, and a cup of sweetened tea laced with brandy in his hand.

"There," she said, stepping back, an expression of satisfaction on her face. "You stay there and rest. You'll feel better if you stay off that leg for an hour or two."

He had opened his mouth to holler at her, when she played dirty and showed him the cuff links. He was so astonished, his holler evaporated. "Where'd you find those?"

"On the floor. I don't know how they got there."

"What floor?" Had she gone into his bedroom, looking for them? The notion of Genevieve Crowfoot in his bedroom wasn't a half-bad one, although he'd prefer her somewhere other than the floor. The bed would be nice.

She dropped the cuff links on the table next to him and waved her hand airily. "Oh, I can't remember offhand, but I'm glad they turned up."

They just turned up? He stared up at her, and she got nervous. "Well, I have some things to see to. Have a pleasant rest, Mr. Rakes." She turned and hurried toward the door.

"Hey," Tobias called. "You can't abandon me here like this."

She whirled around. "Abandon you? But you need to—"

"Bother rest. I need some amusement." He thought hard for a minute, trying to think of some way to keep her in the room with him. "I need for you to"—inspiration struck—"read to me. I haven't had a chance to read the *New York Times* for years. Since you're making me sit here and drink brandy in my tea, you'll have to read it to me." He pointed at his eyes. "Drinking makes me blurry."

He could tell she wasn't convinced, but at least he'd made her smile. "I really do have duties to perform, you know, Mr. Rakes. I can't be sloughing off because—"

"Because the master of the house needs you? What kind of employee are you, anyway?"

She giggled. Tobias was charmed. "Oh, very well. I'll read to you from the *Times*."

He didn't know how long he sat in his chair, lost in a fluff of sheepskin and soft pillows, comfortably sipping tea and brandy and listening to Genevieve read to him. Her voice was musical and soothing and had a delicious rhythm to it.

She spoke in time to the throbbing in his leg for a while, then the throbbing eased, and her voice grew faint, and Tobias couldn't keep track of the article she read.

Genevieve tiptoed to the door as quietly as the proverbial mouse while Tobias was sleeping. She opened the door, slipped out, and closed it behind her. Then she leaned against the heavy oak door and pressed a hand to her ricocheting heart.

Whatever had possessed her to touch him that way—to stroke his forehead like that? And had she really, truly *kissed* his sleeping brow? Good heavens, what a wanton, abandoned woman she was.

"That's how young women get into trouble, Genevieve Crowfoot, and you know it."

Her stern lecture didn't do much good. He'd been in such dreadful pain, and he'd tried so hard not to show it. Genevieve remembered that Benton had been the same way. *All boy* is how her father had described Benton—rather sadly, if Genevieve recalled correctly. Her father would have loved to have had a son. Not that he didn't love Genevieve, but she always knew he wished for a son. Her heart gave a painful throb as it always did when she thought about Benton and her kindhearted father.

Benton had never wanted to admit when he was in pain, just like Mr. Rakes. And poor Mr. Rakes's face had been so ashen and drawn. And his dark hair had curled so beautifully and fallen across his brow so nicely.

"He needed to rest," she said in a firm voice, trying to shake away thoughts of both her family and her alarming behavior.

But she'd never felt so intensely drawn to a man before. When he'd leaned his head back against the cushions and closed his eyes, Genevieve had experienced the most dreadful urge to touch him, to stroke him—like some kind of pet.

She frowned, knowing that her feelings about Tobias Rakes were about as far from her feelings for a pet as they could get.

"Good heavens, this is awful."

As if it weren't bad enough having a family ghost trying

to frighten Tobias Rakes to death, now she had to worry about her own shocking attraction to him.

She felt excessively crabby when she pinned on her hat, took up her wicker basket, and sailed out the door to visit some shops in Bittersweet. Her mood didn't improve when she was attacked by Aunt Delilah after she'd barely even made it through the front door at the grocer's.

"Is it true what Molly said about that dreadful ghost, Genevieve?"

Delilah clamped a hand on Genevieve's arm so tightly, Genevieve feared for her circulation. She frowned at her aunt. "Since I don't know what rumors Molly has been spreading, I'm afraid I can't answer your question, Aunt Delilah." She spoke in a severe tone, hoping in that way to curb her aunt's unruly tongue.

She ought to have known better. Delilah, still clutching Genevieve's arm, leaned close and whispered loud enough for anyone in the store to hear, "She said poor Mr. Rakes had been kept awake half the night listening to the horrid thing rattling chains and moaning and groaning."

Genevieve decided another lecture to the staff was in order. Molly, who was possibly the worst cook in Bittersweet, had no business spreading tales about such an idiotic thing as a ghost. Even if the ghost existed. "And how would Molly know that, pray tell? She doesn't sleep in the castle at night."

"But you do!" Aunt Delilah's eyes opened as wide as they could. Since she was quite myopic, her pupils were large most of the time; now she looked almost avid, as if she couldn't wait to hear a juicy bit of salacious gossip.

Her attitude annoyed Genevieve greatly. "Yes, I do. And there's nothing in the castle that is causing Mr. Rakes the least trouble except Uncle Hubert's legacy of bad management."

Delilah dropped her hand from Genevieve's arm, thank goodness, and stepped away. Genevieve was dismayed to see an injured expression on her dear aunt's face. "But I *saw* it, Genevieve. And so did you. The ghost is there, and I think you're being deliberately mean to me."

Oh, dear. Now Genevieve felt guilty. "I beg your pardon,

Aunt Delilah, but it annoys me that Molly should be telling tales about things she can't possibly know of. Besides, Mr. Rakes is a rational man with a good head on his shoulders. He's not intimidated by idle rumors.''

"They aren't idle." Delilah sniffed to let Genevieve know she was still hurt. "I saw it with my own eyes."

Genevieve heaved a sigh. "Well, the old ghost isn't going to succeed in getting rid of him, no matter what she does."

"Oh, has she done something?"

Taking note of her aunt's once-again eager expression, Genevieve wished she'd kept her mouth shut. "No," she said snappishly. "She hasn't done a thing. For heaven's sake, Delilah, keep your voice down! You don't want the whole village to think we're out of our minds, do you? Ghosts, indeed!"

"Say what you will, Genevieve Crowfoot," Delilah said indignantly. "You and I both know what exists in that awful place, and I think you're being heedless to place yourself in jeopardy merely because that poor man wants to make his father angry."

Genevieve was growing fairly indignant herself. Not only did she resent Delilah for being right about the existence of Granny Crowfoot, but she also resented her reference to Tobias's less-than-noble motives for purchasing the castle. She said "Nonsense!" and knew it to be inadequate.

Delilah sniffed again. "You can 'nonsense' me all you want, Genevieve Crowfoot, but you know I'm right." Delilah moved toward a bin, picked up an ear of early corn, and put it down again. "Anyway, I don't suppose *I* care what happens to that man. I thought he was cold and unpleasant when we met him."

"Fiddlesticks." *Fiddlesticks* was every bit as inadequate as *nonsense* had been, and Genevieve knew it. She felt an irrational impulse to defend Tobias Rakes even though, in many respects, she knew her aunt's opinion of him was justified. He *had* been cold and unpleasant when they'd first met him. And although he was less so now, he could still be touchy and irritable.

Yet he'd endured so much in his life, from the loss of his

mother, to his father's unjust fury, to dreadful injuries. She felt a good deal of compassion for him, when she wasn't wishing she could fling herself into his arms and beg him to have his way with her.

Oh, dear.

She turned to glare at Delilah. "I should appreciate it if you wouldn't give credence to Molly's foolish slanders by spreading them around Bittersweet, Aunt Delilah. Poor Mr. Rakes has enough to contend with without adding empty rumors to his plate."

"They aren't empty!"

Genevieve's temper snapped. "Even more reason to keep them from spreading. For heaven's sake, Aunt Delilah, do you want everyone in Bittersweet to think the Crowfoot ladies are mad? How many people do you think really believe in that ghost? They may prattle on about it and titter and gossip, but if anyone discovers that you believe you've actually *seen* the thing, they'll lock you up! Don't you know that?"

Delilah pinched her lips together and her expression of hurt intensified. Genevieve saw a suspicious glitter in her old blue eyes and chastised herself for her harshness. Yet she'd spoken only the truth. She really didn't want her aunt considered eccentric or crazy by her fellow Bittersweet citizens. Poor Delilah would be crushed if people gossiped about her, and Genevieve knew it.

"I think you're being deliberately cruel, Genevieve Crowfoot. I've never known you to be cruel before." Delilah turned away and lifted her chin.

Genevieve felt awful. "I'm sorry, Aunt. I didn't mean to speak to you harshly. Please forgive me." She was beginning to feel beleaguered when a lovely thought struck her. "Please, come with me, Aunt Delilah. Let me buy us both a cup of tea and a turnover at the bakery. It's Tuesday, you know, and Tuesday is when Mrs. Carvahal makes those wonderful lemon turnovers."

Her aunt brightened slightly. The thought of sweets generally did that to her. Genevieve knew how aggrieved she was when it took another minute or two of cajolery on her part to get Delilah to agree to the treat.

Genevieve was still troubled when she returned to the castle an hour and a half later. The first thing she did was give Molly a stern lecture about spreading rumors and gossip about what went on in the castle. She knew it was only because Molly was proud of her new position, but she still aimed to put a stop to her jabbering. ''Pay attention to your cooking, Molly Gratchett, and let me worry about ghosts. You're the worst cook in Bittersweet, you know, and Mr. Rakes deserves better.''

Molly burst into tears, and Genevieve felt like a brute.

Chapter Six

Molly's cooking improved minimally in the ensuing weeks. She still served overcooked vegetables and had a habit of burning the meat, but Tobias, who wasn't nearly as aloof and grumpy as he'd been at first, was good about laughing off the cook's shortcomings. Genevieve continued to serve his meals, the better to audit and correct Molly's efforts. She sometimes even succeeded in averting disaster—but not very often.

"I used to eat beef that was burned black on the outside and running red on the inside all the time, Miss Crowfoot," he told Genevieve one evening when she gazed in dismay at the unidentifiable piece of leathery meat resting next to a heap of gray English peas on his plate. The peas, of course, ought to have been green—and, indeed, they had been before Molly got hold of them.

"My goodness, really?"

"Absolutely. And as far as green vegetables went, why, we used to have to eat weeds and cactus if we wanted to eat anything besides burned beef."

"Really?" Genevieve's eyes were so wide, Tobias thought he might drown in them.

"It's the way things are done on the frontier."

"Good heavens. How horrible for you."

She looked so genuinely distressed, that Tobias burst out laughing. "I'm only joking about the vegetables, Miss Crowfoot."

Her eyes thinned and she put on an expression of *faux* outrage. "Honestly! You must think I'm a complete simpleton, Mr. Rakes, and all because I've never been to the West."

"Not at all. Not at all. And I'm teasing only about the vegetables, unfortunately. They really did cook meat that way. Texans don't believe in slow cooking."

She dropped her look of indignation and appeared interested again. "Oh, were you in Texas?"

"For a while. Before I was stationed in the Dakota Territory, I was posted in Texas and New Mexico Territory briefly."

"I've read so many stories in the newspapers about the western frontier. It must be something. And the landscape. Why, from the paintings I've looked at, you can see clear to the end of the earth out there."

"It's big, all right. I was out there so long, I actually felt claustrophobic when I finally came back to New York."

"I should think I'd feel lost in all that open space," she said pensively.

"It has that effect on a lot of people. When I first went to Texas, I had the eerie sensation that the unbroken vista was going to swallow me up. The openness gave me a feeling of—oh, I don't know—as if I were no longer attached to the earth or something. Like I might blow away. The wind out there is fierce, too."

"My goodness."

Tobias loved the way Genevieve's eyes opened wide and brimmed with curiosity, and her voice rang with wonder. He'd never been fond of discussing his military career before, mainly because he hadn't seen any point to it. That was before he met this sunny creature who'd never been out of the state of New York, and who seemed to pine for adventure. She was such a receptive audience that he discovered himself remembering things he'd forgotten for years and years.

Not that living in this rambling old place didn't often constitute an adventure. On a given night, Tobias was apt to be awakened by any number of crashings, creakings, moans, groans, and rattles. He had no idea what caused all the noise, but it was disconcerting, especially since he hadn't been able to sleep well for years. And lightweight personal items vanished with irritating regularity as well. Genevieve usually found them again as she went about her daily duties. Occasionally Tobias wondered if Genevieve herself might be pinching his things, but he couldn't imagine why she'd do such a thing unless she was flat out of her mind. Since she showed no other symptoms of mental disorder except a tendency toward nervousness, he didn't think that was it, even if she did jump at the least little noise.

On the other hand, it was sort of fun, living in a supposedly haunted castle. The housemaids went about in pairs because they were afraid of the alleged ghost, and Watkins, his butler, looked like a scared jackrabbit most of the time, although that might be due to the poor boy's fear of his mother.

Tobias did his best to put everyone at their ease, and Genevieve did likewise, but Tobias didn't interfere with their duties. He was more apt to have to stifle his compulsion to utter ''Boo'' in a sepulchral voice when he came upon a servant who'd ventured forth alone. He knew it would be cruel, so he never did it, but he wanted to. The urge surprised him, since he hadn't felt a lick of playfulness since he was ten years old and his mother died.

The one thing that truly puzzled Tobias was that Genevieve, who in all other respects was a sensible woman, also believed in the existence of the ghost. She'd even told him it was the ghost who was responsible for his missing items. To give her credit, she'd looked abashed when she said it.

''I fear the rumors are true, Mr. Rakes.'' Genevieve had muttered earlier when he'd told her that a pair of collar studs had gone missing.

He hadn't been sure what she meant. "What rumors are those, Miss Crowfoot?"

She'd sucked in a deep breath that swelled her bosom enchantingly. "I'm afraid there really is a ghost."

He'd been too stunned to speak.

When the silence dragged on, she'd lifted her head, gazed at him, and sighed again. "You don't believe me, do you?"

"Ah—well—I've, er, never had anything to do with ghosts before, Miss Crowfoot."

Her lips had pinched up, as if his hesitation irritated her. "I've seen it, Mr. Rakes. When we were cleaning out the place, when I was here with Aunt Delilah, we met the ghost. That's why Aunt Delilah refuses to come inside the castle. She's afraid, you see."

"Yes. I see." He hadn't guffawed or snorted in disbelief and was proud of himself.

"I can tell that you don't believe me, but it's the truth. It's the ghost of Granny Crowfoot, who was Charles Crowfoot's daughter. She's furious that a Rakes has bought the castle, and she told me she's determined to make your life miserable until you move out again."

"I see," he had said again, since he couldn't think of anything more cogent to say.

"You don't see at all." Genevieve had frowned heavily. "And I don't really blame you, but it's true all the same. I don't think she can hurt you, but she's the one who's been making all the noise at night."

He had nodded this time, because he didn't think she'd appreciate another "I see."

She'd stared at him for another minute or two, and then huffed out, "Oh, never mind," and walked away.

In all other respects, Genevieve Crowfoot was a superior female, so Tobias didn't hold her belief in ghosts against her. It rankled, though, that she actually, really and truly, *believed* in something so idiotic as a family ghost. Maybe there was a strain that ran through the Crowfoot lineage. Such a tendency toward lunacy might account, in part, for the feud— although the Crowfoots being crazy didn't account for the Rakeses' part in perpetuating the hostilities. Tobias decided he had better use for his brain cells, so he didn't dwell on it.

He was becoming better acquainted with his neighbors, too. When he'd first come to live in the castle, he'd entertained the bitter notion that he'd hide away here, isolated from his fellow man, and spend his days brooding and nursing his wounds and grievances in private. Wesley Armitage had assured Tobias that Ernest Rakes knew of and deplored his purchase of the castle, so Tobias's main aim had already been achieved.

Genevieve Crowfoot, however, wasn't much for hiding away. She'd introduced him to no end of people since he'd moved in. Even bullied him into holding an open house to celebrate the resuscitation of the castle gardens.

"The citizens of Bittersweet have a big stake in the castle, you know, Mr. Rakes."

"They have, have they?" He'd lifted his left eyebrow, hoping in that way to intimidate her into dropping her scheme for a house party. The eyebrow trick had worked on soldiers, and even on Wesley Armitage. Genevieve Crowfoot was made of sterner stuff. She merely lifted an eyebrow of her own, added the little lift to her chin that made her look so cute, and dug in her heels.

"Yes, they have. The castle used to employ a large number of people from Bittersweet. Bittersweet folks used to tend the gardens and the fields and so forth. When the Crowfoots sold the farming acres three or four decades ago, several families were hard put to make a living."

He interrupted her lecture. "That was the Crowfoots' doing, not mine."

"Yes, it was, but until my uncle Hubert came to live here, at least the Crowfoot family kept a good number of carpenters, farriers, blacksmiths, gardeners, and indoor staff employed. Since Hubert took over the running of the place, the whole town has suffered."

"That, may I remind you again, was not my fault."

She stamped her foot. Tobias hid the grin that sneaked up on him. "Of course it's not your fault!"

Because he wanted to see how she'd react, he lifted his

left eyebrow even higher and adopted the superior sneer that had done so well by him when dealing with recalcitrant Cavalry enlistees—and even a few officers. For a second or two, Tobias was pretty sure she was going to holler at him for it, and he experienced a gleeful delight that was all out of proportion to the conversation. She knew her place as his employee, however—a fact Tobias wasn't sure he appreciated in this instance—and muttered, "I beg your pardon, Mr. Rakes. But you're missing my point."

"Ah. Am I?"

There went her scowl again. And her cheeks were as pink as the hollyhocks outside in the garden.

"The point is that you *are* doing a good deal to revitalize the economy in Bittersweet. You're giving people employment, and the whole town ought to be made to understand that. You're doing everyone a tremendous good, Mr. Rakes, and you deserve some credit."

"I've never been much in the habit of currying credit, Miss Crowfoot."

She expelled a breath of pure exasperation. "Well, you should be."

"Oh? Why?"

"In case you didn't know it, Mr. Rakes, the feud that's simmered between our families for the past century and a quarter hasn't bypassed the town of Bittersweet. The whole place has been split into factions during that same number of years. There are Crowfoot supporters and Rakes supporters. The whole thing is ridiculous. By showing the community that the Crowfoots and the Rakeses have buried the hatchet, it will only become more difficult for people to perpetuate the hostilities."

Tobias frowned, not having looked at the matter in this light. "I had no idea."

"Well, of course you didn't. How could you? You ran away and stayed gone for decades." Now she sounded huffy.

Tobias lifted his eyebrow again for the hell of it. "Seventeen years, Miss Crowfoot. That's only a little more than a decade and a half."

"Humph."

"You don't approve?"

"It's not my place to approve or disapprove," she said in a voice reeking with disapproval.

"Anyway, I had good reason to leave."

She sniffed. "So I've heard." She might well have added, "That female," because the unspoken words echoed so loudly in the room.

The hostile look he gave her this time wasn't entirely feigned. She had the grace to blush. "I beg your pardon."

"You seem to have to do that a lot," he said in a voice as dry as dust. "However, you have made some valid points, and I'll think about hosting an open house."

As it turned out, he had no cause to think about it at all, because Genevieve had taken his equivocation as consent. The open house was to be held on Wednesday afternoon the following week, and now she was all a-bustle, getting things ready.

And not only had Genevieve Crowfoot forced Tobias into meeting his neighbors, but now Wesley Armitage visited all the time, too. Wes was a worrywart but Tobias didn't mind too much. The fellow had Tobias's best interests at heart and was quite often useful. He was going to be visiting at noon today to take luncheon and discuss business affairs and investment opportunities.

Until then, and since the house had been taken over by what seemed a platoon of housemaids, all armed with feather dusters, furniture polish, mops, buckets, and brooms, Tobias aimed to escape to the stables. He'd graduated from the chestnut mare to the larger black gelding, which he'd named Rake's Progress—Pickstaff didn't understand the irony of naming a horse after a Hogarth print—and the exercise was doing his leg good. It didn't hurt half as much as it used to, and his muscles, which had nearly atrophied with disuse, seemed to be getting stronger every day.

"Thanks, William."

Small William nodded and gave a grunt that Tobias had realized some time ago meant "You're welcome." The boy released the stirrup he'd been holding. He no longer had to walk alongside the horse as Tobias rode, thank God.

The lad wasn't anywhere near as surly as his father, but he was none too cheerful. Tobias figured one needed to be taught good cheer. He didn't hold William's lack of social graces against him. Hell, Tobias himself had been brought up under the austere guardianship of one of the East's sternest Yankee fathers. He shuddered at the memory.

However, Rake's Progress felt like a well-oiled machine under him, the weather was fine, and hence, Tobias soon ceased thinking about Small William Pickstaff, Old William Pickstaff, his own father, and his unhappy past. He lifted his face to the sun and felt its healing rays soaking into his brain, gently nudging his black thoughts aside.

He rode through the woods on his estate for an hour before his leg reminded him he was no longer a completely whole man. Because he really and truly had come to love the place and enjoyed watching its transformation from an uncared-for, overgrown heap of vine-entangled stones to his own home—the first home he'd ever really had—he decided to ride back along the path that took him around the castle's honey-colored walls.

William Pickstaff was directing two men spreading gravel along the twisting paths through the rose garden as Tobias passed. "The rose beds look good, Pickstaff," Tobias called out. Pickstaff glowered at him and grunted. Tobias grinned.

Genevieve had told him time and again that Pickstaff didn't dislike Tobias any more than he disliked anyone else in the world, and Tobias tried to keep her words in mind every time he had dealings with the sullen Pickstaff. The man was a good worker, and that's what mattered.

In truth, Tobias would have been happy with a surly cook who could prepare a fine meal. It would beat the Dutch out of the cheerful but inept Molly Gratchett.

He grinned at that thought. And then there was Godfrey Watkins, Tobias's erstwhile butler. When they'd first met, Tobias couldn't understand why Godfrey seemed so afraid of him. He'd even tried not to be gloomy around the poor boy because he feared his own glumness was making the butler nervous. Then he'd met Godfrey's mother, and all became clear.

A regular Amazon, Mrs. Watkins. Tobias had met one or two powerful females in his day, but none compared with Mrs. Watkins. He was half afraid of her himself.

He heard a strange, faraway, crunching noise and looked around. Then he looked up at the tower beneath which he was passing at the time—and almost had a heart attack. A huge stonework figure seemed to rock unsteadily over his head for a second or two. Then it lost its grip on its moorings and, with an ominous sound of grinding stone, hurtled down at him from the roof of the castle.

In the split second he had to avoid the falling masonry, Tobias jerked Rake's Progress unmercifully. Startled, the horse whinnied and danced sideways. The figure crashed to earth no more than two yards from them, and Rake's Progress reared in panic. Tobias, who a year ago wouldn't have had any trouble controlling a runaway, frightened horse, lost his seat and fell to the ground. Right on his wounded leg.

"Son of a bitch." Tobias heard the horse thunder away toward the stables, but he couldn't open his eyes just yet.

Then he heard feet running his way, and he made the effort. Damn it all to hell and back again. If he'd reinjured his leg, he was going to shoot himself in the head and get it over with. He couldn't bear living with only one leg. He couldn't do it.

"Mr. Rakes! Mr. Rakes! Oh, good heavens, what happened?"

It was Genevieve's voice, and she sounded nearly hysterical. The tone sounded out of place on her. Tobias, who *really* didn't want her to see how helpless he was, shoved himself up to a sitting position. His leg screamed at him.

Genevieve flung herself down at his side and grabbed his shoulders. She looked terrified. Tobias might have appreciated the way she was holding him if he weren't in such agony.

"What happened?" she repeated, staring at him as if she were gauging his degree of injury.

He waved his hand toward the fallen stonework item—he saw now that it was a griffin. "That gargoyle fell from the tower. Almost killed the both of us. I hope the horse is all right.''

"What?"

Tobias winced. "No need to shout, Miss Crowfoot. I'm right here." In her arms, as it were. If he were still a whole man, he'd be able to do something about that. But he wasn't. That thought was damned near as painful as his leg.

She let him go in a flurry and spun around to stare at the fallen griffin. His disappointment was great, but he decided he couldn't just sit there in the dirt and wait for her to come back and hug him some more.

More people were rushing up now. Marvelous. Just what he enjoyed: an audience to his incapacity. He gestured to Small William, one of the many who had come to his aid. "Give me your hand, William."

The boy did, and with his help Tobias heaved himself to his feet. His right leg nearly buckled under him, but with a great effort of will and even greater pain, he didn't let it.

Wesley Armitage's voice rose above the babble of gardeners, children, and housemaids. "Good God, Tobias, what happened?" He was out of breath when he ran up to Tobias and shoved Small William aside. Sweat poured from his face, and he looked more frightened than Tobias had felt when he'd seen that lump of rock dropping out of the sky on him. The boy resented being pushed aside—for good reason, in Tobias's estimation. Yet he appreciated Armitage's concern.

"I'm all right. That griffin fell from the tower. Almost crushed Rake's Progress and me both."

"Good God." Armitage stared at the griffin, one of whose stone wings had broken off and lay in a heap of rubble a foot or so away from the stone body. Armitage's eyes grew large. "How could something like that happen?"

"I know how it happened," Genevieve declared grimly. "And I'm going to put an end to it."

She whirled around and before Tobias could stop her, she was gone, muttering "Granny Crowfoot" under her breath. Tobias hoped no one else heard her, or they'd probably all panic. Or maybe not. Perhaps they'd all think it was jolly fun to have a ghost who heaved stone statues down onto the heads of Crowfoot Castle's owner. He shook his head, trying to dislodge the image the thought had conjured up.

"Are you all right?" Armitage still sounded scared to death.

"I'm fine," Tobias lied. "I'll just go on into the house and take a dose of the salicylic powders Dr. Johnson sent over. I'll be as good as new in no time at all."

"How's your leg? Did you hurt your leg?"

Damn it, Tobias wished Armitage would shut up. His leg was killing him and he was worried that he'd done it a permanent injury, but Tobias didn't necessarily want the world to know those things. "It's fine," he said shortly, and left it there.

"Well . . ."

Tobias didn't let Armitage question him any longer. "Small William, please go and check on Rake's Progress. He was frightened, and I had to jerk him hard. Make sure I didn't damage his mouth, all right?"

"Yes, sir."

Small William ran off toward Rake's Progress, clearly displaying the much greater interest he had in the horse's health than in that of the horse's owner. His attitude made Tobias grin inside, which was an improvement.

"Give me your arm, Wes. I fear I'm going to have to lean on you." He'd much rather lean on Genevieve Crowfoot, but she was off chasing ghosts.

"Of course."

By the time Tobias limped to the parlor, he was feeling smothered by Wesley Armitage's solicitude. In fact, he had a strong desire to punch the poor man, and he knew the impulse to be irrational.

"I'm fine, Wes," he said for what seemed like the hundredth time.

"Are you sure? What can I get you?"

Tobias thought for a second. He really wanted to get rid of Armitage. "Tea. Go to the kitchen and ask Molly to make me a pot of tea, if you will. I'll take it with the powders." Molly was the only woman Tobias knew who couldn't make tea, so with luck, this request would keep Armitage away long enough for Tobias to begin feeling better.

"Do you have the powders with you? Can I fetch them for you?"

Good. Another excuse to keep the hovering fellow away for a while. "Uh, no. If you wouldn't mind going up to my bedroom, there are some papers of them in the drawer of my night table. Thanks, Wes."

Tobias sank onto the overstuffed chair and had to use both hands to lift his leg onto the ottoman. It really did hurt very badly.

As far as Genevieve could recall, she'd never been this angry in her life. She took the castle stairs three at a time, her corset be hanged, and searched for the damnable Granny Crowfoot with a vengeance. It took her forever, but she finally found her in Tobias's room, pilfering a pocket watch.

"Put that watch down!"

She had the satisfaction of seeing Granny Crowfoot start. Good. She hadn't realized ghosts could be startled until this minute.

"What do you mean by sneaking up on a body like that?" Granny Crowfoot dropped the watch with a chink and scowled at Genevieve, who didn't care.

Pointing a finger quivering with wrath at the ghost, Genevieve ground out, "Do you have any idea what you almost did to that poor man?"

"What poor man?"

"Don't try to be coy, you wretched ghost!"

"Don't you call me names, you young whippersnapper."

"And don't *you* whippersnapper *me*. You almost killed that man!"

Granny Crowfoot's translucent eyebrows drew together. *"What man? You mean that Rakes devil almost died? How? What happened? If somebody tried to kill him, why isn't he dead?"*

Vibrating with fury, Genevieve stomped right up to the ghost. "Do you realize that when you threw that griffin down from the tower, anyone might have been passing underneath?

You seem to want Mr. Rakes out of the way, but what if your spite had killed one of those innocent children working in the garden? What then, you miserable old bat?''

"What are you babbling about, child? What griffin? What tower? And don't call me a bat."

"Ooooh, you make me so *angry!*"

"Yes, I can see that, but I still have no idea what you're talking about."

"Don't lie to me!" Genevieve couldn't remember the last time she'd screeched like that—it had probably been when she was a child and she'd gotten mad at Benton. She was so furious now that tears began to course down her cheeks.

"For heaven's sake, get a hold of yourself, girl. You're too emotional by half. You'll never get anywhere that way. A female needs to keep her wits about her, especially when there's a Rakes male in the vicinity."

"You drive me crazy!"

"Good grief, girl, whatever is the matter with you?"

"I'm calling Father Francis. I don't care if he is a Catholic, I'm sure he'll know how to get you out of this house!"

Granny Crowfoot tutted. *"Don't go yammering on about exorcism again, please. You're being foolish, child."*

"Foolish! *Foolish?* You almost killed him!"

"I did no such thing. I don't know what you're talking about. Has one of the griffins fallen? Those are Crowfoot griffins, you know, and as such, impervious to time—as are we Crowfoots, all."

Granny Crowfoot preened, and Genevieve's temper rose so high, she'd have tried to kill the old ghost if she weren't already dead. "Are you out of your mind? Impervious to time, my foot! That dratted griffin almost fell on his *head!*"

"If such a thing occurred, I'm sure the Rakes fiend himself is behind it."

"Why would he want to drop a stone griffin on his own head?"

"I have no idea." Granny Crowfoot crossed her arms over her transparently buckrammed bosom, lifted her chin, and turned away from Genevieve, pouting for all she was worth.

Practically incoherent with rage by this time, Genevieve

could stutter only fierce, inarticulate growls and hisses for a moment before she burst out, "I want you to stop tormenting that man!"

The ghost whirled around, her expression reminding Genevieve of a sullen schoolgirl. *"I'll be hanged if I will."*

"So help me, if you hurt him, I'll—"

"I couldn't hurt him if I wanted to!"

The words stopped Genevieve cold. Her mouth hung open and her finger trembled as it pointed at the ghost. She dropped her hand to her side. "What? What do you mean?"

The ghost whooshed up to Genevieve. It was all Genevieve could do to maintain her firm stance, but she'd not give Granny Crowfoot the benefit of any satisfaction at all, even that of knowing the spirit's sudden shifts and movements disconcerted her.

"What do you think I mean, you nonsensical child? Don't you think that if it were within my power to do so, I'd have knocked him off before now?"

"You mean you can't?" Genevieve was flabbergasted.

"Of course I can't! If I could have, I would have. I do not want that odious Rakes man—or any other odious Rakes men—in my own dear father's home. My father would be horrified if he knew the demon spawn of a Rakes had bought the castle he built with his own hard-earned money!"

"I had no idea."

"Harrumph." Granny Crowfoot flew to the window and pouted some more.

The sound of footsteps approaching the bedroom jerked Genevieve out of her stupefied contemplation of the ghost's rigid back. She turned just as Tobias Rakes's large form appeared in the doorway. She shot a look in Granny Crowfoot's direction, thinking that the ghost would surely have disappeared, but she discovered the old bat—er, ghost—glaring balefully at Tobias.

"What's going on up here?" Tobias asked. "What are you doing in my bedroom? What's all the yelling about?" He threw his hands in the air, obviously perplexed. Hearing yelling coming form his bedroom, Tobias had limped his way up the stairs to try to find out what all the commotion was about.

Genevieve cleared her throat and folded her hands demurely before her. She took a step back so that Tobias would have an unimpeded view of the window—and of Granny Crowfoot.

"Mr. Rakes, please allow me to introduce you to one of my oldest relations." The drilling she'd been given in proper forms of address made her pause for a moment. Then she decided that if anyone deserved to be introduced properly, it most assuredly wasn't Granny Crowfoot, and she went on. "Granny Crowfoot. Granny Crowfoot," she said, her voice going hard, "please allow me to introduce you to the gentleman whom you've been tormenting these past several weeks, Mr. Tobias Rakes."

Chapter Seven

Genevieve couldn't recall when she'd heard such thick, absolute silence as that which permeated the air of Tobias Rakes's bedroom after she'd introduced the man to the ghost. She should, of course, have done it the other way around, since Granny Crowfoot was—or had been—a woman, and it was polite to introduce the gentlemen to the ladies, rather than vice versa, but Genevieve didn't care.

Granny Crowfoot continued to glare at Tobias. Tobias stared at the ghost, blinking. Then he rubbed his eyes. He remained silent.

The quiet was getting on Genevieve's already fragile nerves. She cleared her throat again. "This, Mr. Rakes, is the creature who has been causing such havoc in the castle since your arrival. She was stealing your watch when I found her—"

"I was not!"

Genevieve spoke more loudly. "She was stealing your watch when I found her."

"I was not stealing it!"

Genevieve didn't react to Granny Crowfoot's second indignant denial, but continued speaking to Tobias. "I regret to say she's a relation—*was* a relation of mine."

"Harrumph," said Granny Crowfoot, obviously peeved. *"I was merely borrowing the horrid man's watch."*

Tobias continued speechless. Genevieve huffed.

"I fear I haven't been able to persuade the ghost to discontinue her rattlings and moanings and pilferings, but I have it from her own lips that she can do you no physical harm, so perhaps, if you can learn to live with the irritation"—she paused to shoot Granny Crowfoot a glower that held, she hoped, a world of meaning—"evidently your physical well-being is not at risk. Except, of course, for the loss of sleep, which can't but be unhealthful."

"Um, I don't think I believe this."

Tobias's voice sounded quite unlike its customary deep, resonant baritone. Genevieve wasn't astonished at that. She did, however, heave another deep sigh. There was so much she had to do to get the castle ready for next week's open house. She truly didn't want to spend any more time in persuading Tobias to believe in the evidence of his senses. Clearly, he saw the ghost. She decided to use that to her advantage and try to get this over with.

"You see her, do you not?" She held an arm out, indicating Granny Crowfoot's sulky form next to the window.

"I'm sure I don't really see whatever that is over there."

"Hogwash! I told you the man was a beast!" Granny Crowfoot's pout intensified.

"You do see it, Mr. Rakes," Genevieve said gently, understanding how difficult this must be for him. "And you hear it, too, don't you?"

"I am not an it." Granny Crowfoot uncrossed her arms and stood. Genevieve guessed she was annoyed at not being believed in, because she went into her expanding routine until her essence filled the room from the window almost to where Genevieve stood by the door.

"I do beg your pardon," Genevieve said with exquisite sarcasm. "She's not an it, Mr. Rakes, she's a ghost."

"Um, there are no such things as ghosts." Tobias didn't sound as though he believed it.

While Genevieve honestly did understand Tobias's reluctance to believe in so odd an entity as a ghost, she'd been through a good deal recently, and her patience crumbled. "Oh, I do wish you'd give up fighting your eyes and ears and accept it, Mr. Rakes. I have so much to do yet, and so much of this day has been wasted already."

"But, you're trying to make me believe that thing's a ghost," Tobias protested, getting a little hot himself.

"Of course I am—because it is!"

"I am neither a thing nor an it!" Granny Crowfoot deflated instantly, leaving Tobias gaping.

"Oh, for heaven's sake, nobody cares *what* you are," Genevieve declared hotly. "You're a pest and a pain in the neck, is what you are, and I'm sick of trying to fight you!"

"Then don't. Get rid of that wretched fiend, and I'll go away."

Tobias held up his hands. "All right. Let's not get into a fight here, ladies. So, say I do believe in you, Miss Crowfoot. Why are you so dead set against my living here? Doesn't the place look better now than it did before I moved in?"

"That's not the point." Granny Crowfoot had resumed sulking. She turned her face toward the wall and refused to look at him.

"Oh, let's just drop it. Granny Crowfoot is determined to keep the feud hot, Mr. Rakes, and I don't know if there's anything we or anyone else can do about it."

"There's not," the ghost said.

Genevieve thought of something that made her so uncomfortable, she almost forgot her grievances against the vexing Granny Crowfoot. "But, if she didn't drop that griffin on your head, who did?"

Tobias didn't seem to want to remove his gaze from Granny Crowfoot. Genevieve guessed she didn't blame him—after all, it wasn't every day you came face to face with a ghost.

"I don't know," he said.

Genevieve turned to Granny Crowfoot. "Do you know who did it? If you really can't hurt Mr. Rakes, then you'd better tell us or, by your silence, you'll be abetting whoever it was who *is* trying to hurt him." She wasn't sure that made sense, and hoped she wouldn't have to try to explain herself.

"I don't know anything at all about any griffin," Granny Crowfoot snapped. *"If a griffin has fallen from the turret, however, I believe it to be your duty, young man, to restore it to its rightful place. That is a Crowfoot griffin, you know."*

"Oh, Good Lord."

"No, Miss Crowfoot, I believe the elder Miss Crowfoot is right in this instance."

Tobias had taken to speaking in a conciliatory tone. Genevieve was sure such measures would hold no sway with the abominable ghost, but she didn't want to say so in case she was wrong. "That's very kind of you, Mr. Rakes." She shot another look at the ghost. "Considering the circumstances and all."

"But perhaps we should go to the scene of the crime and take a look. Maybe we can determine exactly what happened if we investigate further."

"Good idea." Then Genevieve could get back to work. She still had to call on the florist and the baker to make sure their orders for next week's party were progressing properly.

"You should have thought about that in the first place, instead of coming in here and accusing me of doing something so dastardly."

"Oh, stop it!" Genevieve was in no mood to placate a peevish, irritating ghost. "You were stealing his watch when I found you, in case you've forgotten. Besides which; you've caused plenty of trouble. Just because you didn't drop the griffin on his head doesn't excuse all your other sins."

"Sins?" The ghost looked mightily offended.

Walking toward the door, Genevieve said, "She's the reason all of your personal items kept disappearing, Mr. Rakes. I don't think you believed me when I told you so at first, but you can see now that I was right."

"Borrowing. Mere borrowing," Granny Crowfoot muttered.

"Borrowing, my foot! Pilferage is pilferage, you dreadful old ghost."

"Now, now, ladies, let's not argue about this."

Tobias took Genevieve's arm and put it on his coat sleeve. She felt the muscles ripple under her fingers, and got weak in the knees. "You're right, of course," she murmured, feeling light-headed.

"About time somebody did something sensible."

"Would you care to come with us?" Tobias asked politely as he and Genevieve moved toward the door. Genevieve admired his restraint.

"No, I would not," the ghost declared. *"I wouldn't be caught dead in the company of a Rakes."*

Tobias bowed. "Inapt phrasing, I fear, Miss Crowfoot, since you evidently are dead in my company. By the way, you sound exactly like my father."

Granny Crowfoot uttered an indignant *"How dare you!"* and shot up the chimney. Genevieve was very glad to see her go.

Tobias didn't really believe he'd just met a ghost. Such things as ghosts simply didn't exist. The kinds of people who believed in ghosts went to the Transcendentalist Church, read Madame Blavatsky's ludicrous trash, attended seances, and were generally as nutty as fruitcakes. Tobias might be wounded in body, but his mind was sound.

So why had he been able to see the wall and window through that creature to whom Genevieve Crowfoot had lately introduced him? And had the thing then expanded to fill half the room? And had it then shot up the chimney like the smoky trail of a war rocket? Tobias didn't quite dare let himself contemplate these things for fear he might discover he had lost his mind.

It was much more cozy to have Genevieve Crowfoot's hand resting on his arm, warm and reassuringly human. She walked close to him, too.

"You shouldn't have negotiated all those stairs, Mr. Rakes. You suffered a terrible fall, and should be resting now."

Aw, how sweet. Tobias didn't have to pretend in order to make his limp more pronounced. He'd been trying not to limp before. Now he decided he might as well garner all the sympathy from this darling creature as he could. "I'll be all right," he said, his voice fairly throbbing with nobility. He hadn't known it could do that. "You don't mind if I lean on you a little bit, do you?"

"Of course I don't. Here, let me prop you up some more."

And she put her arm around his back and prepared to take his weight. In order to do so, she had to stand right smack next to him. Indeed, her bosom pressed against his back delightfully. Tobias sighed with pleasure and didn't even feel guilty. He honestly was in a good deal of pain.

"I'm not sure I believe Granny Crowfoot about her not throwing that griffin at you," Genevieve announced in a disapproving voice. "She's a high-handed, overbearing woman."

Lord, he really didn't want to talk about a ghost as if it existed. On the other hand, he'd seen it with his own eyes, which were, the last he'd checked, in the head of a sane man. It was difficult not to believe something one saw for oneself. He decided to pretend he believed in it for Genevieve's sake, and hold off a firm decision until later. When he woke up.

"Yet, do you think a . . . ghost . . . would be able to lift so heavy an object as that griffin? Ghosts are rather insubstantial themselves, don't you think?"

"Well, maybe." To Tobias, it sounded as though she'd been rather hoping to be able to pin the blame on the ghost.

"Besides, you told me that she was unable—for whatever ghostly reason—to do real harm to anyone. Do you think she was lying?"

"I don't know. I wouldn't put it past her." Genevieve's voice sounded awfully grim. Tobias had never heard her sound thus.

"Why don't we assume she was telling the truth, just in case," he suggested gently.

She huffed, but agreed. Tobias thought she was adorable in all her indignation and ghostly prejudices.

"The thing fell from the tower closest to the rose garden," he said to distract himself from the rush of arousal speeding through him.

"I don't think you should climb any more stairs," Genevieve said severely. "I'll go up there and look around."

"Nonsense. I'm not completely helpless, Miss Crowfoot." Indeed, his leg did hurt him rather badly but he wasn't about to let Genevieve leave him just yet. He was enjoying her undivided attention and gentle ministrations too much for that.

"I know you're not, but you suffered a bad fall, and should be—"

"Resting. I know. But if those gargoyles are loose, I want to know about it. I'll have to have them taken down or re-inforced. I don't want one to fall on anyone else. The thing could have hit one of the children working in the garden. Or you." The thought came to him suddenly, and it made his blood run cold.

"Hmm. Perhaps you're right, although I don't like the idea of you climbing any more stairs. You've done enough damage to your poor leg as it is."

Tobias could think of several ways in which Genevieve Crowfoot might distract him from the pain in his leg, but he didn't want her to slap his face and leave him stranded, so he didn't mention them. He settled for an ambiguous "hmm," and left it at that.

He regretted his rashness in insisting he climb up to the tower before they were halfway there. His leg didn't enjoy the exercise one little bit and, therefore, neither did Tobias. He gritted his teeth and bore it, though, as he'd been bearing things these seventeen years and more. At least he had the comfort of Genevieve's soft body pressed against his, which almost made the agony worth it.

"Here we are." Genevieve's voice carried a tone of worry, as if she could tell that he was pretending to be hale. "Let me open the door for us."

He let her. Vanity could only be pushed so far.

As soon as she opened the door, Tobias could tell that it had been no ghost who'd shoved the stone griffin down on him. Footprints were plainly visible in the dust created when the griffin had been sawed from its base. The tools the villain had used to dislodge the gargoyle lay in a heap next to the window, as well.

"Merciful heavens! I do believe someone was actually try-ing to kill you." Genevieve sounded appalled.

Tobias was fairly appalled himself. He stared at the footprints and the tools—even walked over and picked up a
chisel and saw—and tried to think of another explanation for
this scenario. He couldn't come up with one. Nevertheless,
the notion that someone was out to murder him was too much
to accept without a struggle, so he struggled.

"Have there been any workmen up here?" He looked up
and fairly pleaded with Genevieve with his eyes. "Did anyone set them to repairing the roof or anything?" The lack of
conviction he felt was plain to hear in his voice.

Genevieve shook her head. "No." Her own voice was no
more than a whisper.

"Hmm. Well then, it looks as though our ghost has an
accomplice."

"Oh, but—but . . ." Her protest faded and died.

"Can you think of another explanation for all this?" Tobias swept a hand out to include the tools, the footprints, and
the pristine pink of the stone where the griffin had been
hacked away from its base.

"No, but—" Again, Genevieve failed to produce a solu-
tion that would absolve whoever had dropped the griffin
from attempted murder.

"No. Neither can I. I wish I could."

"So do I."

"You know the people in Bittersweet much better than I
do, Miss Crowfoot. Can you think of anyone who has a large
enough grudge against my family or me to commit homi-
cide?"

"No," said Genevieve, horrified. Then she shook her head
again. "I mean, there are factions in the town—pro-
Crowfoot and pro-Rakes—but I can't imagine that anyone
would be crazy or hateful enough to kill you because of a
problem our great-great-great-grandfathers had with each
other."

Tobias, who had seen entire wars waged for the sake of
nothing better than false assumptions, wasn't sure he shared
Genevieve's conviction. "Do you have any idea who belongs
to which faction?"

"Of course. But even those who are hot to defend one

side or the other are still civil to each other—most of the
time. Are you sure you don't have enemies elsewhere?''

He stared at her blankly. "Enemies? Why should I have
enemies?''

"I don't know. What about your father?''

"My *father?*''

She looked disconcerted and a little embarrassed. "Oh,
dear, I'm sorry—but, I understood that the two of you were
at odds with one another.''

'' 'At odds' is a far cry from murder, Miss Crowfoot. I'm
sure my father would welcome me with open arms—well,
perhaps not open arms, since he isn't a demonstrative man—
but he'd be pleased to have me back in the family fold, such
as it is, if I'd grovel to him. He even wrote a letter demand-
ing I return to the family. He's hoping I'll play the prodigal
son, I believe.''

She stared at him for a moment, then murmured, "How
sad. I can't imagine how awful it would be to be estranged
from my family, Mr. Rakes. I miss my own parents dread-
fully.''

Now, while it was true that Tobias was happy to have
Genevieve's sympathy for his physical ailments—up to a
point—it was also true that the estrangement between Tobias
and his father was a raw sore on his soul, and one he didn't
appreciate people witnessing. He said brusquely, "Nonsense.
The old man's a tyrant, and I was a young fool.''

"Oh, but it wasn't your fault.''

He squinted at her. "What do you know about it?''

Blushing, she said, "Nothing. Not really. But I do know
that an impressionable young boy of seventeen could easily
be lured into the clutches of an unscrupulous older woman
with ulterior motives.''

His cynicism was rising by the second. So was the sarcasm
he wielded to hold the world at bay. "And how, pray, would
a sheltered young lady like Miss Genevieve Crowfoot know
anything about unscrupulous older women with ulterior motives?''

Her blush deepened. "There's no need to be scornful, Mr.
Rakes. I may not have traveled in the world much, but I have

known many young men in my day, including my cousin Benton, who formed just such an attachment. He, unlike you, had parents who understood the nature of the problem and did not condemn him for it.''

"Lucky Benton.''

Genevieve's eyes suddenly filled with tears, and she spun around. Unnerved by this atypical show of vaporishness, Tobias said sharply, "You needn't cry, Miss Crowfoot. I'm sure Benton is a much better man than I, and deserves your tears, but he's not here to benefit from them.''

"No,'' she said tightly. "He's not here. He's dead. As are my mother and father.''

Wonderful. Tobias silently cursed himself as an ass. "I beg your pardon, Miss Crowfoot. I had no idea. You and he were close, I take it.''

"Yes.'' She seemed to pull herself together and turned to face him once more. "Yes, we were very close, and his death was unexpected and quite cruel. He died of pneumonia, you see, and the end was terrible to watch. In effect, he suffocated.''

"I'm sorry.'' He didn't know what more he could say, and wished the subject had never come up.

Genevieve's thoughts were evidently more elastic than his. He saw her eyes, which had just been filled with tears, narrow in thought. "You know, Mr. Rakes, you might have enemies you don't know about. What about that adventuress you eloped with? Did she have family who might hold a grudge?''

Well, now, *that* was a corker. Tobias had never even bothered to consider such a thing. He did now. "I'm not sure. She had a brother here in Bittersweet, I think.''

"What about her—'' Genevieve stopped suddenly and blushed again. Tobias suspected what was coming and decided not to help her along. She was quite charming when she blushed. After taking a big breath, she forged onward, "What about her husband? Is he still living?''

"I believe he is.'' He left it there, wanting to know what Genevieve would pop out with next.

"Er, do you suppose he might still be angry with you?''

"Perhaps. I understand he wasn't awfully pleased when Madeline and I ran off together."

"I should think not."

He finally couldn't stand it any longer, and allowed his grin to break through. "They weren't a happy couple, you know, Miss Crowfoot. If they had been, Madeline wouldn't have bothered to make me fall in love with her. She only did it to get away from her husband."

"Oh." She tilted her head and peered at him, reminding him of a pretty little bird. "How do you know that?"

"Because as soon as we'd left New York and traveled into New Jersey, she dumped me for another man. He was the one she'd wanted all along, but she used me to take her to him."

"Why, the wicked hussy! What a cruel thing to do to a sensitive young boy."

Now she was all indignation and pink cheeks on his behalf. Tobias felt a strong surge of lust. He tried to tamp it down, but it didn't want to be tamped. He tried harder. "I don't know how sensitive I was, Miss Crowfoot. I believe you're endowing my younger self with more credit and nobility than it deserves."

"I doubt it." She seemed to collect herself. "But you shouldn't be standing about chatting. We can discuss this downstairs where you can sit and elevate that leg. I'll bring you a dose of laudanum to dull the pain."

Genevieve's words brought reality back with a thunk. Tobias remembered that he'd sent Armitage on an errand to secure some salicylic powders, and he sighed. "You're right, Miss Crowfoot. As delightful as it is to spend time chatting with you, poor Wes is probably pulling his hair out, wondering what's happened to me."

"Mr. Armitage?"

"Yes. I sent him off to get me tea and medicine."

"Oh. Let me help you downstairs, then. Perhaps you and Mr. Armitage can discuss the griffin situation while I continue preparing for the party." She had walked to his side and put her arm around him. Now she looked up at him.

"Unless you want to call off the party because of this incident, of course."

Her eyes were so big and beautiful, and she was so close and smelled so sweet, that Tobias almost lost the train of the conversation. He managed to hold on to his sanity long enough to say, "By no means, Miss Crowfoot. I believe we should invite the whole town and observe everyone closely."

She licked her lips. Tobias got the impression that she, too, was having trouble concentrating. "Yes," she said softly. "Yes, that's a—ah—the town. Yes."

"Observation," he murmured. "Detective work."

"Detec—yes. Of course."

His leg throbbed as if a drum-and-bugle corps had taken up band rehearsal in it, someone had tried to kill him within the past half hour, and he and Genevieve weren't even on a first-name acquaintance yet, but Tobias's insides didn't care. All they knew was that Genevieve Crowfoot was here, pressed against him, she was lovely and soft and sweet and seemed at the moment about the closest thing to heaven Tobias would ever know. So he kissed her. And she kissed him back.

Tobias had kissed any number of women in the past seventeen years, since his introduction to the joys of the flesh in the arms of the sultry, devious Madeline Riley. During his travels, he'd had women in Brazil, women in Africa, and women on the frontier. Since his involvement with Madeline, he'd never fancied more than a quick tumble with any of them. If he'd been older when he'd met Madeline, he wouldn't have wanted more from her, either. He told himself he didn't want more than that from Genevieve Crowfoot, either, but he wasn't sure he believed it.

No. That was merely the months of pain and exhaustion talking. Of course he didn't want more than a quick tumble from Genevieve. He kept telling himself so as she melted in his arms, holding him tightly, her fingers digging into his back, her breasts squashed against his chest. Her lips were like honey. They were like wine. They intoxicated him, and he dipped his tongue into her mouth to taste her more deeply.

Her tongue sparred with his, and he heard her whimper softly.

His hands began to wander even as he told himself that he wasn't in the habit of seducing virgins, that such despicable practices invariably led women to ruin and men to marriage, that he didn't want to be married, and that he valued his freedom too highly to allow himself to be suckered into falling for yet another woman's lures.

His arousal was so intense that he couldn't seem to get close enough to Genevieve's warmth. In truth, there was only one way to slake such hot lust, and that was to plunge into the act of love—that is, the act of sex—itself. Which, of course, he told himself as he lifted Genevieve's skirt and put his palm to her womanly, cotton-clad rump and pressed her against his almost painfully erect member, was impossible with this woman. She was a virgin. She was his housekeeper. She was a Crowfoot. She was—

"Tobias? Tobias, are you up here somewhere?"

Damn Wesley Armitage to perdition. Tobias groaned and tried to ignore Armitage's voice.

Genevieve, on the other hand, gasped loudly and began to struggle.

Feeling drugged, Tobias slowly came to his senses. He found Genevieve staring up at him as if she couldn't quite believe they'd just shared such a passionate embrace. He could believe it. He was hard as a rock and aching for her.

She whispered, "Oh, my," and pressed two fingers to her lips.

Tobias fought his impulse to grab those fingers away and replace them with his lips once more. There could be no more of that nonsense today. Whatever had possessed him? He dragged his gaze away from Genevieve, who had begun furiously patting at her hair.

"We're up here," he said, croaking slightly.

"Where?"

"Here." Shit, Tobias didn't want Armitage up here. Not while Tobias was still suffering from unsatisfied lust. Still holding lightly to Genevieve's shoulders, he looked down and asked urgently, "Are you all right?"

She nodded. He wasn't sure if she could speak or not, but there wasn't any time to ask her, because Armitage's footsteps sounded from right outside the tower door.

"Are you in there, Tobias?"

"Yes."

Genevieve scuttled away from him, clear to the other side of the room, where the tools and footprints resided. Tobias felt as if she'd abandoned him, which he knew was a ridiculous way to feel.

The door opened, and Armitage's face appeared. He looked frightened. Tobias didn't stop to analyze why Armitage should be frightened. He tugged once at his jacket and said, "Here we are, Wes. Come on in." He wanted to kick the interloper down the castle stairs.

"You didn't come back," Armitage said, easing his way into the room. "I was worried about you." He glanced over to Genevieve and his eyes thinned. "What are you doing up here?"

Tobias wondered why Armitage's voice should have gone hard and suspicious. Then he decided it was because, in spite of what Armitage had told Tobias, the lawyer was sweet on Genevieve Crowfoot. Tobias considered such a condition to be merely sensible, given Genevieve's potent charms.

Before Tobias could formulate an answer—his brains having been virtually scrambled by Genevieve Crowfoot—she spoke. "Someone tried to kill Mr. Rakes by dropping that griffin on him. Look over here, Mr. Armitage."

"What?" Armitage's eyebrows dipped. "That's absurd, Miss Crowfoot."

The scorn in the lawyer's voice brought Tobias back to the here and now. "Absurd, is it? Take a look at the evidence, Wes." Tobias limped to where Genevieve stood, gesturing for the lawyer to follow. "See here? This is where the griffin was chopped away. I'm surprised no one heard whoever it was doing it."

Genevieve shook her head. "No. There's an entire floor and more between this turret and the ground floor, where all the activity is being carried out today. No one would have been close enough to hear. Whoever did it chose his day well."

"Good God," Armitage whispered. "I can't believe it."

"I fear I'm going to have to believe it," Tobias said dryly. "And I'm also going to have to keep my eyes open. If someone hates me enough to drop a stone griffin on my head, I don't suppose he'll stop now."

"But why would anyone do that?"

"Your guess is as good as mine. Miss Crowfoot and I have been discussing it."

He peered at Genevieve. So did Armitage. She looked as though she'd recently been thoroughly kissed. Her color was high, her lips were rosy and slightly swollen, and she looked guilty as sin. Tobias sighed. Hell, he knew better than to kiss a virgin. When he glanced at Armitage again, he saw that the lawyer was drawing some obvious conclusions. He didn't look as though he liked them much, either.

Well, too bad. Tobias said in his best captain's voice, "Let's go downstairs, shall we? We can discuss the implications of this incident while Miss Crowfoot finishes preparations for next week's festivities."

Armitage gaped at him. "You mean you're going ahead with the party?"

"Oh, yes." Tobias gave him a thin smile. "I'm not dead, after all."

"Not yet," the lawyer said, his tone brittle.

"Exactly."

Wishing he could go to bed—preferably with Genevieve Crowfoot—and sleep for a year or so, after performing various athletic maneuvers with her, Tobias walked to the door and held it open. Genevieve hurried out first, followed by Wesley Armitage. Tobias glanced once more at the evidence of the crime, then sighed and shut the door.

Chapter
Eight

Genevieve fanned herself with her hand as she preceded Tobias and Wesley Armitage down the turret stairs. Her face felt as if it were about to burst into flames. How could she have allowed herself to kiss Tobias Rakes in that abandoned fashion? Thank heavens they'd ceased to paw each other by the time Wesley Armitage found them—but how could she ever face Tobias again? She was supposed to be his house-keeper, not his mistress, for heaven's sake.

It was all because she'd lost sight of her purpose for seeking employment in the castle. She had to stop thinking about her housekeeping job here and pay attention to finding the treasure. She hated to admit it to herself, but she was beginning to doubt any treasure existed. Surely Granny Crowfoot, who could fly right through solid walls when she took it into her contrary head to do so, would have found it by now if there were one.

Not necessarily, she told herself, pleased to have her thoughts diverted from her shameful behavior with Tobias Rakes. After all, Granny Crowfoot didn't have any interest in treasure. Why should she pay attention to one if it existed? Anyway, it must be well hidden, or someone would have found it by this time. And if anyone had discovered a treasure hidden in Crowfoot Castle, the entire town of Bitter-sweet would have heard about it, because there was no such thing as a secret in so small a town.

Which meant the kiss she and Tobias had shared would be common knowledge by this time tomorrow if Wesley Armitage figured out they'd been kissing. Genevieve stumbled on the last turret step when that unhappy thought struck her.

"Are you all right, Miss Crowfoot?" Armitage left Tobias's side and hurried to Genevieve.

She managed an indifferent smile for his sake. "Yes, thank you, Mr. Armitage. Clumsy of me to trip."

"Nonsense. This has been a trying day for you as well as for Tobias."

"Yes. Yes, it has been." Genevieve studied the lawyer's face. He didn't appear to be unduly shocked, but only looked worried. She hoped that meant he was contemplating the nature of the griffin incident and not the sin of the flesh he'd interrupted in the castle turret. Not that they'd had time to do much sinning beyond that truly stunning kiss, but—Oh, good heavens. Genevieve *had* to get a grip on herself.

Armitage looked over his shoulder at Tobias. "You shouldn't have walked up all those stairs. You'd already hurt yourself enough for one day without aggravating whatever damage the fall did with all that climbing. I don't know what Dr. Johnson will have to say about it."

"Dr. Johnson doesn't have to know."

"I felt it advisable to send a boy to the village to fetch him, Tobias. No sense in taking chances. I understand sometimes blood clots can develop from wounds and cause apoplectic fits."

Genevieve gasped.

Tobias said, "My, what an appealing prospect," in a sour tone.

"I beg your pardon." Armitage looked embarrassed, as if he wished he'd kept his worries to himself.

"That's all right, Wes. I know you have my best interests at heart."

"Yes, I do."

"Did you find those powders in my room?"

"Yes. I set them on the table next to your chair in the library. I thought you could take them with the tea that cook of yours said she'd send up to you." Armitage looked not entirely pleased, and Genevieve guessed the cause.

"Oh, dear. Did you ask Molly to make tea?"

"Yes." Armitage opened the door to the library and stepped aside so that Genevieve and Tobias could enter. "I must say, she seemed to have quite a few problems with it. Is she, ah, simpleminded or something? I can't say that I know the Gratchett family well."

The notion of Molly Gratchett, the sharpest tack in the Gratchett tool chest, being simpleminded, tickled Genevieve. For a moment she forgot about her recent lapse of propriety and burst out laughing. "Good heavens, no, Mr. Armitage. It's only that Molly's family has some rather odd notions about tea, evidently left over from the Revolution. Only women and sick old men, you see, drink tea. Everyone else is supposed to drink water, grog, or, now that it's readily available, coffee."

"Is that what her problem is?" Tobias grunted in pain as he lowered himself into his chair. "I'd wondered. Her family doesn't believe in serving soft-cooked eggs or underdone meat, either, I take it."

Feeling defensive—after all, it had been her sympathy for Molly that had led to the girl's being hired by Tobias— Genevieve said, "She's learning, Mr. Rakes. I'm sure she'll be a superb cook one of these days."

Tobias gave her one of those smiles of his that entered through her eyes, ricocheted around in her body until her flesh tingled, and landed somewhere in her heart. Good Lord, she had to get over this. And fast, or she'd be ruined beyond redemption. She knew herself, and she knew good and well that she wasn't the prim and proper spinster everyone believed her to be. There were untapped passions lurking in her bosom, and Tobias Rakes, unfortunately, had just the combination of physical and mental assets to tap them.

On that awful thought, Genevieve rushed to the tea tray and began fixing Tobias a cup of tea with sugar and cream.

"Where are those powders, Mr. Armitage? Perhaps I should stir them into the tea."

"Will it make the tea taste bad? I think I'd rather stir them into some water, and then down the tea after I take my medicine."

"I'll get a glass from the kitchen," Genevieve said, glad for an excuse to leave Tobias for a minute. Perhaps she could collect herself on the short trip to the kitchen and back.

"Nonsense, Miss Crowfoot. You stay here with our patient, and I'll fetch the water."

Before Genevieve could protest, Armitage had left the room, taking the packet of powders with him. Drat the man for being so blessed efficient. Well, in that case, Genevieve would just behave like a lady. It was a little late for that, perhaps, but there you go.

"Here you are, Mr. Rakes. I put two lumps of sugar in it. I trust that's all right with you."

"Thank you, Miss Crowfoot." He took the cup and saucer from her hands. She was amazed they didn't shake.

Then she made the mistake of looking into his eyes. They were twinkling like stars, and held more humor than she'd previously believed was in him. She clasped her hands together to keep them from reaching out to him.

"Will you forgive me for my lapse in manners upstairs, Miss Crowfoot? I was a beast to take advantage of you that way."

A beast, was he? Well, that was one interpretation of the event. She turned away, feeling unaccountably melancholy all of a sudden. At once, she took herself to task. What did she expect? He was a man of the world; she was a country hick. Even if she did live in New York state. There was, and she knew it, a world of difference between Bittersweet, New York, and New York City, where the sophisticated crowd frolicked. Although she hated admitting it, Genevieve knew she was about as sophisticated as her Aunt Delilah.

"Think nothing of it, Mr. Rakes." She forced herself to sound both cool and casual. "I'm sure it was a mere—" It was a mere what? a mere bomb blast? a mere earthquake? "Nothing to either of us." Good grief, if she told any more whoppers like that one, God would get her for sure. With a monumental effort, she turned and smiled at him—a cool smile, a we're-both-old-enough-to-remain-unshaken-by-such-trivia-as-kisses smile. She wished it were an honest smile. In truth, she'd been shaken to her toes by that kiss.

"A mere nothing?" The twinkle in Tobias's eyes died and was replaced by something cold and dangerous.

Genevieve was taken aback. She recovered quickly by telling herself he was merely surprised she'd understood the nature of their kiss so readily. She only wished. Because she wasn't sure what to say, she gave a small shrug.

They were spared further conversation when Dr. Johnson's voice, loud and grumpy, came to them from the hall. Genevieve hurried to the door to let him into the library. "In here, Dr. Johnson."

A big, burly man, with elegant whiskers of which he was inordinately proud, Dr. Johnson entered scowling. "What's this I hear about you falling from horses, young man? Don't you know better than to jeopardize the progress you've made by riding?"

"The riding didn't hurt it, Doctor. It was the falling-off part that hurt." Tobias straightened in his chair. He looked put out by all the attention his fall seemed to be garnering. "I'm sorry Armitage sent for you. I'm fine, as you can see. All I need is a little rest and some of those salicylic powders."

"I'll be the judge of that."

Armitage scurried up to Tobias, glass in hand. "Here, Tobias. I stirred the powders in already."

"Don't touch that glass, Mr. Rakes."

Armitage was so startled by the doctor's gruff command, that he spilled some of the water. "I beg your pardon?"

Genevieve wondered why the lawyer seemed so nervous, and chalked it up to his having done something Tobias didn't like by calling the doctor. Men. She'd never understand them. Armitage drew the glass toward himself, cradling it against his chest as if it were precious. She shook her head, wondering if he were trying to garner favor with Tobias. She didn't think he'd be able to do it that way. From what she'd observed of him so far, Tobias Rakes seemed to appreciate people with an independent streak. She didn't think he'd like anyone toadying up to him.

Dr. Johnson waved the glass—and Wesley Armitage— away. "Take that stuff out of here, Armitage. Mr. Rakes needs something stronger than salicylic powders now. I'm giving him a dose of morphia, and I don't intend to entertain any arguments." The last part of his sermon was delivered to Tobias, who frowned up at him.

Genevieve detected some bitterness in Tobias's expression, and she felt a spurt of sympathy for him. After all, he'd been on his own since he was no more than a boy, and he'd served as an explorer in Africa, a merchant seaman, and a soldier on the frontier. He didn't seem to her like a man who'd take kindly to mollycoddling. She cleared her throat. "Perhaps we should leave Mr. Rakes with Dr. Johnson, Mr. Armitage."

"Wait a minute, you two. We need to talk about that damned griffin."

Genevieve drew herself up straight, turned, and cast a cold glance at Tobias. "And we shall. After you have rested for a bit. As you well know, I still have much work to do to prepare for the open house next week, since you refuse to cancel it." There. That would teach him to swear at her.

The dangerous look he'd sported for the past several minutes vanished, and he grinned. Genevieve's heart nearly gave out from the sheer suddenness of the change a smile made in his aspect. She turned abruptly and spoke to Armitage. "Let me take that glass, Mr. Armitage. I'll return it to the kitchen."

"No, no," he said, looking and sounding apprehensive. "I'll take care of it."

And he hurried off, leaving Genevieve to wonder what had him in such a pucker. Without a backward glance at her employer, she exited the library, looked down the hall both ways, saw no one lurking, and collapsed against the wall. She had to stay there for several seconds before she felt strong enough to return to her duties. Tobias Rakes's smile ought to be outlawed.

Before she set off for the village of Bittersweet to check on the florist and the caterer—neither she nor Tobias had wanted to risk the town's health to the tender mercies of Molly Gratchett's cooking skills—Genevieve went outside to inspect the work being done on the grounds. She didn't want the people she'd hired to slough off in their duties in their excitement over discussing Tobias's accident. They weren't. Thanks to the combined efforts of the Amazonian Mrs. Watkins and the sour Mr. Pickstaff, all were working like beavers.

Genevieve was especially pleased with the sunken garden, an area not far from the rose garden and accessed by stone steps. The sunken garden had been built early in the century by one of her ancestors, and it contained a pool with a fountain and grassy swards dotted with flowers. Violets peeked up from between rocks in the shade of several trees, and roses and honeysuckles bloomed here and there, scenting the air.

This was one of the first gardens Genevieve had tackled in her tenure as housekeeper, and it looked beautiful now under the summer sun. When Genevieve had first set to work on it, the pool hadn't been filled with water for decades. A mountain of debris had to be hauled out of it. Mr. Gratchett, Molly's father, and as skilled a plumber as Molly was unskilled as a cook, had repaired the piping. Now water splashed into the sparkling pool from a stone flower held by a stone cherub. A wooden tub planted with water lilies had been set in the pool, and huge blossoms now bloomed in the water. Large lily leaves made wonderful resting places for frogs. A bridge spanned the pool, and stone benches had been scrubbed of years' worth of filth and set on the grass.

The sunken garden had become Genevieve's favorite place in the entire world. She didn't think Mr. Rakes had even seen it yet, and she was eager that he should approve. She clattered down the stone steps and was surprised to see Small William Pickstaff, a sullen expression on his face, raking up the few leaves that lay on the grass.

"Good afternoon, Small William. I thought you'd be in the stables still."

The boy looked up, frowning. ''M'father told me to rake up them leaves, Miss Crowfoot.'' He gestured at the small pile of leaves at his feet. From his tone, Genevieve surmised he'd rather have been left to the horses.

''I see.'' She didn't know why she should feel uneasy about Small William's present occupation. After all, it wasn't her business what Old William set his son to doing. Because she was uneasy anyway, she asked, ''Is Rake's Progress all right, Small William? Did he suffer any ill effects from his accident?''

The boy returned to raking, evidently feeling he'd fulfilled his social obligations for the present. ''He's all right.''

''He wasn't hurt?''

''Naw.''

So much for that. Genevieve stood and watched the boy for a moment. Small William continued doggedly doing his job and didn't acknowledge her presence again. She realized the reason for her unease was that someone—some human being—had been behind the toppling of that griffin. Someone other than Granny Crowfoot wanted Tobias Rakes dead, and someone in the Pickstaff family could as easily be the perpetrator as anyone else. The realization made her shiver.

''Don't be stupid,'' she advised her fanciful self.

Small William squinted up at her, and Genevieve realized she'd spoken aloud. Because she felt silly for it, she smiled at Small William. He shrugged and bent once more to his task.

Genevieve watched the boy for another moment before deciding she had no business standing here, contemplating one of the moody Pickstaffs. There was too much to do, much too much time had been wasted already, and Tobias was safely in Dr. Johnson's care. No one would dare hurt him with the indomitable Dr. Johnson hovering over him— unless Dr. Johnson was the villain in the piece.

Good heavens, she'd drive herself mad if she kept this up. She gave herself a mental shake. ''I'm glad the horse is all right.''

Small William didn't respond.

A little testily, and because she couldn't help feeling edgy,

Genevieve added, "Mr. Rakes is all right, too.

This time Small William gave her a grunt. She was obviously not going to wring a confession out of him this way—if he had anything to confess—so she said a brisk good-bye and set out for town. The boy didn't return her good-bye.

Genevieve had barely stepped outside the castle gates before she heard someone scurrying after her. She turned and sighed deeply when she saw it was her aunt coming from the cottage. Delilah had taken it into her head that Genevieve was going to be ruined if she remained in the castle. While Delilah was too frightened of Granny Crowfoot to venture inside the castle herself, she seemed to delight in attacking her niece every time Genevieve went to town. Genevieve braced herself.

"Oh, Genevieve! I heard about Mr. Rakes's accident. Is he all right?"

"News certainly travels quickly around here." Genevieve waited for her aunt to catch up with her. She might as well; there was no avoiding her now.

"Yes, it does. Mildred Hotchkiss brought me the news. She'd heard it from Dr. Johnson's nurse, Glynis Phipps." Aunt Delilah caught up with her, slapped a hand to her chest, and commenced panting.

"Mmmm." Genevieve didn't care to stand waiting while Delilah caught her breath, so she moved on.

Undeterred, Delilah hurried along with her. "It was that beastly ghost, wasn't it?" she queried in a hushed tone.

"No, it was not the ghost." Genevieve knew she shouldn't be annoyed with her aunt. After all, it wasn't every day one met a ghost. She didn't suppose it was her aunt's fault that she'd been frightened by Granny Crowfoot. "A griffin fell from the tower." She decided not to mention that the griffin had been hacked from its moorings and then pushed by a human hand.

"I knew it," Delilah declared, plainly titillated. "Someone's trying to kill the poor man."

Genevieve stopped walking. "Who told you that?"

Delilah's eyes went round. "Why, what other explanation could there be?"

"Hundreds," Genevieve declared stoutly, although she couldn't think of a single one at the moment—but that was only because she'd seen the footprints and the tools in the turret room.

Delilah shook her head. "I don't think so, dear. Mildred and I talked it over, and we both decided that someone's out to kill him." She spoke in an excited, hushed voice, chock-full of drama and intrigue.

Genevieve, on the other hand, made sure her scorn was plain. "Oh, dear heaven. I do hope the two of you won't stir up a load of idle gossip in the village, Aunt. Neither the Rakes family nor the Crowfoots need more scandal attached to their names."

"Why whatever do you mean, Genevieve? What kind of scandal could accrue to us if somebody is trying to murder Mr. Rakes?"

"For heaven's sake, Aunt Delilah, use your head! Who do you think people are going to believe is trying to do something like that?"

Delilah blinked at her. "Certainly not *you*, Genevieve!"

Exasperated now, both because of her gossipy aunt's presumption and by the knowledge that, by heavens, people *were* going to think a Crowfoot was behind the attempt to kill Tobias Rakes, Genevieve said, "Why not? Who else would want a Rakes dead?"

"I have no idea, dear, but we don't." Delilah looked confused. "Do we?"

"Of course we don't! But don't you see? If you run around spreading tales, other people will think so."

"No one would ever think such a thing, Genevieve. I'm sure of it."

"Ha! Just you wait, Aunt Delilah. I'll bet you anything that after Mildred left the castle cottage, she hightailed it into town, and now everyone in Bittersweet thinks I've made an attempt on Tobias Rakes's life. I can see them now in my mind's eye." She tapped the side of her head.

"Oh, Genevieve, no!" Delilah sounded honestly horrified—much too late, in Genevieve's opinion.

"Oh, Delilah, yes," she said, a sharp edge to her voice.

And she was right. They'd no sooner set foot on the cobbled main street of Bittersweet than Genevieve saw Mrs. Carvahal, the baker, chatting with Glynis Phipps. As soon as the two women saw Genevieve and Delilah, they stopped speaking. Mrs. Carvahal looked guilty. Glynis Phipps merely seemed curious.

Genevieve was in no mood to shrink away from spiteful tongues. She walked boldly up to the two woman, Delilah trailing nervously in her wake. "Mrs. Carvahal! You're just the person I wanted to see." Genevieve gave her a cheerful smile and hoped the baker would choke on it.

Mrs. Carvahal tittered nervously. "About the food for next week's do, I expect."

"Indeed. If you and Miss Phipps don't mind my interrupting your chat"—she gave them both a meaningful look—"perhaps we can go over everything one last time."

"Of course. We were just chatting about—ah—"

"I was telling her about Mr. Rakes's terrible accident this morning, Genevieve," Glynis Phipps said.

Glynis was nearly as powerful a female as Mrs. Watkins. Genevieve knew she'd not flinch from calling a spade a spade—or even from calling a club a spade if she'd made up her mind it was one. Genevieve decided to take the nurse by the stethoscope. She turned and deliberately stared down her nose at Glynis. "Yes, it was a terrible accident, and Mr. Rakes might have been seriously injured. Fortunately, he wasn't. Dr. Johnson is tending him as we speak."

"Did he need stitches?" Mrs. Carvahal asked breathlessly.

"No, he did not. Dr. Johnson prescribed rest." Genevieve decided not to mention the dose of morphia.

"Oh. Well, let's go to the bake shop." Mrs. Carvahal sounded disappointed.

"Certainly." Genevieve gave Glynis Phipps a haughty nod. Glynis seemed remarkably unaffected by her haughtiness, which irked Genevieve. She wished she had a reputation for sternness rather than good humor. Sternness would stand her in much better stead at the moment.

Well, it couldn't be helped. She glanced at Delilah and hoped her expression said "I told you so." Delilah appeared suitably guilty, for all the good that did either of them.

Mildred Hotchkiss and Glynis Phipps had done their work well. There was apparently not a single citizen in Bittersweet who hadn't heard about Tobias's accident. Most of those citizens seemed to believe the griffin's fall had been no accident, and Genevieve didn't think it was her imagination making her suppose several of them were looking at her somewhat askance. She did know it was her imagination making Delilah seem to shrink as they made their way from business to business in Bittersweet.

She was quite irked by the time she'd finished her chores in town, and she and Delilah had set out for home again. "There. Do you see what your gossiping has done now, Aunt?"

"It wasn't *my* gossiping, Genevieve," Delilah said, as hotly as she was able, which wasn't very by this time. Delilah Crowfoot was easily intimidated.

"You should have tried to quell it the moment Mildred Hotchkiss brought it to you."

Delilah looked hurt. "That's not fair, Genevieve. You know it's impossible to quell Mildred Hotchkiss."

This was true, but Genevieve still felt put out with her aunt. It wasn't pleasant to realize that people one had known all one's life were now calling one a murderess behind one's back. An attempted murderess, she amended quickly.

The notion of Tobias Rakes being murdered hit her suddenly, causing a spasm to shudder through her. Good Lord! Someone was trying to kill him. And rather than focusing their attention on who might possibly be at fault, the nonsensical folks in Bittersweet were finding it more amusing to speculate about Genevieve being behind the vicious attack.

This was terrible. "I won't let them get away with it," she declared.

"You won't let who get away with what, dear?"

"I won't let the citizens of this town get away with thinking I'm a murderer."

"Oh." Delilah accepted that without comment.

"The very idea is absurd," Genevieve went on, getting madder by the moment. "I can't believe anyone could seriously consider me as a candidate for slaughtering another human being."

"Indeed," said Delilah.

"I mean, how absurd! Anyone who knows me knows I don't hold grudges. I've always, always done my best to stifle talk about the family feud. You know I have, Aunt Delilah!" She glared at her aunt because there was no one else around to glare at.

Delilah seemed to shrink even further. "Yes, dear. I know you have."

"It's all stupidity and narrow-mindedness. The very idea is outrageous."

"Certainly it is."

"Why, I should sue Mildred Hotchkiss for slander!"

"Oh, I don't think you should do that, dear."

When Genevieve glanced at Delilah again, she saw that her aunt had gone pale, as if she feared Genevieve might actually bring charges against Mildred Hotchkiss. The notion was so silly, Genevieve's anger evaporated and she laughed.

"I don't really mean it, Aunt. I'd never sue Mildred for slander, even if I do resent her spreading such silly tales."

Delilah looked relieved. "I'm so glad, Genevieve. Slander is such an ugly word."

"Humph. It's not as ugly as murder, if you ask me, and Mildred Hotchkiss is the one spreading that tale."

"Well, you know how she is, dear."

"Yes. I know."

They walked up the path to the cottage door in silence, Genevieve nursing her psychic wounds, Delilah mulling something over that Genevieve couldn't even guess at. She stooped to kiss her aunt on the cheek when they reached the door.

"Won't you come in for a cup of tea, dear?"

"No, I don't have time today, Aunt Delilah. I need to get back to the castle. There's lots left to do."

"All right." Delilah appeared disappointed.

"You will come to the open house, won't you, Aunt Delilah? Surely Granny Crowfoot won't bother you with all those other people present."

"Well . . ." Delilah appeared frightened for a moment, then said, "I suppose so, dear, if it will make you happy."

In light of Delilah's terror of ghosts, Genevieve considered her compliance sweet. She ceased thinking so as soon as her aunt's next words smote her ears.

"*Were* you the one who pushed the griffin from the tower, Genevieve?"

Chapter Nine

"I can't believe my own aunt asked me such a thing!" Genevieve stopped her heated pacing and glanced at Tobias, a guilty expression on her face. "I know I shouldn't be yelling in your library, Mr. Rakes, especially since you're trying to recuperate from your ordeal."

Tobias, sunk in his overstuffed chair and with his leg propped on the ottoman, waved his hand and murmured, "Think nothing of it, Miss Crowfoot. I don't mind at all." He didn't, either. He'd seldom experienced such emotional outbursts, both happy and wrathful, as those Genevieve seemed prone to. He discovered he enjoyed her openness, rather as he enjoyed fresh spring breezes. The emotional rigidity of his own life seemed dull and colorless by comparison.

"It's only that I'm *so angry*," Genevieve continued, quite unnecessarily in Tobias's estimation. Anyone looking at her could tell she was every bit as angry as she claimed to be. She'd been stomping up and down the room in front of Tobias's chair ever since she'd stormed back to the castle, fury propelling her. "My own aunt!"

Although Tobias had seen Genevieve peeved once or twice, he'd never seen her in an all-out rage before. He thought she was darling, which astonished him, since he'd never been attracted to stormy females. He decided his feelings in this instance were prompted by the incongruity of the usually good-natured Genevieve Crowfoot being in such a temper. Besides that, her inner anger had manifested itself in a delightful color to her cheeks, and an attractive swelling of her generous bosom. While Tobias acknowledged himself to be somewhat physically incapacitated at the moment, that didn't mean he couldn't appreciate pulchritude when it paraded itself in front of him.

Wesley Armitage, on the other hand, appeared almost frightened by Genevieve's uncharacteristic temper tantrum. "Er, I'm sure she didn't mean it the way it sounded, Miss Crowfoot," Armitage ventured, sounding not sure at all.

Genevieve rounded on Armitage, causing him to shrink back against his sofa cushion. "She did, too, mean it! That's what's so galling about it! She honestly believed I'd be capable of such a thing!"

"You look mad enough to heave any number of griffins at the moment," Tobias commented mildly, mostly to see what she'd do.

What she did was suck in such a huge breath, that he feared for her bodice buttons. In truth, he watched them avidly, hoping. Unfortunately, they held fast.

"If," Genevieve said in a voice shaking with passion, "I ever became angry enough to do someone a physical harm, I hope I won't be sneaky about it. I hope I'd have enough gumption to march right up to him and shoot him." She turned abruptly and resumed pacing. "If I had a gun, which I don't. But at least I'd slap his face or something. I'd never drop a griffin on his head!"

"I'm glad of that." Tobias smiled at her when she whirled around and frowned at him. He almost wished he could provoke her into slapping him. He could imagine all sorts of scenarios that might transpire in such a case—if he were physically able, which he wasn't. He sighed with regret.

Armitage, who apparently hadn't left Tobias's side, seemed uncomfortable in a room filled with such potent feminine intensity. "Er, you know what elderly ladies are like,

Miss Crowfoot," he stuttered. "I'm sure she didn't—er—that is to say, I'm sure she doesn't honestly believe you capable of doing Tobias injury."

Genevieve snorted. Then she whirled around again, making Armitage blink and Tobias grin. "What about the Pickstaffs? Do you think one of them might have done it?"

"The Pickstaffs?" Armitage repeated blankly.

Tobias shrugged. "I don't think Small William would have had time to drop the griffin and get back to the stables, which is where he came running from after the griffin fell. And Old William was supervising the gardeners at the time."

"Did you see him?" Genevieve looked almost hopeful.

Tobias was sorry to burst her faint bubble of hope. "I'm afraid I did, Miss Crowfoot."

"Oh." Genevieve was clearly disappointed. "What about Mrs. Watkins? She certainly has a hardy enough constitution and a strong enough will to do such a thing as heave a griffin. Has she ever indicated that she dislikes you, Mr. Rakes?"

"Not so as you'd notice. At least, she's always stern with me, but she seems to be stern with everyone."

"Yes. You're right about that. I don't think she's ever mentioned being on one side or the other in the feud, either." Genevieve scowled, picked up the fireplace poker, and stabbed an unburned log with it. The log was fresh, and the pleasant scent of pine wafted from the fireplace. Tobias wondered if Genevieve would be happier stabbing something more animated than a log in her present state of agitation, but thought it prudent not to ask. She might decide to stab him.

Genevieve obviously didn't like her theory being poked full of holes. She looked put out with him. Again, an explosion of pleasure filled Tobias. He'd never had such fun with a woman out of bed—and he'd only kissed her. He wondered what Genevieve would be like in bed. Would she be as passionate sexually as she was morally? The notion appealed to him very much, and he decided he'd really like to find out.

Unfortunately, it had taken all of his strength to kiss her. He'd have to wait a while before he attempted anything more strenuous than a kiss.

In a way, he was grateful to Genevieve's aunt. If Delilah hadn't propounded such an implausible question to Genevieve, she might still be embarrassed about that kiss. Tobias sighed, remembering the kiss with great pleasure.

"There has to be an explanation," Genevieve declared. "But until we discover what it is, you must take great care, Mr. Rakes. I believe you ought never to go out alone, for one thing. For another, perhaps you should hire some men to act as sentries at night or something."

"Don't be ridiculous, Miss Crowfoot." Tobias spoke more sharply than he perhaps should have, because Genevieve stiffened like the poker she was still jabbing at the fire. "I assure you, I can take care of myself. I've been doing so for a good many years now."

"Yes, I'm sure you have." Genevieve, too, spoke sharply. "But you didn't have anyone trying to kill you then."

"Tell that to the Sioux," Tobias said dryly.

"Oh, don't quibble! You know very well what I mean!"

Tobias took refuge in his lifted eyebrow again, and Genevieve blushed. "I beg your pardon. I know I shouldn't speak to my employer in such an intemperate way."

"Indeed."

The one word set her off again. "But you know very well what I mean, Mr. Rakes. There's someone in Bittersweet who is trying to get rid of you, for heaven's sake! You must look after yourself."

Tobias considered asking if Genevieve would like to be his bodyguard, but wasn't sure she could be trusted in a room with a poker.

"Perhaps that's not the case," Armitage said, saving the day, in Tobias's estimation. He and Genevieve looked at him, and Armitage shrugged self-deprecatingly. "I mean, maybe it wasn't intended as an attempt on your life, Tobias. Perhaps it was an accident."

Genevieve looked as skeptical as Tobias felt. "How could it have been an accident? Someone went to a good deal of trouble to hack that griffin away from the crest and shove it off the turret."

"Well, yes, but perhaps there's a less deadly—though still illegal—explanation."

"Like what?" Tobias wanted to know.

"I—I don't know. But if someone were, say, trying to steal the griffin, he probably wouldn't confess to it, because although theft is a less serious crime than murder, whoever it was still wouldn't want to admit he'd done it."

Tobias contemplated Armitage's proposal. It didn't sound too bad, except that he couldn't imagine a reason anyone in his right mind would want to steal a stonework griffin.

"But what was his motive?" Genevieve said, speaking his thoughts aloud. "What might the motive be for stealing a Crowfoot griffin?"

"I'm afraid I don't know, Miss Crowfoot. It was only a suggestion."

Armitage wasn't up to Genevieve's fighting weight when it came to debate and discussion, Tobias noticed with wry amusement. The lawyer seemed to shrivel against the sofa cushions once more.

Pacing again, Genevieve pondered Armitage's suggestion. After a moment or two, she said, "Well, it's a thought. And it's certainly no more foolish than my aunt's."

"Thank you," Armitage mumbled.

Genevieve stopped pacing abruptly. "I really can't stay here discussing this matter any longer. There's still too much to do for the open house next week. See if you can get some more sleep, Mr. Rakes. I'm sure it will be good for you."

And with that she sailed out of the room. Tobias and Armitage stared after her, thrown slightly off kilter by her sudden departure. Tobias murmured, "Mercurial."

Armitage said, "Indeed."

Tobias liked the word in reference to the bright and lively Miss Crowfoot. He drifted off to sleep under the influence of it.

For a day or two after the griffin incident Tobias's leg felt as if it had been kicked by an army mule. "Damn," he muttered as he eased himself out of bed one day. "I'm glad that damned open house isn't happening today. I'd never make it through.''

He had awakened that morning with pleasant images of a naked Genevieve prancing in his head. He chastised himself for succumbing to what he was sure must be a schoolboy infatuation with his housekeeper, but that did nothing to assuage his rampaging lust.

Those images, however, as well as some others of the two of them together, were much more pleasant than the incident that beset him as he headed to the dining room for breakfast. He had no sooner limped to the head of the grand staircase than he grasped the banister and it gave way. If he hadn't been leaning heavily on his cane, he'd have fallen clear over the railing and bashed his brains out on the flagged entryway.

As it was, the wooden banister clattered to the floor beneath, causing a racket like a thunderstorm in the echoing entryway. Staff came running from all over the castle.

"Good heavens!"

More startled than he cared to admit, it took Tobias a moment to realize the exclamation had come from Genevieve. When he peered over the no-longer-banistered landing, he saw her gazing up at him, patently horrified. Her eyes looked huge as they stared at him, and he felt almost trapped in them for a moment.

"Good Lord," she whispered. "What happened?"

"I think our griffin tosser has been at it again." Tobias was proud of the tone he achieved, which was wry and slightly amused.

"Oh, my God!"

Before Tobias had completely recovered his composure, he saw Genevieve dashing up the stairs toward him. He barely had time to brace himself before she hurtled into his arms. She must have realized what she'd done, unhappily, because she drew away again instantly. Tobias was disappointed and let her go reluctantly. "I'm all right, Miss Crowfoot."

Her cheeks were rosy with embarrassment, and she pressed a hand to one of them. "I beg your pardon, Mr. Rakes. I can't believe such a thing has happened to you—

and only two days after that griffin almost fell on your head!"

"Think nothing of it, Miss Crowfoot." Tobias wished she'd fling herself at him again. He'd be better prepared this time. In spite of his aching leg.

"Something terrible is happening in Crowfoot Castle," Genevieve declared. "And we must discover who's behind it."

"Good idea," Tobias said, meaning it sincerely.

But they didn't. In spite of all their conferences and discussions, during which Genevieve revealed some papers she'd discovered regarding the feud, they came up with nothing that pointed to any specific person.

"I don't understand it," Genevieve said, sounding grumpy.

Tobias was sipping from a tumbler of brandy, and Genevieve was demolishing a cup of hot chocolate and a plate of macaroons. It was the evening before his open house, and his leg had recovered from the jostling it had received in his fall from Rake's Progress. Tobias eyed Genevieve over his tumbler's rim, thinking that her eyes were much the same color as the liquid in his glass. He liked that thought.

Genevieve bit savagely into a macaroon and took another gulp of chocolate. "I mean, I've searched into the sordid secrets of every citizen of Bittersweet, trying to find any kind of connection, and I haven't been able to discover anything about anyone."

"That's comprehensive," Tobias murmured, wondering how long he could keep her here in his library, chatting. He always hated it when the day came to an end and Genevieve and he went up to their separate bedrooms. What was worse, he then generally spent upwards of an hour in bed, unable to sleep for trying to come up with ways to get Genevieve to share his bed with him. So far, he'd been unsuccessful.

She glanced at him uncertainly, as if she suspected him of sarcasm. He kept his expression mild, and she went back to her chocolate. "I can't imagine who it is."

"You don't suppose the old place is just falling down around us, do you?" he posited, knowing that was too simple an answer to explain away the accidents plaguing the castle.

"Not for a minute," Genevieve declared.

"No, I don't, either." Tobias took another sip of brandy, feeling gloomy.

"But I can tell you this much," Genevieve said, sounding staunch and loyal. "And that is, I won't rest until we've discovered who's behind it all. Whoever it is will surely make a mistake one of these days, and then we'll have him."

"Or her."

She blinked at him. "Of course." It didn't sound as if she wanted to contemplate the possibility of a female being the source of his problems.

He lifted his tumbler in a toast. "You're a good person to have on my side, Miss Crowfoot. I could have used more soldiers with your determination and allegiance."

She blushed, and Tobias was hard-pressed to remain in his chair. He wanted to leap out of it, stomp over to her, and ravish her. Right here on the library carpet. It was a damned good thing he was in no fit condition to leap and stomp, because he had a feeling he'd be perfectly fit to ravish.

By the time she awoke on the morning of the open house, Genevieve's outrage over her aunt's question had abated, and memories of the kiss she and Tobias had shared had returned in full. Thanks to the dreams she'd had for the past week, that kiss had taken the topmost spot in her mind. She thought about it waking and sleeping. Images flashed through her head at all sorts of inconvenient times, and she knew she'd have to guard herself against succumbing to her passionate impulses again. She was unequal to withstand the lures of so obviously practiced a man of the world as Tobias Rakes. She'd been doing her best to avoid him during the week, except when absolutely necessary, because she didn't trust herself.

"Thank heavens he's injured," she muttered as she donned her starched white apron. She realized immediately how unkind her thought had been and felt a little guilty about having had it—but it was the truth. If Tobias Rakes were a whole man, Genevieve would probably be a fallen woman by now. She knew good and well she wouldn't have tried to stop his assault in the tower room.

"Assault?" she said with a snort. "That was no more an assault than that griffin or the banister railing was an accident."

On that daunting note, she left her room, descended the stairs, and resumed her generalship of the household staff. The guests would begin arriving at noon, and Genevieve wanted to make good and sure everything was in readiness. She aimed to set the Bittersweet rumor mill on its ear by showing everyone in town that the Crowfoots and the Rakeses had finally settled the century-old differences between them in an amicable fashion. Her mind wandered to the kiss again, and she reprimanded herself. "Not *that* amicably."

Tobias, she soon discovered, didn't share her goal of amicability. He was grouchy as a wounded tiger and grumbling.

The first thing he said to her when she saw him in the dining room, dishing up breakfast from the sideboard, was, "I'll be glad when this day is over." He said it with a scowl, too.

The second thing he said was, "I spent a damnable night—couldn't sleep for love nor money because of that damned ghost—and I feel like hell this morning. And my leg hurts, too."

Tamping her temper down—one temper tantrum a week was her limit—Genevieve said mildly, "I'm very sorry to hear it, Mr. Rakes. Would you like me to fix you a posset of some sort? Would you like me to send for Dr. Johnson?"

"God, no."

"Would you care for a dose of laudanum or some of your salicylic powders?"

"No! Leave me alone, for God's sake. Please." Tobias sucked in a big breath and let it out slowly. "I beg your pardon, Miss Crowfoot. I didn't mean to snap at you."

"Think nothing of it, Mr. Rakes." She gave him one of her icier smiles. "I'm sure you must be in some pain this morning."

"Yes," he said. "I am. But I shouldn't have taken it out on you."

True enough, Genevieve thought, although she didn't say so aloud. She merely nodded and left the room, deciding to take some toast and tea in the kitchen where the company was sure to be merrier.

In that she discovered she was mistaken. Molly was in a state, and so were the rest of the housemaids, several of whom had been hired specifically for this occasion. Genevieve soon realized that Molly's state had been precipitated by Mrs. Carvahal, who had been lording over the hapless Molly the fact that she was a better cook. Genevieve found the poor girl sobbing in a corner beside the stove, with her apron over her head. It took forever to calm her down again, and by the time Genevieve finally got to eat her toast and tea, she had a raging headache and wished she could go back to bed.

"And it's not just that she's so mean about the cooking," Molly whimpered, blowing her nose on a napkin. "But I found Gray Baby this morning." Gray Baby was a stray cat Molly had been feeding since she started cooking at the castle.

Rubbing her temples and longing for some of Tobias's salicylic powders, Genevieve said, "Don't you find Gray Baby most mornings, Molly?"

The girl nodded. "But this morning she was *dead!*"

That did put a different light on things. Genevieve was sorry to hear about the cat. "How did she die?"

"I don't know. She was just dead. Out by the stables. Stiff as a board. It looked like there was some foam around her mouth. She must have died a few days ago, because she didn't come when I called all week."

"Where's the cat now?"

"Small William took her off. He said he'd bury her in the garden."

"That's good." Genevieve would have liked to view the corpse, not because she had any interest in dead cats, but because the cat's sudden demise seemed suspicious to her. As far as she knew, Gray Baby had been as healthy as a horse only a few days ago. And that foaming-around-the-mouth business might have been caused by something more sinister than mere chance. It sounded, in fact, suspiciously like poison to Genevieve.

However, there was no time to think about possibly poisoned cats now. She had work to do and, as soon as she'd swallowed her toast and tea, she got at it.

Unfortunately, her headache had managed to get a firm grip on her and did not seem to be abating. She didn't want her own incapacity to interfere with her duties today of all days and therefore, she hunted down Tobias. He didn't seem pleased to see her, but glanced up from the book he'd been reading with a frown on his face. "Yes?"

The one word slightly daunted Genevieve. "I'm sorry to disturb you, Mr. Rakes. I don't mean to interrupt your reading, but I wondered if I might have a dose of your salicylic powders."

His expression softened significantly. "Are you unwell, Miss Crowfoot?" In fact, he looked concerned, which Genevieve appreciated.

She smiled. "Merely a headache from all the hustle and bustle, I suspect."

"Indeed." He frowned again. "Certainly. The powders are in my bedside stand. Please forgive me for not standing. My leg isn't well today."

"I'm sure it couldn't be, after the jarring it's taken lately."

"Yes, but it's going to have to be sound this afternoon, during the blasted party." He glared at her as if the party were all her fault—which it was.

Genevieve reined in her own frown, as well as a sarcastic retort. "Thank you for the powders."

His smile almost made up for his rude comments about the open house. "No need to thank me, Miss Crowfoot. You're the one who's doing all the work. I'm just sitting here aching and moaning."

Genevieve got the distinct impression he resented his incapacity today more than he generally did. She understood. He was a man accustomed to command and to doing things. It must be galling to have to sit still and watch everyone else working around him. In fact, she had a sudden, almost over-whelming, urge to trot over to his chair and kiss him in sympathy. Good heavens, what was the matter with her?

She was still shaking her head when she reached into To-bias's nightstand and withdrew one of the folded papers filled with fine white powder. She marched herself downstairs, stirred the powder into some water, and took a sip. The stuff was perfectly vile, but she forced herself to take another sip.

It was while she was bracing herself to swallow a third sip that Small William burst into the kitchen to relate the news that the grocer's horse had gone lame and if Genevieve wanted the iced champagne delivered, Small William was going to have to take Old Toby down and hitch him to the grocer's wagon. Genevieve abandoned her powder-laced wa-ter with a grimace, deciding she'd rather have a headache than drink any more of the wretched medicine. She didn't wonder that Mr. Rakes was so moody, if he had to drink concoctions like that every day.

"Of course you may take Old Toby into town, William. What were you doing before you got word about the grocer's horse?"

"Helping Dad gather flowers for Mrs. Watkins. She ain't going to be happy."

That was an understatement, and Genevieve knew it. She sighed, resigned to her fate today. "I'll talk to Mrs. Watkins, Small William. You get Old Toby to town. I'm sure I, at least, am going to need at least one glass of champagne be-fore the day's over."

The boy didn't crack so much as a grin at Genevieve's small joke. He only nodded and hurried off toward the sta-bles. Genevieve dumped the disgusting mixture she'd been drinking into a pot of geraniums on the windowsill. She didn't think salicylic powders could hurt geraniums, even if they did taste like poison. She stopped pouring suddenly, alarmed by the word her mind had chosen to describe what she'd been drinking.

"Don't be foolish, Genevieve Crowfoot." She finished emptying the water into the pot, set the glass in the sink, and went off to soothe Mrs. Watkins's ruffled feathers. She was

just in time. Mrs. Watkins had already reduced two housemaids to tears, and poor Godfrey was in a hand-wringing
state of agitation as Genevieve walked up.

And so the morning went. By the time guests began to
arrive—and it didn't look to Genevieve as though anyone in
town had declined Tobias's invitation—her stomach was
aching along with her head. She hoped she wouldn't be sick,
and tried to fool her body into feeling better by ignoring it.
She was nominally successful in the endeavor.

Tobias, on the other hand, felt rotten. He stood at the window
wondering how he had gotten himself into this mess. He
didn't enjoy big parties, and this was one of the biggest he'd
ever seen—and it was only an hour or so old. What's more,
it was taking place in his own personal home and grounds.
At his invitation. Lord, the things a man could be tricked
into doing by a clever female if he dropped his guard for as
much as a second or two.

What's more, he'd been startled when Genevieve came to
him asking for salicylic powders. He'd begun to think of
himself as the only one in his circuit who had aches and
pains. To have Genevieve Crowfoot, of all people, complain
of a headache disturbed him, although he wasn't sure why.
Perhaps it was because he'd started thinking of her as his
own personal bright and shining star.

That notion was even more hideous than thinking his leg
would never heal properly. In fact, it made him downright
bilious. He was thirty-four years old, for the love of God,
and he hadn't depended on another human being for seventeen years. Even when he was a boy, he'd learned not to
depend on others. He'd depended on his mother, and look
what happened. She'd died. Then he'd tried to depend on his
father, only to be rebuked and scolded—a ten-year-old boy,
for Pete's sake. If Tobias ever had children, God forbid, he'd
sure as the devil never rebuke and scold one of them for
being sad about his own mother's death.

And then, to top off his youthful follies, he'd eloped with
Madeline Riley. If ever an affair was doomed from before

the beginning, it was that one. What a jackass he'd been. He'd played right into the conniving harpy's talonlike hands. He shuddered now, just thinking about it.

"Are you all right, Tobias?"

Wesley Armitage's timid question brought Tobias back to himself. "Yes," he snarled. "I'm fine." He noticed Armitage's reaction and regretted his brusqueness. "Forgive me, Wes. My leg hurts."

"I'm sure it does," the lawyer said, sounding solicitous. "Would you like to sit down for a while? You've been standing there for a while now."

"Actually, I'd like to escape for a few minutes. Miss Crowfoot told me about the sunken garden. Where is it, do you know? She seems pretty keen on the thing. Maybe no one will be there."

"I'll ask."

So Armitage scurried off to ask the location of the sunken garden, and Tobias was left to fend for himself among a herd of strangers. Hell's bells, he couldn't even depend on his own lawyer to defend him from his encroaching neighbors. What was the world coming to? Nevertheless, he smiled and nodded and chatted with the locals, playing the country squire for all he was worth. Thanks to his maternal grandmother, he was worth a great deal.

That thought soothed him slightly until he caught sight of Genevieve, talking to Tobias's inept butler. Hell, his whole staff was inept except for the Pickstaffs and Mrs. Watkins. And, of course, Genevieve herself. However, he actually found his bumbling staff rather endearing—and amusing.

His amusement died when he studied Genevieve's face. She looked pale. Almost sickly. As he watched her, she withdrew a handkerchief from her pocket and dabbed at her brow with it. Was she sick? She'd complained of a headache; perhaps that was only a precursor to something more deadly. His heart lurched painfully. He told himself it was because he didn't like to see anyone looking unwell, but he was pretty sure he was lying to himself.

When Armitage came back, however, Tobias wrenched his

attention away from Genevieve. She was fine, he told himself. Fine.

"It's over that way," Armitage said, pointing toward the rose garden.

"Let's take a look."

So they did. And, when he got there, Tobias had to agree with Genevieve. The sunken garden was really quite lovely. He particularly liked the stone bridge spanning the pond. He and Armitage walked across it, stopping in the middle to look into the water. Carp and goldfish swam amid the water lilies.

"What happens to the fish in the wintertime?" he asked Armitage.

"I'm not sure. I think they're taken out and stored in one of the greenhouses."

"Hmmm. Enterprising of someone. One of the Crowfoots, no doubt—although I'm sure it wasn't Hubert."

"No doubt."

Tobias wondered if any of his relatives had been this innovative when it came to gardens. He didn't think so. The only thing his father seemed to value was money. Beauty had never stirred him an inch.

"Oh, Mr. Rakes! You shouldn't have walked so far."

Tobias swung around, startled by Genevieve's worried tone. In turning, he wrenched his leg and cursed softly. Armitage grabbed his arm, which increased his annoyance.

"I didn't hear you approach, Miss Crowfoot."

His voice was cold and curt, and Genevieve didn't appreciate it. She was feeling decidedly unwell, didn't understand it since her health was usually prime, and didn't care to be snapped at when she was merely showing her solicitude toward a man who had suffered a grievous injury and who, what's more, was evidently the object of someone's murderous intentions. She walked across the bridge and joined the two men.

Tobias frowned at Armitage. "You needn't hover over me, Wes."

"Sorry." Armitage dropped Tobias's arm in a hurry.

Genevieve drew back from her employer, annoyed by his

abrupt tone. "He wasn't hovering. He was merely showing concern for your welfare."

Tobias huffed with impatience. "I'm sorry I barked at you, Wes. What is it, Miss Crowfoot?"

Rather testily, Genevieve said, "I merely wanted you to know that a gentleman from your father's household has arrived and wishes to speak to you." She twitched the bow at her waist, which had a tendency to sag, and glowered at him.

The information she'd brought seemed to surprise Tobias, and he didn't give any indication of having noticed her tone of voice. "Someone from my father's household? Did we invite my old man?"

"We sent invitations to everyone in Bittersweet. Your father's name was among them. If you will recall, I asked you about it specifically."

"Oh, yes."

Again, Tobias appeared to pay no attention to her tone of voice. Genevieve, for whom it was no small feat to sound testy, especially when she felt unwell, found his lack of recognition in this instance galling.

"Who is it?"

"A Mr. Forster."

"Forster. Oh, yes, I think I remember him. He's my father's attorney, I believe. Where is he?"

"In the house. He said he'd await you in the entry hall, next to the champagne punch."

The entire household, inside and out, had been decorated for the festivities, and there was food and drink set up in the enormous flagged entryway, in the parlor, and outside, on the terrace, shaded from the sun.

"Thank you, Miss Crowfoot. I'll go to him."

Although she didn't want to because she was mad at him, Genevieve said grudgingly, "I'll take you to him."

"Thank you." Tobias, contrarily, sounded humble. Genevieve shot him a look and noticed his eyes twinkling at her. She was in no mood to be appeased, but walked stiffly at his side. Unfortunately, she had to unbend her royal manner in order to greet Bittersweet visitors, who were fascinated by the castle. No one who wasn't a Crowfoot had been allowed onto the castle grounds in decades, thanks to Hubert Crowfoot's misanthropic eccentricity.

In spite of her headache and queasy stomach, Genevieve performed her duties as hostess, smiling at everyone and greeting old friends. Delilah had condescended to come to the party, although she wouldn't go inside the castle itself. She hovered on the terrace in the shade, gossiping happily with everyone and only shooting terrified glances from time to time at the castle itself.

Delilah tried to waylay Genevieve on her trip to the entryway, but Genevieve wouldn't be waylaid. She intended to eavesdrop on the conversation between Mr. Forster and Tobias, even if it was impolite of her to do so. She'd been thinking for some time that it would be nice if a reconciliation could be arranged between father and son, even if she did disapprove of the elder Mr. Rakes's behavior on the occasion of his son's youthful folly.

Genevieve believed that understanding and kindness almost invariably worked better than bitterness and recrimination. When it came to dealing with impressionable adolescents, one couldn't afford to be stiff-necked and rigid. That didn't mean one shouldn't hold to one's standards, but blaming a young man for falling in love was like blaming the sun for shining. No young man of spirit would easily forgive a parent for being right in calling him a fool.

"There he is," she murmured to Tobias as they crossed the flags in the entryway. A tall, gaunt man, clad all in black and looking every inch a tight-lipped Yankee, stood beside the front door, as still as a statue. He frowned at the people milling around him as if he disapproved of their levity.

"I see. Yes, I recognize him." Tobias moved away from Genevieve, who followed more slowly, not wanting to be in the way, but curious as to why Forster, and not Mr. Rakes, had come. "Forster," Tobias said. "Good to see you."

"Mr. Rakes." Forster bowed formally.

"I see my father didn't deign to come."

Tobias's voice sounded extraordinarily bored and cynical to Genevieve. She recalled hearing that same inflection in his voice on the day they'd met, right here, in this same entryway. She hadn't heard it again until right this minute. From this curious incident, she gathered that, while outwardly Tobias seemed relaxed and hospitable, inside he remained tense in front of a representative from his father. She judged that he considered Forster in the same manner as he would a representative from an enemy camp.

"The older Mr. Rakes hasn't been well recently, Mr. Rakes." The two men shook hands. "But he wanted me to come. He wanted to know if you received his letter."

"I received it." Tobias smiled. Cynically.

Genevieve, who was feeling weak as well as quite curious, sat in a chair set against the wall. She fanned herself with her hand.

"Your father didn't receive a reply," said Forster.

"That's because I didn't send him one. His letter was a command, Forster. I don't respond to commands in civilian life. Never have. I'm surprised my father didn't remember that."

It looked to Genevieve as if it cost Forster some effort, but he unbent slightly. "He didn't mean it that way, Mr. Rakes. He's an old man, and he's set in his ways. He was hoping to make amends."

Tobias didn't unbend an inch. "Amends? He has a funny way of showing it. He made no mention of remorse. He commanded my attendance upon him, and that was that."

Forster sighed, something that seemed foreign on a man of his bearing. "I fear he's not learned pretty manners in his lifetime, Mr. Rakes. I do know that he regrets the estrangement between you, and would like to resolve it."

"If he wants to resolve it, he can show up at my house himself. I sent the invitation. He evidently chose not to accept it." There wasn't a hint of compromise in Tobias's voice. "He threw me out and cut me off. I'm sure he thought I'd fail in life and was looking forward to seeing me crawl back and beg his forgiveness. But I didn't fail." He made a gesture intended to encompass the entire castle and grounds. "As you can see—and as you can report to him."

Genevieve's head began to swim. She was trying very hard to follow the conversation between the two men. She cared about the outcome for some reason. But a strange, numb sensation had begun to take hold of her fingers and toes. Cold perspiration broke out on her forehead. She wondered if she were really getting sick. She glanced to her right. Was it her imagination, or was that geranium dying? It had seemed perfectly healthy this morning.

From what seemed like very far away, she heard Tobias's voice, hollow and worried.

"Miss Crowfoot? Miss Crowfoot!"

She opened her mouth to tell him she'd be fine in a moment. Nothing emerged but a soft moan. And then the world went black.

Chapter Ten

"No, I won't sit down, damn it. Stop pestering me."

"I beg your pardon."

Tobias was sorry he'd snarled at Armitage, but the man was driving him mad with his solicitude and suggestions. Damn it, if Tobias wanted to sit, he'd sit. At the moment his nerves were rattling a hell of a lot harder than his leg was aching, so he continued pacing the Persian carpet in the hallway outside Genevieve's room. The sound of his guests, happily oblivious to Genevieve's illness, rose up from the gardens along with the fragrance of the roses and honeysuckle, making Tobias want to shoot them all.

He wasn't generally this irrational and couldn't account for his present state of worry. He tried to chalk it up to the fact that Genevieve didn't seem to be the fainting-spell type, but he had a sinking suspicion the cause of his distress went deeper than that.

"Thank God Dr. Johnson was here when she fainted. What the devil can be wrong with her? She looked like hell, and she was sweating like a pig."

Armitage shook his head. He looked worried too, but then Armitage always looked worried. Tobias had never seen a man who looked so worried so often, in fact. He didn't understand what the fellow had to worry about all the damned time. At the moment, Tobias was so worried he wanted to bellow and break things, but that was because Genevieve was sick. Instead, he paced.

The door to her room opened and Dr. Johnson emerged, wiping his hands on a towel. Tobias hurried to him, barely restraining the urge to grab the doctor by the lapels and shake a prognosis out of him.

"What's wrong with her? What happened? Why did she faint? Will she be all right?"

Dr. Johnson looked grave, a circumstance that made Tobias's heart palpitate wildly. "She's very sick. Mrs. Watkins and Delilah Crowfoot are in there. The poor girl's lost her breakfast, which is probably a good thing, since it will eliminate the primary source of the trouble. She must have eaten something that disagreed with her."

"You mean food?"

Both Tobias and Dr. Johnson turned to look at Armitage, who immediately became embarrassed.

"I mean, do you suppose it was something she ate at the party?"

"What?" A good deal startled by the thought, Tobias left Dr. Johnson's side and went to peer out of the hall window. He and Armitage had managed to get Genevieve upstairs without causing a stir. Then Tobias had hunted down her aunt. Delilah had refused to enter the castle until he'd explained that Genevieve was sick. Then she'd entered, but she'd looked like a scared rabbit and clung to him so hard all the way upstairs, he was sure he'd have lasting bruises.

The notion of Genevieve having become ill after eating something at his party, however, gave him a turn. "Good God, you don't mean to tell me there are going to be hundreds of sick people running around Bittersweet, do you?" He held the curtain back and tried to estimate the number of citizens partaking of his generosity. It wouldn't seem so much like generosity if they all got as sick as Genevieve. "The whole town will hate me if that happens. It won't just be the Crowfoot faction."

Dr. Johnson shook his head. "I don't think it's party food.

If it were something she'd eaten at the party, I expect we'd know it by this time. The citizens of Bittersweet aren't exactly shy when it comes to gorging themselves on free food. If any of it were tainted, more folks than Miss Crowfoot would have become ill by this time.''

"But what could it have been?" Armitage asked, sounding shaky.

Dr. Johnson's shaggy head shook again. "If I didn't know better, I'd think it was arsenical poisoning. The symptoms are the same.''

Armitage paled.

Tobias, shocked, uttered once more, "Good God!''

"There's no way she could have ingested anything containing arsenic, is there?''

Tobias glanced from the doctor to Armitage, who stared back, looking like he might join Genevieve in a faint.

"I can't think of a thing," Tobias said at last.

Genevieve's door opened again, and Delilah stepped out. She didn't appear to be very happy. Mrs. Watkins was right behind her.

"But she's my niece," Delilah protested to the more formidable Mrs. Watkins in an indignant, albeit quavery, voice.

"I don't care who she is. I don't want you in that room fretting and fussing and jabbering about ghosts!" Mrs. Watkins turned and went back into the room, shutting the door with a sharp bang behind her.

Delilah burst into tears, and Tobias felt honor-bound to put an arm around her and offer her the comfort of his clean linen handkerchief. Such behavior was completely unlike him. Hell, he was used to dealing with soldiers, and soldiers didn't cry. At least they didn't cry in front of people and for no better reason than that they were worried about their nieces and afraid of ghosts. Soldiers cried only when their arms or legs were blown off and stuff like that.

"Here, it's all right, Miss Crowfoot. I'm sure your niece will be fine in a little while. I'm afraid Mrs. Watkins is a bit, ah, overbearing.''

Delilah let out with a wail. Tobias wished she'd go somewhere else and cry. He looked up and saw Armitage staring at them and decided to get some good out of the man. "Wes," he said quietly. "Will you please help Miss Crowfoot downstairs." He thought furiously for a second. "Take her to the kitchen and give her some tea or something." Tea sounded useful. Medicinal, even.

He was startled when Delilah cried, "No! I don't want tea in the k-k-kitchen. I want to get out of this awful place."

This awful place? Well, there was no accounting for taste. Tobias looked at the lawyer and jerked his head in the direction of the stairs. "Wes?"

Armitage popped up from the bench he'd been sitting on. "Of course. I'll be happy to help Miss Crowfoot downstairs."

"But what about Genevieve?" Delilah moaned. "I can't abandon her like this!"

"I'll let you know as soon as we hear anything about her condition, Miss Crowfoot," Tobias assured her. A brilliant idea occurred to him. "Why don't you go downstairs and see if you can keep the party going. Miss Crowfoot has told me often that you're a wonderful hostess, and I'm sure she'd appreciate your taking over for her in this crisis."

Delilah brightened minimally, blew her nose, and looked up at Tobias with big, hopeful eyes. "Did she really?"

No, of course she hadn't said any such thing, but Tobias didn't have any qualms about lying for a good cause. "Indeed she did. And she needs you to be strong now, for her sake."

Delilah nodded and squared her small, plump shoulders. "Of course. Thank you, Mr. Rakes. You're very kind."

Kind, was he? He frowned at Armitage, who gently took Delilah's arm. "Here, Miss Crowfoot. Lean on me."

"Thank you so much." She gave Armitage the sort of smile women usually reserved for heroes.

As Delilah tottered away, leaning heavily on Armitage, Tobias heard her say, "You know, Mrs. Watkins may say what she pleases about the ghost, but I've seen it, Mr. Armitage. I've seen it with my own eyes." Her voice throbbed with intensity. "And one can't help but believe in what one sees, can one?"

"Of course one can't," Armitage murmured soothingly.

Tobias was glad Wes was the one having to deal with the scatty Delilah Crowfoot. Tobias himself would probably have lost his patience and barked at her, and that would have done no good at all. He turned back to Dr. Johnson. "How is she, really, Doctor? Will she be all right?"

"I think so. She couldn't have ingested much of whatever it was, but if I were you I'd look the place over and see if there isn't a stash of something containing arsenic somewhere. Perhaps the gardening staff used it for killing dandelions, or one of the maids put some out to kill rats or something."

"Maybe." Tobias didn't like the sound of this. Damn it, first a griffin falls, then a banister railing breaks off in his hands, and then Genevieve gets sick in a manner reminiscent of poisoning.

"I don't want to cause you alarm," Dr. Johnson continued gruffly. "But I don't like coincidences much, and there have been a few too many accidents around here for my taste."

"Only three," Tobias said, but he didn't like it, either.

"Hmph. Well, I'll be back to take another look at her before I go home today. In the meantime, take care of yourself." Her jerked a thumb at Genevieve's door. "And her."

"Thank you. I will."

In that endeavor, as soon as the doctor left, Tobias very quietly opened the door to Genevieve's room. Mrs. Watkins shot him a look that as much as said it was shockingly improper for him to be visiting a single lady's bedroom and, what's more, she didn't approve. Since Tobias was Mrs. Watkins's employer, he paid her no mind.

He didn't make a sound when he walked across the thick Turkish carpet to Genevieve's bed. His heart lurched when he looked down at her. She was asleep, and as pale as newly fallen snow. Gone was the blush of roses that so often kissed her cheeks, and her face looked haggard.

"Do you think she'll be all right?" he asked, alarmed by how truly ill Genevieve looked.

"The doctor thinks so," Mrs. Watkins answered.

The way she said it, in a funereal tone that evoked mental

images of graveyards at midnight, gave Tobias the impression she didn't share the good doctor's optimism. He searched the older woman's face, and tried to make himself believe that she was only possessed of a dramatic turn of mind—one of those people who thrived on disasters and tried to make the least little accident into a catastrophe. He hoped to hell he was right.

"Is there anything I can do?"

She frowned at him, as if silently telling him he could leave if he really wanted to do something useful. Tobias decided to overlook her unspoken message.

"No, I don't believe so."

He nodded. He really wanted to be alone with Genevieve, if only for a little while, and if only while she slept. Since he was the boss, he decided to arrange things the way he wanted them. "I'd appreciate it if you'd go downstairs and see that everything's going smoothly with the party, Mrs. Watkins. I'll stay here with Miss Crowfoot and make sure she doesn't take a turn for the worse."

The scowl she gave him might have made a less sanguine employer than Tobias fire her on the spot. Nevertheless, she stood, fluffing her skirts out in a way that left him in no doubt as to how indelicate she considered his request. Her tight little, "Very well," confirmed his opinion. She might as well have said, "On your head be it."

That was all right with Tobias. He was used to taking responsibility for his own actions and those of others. Hell, he had been since he was seventeen.

Mrs. Watkins left the room, taking with her the basin into which Genevieve had been sick. Tobias didn't even have time to appreciate the domineering woman's absence before Granny Crowfoot showed up. Tobias groaned softly, as little pleased to see the ghost appear as he had been glad to see Mrs. Watkins disappear.

"Did you do this?" he demanded before the ghost had even settled completely into her translucent human shape.

She bridled. *"How dare you ask me such a question? Only a damned Rakes man would dream of saying such a thing to me."*

"To hell with the Rakeses and the Crowfoots. I want to know if you poisoned Genevieve, damn it!" It took great effort, but he didn't holler at her, keeping his voice pitched at a harsh whisper in deference to the ill woman on the bed.

Granny Crowfoot went into her puffing-up routine. Tobias remained unimpressed.

"*I*," declared Granny Crowfoot in the voice of doom, "*would never, ever harm a hair on that child's hair.* She *has gumption.*" She deflated again with a whoosh. "*Unlike some of the other Crowfoot women I could mention.*"

"Obviously, you're not referring to yourself."

"*Of course I'm not. I'm talking about that silly aunt of my dear Genevieve's.*"

"When exactly did she become your dear Genevieve? The last I remember, you two were going at it tooth and nail."

"*That's merely because the girl has spirit,*" said the spirit.

"I see." Tobias sat on the chair Mrs. Watkins had lately vacated. Since he'd seen Mrs. Watkins bathing Genevieve's forehead with a washcloth dipped in the bowl of water residing on the bedside table, he figured he might as well do likewise. He really wasn't much of a nurse, but he was very worried about Genevieve and didn't want to neglect any duties.

"*The poor child needs better people around her than those you provide in this castle.*"

"What do you suggest? Leeches and cupping? Those things went out of style a century ago."

"*Don't speak to me in that tone of voice, young man.*"

Tobias grunted.

"*Medicine may have advanced slightly since my day, but the castle certainly hasn't. It isn't run the way it was in my father's day, I can tell you.*" The ghost sniffed as she hovered over Genevieve.

"No, and it isn't run the way it was in Hubert Crowfoot's day, either, in case you've forgotten." Tobias glowered at her, wishing he could do something to get rid of her, like swat her with a flyswatter, or blow on her and make her essence dissipate into the ether or something.

"Every family has one or two loose links," Granny Crowfoot said with another disdainful sniff.

Tobias thought about his father, and didn't respond.

"I was lurking when that silly aunt of hers and that dreadful doctor were in here fussing over her, but all they did was dither, and I never heard either one of them or that ghastly Watkins woman mention a diagnosis. What caused her illness? Does that stupid man know?"

Tobias decided to be bold with the old bat and perhaps shock her into confessing if she'd had a hand in this. "He thinks it was arsenical poisoning."

"What?"

Immediately Tobias regretted his boldness. "For God's sake, keep your voice down. She's trying to sleep."

Genevieve groaned and lifted a hand to her brow. Tobias wished he could pick her up and hold her in his arms.

"Who in the world would ever want to murder this sweet child?"

It was an improvement. At least the lousy ghost had taken to hissing instead of yelling. "I have no idea, but whoever it was is likely to succeed if you don't keep your damned voice down. She needs to rest, damn it."

"Don't you swear at me, young man. Show some respect. I'll have you know I'd be a hundred and fifty years old if I were alive today."

"Well, you're not alive today, and you're being too damned loud."

Granny Crowfoot huffed indignantly.

Genevieve's eyelids fluttered. She looked so weak and helpless. It made Tobias's heart hurt to see her thus. "Genevieve?" he said softly. "Miss Crowfoot?" He thrust the washcloth back into the bowl of water and leaned closer to her, lightly resting his bare palm on her forehead. Her skin felt cool and clammy. He wasn't sure that was a good thing, but at least she wasn't feverish.

"M-Mr. Rakes?" Her eyes flittered open. They were huge and dull and looked as if they'd sunk into the skin around them.

"Yes, Miss Crowfoot. Don't worry. I'm here."

Granny Crowfoot huffed again. Tobias shot her a murderous scowl that she ignored completely, which didn't surprise him a whole lot.

"What happened to you, child?" the ghost asked, materializing on the other side of Genevieve's bed and making her turn her head quickly—too quickly, apparently, because she groaned again and lifted a hand to her forehead. Since Tobias's hand was there already, he grabbed hers and lifted it to his lips. Genevieve looked mildly shocked—she was probably too weak to react more strongly.

"Let that child go immediately," Granny Crowfoot commanded. *"How dare you take advantage of her in her present condition?"*

"I'm not taking advantage of her," Tobias said, furious with the old busybody. "I'm offering her comfort and solace."

She huffed yet a third time.

Genevieve whispered, "He's not taking advantage of me."

"Thank you." He did, however, release her hand, feeling that it had perhaps been unwise to kiss it. He didn't want anyone, least of all Genevieve herself, to get any ideas about his intentions since he didn't really have any. Not regarding Genevieve Crowfoot, he didn't. She was a respectable woman, and Tobias's ambition was to stay as far away as possible from respectable women.

"Somebody attempted to poison you," the ghost declared flatly.

Tobias wished she were a living man. He'd poke her in the nose and throw her out the window.

"Wh-what?" Genevieve looked as startled as someone in her condition could look.

"No one knows what happened," Tobias said, glowering at Granny Crowfoot, who glowered back. "Dr. Johnson said the symptoms are like those of arsenical poisoning, but he doesn't know, really. Besides, why would anyone want to poison you?"

"I don't know." Genevieve moaned again softly, as if she

couldn't help herself. Her paleness and weak appearance troubled Tobias greatly.

"Can you recall eating anything unusual?"

"No. Nothing." Genevieve closed her eyes, as if she were too weary to hold them open a second longer. "My head hurts awfully," she murmured.

Since she'd mentioned her head, Tobias put his hand back on it. He liked touching her. She turned her head slightly so that her cheek rested against his palm. Her flesh felt soft and sweet, and Tobias wished he had the right to touch her any time he felt like it.

"You mentioned a headache this morning. Did you take any salicylic powders? They evidently didn't work."

Her eyes opened again. "I did take some of your powders. I'd forgotten."

"Perhaps you were sick even then, and that's why they didn't work." The urge to kiss her was so strong, it was all Tobias could do to hold back.

Her expression turned grave and her eyes narrowed, and his urge to kiss her receded.

"Perhaps they did work," she said.

It took him a second to catch her meaning. When he did, he sat bolt upright and withdrew his hand from her cheek. "Good God."

"What do you mean, perhaps they did?" Granny Crowfoot demanded.

"But how? Why?"

Genevieve said softly, "I don't know. I don't understand any of it."

"Neither do I! What are you two talking about?" Granny Crowfoot, never happy to be left out of a discussion, raised her voice.

"Keep your voice down," Tobias told her.

"I won't until you tell me what you're talking about," she told him back.

"Damn it, quit yelling. Can't you see Miss Crowfoot is still ill?" He wished he could capture the old ghoul and stuff her into a bottle, like a genie. He'd never uncork it in this lifetime.

"Don't you swear at me, young man! I want to know what the two of you are yammering about."

"Please," Genevieve whimpered. "I'll tell you if you'll please only lower your voices. My head feels like it's going to explode."

Immediately contrite, Tobias whispered, "I'm very sorry, Miss Crowfoot."

"You should be," Granny Crowfoot barked.

He scowled at her, which had about the same effect his scowls usually had on her.

"You see," Genevieve hurried on, obviously hoping to forestall another spat, "we think perhaps the salicylic powders I took from Mr. Rakes's bedside drawer had been doctored with arsenic."

"Oh," said the ghost.

"What I want to know is who would have done such a thing?"

"And why?" added Genevieve.

"And when?" Tobias kept glaring at Granny Crowfoot, hoping she'd take his meaning—or, better yet, take herself off.

She did one of those things. *"Well, it certainly wasn't me. What do you take me for, anyway?"*

"I'd better not say," Tobias said, not bothering to conceal his animosity. Not that he'd ever bothered to conceal it before.

She puffed herself up again. *"You, young man, are no gentleman!"*

"I never claimed to be a gentleman."

"Please," Genevieve said, sounding desperate. "There's no point in arguing." Her eyes thinned as she thought. "Right before I fainted, I seem to recall looking at a geranium into which I poured the water with the powders this morning. If it wasn't an hallucination, I think the poor thing was dying."

"Good God."

She looked up at him, her eyes beginning to sparkle ever so slightly. "Perhaps you can look at them and see if it was my imagination."

"I certainly will."

"I think you're both insane. Who would want to hurt our precious Genevieve?"

Our precious Genevieve? Tobias glared at the ghost again, unable to believe his ears.

Sounding as though she were hurrying in order to forestall another quarrel, Genevieve said, "Is there some way a chemist can test those other packets of salicylic powders to see if they contain poison?"

Although he didn't much want to, Tobias left off scowling at the ghost. As annoying as the old hag was, Genevieve was right to keep them to the point. "I think so. I believe there are chemical tests that can be run on them."

"Who in Bittersweet could do that? Do you know of anyone?"

He shook his head. "You know more people in Bittersweet than I do. The druggist, I suppose. Maybe Dr. Johnson."

"I don't think you should ask Dr. Johnson. He's the one who prescribed them, don't forget."

Tobias blinked down at Genevieve, who looked back at him steadily. "But why would he . . . ?"

"I don't know."

"Do you mean to tell me you think the doctor did this to you?" Granny Crowfoot exclaimed. *"Why, the next time I see the man, I'll haunt him to within an inch of his life!"*

"You'll do no such thing," Tobias told her. "It seems unlikely to me that Dr. Johnson would have done anything so obvious."

"I agree," said Genevieve. "But I still think you shouldn't have him analyze the powders, because word might get out in town, and then there would be a terrible lot of gossip. In fact, I think you should take them to another town entirely. Just to be on the safe side."

The import of her words fairly stunned Tobias. "Good God, someone really is trying to kill me, isn't he?"

"Or she."

"Or she," Tobias agreed. He didn't want to. "But who?"

"I don't know." She shut her eyes again, as if she were

too exhausted to keep them open. "But it's obvious that someone doesn't want you here."

"*No one wants him here,*" said Granny Crowfoot.

Genevieve sighed.

Tobias turned toward the ghost. "So far, you're the only one whom we *know* has tried to get rid of me. I wouldn't put it past you to add poison to my medicine. Those packets are light enough for you to carry."

Granny Crowfoot began inflating once more. "*Me! Why, you insolent young whippersnapper. I ought to—*"

"Can the dramatics, dammit!" Patience had never been Tobias's long suit. Now he lost his entirely. "You know you're the only one we've caught doing anything to get rid of me."

"*Well,*" Granny Crowfoot said, deflating. "*Perhaps that's so, but if you'll recall, I've already told my dear great-relative here that I couldn't harm you if I wanted to, which should be obvious by this time, since you're still here and healthy.*"

"Yes, I know what you've said. But I don't know if it's true."

"*I am not in the habit of lying, young man!*" She sniffed, crossed her arms over her bosom, and turned her back on them. "*Besides, I can't leave the castle.*"

"Dammit, you dropped leaves on my head from a tree that's a good hundred yards outside the castle. If what you just said isn't a lie, I'd like to know what is."

She swiveled her head around. Since she did so without turning the rest of her body, the effect was relatively grue-some. Tobias didn't react, since he suspected she wanted him to.

"*I* meant *I can't leave the castle grounds,*" she said. "*That's* what *I meant when I said I can't leave the castle. You may consider the structure alone to be a part of the castle, but I, as a Crowfoot born and bred, consider the entire—*"

"All right, all right," Tobias interrupted. "I get your point, but I still don't know if I believe you."

A soft moan from the bed captured the antagonists' attention. Immediately Tobias felt contrite. "I'm sorry, Miss Crowfoot. We shouldn't be arguing like this in your sickroom."

"If you'll take the rest of the powders in your bedside stand to Watertown, perhaps you can find a druggist or a chemist there who can test them for you. I do think it ought to be done."

"You're right," said Tobias, studiously ignoring Granny Crowfoot.

"Of course she's right," said the ghost, who evidently didn't care if he ignored her or not. *"She's a Crowfoot."*

Tobias rolled his eyes. His spirits lifted slightly when Genevieve smiled a very small, very wan smile.

"You ought to get back to your guests," she said.

He didn't want to get back to his guests. He wanted to stay here and hold Genevieve's hand. Since he suspected his desire was a weakness and did him no credit, he said, "In a minute."

Before his minute was up, a soft knock came at the door. Genevieve, who'd been resting with her eyes closed, opened them again. Tobias sighed and released Genevieve's hand. Granny Crowfoot muttered something under her breath and vanished.

"Thank God," Tobias said before he stood up.

He was pleased when Genevieve giggled.

The door opened, and Mrs. Watkins's solid form entered. She looked most disapproving. "How is she doing?" From the expression on the woman's face, anyone would think Tobias had spent his time alone with Genevieve making mad, passionate love to her. Not that they'd been alone. Or that he would have made love to her in her present condition.

"She's awake," he said, deciding he'd be better off if he didn't acknowledge Mrs. Watkins's expression, but instead merely address her question. "I think she'll be all right with rest."

"Good." Mrs. Watkins stalked over to the bed and looked down upon Genevieve, as if she were trying to make sure Tobias hadn't lied to her about the patient's condition. Her expression eased somewhat. "Yes, I believe she'll do. But she needs to sleep some more."

With another sigh, Tobias rose. "I suppose I'd better get back to my guests."

"I should think so." Mrs. Watkins frowned at him. He almost wished for Granny Crowfoot back.

He was about to turn and leave the room when he felt Genevieve clutch his hand. Surprised, he glanced down at her, and nearly lost control of himself when he saw her soft, sweet smile.

"Thank you, Mr. Rakes. I appreciate your concern."

Not having a clue what to say, Tobias only nodded curtly, gave her hand a gentle squeeze, and left the room. He felt disoriented and light-headed, which was idiotic. The woman had only smiled at him. There was no reason for him to feel giddy because of a smile.

Idiotic or not, the giddiness stayed with him for a full ten minutes after he rejoined his guests and tried to concentrate on what people were saying to him. He wanted to be back upstairs in Genevieve's room, holding her hand some more. Definitely naked.

Chapter Eleven

During the hours remaining of his open house, Tobias decided to set out for Watertown the very next morning. No sense in dawdling, since it now seemed clear that someone truly was trying to do away with him. If he discovered arsenic in the powders, he'd have proof positive that whoever had been staging all the incidents intended his death. He supposed that made more sense than someone wanting to kill Genevieve, although he couldn't imagine why anybody would want him dead, either. None of it made any sense to him.

He'd considered assigning Armitage the duty of having the powders analyzed, but when he pondered the matter further, he decided he'd be better off taking no one into his confidence. He didn't think the day would ever end or that his guests would ever leave, but he gritted his teeth and bore it, and succeeded in not shouting at anyone.

The doctor paid a final visit to Genevieve at about eight-thirty that evening. Then the gruff old man left, and Tobias hoped his departure would signal for an exodus of his other guests to start. It didn't. Instead, folks hung around for what seemed like forever.

He nearly had to hog-tie Delilah Crowfoot and throw her

through the castle gate to get her to leave, even though she refused to go inside the castle itself. She begged him to have Genevieve transported to the castle cottage so she could look after her. Tobias refused, trying his best to be tactful about it. Fortunately, Dr. Johnson, exiting the castle at that very moment, came to his aid.

"The girl isn't fit to be moved, Delilah Crowfoot. For heaven's sake, she's had a terrible bout of food poisoning." The doctor cast a significant look at Tobias, who nodded his approval. No sense in worrying Delilah any more than she was already worried, and the mention of poison would assuredly frighten her. Tobias had no very great faith in Delilah's strength of character. She wasn't like her niece at all in that regard.

Tobias nobly hung around until the last remaining clump of people, including Wesley Armitage and the mayor of Bittersweet, finally trundled off. The very last of his guests left no earlier than fifteen minutes before midnight. It had been a damned long day. From all appearances, the open house had been a huge success, although Tobias was so frustrated toward the end of the evening that he nearly yelled at everyone to go away.

As soon as the gates closed behind Armitage and the mayor, Tobias tore into the castle, climbed the stairs as fast as his injured leg would allow, and charged down the hall to Genevieve's bedroom. It was midnight by that time, and Tobias was glad to see her looking much stronger when he peeked into her room—just to check on her welfare because she was in his employ, of course.

She saw him standing in the door and smiled. "Oh, hello, Mr. Rakes."

Tobias swallowed and wondered why his heart had taken to hammering so blasted hard. "Hello, Miss Crowfoot. How are you feeling now?"

"She's not well."

This from Mrs. Watkins, who looked as if she expected Tobias to leap on the bed and ravish Genevieve in front of the housekeeper's very eyes. Which didn't sound like a bad idea at all to Tobias.

Genevieve, blithely ignoring the gorgon at her bedside, sweetened her smile up a notch. Tobias felt his insides turn to mush. "I'm much better, thank you. Would you care to come in for a minute? I'd love to hear how the party went after I abandoned you."

"Humph," said Mrs. Watkins, looking as suspicious as she sounded.

In spite of Genevieve's formidable nurse, Tobias entered her room, a little reluctantly.

He wasn't nearly as reluctant to enter it as Mrs. Watkins was to allow him to do so. Nevertheless, Genevieve prevailed—which probably proved something about the relative efficacy of honey and vinegar if he cared to pause and to ponder it, but he didn't have time for that now. So here he was, in Genevieve's room.

What's more, Mrs. Watkins wasn't. Five minutes after he arrived, she left in something closely resembling a huff, although Tobias wasn't certain. He was very glad to see Genevieve sipping some broth and eating a piece bread and butter, however.

Now he paced the carpeting at the foot of her bed, not quite trusting himself to sit in the chair next to her. The erotic urges he'd been experiencing with regard to Genevieve's person only seemed to get stronger every time he saw her. Therefore, he kept his hands clasped behind his back as he paced, and tried not to look at her too often. When he did look at her, he was annoyed by her own apparent serenity. She, obviously, didn't suffer from the same attraction to him from which he suffered in regard to her. Yet one more validation of his theory that God favored irony in the running of things. He propounded a question.

Genevieve pondered it for a moment or two while she chewed. "I'm sure Mr. Armitage is a very nice man, and that his integrity is above reproach, but I don't like the idea of any more people knowing about our suspicions than absolutely necessary."

"You're right." So that made it Genevieve and him, alone, in on their suspicions. A couple, as it were. He wished he hadn't thought of their pairing in exactly that way.

"I'm not sure what to do if we find the powders contain arsenic, though."

"Neither am I."

Tobias watched Genevieve take a little bite of bread and butter and couldn't stand watching her lips move that way. He turned and paced in the opposite direction. "We'll have to keep a close watch on everyone, I guess."

"I suppose so." Tobias frowned at nothing in particular. "I only wish we knew who to watch."

"So do I." Genevieve frowned, too, as she dipped a piece of bread into her broth. "It must be someone who has a personal grudge against you, but I can't think who it could be since you haven't lived in Bittersweet for so many years. I mean, you haven't lived here long enough to develop enemies, even if you were the type who'd do so."

Tobias stopped pacing and frowned at the pattern on the carpet. "Unless it's someone who's crazy."

"I should think that's unlikely."

He transferred his frown to Genevieve in time to see her take a delicate sip of broth from her spoon. Her lips were puckered in an extremely appealing way, and he wished he hadn't noticed. Damn, maybe he was just randy. He hadn't slept with a woman since shortly before that arrow had smashed into his leg bone, and that was nearly a year ago. Lordy, he hadn't gone without a female for this many months since his seventeenth summer. Small wonder he was so attracted to Genevieve.

He had a feeling that explanation wasn't quite it, but he didn't care to dwell on it. "You really think insanity is less likely than a murderous grudge?"

She chewed a bite of bread thoughtfully as she mulled over his question. Tobias was glad to see that a little color had returned to her cheeks.

"I don't know. We don't even *really* know that someone's actually trying to kill you, although it does look that way, doesn't it?"

Tobias hesitated. He hated to give weight to the notion that someone was attempting to achieve his death, but he had to admit things pointed in that direction, especially if his salicylic powders had been doctored with arsenic. Feeling uncomfortable about it, he muttered, "I guess."

Genevieve took a fairly energetic bite of bread and butter. "My money's on the Pickstaffs," she said after she'd swallowed it.

"But why?"

She shrugged, sending the sleeve of her lacy dressing gown slipping and exposing her shoulder and a very, very small swell of bosom. Tobias wrenched his gaze away from the flesh thus exposed, too late to prevent the physical reaction he'd been having all too frequently in Genevieve's presence. When he dared look at her again, she'd tugged the gown up to cover herself. He wanted to stomp over there and pull the whole damned thing over her head and feast his senses on her naked flesh.

He turned abruptly and walked to the fireplace in order to put more distance between the two of them. Laying his arm atop the mantel and leaning against it to take weight off of his leg, he stared into the grate, trying to ignore thoughts of Genevieve's lovely skin.

"I'll keep my eyes open, you can be sure of that, Mr. Rakes. If I see anything in the least suspicious, I'll let you know. I think you should do likewise. Perhaps we should have daily conferences or something of a like nature."

He lifted his head and dared to glance at her again. "That's probably a good idea. Morning or evening?"

She frowned prettily. "Evenings, I should think. After supper, perhaps."

He nodded, wishing with all his heart that her frown wasn't so pretty. He also wished he could forget the hint of swelling flesh he'd seen for both far too long and too short a time. "Sounds all right to me." And, if they should happen to decide to confer in his bed, that would be nice, too. He didn't suggest it, since he didn't want to upset her. Hell's bells, she'd been poisoned already today. She didn't deserve to have to entertain lewd suggestions as well, no matter how good they sounded to him.

He did wonder, however, if he could somehow connive to get Genevieve Crowfoot into his bed without suffering any permanent consequences. Like marriage, for instance. The mere thought of marriage made him shudder. Not that he had anything in particular against the institution itself. He was sure some people took to it like ducks took to water.

But Tobias couldn't help recalling how unhappy his mother, who had otherwise been a cheerful person, was every time she'd been in the company of his father. He didn't want to be unhappily shackled to anyone, even someone as appealing as Genevieve Crowfoot. And the thought of being the author of another person's misery, as his father had been of his mother's, gave him a sick feeling in his gut.

Good God, why was he thinking about marriage at a time like this? He turned his head again and resumed staring at the fireplace grate. "We can meet in the library," he suggested, trying to think of someplace as far away from a bedroom as possible.

"That's a good place."

Yes, it was. There wasn't even a sofa in his library. And, while it might be possible to carry out a seduction in a leather chair or on top of his desk, it would be a damned sight more difficult there than on a sofa. He nodded, lifted his head, and noticed that she'd finished her broth and bread.

"Would you like me to take that tray away?"

"Thank you. It would be kind of you. I'm still feeling a little shaky."

"You've been through an ordeal," he murmured, steeling himself as he approached her bed.

She smiled up at him. "It has been quite a day."

Her smile did something to him. He wasn't sure what it was, but it was powerful, unexpected, and it knocked the good sense right out of him. He took the tray from her lap and consigned it to the bedside table. Then he sat right on the bed, leaned over Genevieve, trapped her in his arms, and kissed her. She uttered one tiny gasp that might have been a protest, but he paid no heed. Resistance, at that moment, was beyond him.

Resistance was beyond Genevieve, too. She could hardly believe it when Tobias sat on her bed, and she hadn't even fully taken in that remarkable circumstance, when he grabbed her and began kissing her. Her body melted instantly, even as her brain told her to resist. Treacherous things, bodies.

Once or twice in her life, Genevieve had allowed a young man to kiss her, just to see what it was like. She had long since decided she could live without kisses. That was before she'd been kissed by Tobias Rakes. Even in her weakened condition, she clung to him. She'd never felt so alive and at the same time so helpless.

"You taste good," he mumbled when his lips left hers and traveled to her throat.

Genevieve's head fell back. Every cell in her body seemed to have taken to dancing and tingling. Her breasts felt heavy, her nipples beaded, and her skin was suddenly so sensitive, she writhed to feel Tobias's against it. A throbbing pressure built low in her belly and traveled every which way, eventually puddling between her legs and making her squirm. Her fingernails dug into his shoulders. She had a brazen urge to rip the coat from his back, tear his shirt to shreds, and press her naked breasts against his chest. Then she wanted to do the same thing with the rest of his clothes. She wanted to see him in all his masculine glory, scars and all, and to run her hands over every inch of him.

Obviously, she'd been wrong about not needing kisses. She'd just never been kissed by the right man until now. Tobias's kiss was—well, really quite stunning.

His hand closed over her breast, and, shocked by his forwardness, she nearly screamed. "Good heavens!"

However, she was unexpectedly crushed when he sat up with a jerk and withdrew his hand. Of course, Genevieve thought to herself, what did she expect him to do when she had so obviously protested to his touch. She hadn't meant to yell. In fact she quite liked Tobias touching her there—it had just surprised her, that's all. She blinked at him, too dazed to say anything. He blinked back at her, looking pretty dazed himself. He licked his lips. She licked hers.

Then he uttered a growl the likes of which Genevieve had never heard, and drew her back into his arms. She was very glad of it. She was even more glad when his hand returned to her breast. She thrust her bosom at him, wishing he had more than two hands to put to the purpose.

Neither of them heard the door open. They did, however, hear Mrs. Watkins's scandalized, *"Well!"*

Tobias was up and across the room like a shot. Genevieve, her head racing as it used to do when she and Benton had been caught in a mischief, dove under the covers.

She emerged a half second later, holding a sheet over her bosom with one hand. In her other hand she clutched a napkin. "Here it is, Mr. Rakes. Thank you for helping me look for it. It must have become entangled with the bedclothes." Considering the state of absolute absorption she'd been in when Mrs. Watkins interrupted, Genevieve was quite proud of herself for that one. She chalked up her quick thinking to her days spent getting into trouble with Benton.

Mrs. Watkins didn't look as though she believed Genevieve's ruse for a minute. Well, too bad for her. Genevieve lifted her chin and smiled at the woman. "I dropped my napkin."

"My eye," said Mrs. Watkins, grinding the words out between her teeth.

Genevieve was amazed to see that she looked even more disapproving than usual. She hadn't believed such a thing possible until this minute. No wonder Godfrey was such a timid young man. Genevieve would probably be timid, too, if she'd been raised with so much sternness and disapproval. She hadn't been, thank God, so she was able to withstand Mrs. Watkins's look with fair grace.

She was able to assume better grace than Tobias, at any rate, she noticed when she darted a glance at him. He looked as if he'd been caught with his hand in the cookie jar—or on her breast—and he also looked as if he hadn't had a partner in crime with whom to connive, as she'd had in her childhood. She decided to ease the moment with a stab at humor.

"I think we've shocked Mrs. Watkins, Mr. Rakes. I do believe she suspects that we were engaged in improper behavior." Genevieve put on her I-can't-believe-you'd-ever-think-such-a-thing face, the one she'd practiced to perfection with Benton. Benton had always been better at it than she, but Genevieve was no slouch.

Tobias, on the other hand, still looked like he'd been caught red-handed in a felonious deed. Genevieve shot him a frown when Mrs. Watkins wasn't looking, silently commanding him to start pretending. Genevieve didn't want the entire community of Bittersweet to be gossiping about her come morning. After looking stunned for another second or two, Tobias seemed to pull himself together.

"Er, yes. That is, no, we weren't engaged in anything improper."

He forced out a chuckle, although it sounded as though it was strained almost beyond mortal endurance. He gave Genevieve an odd look, and a shiver shook him. After he cleared his throat and squared his shoulders, he looked slightly more the thing. Thank heavens. Genevieve had begun to wonder if she'd been sinning with an amateur—when she knew good and well he'd had more experience in amour than she had. In reality, he couldn't very well have less.

She gave him a conspiratorial smile and a small nod to lend him courage. In return, he gave her another odd look. Genevieve forced herself not to frown; she didn't want Mrs. Watkins to get any more ideas than she already had.

"I never," said the lady, clumping over to Genevieve's bed and snatching the napkin from her fingers.

It crossed Genevieve's mind to ask her how Godfrey had been born, if Mrs. Watkins had never, but she decided she'd better not. The woman was a prude and a fusspot, but Genevieve didn't want to alienate her forever, or her own reputation was liable to be tattered. "Honestly, Mrs. Watkins. Mr. Rakes was helping me with my dinner tray. It was heavy on my stomach, which still isn't feeling too well." Hoping to play on the older woman's sense of fairness, she added, with a little dip in her voice, "It's been a difficult day for me. I don't believe I've ever been so sick in my life."

It worked. Mrs. Watkins maintained her stern expression for another fifteen seconds or so, then relented. "Yes. Well, I'm sorry you were ill, Genevieve, but you and Mr. Rakes ought to know better than to stay in a bedroom alone together with the door closed. It's just not done."

Mrs. Watkins turned her head to give Tobias another scolding look. Genevieve was pleased to see that he'd finally recovered himself and now gave the appearance of a man sorely tried and one who was, moreover, now feeling both meek and slightly offended. Wherever he'd been for the last seventeen years, he'd evidently had some practice in deception, too.

"It may not be done," he said, lifting that left eyebrow of his, "but as Miss Crowfoot's employer, I believe I owe her the courtesy of ensuring her welfare."

Genevieve was impressed with the haughty tone he achieved. So was Mrs. Watkins, who seemed almost flustered for perhaps ten seconds. Nothing could fluster Mrs. Watkins for long, however, and she recovered with a sharp, "Humph."

Tobias returned to the bed. Genevieve felt shy when he gazed down at her, his expression softer than any she'd yet seen on his face. Because she didn't want to give Mrs. Watkins any further fuel for her speculations, she said, "Thank you for checking up on me, Mr. Rakes. As you can see, I'm feeling much better than I was earlier."

"Yes, I see."

His smile was so warm, it made her blush. She looked away quickly. "I'm sorry I deserted you during your party."

"Think nothing of it. Your aunt was kind enough to carry on as hostess. Several people asked after you, however."

Thoughts of kisses flew right out of Genevieve's head. She peered up at him, alarmed. "Oh, dear! I hope you didn't tell them the truth."

Mrs. Watkins looked at her strangely. Genevieve cursed her ready tongue. "That is, I hope you didn't tell them I'd become ill with food poisoning. They might think there was something wrong with the food."

"Well, there was, wasn't there?"

Genevieve wished she hadn't opened her mouth. She frowned at Mrs. Watkins. "Certainly not. Not here, at any rate. It was something I ate in—in—" Oh, dear. A quote having something to do with what happens when one first starts practicing to deceive flitted through Genevieve's head, although she couldn't remember all of it.

"Miss Crowfoot ate a pastry Mr. Armitage brought from Bittersweet, Mrs. Watkins." Tobias chuckled again, this time with more success. "I'm glad I didn't have time to eat mine."

Genevieve chuckled, too, and blessed the man for his quick thinking. "Yes, it would have been awful if the host of the party had become sick."

Mrs. Watkins said "Humph" again.

Tobias waited in Genevieve's room, feeling awkward and in the way, for several more minutes, hoping Mrs. Watkins would go away so he and Genevieve could resume what they'd been doing when the old busybody had interrupted them. Unfortunately, Mrs. Watkins showed no inclination of leaving them alone together, and Tobias eventually gave up and departed.

In spite of his intense frustration, he consoled himself with the knowledge that things were probably better this way. If he and Genevieve hadn't been interrupted, they'd have made love, and then where would they be? Besides blissfully sated, they'd be forced to marry each other, was where they'd be.

Tobias was surprised the notion didn't hit him with greater repugnance than it did. Hell's bells, he *really* didn't want to get married.

Although, it must be admitted, if he married a Crowfoot, it would infuriate his father. Tobias grinned, not having considered the matter from that angle before. He was still grinning when he entered his own bedroom, where a freezing blast of air hit him a split second before Granny Crowfoot appeared in a cold flash of fury.

"How dare you take advantage of that sweet child!" the ghost shrieked, sounding more like a graveyard specter than he'd heard thus far.

Tobias groaned. He didn't need this. "Go away."

"I won't go away. You're going to ruin that girl if you keep on in this way. I knew it! I knew you were a filthy pig and a reprobate who only wanted to have your wicked way

with my great-great-great—'' The ghost paused to think for a second, apparently having lost count of her greats.

Taking advantage of her momentary confusion, Tobias said, ''I don't 'only want to have my wicked way with her,' for God's sake. What a ridiculous thing to say.''

Granny Crowfoot gave up on the greats. *''Oh? Then what, pray tell, are your intentions, you big lout?''*

''Big lout? Good God.''

Tobias yanked off a shoe and slammed it to the floor, feeling doubly frustrated. First he'd been thwarted in his effort to seduce Genevieve, and now he learned this wretched ghost had witnessed the whole sordid episode.

''Well? Are you afraid to answer me?''

He looked up from untying his other shoe. ''I have no fear of you, nor have I any obligation to answer you, because you have no business asking. What Miss Crowfoot and I do together is no one's business but our own.'' He felt better for having taken a firm stand with the ghost even if, in his heart of hearts, he was confused as all hell about Genevieve and his intentions toward her. And hers toward him.

He wished now that he hadn't lost control of himself. She'd probably expect a proposal tomorrow, and Tobias didn't know that he wanted to propose. All things considered, being married to Genevieve sounded a lot better than several hundred other things he could think to do with himself, but he hated being pressured. Had hated it ever since Madeline had pressured him into running away with her, and he'd been ass enough to do it, thereby ruining his life.

The ghost whooshed right up in front of him, making him jerk back. Damn, she was quick. And cold.

''I may not be able to do you physical harm, young man, but if you touch a hair on that child's head, I shall haunt you until I drive you mad. Do I make myself plain?''

This was ridiculous. Tobias stood up abruptly, sharing space with the ghost for an instant. It was an odd sensation, cold and creepy and excessively unpleasant, but he wasn't about to let her know that. He barked out in his best military tone, ''Don't threaten me. I don't take well to being threatened. Miss Crowfoot and I will conduct our own business without any interference from you, and I don't want to hear another word about it. Now get out of here, and let me sleep.''

He hadn't spoken that forcefully since he'd held the gun to the doctor's head and commanded him not to amputate his leg. His forcefulness had worked wonders with the doctor. Tobias was obliged to admit his success wasn't quite as good with Granny Crowfoot, who merely drew back and glowered at him.

"I'm not threatening you, you big oaf. I'm only telling you what will happen if you trifle with my great-great-great—" She ran out of greats again, which gave Tobias another opening.

"I'm not trifling with her! Damn it, leave me alone, you bag of bones."

"Bag of bones? Bag of bones?" Granny Crowfoot blew herself up until she filled the room from the bed to the doorway. Tobias sighed heavily, wishing he'd controlled his language better. He'd been taught to respect his elders and to speak to them with courtesy. Of course, when his mother had been teaching him manners, she hadn't known he'd end up squabbling with a batty old ghost.

"Will you please vanish now," he pleaded. "I'm sorry if I offended you, but I'm tired. It's been a hard day, my leg is throbbing abominably, and, believe it or not, I'm very worried about Miss Crowfoot."

"Just understand this, young man." Granny Crowfoot waggled a ghostly finger at him. *"If you even try to leave this room and sneak into Genevieve's during the night, I'll raise such a racket that they'll be able to hear it in Bittersweet."*

Tobias dropped his head back and stared at the ceiling. "I won't sneak into Miss Crowfoot's room." Lord, he was weary. He doubted that he could execute a proper seduction if he tried at this point.

The ghost huffed angrily. So that made two females who believed him to be a vile scoundrel: Mrs. Watkins and Granny Crowfoot. Maybe three. He hadn't been able to assess Genevieve's state of mind before being driven out of her room by Mrs. Watkins.

Thankfully, Granny Crowfoot vanished as quickly as she'd appeared, leaving Tobias to stare into the empty space she'd occupied and wonder how it was possible to irritate so many females in so short a time.

His state of exhaustion was acute, however, and he wasn't able to devote too much time to worrying about it. As soon as his head hit the pillow, he slept.

Chapter
Twelve

Tobias drove the buggy to Watertown the next morning. He didn't want to do it, and he fretted the whole time he was away from the castle for fear Genevieve might take a turn for the worse, but he didn't want to entrust the salicylic powders to anyone else.

"I wish you wouldn't," Genevieve told him when he asked if she thought he ought to let Small William know where he was going in case he needed to be sent for. "I think the Pickstaffs are most likely the ones behind all the attempts on your life, quite frankly. Even if Small William isn't doing anything wrong, he'd tell his family you'd gone to Watertown, and that might start them all speculating."

He eyed her from by the fireplace in her bedroom. She looked much better this morning. So much better that he didn't dare go too near the bed for fear of what he might do. His leg wasn't hurting much at all, and he didn't want lack of pain to give his body ideas that his mind wasn't strong enough to resist.

"You're probably right," he said, wishing she didn't look so tasty, sitting propped up in her bed in her lacy dressing gown, with the sun streaming through her window making her hair gleam like fire.

"Well, I don't know if I'm right about the Pickstaffs, but I do think I'm right about not telling anyone where you're going or your purpose in doing so."

Tobias sighed, and knew he had to get out of the room fast. Perhaps it was better that he'd be gone most of the day. At least he wouldn't be tempted by Genevieve Crowfoot into indiscretions.

He was startled when he descended the grand staircase and found a pile of correspondence lying on a silver salver on the front table and a half dozen bouquets of various sizes cluttering up the entryway. Poor Godfrey looked flustered as he turned away from the front door, holding yet another flower arrangement, this one a rather ghastly one consisting of some orange and blue flowers that looked like birds of prey to Tobias's untrained eye.

"Good Lord, Godfrey. What's going on here?" Tobias eyed the room skeptically. It reminded him of a funeral parlor.

"Thank-you notes and flowers," Godfrey said, staggering over to a stone bench with the heavy flower arrangement.

Tobias squinted at it. "What the hell are those things? I've never seen anything like them."

"I don't know. They're from the mayor, so they're probably expensive. My mother could probably tell you what they are exactly."

"Probably." Tobias, not eager to subject himself to one of Mrs. Watkins's disapproving scowls so early in the day, opted not to search her out and ask her. He headed for the dining room instead, in the hope of fortifying himself for his journey. Watertown wasn't far from Bittersweet, but he still wasn't eager to leave Genevieve alone all day. Not, of course, that she'd be alone, or that he could do anything for her even if he didn't make the trip to Watertown.

Thinking about Genevieve only confused him, so he forced himself to concentrate on his bacon and eggs and—"Good Lord," he muttered, eyeing the pallid mass of breaded and fried meat lying in a dish he'd just uncovered. "What is this stuff?"

"Tripe."

The stern voice of Mrs. Watkins drew Tobias's attention away from the revolting-looking offering that seemed out of place on the silver serving platter. "Oh, yes," he said, gazing down again at the tripe. "I recognize it now. My father favored pickled tripe for breakfast." Which was another good reason to make sure it was never again served in Tobias's home. He thought about telling Molly Gratchett himself, and decided the task was beyond him. He'd wait until Genevieve was back at work and ask her to talk to the cook.

Grinning at his own cowardice, Tobias took his plate to the table and dug into his breakfast. After breakfast, he had Small William harness the horse to the surrey, and he took off to Watertown, his coat pocket stuffed with papers containing salicylic powders.

"And arsenic," he said that evening, gazing at Genevieve who sat in a leather chair in his library. "Dr. Johnson was right. The reason your symptoms reminded him of arsenical poisoning is because you'd ingested some with the powders." Tobias's whole body, inside and out, went cold at the thought.

"It's a good thing I didn't finish that glass of water. I didn't have time. That poor geranium is as dead as a doornail." Genevieve shuddered and rubbed her hands over her arms, as though they'd sprouted gooseflesh.

Tobias wished he could rub her arms for her. She seemed to have recovered fully from her ordeal, apparently having obeyed Tobias's request that she rest today.

"You're certain the chemist said arsenic? He didn't say it only appeared to be arsenic?" She gazed disconsolately at him, as if she'd been hoping the chemist was wrong.

"Arsenic. No doubt about it." Tobias was fairly disconsolate himself. He didn't like the notion that someone was trying to murder him. "It is me they're after, don't you think? I mean, it isn't someone out to get you, is it?"

He knew how foolish the question was even before the expression on Genevieve's face told him so. He forestalled her.

"You're right. Of course it's me they're after. Those were my powders, after all."

"Yes. And the griffin was dropped on your head, and it was the banister you'd be sure to grasp that had been weakened. So now we have to be doubly on our guard."

Tobias stared out the window at the setting sun. "You know what puzzles me is that stupid ghost. I mean, she can go anywhere invisibly. Why hasn't she ever noticed what's going on around here?"

Genevieve shrugged. "Perhaps she has. She's not one of your more ardent admirers."

"Very true." He grinned, in fact, thinking about it.

"I am not a stupid ghost!"

Tobias sighed. "I might have known."

"Oh, Granny Crowfoot, I'm so glad you're here." Genevieve beamed at the ghost, who materialized in a seated position on the edge of Tobias's desk, eyeing Tobias balefully.

"That makes one of us," muttered Tobias.

The ghost gave him a vicious scowl. *"You, young man, are a rude, impudent pup. I'll have you know, I'm a good deal your elder, and I'm shocked—shocked—that your parents didn't teach you any better than to call one of your elders stupid."* She sniffed.

"You don't seem to think it's rude of you to call me names," Tobias pointed out sourly.

"That's different."

"I do wish you two would stop squabbling," Genevieve broke in. "We have some serious business to discuss." She turned to the ghost. "Granny Crowfoot, the chemist in Watertown found arsenic in Mr. Rakes's salicylic powders!"

The ghost lifted an eyebrow, giving her transparent face an interested, although not at all appalled, expression. *"Is that so?"*

Tobias eyed the ghost with distaste and decided he wasn't surprised by her attitude. She'd probably dance a jig if whoever was after him succeeded in doing him in. "Yes, that's so. I don't suppose you'd tell us if you saw anyone fiddling around in my belongings."

Granny Crowfoot smirked at him. *"Of course I wouldn't. While I can't hurt you myself, there's no law that says I have to tell you if I see anyone else trying to hurt you."*

"What a horrid thing to say! I can't believe a relative of mine can be so unfeeling."

Genevieve looked angry enough to paddle the ghost's rump if such a thing could be done. Tobias realized he enjoyed having someone on his side, especially someone like Genevieve Crowfoot. His soldiers had always respected him, and they'd carried out his commands with little grumbling, but until he met Genevieve, he hadn't understood how delightful it could be to have a strong-willed female champion him. He liked it a lot.

Granny Crowfoot merely sniffed again and looked like she didn't enjoy being scolded by someone a hundred years younger than herself.

"If whoever is behind these attempts on Mr. Rakes's life ever succeeds in killing him, what do you suppose will happen to your precious castle?" Genevieve continued, warming to her subject and shaking a finger at the ghost. "There aren't many people around here who'd be willing to sink the money into it that Mr. Rakes is doing, you know. Even Mr. Armitage, Mr. Rakes's own attorney, advised him to tear the thing down and build a modern house in its place."

"He never!" Granny Crowfoot shot up from the desk until she hovered against the ceiling.

Tobias noticed that the notion of the castle dying struck the old ghost with much less satisfaction than thoughts of his own demise. He shook his head, marveling.

"Oh, yes, he did," Genevieve insisted. "The very first day I met Mr. Rakes, he was with Mr. Armitage, and Mr. Armitage was plainly trying to discourage him from buying the castle."

"Well, of course. Anyone with an ounce of common sense and discernment would advise a Rakes against purchasing the ancestral home of the Crowfoots."

"Ancestral home of the Crowfoots," Tobias muttered. "God give me patience."

"Believe me, there was no excess of sensibility guiding

Mr. Armitage's suggestion," Genevieve continued, her voice going stern as she gazed up at Granny Crowfoot, whose essence still clung to the ceiling. "He was merely interested in saving Mr. Rakes a bundle of money. In case you didn't know it, it's costing him a fortune, getting this old pile of stones into some kind of livable shape after a century of neglect by your exalted Crowfoot relations."

"How dare you speak of your own kin in that disrespectful tone?"

"Don't give me that wounded-dignity nonsense! You know very well it's true. Mr. Rakes is the only gentleman I know who'd bother to put this place into some kind of order. Anyone else would have ripped it apart before now, and you know it!"

"I know no such thing!"

The living and the dead Crowfoot ladies had raised their voices until they were now virtually shouting at one another. Although he was rather enjoying the show, Tobias decided he'd better try to calm them down or the castle staff might rush in to see what was happening. "Ladies," he said gently, "let's not quarrel."

Granny Crowfoot turned on him. *"What do you know about it? How dare you interfere!"*

Genevieve, too, whirled around, as if she didn't appreciate his interrupting the argument. She even opened her mouth—to shout at him this time, he guessed—when she seemed to catch herself. Her mouth shut with a snap. Then she grinned. "For heaven's sake, how silly we're being."

He grinned back, glad she wasn't mad at him. "Think nothing of it. The provocation is intense." He jerked a thumb toward the ghost.

Genevieve giggled. "Yes, it certainly is."

Granny Crowfoot swooped down from the ceiling to stand on the desk, where she glowered over them both. *"I presume that to be a slight against me?"*

Tobias picked up a book and leafed through it. "Actually, it's not slight at all."

His heart sang when Genevieve giggled again. Granny Crowfoot, on the other hand, was not amused. In fact, she went into her slamming around the room routine, rocketing this way and that, leaving a trail of smoky stuff behind her, until she made one last, incredibly fast circuit around the room, stirring up such a wind that papers flew all over the library floor. She even managed to dislodge a couple of light-weight books and send them tumbling. Then she shot up the chimney.

Tobias watched her, feeling tired and jaundiced. "She sure does put on a show when she feels like it, doesn't she?"

Genevieve shook her head in disbelief. Unless it was disgust. Tobias would have begrudged her neither. "She certainly does. What a mess." She glanced at the papers and books strewn around the room.

"Let me call Godfrey. He can get one of the maids to pick them up."

"Don't be silly. I can do it. But don't you try it. You don't want to strain your leg unnecessarily with a lot of bending and squatting."

Although he didn't enjoy having his infirmity pointed out, especially by the woman about whom he'd been having delectable sexual fantasies, Tobias knew she was right. He sighed. "All right, but please let me get Godfrey or a maid to help."

"There's really no need."

"Nevertheless . . ." Tobias went out to search for assistance, leaving Genevieve kneeling on the floor, scooping up papers.

In her zooming, windy fit of indignation, Granny Crowfoot had managed to disturb quite a few of the library's furnishings. In one of her circuits, she'd even shot through the old-fashioned globe—the one showing the world as it was judged to be a hundred years prior. Her flight had knocked it from its stand and sent it rolling into a corner, under one of the long, green velvet draperies. Ultimately it ended up lodged next to the molded-metal gas heater one of her ancestors—probably Hubert, although he hated spending money—had installed.

Genevieve rescued the globe from the corner and carried

it over to its stand. She was about to replace it, when she noticed something she'd never seen before.

"My goodness." She squinted down at the globe stand. "It's got hinges."

After consigning the globe to Tobias's chair, Genevieve studied the globe stand, pressed the catch, and lifted the lid. There, rolled up and looking as though they hadn't been disturbed for a century, were several old parchments. She lifted one of them out cautiously, hoping the antique, dry material wouldn't rip or crumble in her fingers. When she carefully unrolled one of the scrolls, she gasped. "House plans!" She'd found the original plans to Crowfoot Castle.

Genevieve heard voices coming from outside in the hallway, and quickly rolled up the parchment and replaced it in the globe stand. The next time Tobias went riding, however, she aimed to come back in here, retrieve those plans, and study them. If she could discover a secret room—or any indication that the original plans of the castle had been altered in any way—perhaps she could discover the location of the treasure.

As she hurried to retrieve the globe from the chair and set it carefully back onto its stand, she realized that she'd nearly lost sight of her reason for wanting to be hired to work in Crowfoot Castle. She'd been concentrating on her job and her employer instead of the treasure. This would never do.

The door opened and she swirled around, salvaging a smile from somewhere. "Oh, hello, Godfrey. Thanks for helping me."

Godfrey stood in the doorway, surveying the wreckage of Tobias's library. Genevieve guessed she should have anticipated such a reaction from anyone who hadn't met Granny Crowfoot. She glanced at Tobias, wondering if he'd thought to create an excuse for the mess. She grinned to herself when she saw from the expression on his face that he hadn't. In fact, he glanced up at her, looking as helpless as a seasoned cavalry officer probably ever could.

With a laugh, she ad-libbed, "Mr. Rakes had the window open, Godfrey, and a huge gust of wind came up. I've never seen anything like it."

Godfrey obviously didn't know whether to believe her or not but, given his experience of females up until this point in his life, Genevieve imagined he'd had little practice in questioning anything a woman said to him. If he ever questioned his mother, she'd probably wallop him, even though he was now a good foot taller than Mrs. Watkins. Genevieve gave him one of her best, sweetest smiles, and was pleased to see him swallow and nod.

"Er, yes, ma'am." He scratched his head. "I never seen a wind like that either."

"It was a sudden gust. I'd been looking out the window—smelling the honeysuckles," Tobias added, looking pleased with himself for his improvisation.

Genevieve was pleased with him, too. "Yes indeed. The honeysuckles smell so sweet this time of year. And the gust was sudden. Very sudden."

"And gusty."

Godfrey glanced from one to the other of them, and Genevieve had to press her lips together so she wouldn't laugh with delight. She hadn't had this much fun perpetrating a deception since Benton was alive.

The butler, not accustomed to questioning authority or considering reasons for orders, gave up wondering. He got down on his hands and knees and began picking up papers. So did Genevieve. She looked up once and saw Tobias watching her with such an odd gleam in his eyes that she didn't dare look at him again until the papers were all off the floor.

"I'll put all of this stuff away," Tobias said when they were through. "You two have done the hard part."

Godfrey passed the back of his hand across his forehead, wiping away perspiration. "Oh, no, sir. You shouldn't have to do that." He looked faintly horrified. The poor boy had been taught well, Genevieve thought.

"Don't be silly, Godfrey. Neither of us would have any idea where Mr. Rakes keeps his papers. I fear he'll have to sort them out, since we don't know anything about his business." She gave the poor beleaguered butler another sweet smile. "It's all right, Godfrey. It truly is. Your mother wouldn't expect you to know where these papers go."

"She wouldn't? Are you sure?" Godfrey looked at her as if he didn't dare to believe such good news.

Tobias's deep, rich chuckle made Genevieve feel like flinging herself into his arms. No surprise there, unfortunately. She braced herself on the desk instead and wished she'd stop having these inconvenient reactions to his physical presence. If she didn't watch herself, she'd be succumbing to his practiced charms, and then where would she be? In a hospital for Magdalenes, probably. The thought made her heart squeeze before she regained control of her mental wanderings.

"Of course she wouldn't, Godfrey. Come along now. Let's leave poor Mr. Rakes to tidy up this mess. I think I should probably get to sleep early, since I'm supposed to be recuperating."

"Yes," Tobias said, so quickly that Genevieve gave a start of surprise. "That's right. You need your rest. Forgive me for allowing you to bend over and pick all of those papers up, Miss Crowfoot. I wasn't thinking, or I'd never have been so inconsiderate."

She blinked, thinking it odd that he should appear to be genuinely remorseful. "It's nothing, Mr. Rakes. Truly. I'm perfectly well again."

"Nevertheless, I was thoughtless. The old bat was right about that, I guess."

"The old bat?" Godfrey's eyes went wide. Genevieve presumed he thought Tobias's remark had been in reference to Mrs. Watkins, and she almost giggled again.

"Merely a figure of speech, Godfrey," she assured him.

Tobias, however, remained frowning. "Yes. A figure of speech. But, I do apologize, Miss Crowfoot. And I expect you to rest again tomorrow. You've been through an ordeal."

She thought about protesting, but saw at once that another day of rest would provide her plenty of time for snooping into the globe stand. "All right, Mr. Rakes, although I'm really fine."

"Nevertheless," he said, still frowning.

He appeared truly worried, and Genevieve was touched.

In fact, she wished she could walk over to him, put her arms around him, and kiss him silly for being so sincere in his concern for her welfare. Since such a pleasant good-night kiss would have shocked Godfrey Watkins out of his few remaining wits, she did no such thing, but only smiled meaningfully at Tobias as she and Godfrey left him to his papers. She presumed Tobias took her meaning, when she saw him swallow hard and stare after her right before she closed the door.

"I appreciate your going to all this trouble, Wes, but you really didn't need to do it. I'll be happy to visit you in town. I'm getting around much better these days. Hell's bells, I don't even need my cane half the time any longer." Tobias smiled at his attorney although, in truth, Armitage's constant attendance at the castle was beginning to wear on his patience. This was especially true since Tobias believed the attorney's true purpose in visiting daily had more to do with Genevieve than with him. Tobias didn't like the notion of Wesley Armitage courting Genevieve. Or of anyone else courting her, for that matter.

"I don't mind coming here, truly, Tobias." Armitage clutched a sheaf of papers to his breast and looked around doubtfully.

Tobias indicated for him to set the papers on the hall table while he waited in the open doorway. They stepped outside to the porch together. "I'm just setting out to take a ride around the estate, Wes. Care to join me? I want to see how the men are coming with the forest. It was so overgrown, the town fire marshal was worried about the whole place burning down during the hot weather. I remember how summer lightning used to cause fires when I was a boy here."

Armitage nodded. "Yes, that's true."

"Want to come with me? We can talk about business as we ride." Tobias hoped the attorney was too stuffy to go riding with him, because he wanted to be alone this morning. He'd been tossing something over in his mind all night long—something fairly astonishing—and he needed to consider it in the clear light of day. Alone. Without distractions from a fusspot lawyer.

"Er, no. No, I guess I won't take you up on that offer," Armitage said. "When will you be back, do you suppose?"

Tobias shrugged. "An hour or so, I imagine. Want to wait here? I'll be more than happy to ride into town to visit your office and discuss whatever you want to discuss." He swept his arm in an arc to take in the extensive castle grounds, which were looking more beautiful as the days passed. "I'm going to have them run a telephone line to the castle as soon as I can get it arranged. Then you won't have to be coming out here all the time. We'll be able to make appointments via the telephone."

Armitage appeared skeptical. "A telephone? Here?"

"Certainly. Why not?" Hell, he could afford a few luxuries, thanks to his grandmother, bless her heart. Tobias had a fleeting wish that Armitage weren't quite so conservative. Telephones were commonplace these days; Tobias couldn't understand why the lawyer would object to his getting one installed.

"Oh, no reason. I guess I just never thought about the castle coming into the nineteenth century, is all." Armitage smiled, as if he realized he was being silly.

Tobias laughed. "It's almost the twentieth century. I'd say it's about time the castle made it into the nineteenth."

"You're right, of course." Armitage stopped speaking and looked around, as if his mind was reviewing all the innovations of the nineteenth century in relation to Crowfoot Castle.

Somewhat impatiently, Tobias said, "I'll be off now, Wes. Will you go back to town or wait here?"

The lawyer started slightly. "Oh. I guess I'll wait for you here. I'd like to go over the place and see how all the work's progressing. Is Miss Crowfoot better, by the way?"

"She's fine now." Exceptionally fine, in fact. Tobias didn't say so. He wished Armitage hadn't asked.

"Good. Er, which way do you plan to ride, if you don't mind my asking? There are so many paths and so forth around here."

"That's true. I'm going over toward the west today. There's a road through the forest. I want to make sure the workmen have cleared most of the underbrush out of there."

Armitage nodded and didn't appear to be in the mood to ask any more questions, so Tobias made his escape. He waved his riding crop as he strode toward the stable. He didn't need his cane any longer—at least not all the time. "Be back in an hour or so."

"Have a good ride."

When Tobias walked off, Armitage was still standing on the castle porch, staring around him as if he were lost in a fog of contemplation.

Tobias watched Small William Pickstaff saddle Rake's Progress, and tried to imagine the boy poisoning his salicylic powders. His imagination wasn't good enough, so he turned it to imagining Old William doing so. That was a little easier, but not much. With a sigh, Tobias smiled at the boy, who held the stirrup and didn't smile back.

Genevieve was probably right about the Pickstaffs, no matter how unlikely it seemed. After all, she knew them better than he did. Still, while he could feature Old William shooting someone, it was difficult to imagine the old guy plotting devious stratagems and using so underhanded a method as poison to perpetrate a crime. Or even, Tobias had to admit, hacking a griffin away from its base and shoving it from a castle turret.

He could almost feature the old man sawing through the banister railing in order to make Tobias fall onto the flagged entryway and bash his brains out, but even that was fairly indirect. Tobias couldn't quite see the older Pickstaff as a deep, surreptitious thinker. If someone were to take a potshot at him in the woods, then perhaps he might believe—

Less than a second after that notion entered his head, a shot rang out in the deep woods. Immediately afterward, Tobias heard the unmistakable whistle of a bullet and a thunk as it sank into a tree no more than two feet away from him. He rolled from Rake's Progress's back and flattened himself out on the forest floor, his heart racing like a spooked jack-rabbit.

"Goddamn son of a bitch."

The horse reared and then, panic-stricken, thundered back the way they'd come. Tobias muttered under his breath, but he didn't dare stand up until he'd determined exactly what was going on in his woods.

Chapter
Thirteen

Genevieve, feeling both lazy and excited, took breakfast in bed the morning after she discovered the castle plans in Tobias's globe stand. Because she feared her mood might give her away, she waited until she saw Tobias ride off on Rake's Progress before she made her way downstairs. Since she'd observed Wesley Armitage's buggy outside, she decided to see what he was up to before she began snooping through the castle plans in Tobias's library.

She met Godfrey as soon as she'd descended the stairs. "I saw Mr. Armitage's surrey, Godfrey. Is he still here?"

"No, Miss Genevieve. He said he'd go back to town for a while and return this afternoon. He said he'd just leave those papers for Mr. Rakes to study." The butler gestured toward a stack of papers on the hall table.

Genevieve eyed the papers, silently thanking Wesley Armitage for this uncharacteristic gesture of untidiness. Usually the man wouldn't dream of leaving castle papers lying about. "I'll take them to Mr. Rakes's library, Godfrey."

"Yes, ma'am."

She picked up the bundle and carried it to the library. Once inside the room, she locked the door, figuring she could always make an excuse for having done so if anyone attempted entrance. Then she dumped the stack of papers on Tobias's desk and made straight for the globe.

Tobias was extremely glad his leg was so much stronger by the time he made his way back to the castle grounds. After he'd ascertained that his assailant hadn't stuck around to be sure he'd accomplished his fell purpose, Tobias had kept to the thick woods and walked home. In truth, he didn't even know for certain that it was an assailant. It might have been a hunter out to bag a rabbit or something.

"Don't be an ass," he advised himself grumpily as he limped up to the castle steps. "That bullet was meant for you, and you know it."

For the first time in a year, his limp wasn't occasioned by that blasted Sioux arrow, but by blisters. Riding boots and walking boots were two different animals, and Tobias hoped never to have to prove the point by example again. "You can thank your lucky stars that whoever fired that one shot was too timid to try it again. And that he wasn't a better shot."

But who was it? Tobias didn't have any idea. As soon as he'd shoved the castle doors open, he headed directly to a chair, sat, and tried to tug his boots off. He was having a hell of a time of it when Godfrey hurried into the entryway, looking harassed.

"Mr. Rakes!"

Tobias looked up from his boots. "Oh, good. Help me with these damned boots, will you?"

"But—but sir! But sir, no one knew where you were."

Tobias squinted at his butler, who seemed even more agitated than usual at the moment. "What is it, Godfrey? I went riding. Everyone knew that."

"Yes, sir, but your horse came back alone. We were all afraid you'd fallen off and been hurt. The whole household is in an uproar."

Fallen off? A cavalry officer? Tobias refrained from biting Godfrey's head off only because he was sure the poor boy's mother already had. "I had a little accident is all, Godfrey.

I'm fine.'' Except for the blasted blisters on his feet. ''But I'd appreciate some help getting these boots off, if you don't mind.''

''Oh!'' Godfrey jumped as if someone had goosed him, and continued to stand in the doorway, wringing his hands and staring at Tobias.

Tobias sighed, wishing the poor lad wasn't quite so nervous. All things considered, while Tobias appreciated Genevieve Crowfoot's good heart, he'd almost rather have a well-trained staff. Strays and misfits were all well and good in their proper place, but he wasn't sure that place was in his house. He lifted his booted foot. ''Please?''

''Oh! Oh, certainly, sir! I beg your pardon.'' Godfrey lunged at Tobias, almost tripping over his own feet as he did so.

Tobias sighed again, but it was a relief to have someone tugging on his boot as he pulled his foot back. Godfrey fell on his rear end when the boot finally gave up its hold on Tobias's foot. Instead of laughing, which he thought would be too cruel, Tobias asked mildly, ''Where's Miss Crowfoot?'' If the whole household was in an uproar, he didn't see any sign of it. Hell, if they all thought he'd been injured, she was the first person he'd expect to see in a dither. The knowledge that she evidently wasn't dithering put him in an even worse mood than his blisters did.

''We haven't been able to find Miss Crowfoot, sir,'' Godfrey told him, reaching for the other boot.

''You haven't been able to find her?'' What in Hades did that mean?

''No, sir. I looked all over the place for her, but I couldn't find her. Last I saw, she'd taken those papers Mr. Armitage left to the library, but she wasn't there when I looked.''

''Oh.'' Tobias lifted his other leg for Godfrey's sake. This was the wounded one, and he braced himself on the chair so as not to cry out in pain when the butler tugged.

''Yes, sir. I wasn't sure what to do when I couldn't find her, but my mother finally took charge.''

"No surprise there," Tobias muttered through gritted teeth.

Godfrey didn't even crack a smile. "Yes, sir. She sent Small William and Old William off to search for you in the woods."

"She did, eh?"

"Yes, sir."

Shows how much Mrs. Watkins, in spite of her powerful nature, knew about anything, Tobias thought, suppressing a holler of agony when Godfrey finally wrenched the boot from his foot. "Please tell the staff I'm fine, Godfrey. Thank them for worrying about me." Was that a silly thing to say? Taking note of the faint smile on Godfrey's face, Tobias guessed it wasn't.

"I'll take these boots out back to be cleaned, sir."

"Thanks, Godfrey. I'm going to go upstairs and change." And he wasn't going to put on another pair of shoes, either. Damn it, he was master here; he'd go barefoot if he wanted to. Especially since his blisters hurt like crazy. He turned and, before Godfrey could escape, asked, "I don't suppose there's any calamine lotion anywhere around this pile of bricks, is there?"

Godfrey looked blank, an expression Tobias was used to seeing on the butler's face. "Calamine lotion? Er, I'll ask my mother, sir."

"Thanks, Godfrey." Tobias headed up the stairs, trying not to limp any more than he had to. Lord, it was galling, these constant attempts on his life. And where the hell was Genevieve when he needed her?

He paused, a startling thought having walloped him. Genevieve. Could she be the one? Could she—

"Don't be an ass, Rakes." Disgusted with himself for thinking such a thing for so much as a second, Tobias stomped up the stairs.

As soon as he'd changed into more comfortable clothes and a fresh pair of socks—he refused to wear shoes—he went off in search of Genevieve. He had something very serious to discuss with her. Something aside from that damned gunshot.

Genevieve was fairly jumping for joy, although she didn't utter so much as a single whoop because she didn't care to have anyone else in the castle know what she was up to. She'd found it. She'd discovered the only place in the castle she hadn't searched before, because it was hidden. Actually, it still was hidden, and she didn't know *exactly* where it was, but she intended to remedy that situation as soon as she could.

"The crafty old devil," she muttered as she tapped on the wall next to where her ear was pressed against it. She was in the very attic in which she and Delilah had first met Granny Crowfoot. That seemed like such a long time ago, although it wasn't more than a couple of months, really. "You may have been a patriot and a noble soul, Charles Crowfoot, but I'll bet you were a mercenary money-grubber and a skinflint at heart."

Genevieve jumped away from the wall and looked around quickly, hoping Granny Crowfoot hadn't heard her. No ghost appeared, so she breathed a sigh of relief and went back to her search.

Pressing her ear against the wooden paneling once more, she tapped again, hoping to hear a hollow sound and thereby discover exactly which wall concealed Charles Crowfoot's secret hiding place. She knew this room was smaller than specified in the castle plans because she'd measured them all, but she couldn't tell from scrutinizing the old parchment exactly where the room had been divided.

She was so engrossed in her task that she didn't hear the attic door open. Nor did she hear Tobias step into the room, notice what she was doing, stop still, tilt his head to one side, frown, and consider her for several seconds. She did, however, hear him when he said, "What in the world are you doing, Miss Crowfoot?"

"Ack!" Genevieve spun around, her fist tightening on the aged parchment in her hand. At once, she realized what she'd done and loosened her grip on the castle plans. "Mr. Rakes! You gave me such a start." She glanced at his feet, and she joined him in a frown. "Why are you sneaking around in your stocking feet? You nearly gave me a palpitation." How unfair of him! Even as a part of her mind told her she was being irrational—after all, Tobias owned the place; if he wanted to run through it naked and barefoot, she supposed it wasn't her place to object. However, she still felt aggrieved that he, of all people, should have caught her searching for Charles Crowfoot's buried treasure.

"I wasn't sneaking. You, however, look as if you might have been doing something covert." His gaze locked on the now-wrinkled parchment in her hand, his scowl now replaced by a faintly puzzled expression.

Blast. Genevieve looked at the parchment, too, and wondered how she was going to get out of this one. "I was— er—oh, dear."

"Yes?"

"Um, I was checking the dimensions of the rooms in the castle because I found the old plans in the globe stand yesterday." She held out the parchment and smiled gamely, hoping he'd accept a partial explanation.

"Why would you want to do a thing like that?" he asked, dashing her hopes at once.

Fiddlesticks. Genevieve glowered at him for a moment until the humor of her situation struck her. For pity's sake, what did she care if he knew what she was doing? While at first she'd considered Tobias Rakes a cold, unfeeling, hard man, she'd come to know him much better by this time. He was a fair-minded man, and would surely share her deceased relative's treasure with her, if indeed there was one. She'd be no worse off in that case than she was right now. Besides, it might be fun to take him into her confidence. She hadn't had a partner in crime since Benton died.

She stood up straight and looked him square in the eye. "I'm searching for buried treasure."

His eyes popped wide open. "You're doing what?"

She grinned and held out the parchment. "I'm searching

for buried treasure. Actually, I don't think it's buried. I think old Charles has a secret room or compartment hidden up here somewhere, and I'm trying to find it."

"Good God." After a moment, during which he appeared thunderstruck, Tobias resumed frowning and walked over to her. She handed him the old parchment without another word.

The thick paper crackled as he unrolled it. "Well, I'll be. These do look like the plans to the place, don't they?"

"They do indeed."

He glanced up from the paper and searched Genevieve's face. "But what's this nonsense about a treasure?"

Her grin broadened. "It may be nonsense, really, but when Aunt Delilah and I were cleaning out the place before you bought it, I discovered a tattered old scrap of paper that referred to it, and I've been trying to find it ever since." She tossed her head, feeling a little defiant. "That's why I hoped you'd hire me as housekeeper—so I could keep looking for it since I didn't find it before you moved in."

His expression fell so rapidly that Genevieve wondered what she'd said to upset him. "That's the reason, is it?" He sounded disappointed.

She experienced a strange compulsion to deny it, even though it was the truth; at least a part of it. "Well, and I love this old place, too. And I really did need the job."

It didn't look to her as if her words had eased his disappointment much. "Oh. I thought perhaps you enjoyed living here."

"Oh, I do. I truly do, Mr. Rakes, especially since you're going to so much trouble to restore it to its former glory. I love it here."

His head cocked to one side, he continued to survey her face in a manner that made Genevieve nervous. "You love it here, do you?"

Since her mouth had suddenly turned cotton-dry, she only nodded. She licked her lips, then wished she hadn't when she saw his gaze stray to them. A funny, fluttering sensation began to course through her, making her even more nervous.

"And do you find me a hard taskmaster?"

"Mercy no. You're kindness itself, Mr. Rakes. Surely you know that."

"Actually, I didn't. I'm used to being in the army, where I give a command and it's carried out. I'm not used to making requests and being polite."

"Oh." Genevieve swallowed. Her hands itched, so she thrust them behind her to clasp each other. "Well, you've adapted very well."

His grin caught her off guard, it was so sudden and so beautiful. She'd noticed before that, while his face generally had a grim cast to it, when he smiled, it softened beautifully. In fact, his grin made her feel a little wobbly.

"I'm glad you think so, Miss Crowfoot. I do try not to be spit-and-polish in my own home."

"Th-thank you."

"Thank *you*."

His gaze went back to the house plans, thank God. Genevieve expelled a huge breath and began to relax slightly.

"But I am curious about this supposed treasure. You say Charles Crowfoot hid it here somewhere?"

Mortally glad he'd changed the subject, Genevieve nodded. "Yes." She was fairly certain she wouldn't swoon or throw herself at him if they could talk about something other than how much she liked living with him. Which was a perfectly shocking way to think of their living arrangements, and she wished she hadn't.

She cleared her throat and forced herself to think about Charles Crowfoot's putative treasure instead. "That is to say, I don't really know, but I figured it wouldn't hurt to look for it." She cast him a quick glance. "I hope you don't mind."

"Mind? Why should I mind? This sounds like the most fun I'm likely to have around here for a while. Someone took a shot at me in the woods today."

"*What?*" Forgetting all about treasure, secrecy, Charles Crowfoot, and her tendency to want to make mad, passionate love to Tobias Rakes, Genevieve grabbed his arm in both of her hands.

In one fluid motion, Tobias thrust the castle plans away from him, and they fluttered to the floor. He took Genevieve in his arms and gazed down into her huge, frightened eyes. "I fear it's true, Miss Crowfoot. Someone shot at me. I've had experience with such things, you know, and it was impossible to mistake the shot for anything else. I immediately slid from Rake's Progress and flattened out on the ground to make a more difficult target. Since the horse isn't experienced at all with gunfire, he galloped straight back to the castle. I had to walk home. Which explains why I was sneaking around in my stocking feet, as you so cleverly phrased it. Blisters."

"Oh, my." Genevieve was beginning to feel breathless. "Blisters."

"Blisters."

"I'm sorry."

"So am I."

He cleared his throat. "Since no further shots were fired, I presume the assailant either frightened himself or could no longer get a clear aim at me once I was down from the horse."

"Good heavens."

"Indeed."

"How frightened you must have been."

He chuckled low in his throat, and the effect of the sultry sound was to give Genevieve's palpitations gooseflesh.

"It wasn't much fun. I kept to the woods and was very careful making my way home, believe me. Whoever it was evidently gave up, because I didn't hear anything but the usual squirrels and birds."

"I'm so glad you are all right."

"I'm awfully happy about that myself," Tobias said, as a wry grin played across his face.

She forced herself to glance away from him. She felt so odd in his arms. So very, very odd. She licked her lips again, scrambling like mad to think of something to do or say that wouldn't give away her state of agitation. She wanted to press herself against him and beg him to have his way with her, which wouldn't do at all. "Do—er, do you mind about the treasure, Mr. Rakes?"

"I don't suppose I could prevail upon you to call me Tobias, could I? I know it's a silly name, but I had nothing to do with it.''

Before she knew what she was doing, Genevieve had lifted a hand and pressed it against his cheek. ''I think it's a lovely name. Beautiful.''

''Would you object to using it when you speak to me?''

''Object to calling you Tobias?'' Genevieve was embarrassed when her voice went up and she squeaked slightly at the end of his name. What was wrong with her? She had a dreadful suspicion she already knew what was wrong with her, and was refusing to face facts. ''I shouldn't object at all, if you will call me Genevieve.''

''Genevieve. It's a beautiful name. Almost as beautiful as you are.''

Merciful heavens, had he really said that? Genevieve had become so used to thinking of herself as a spinster that she couldn't come to grips with this extraordinary man thinking of her as a woman. A beautiful woman. Her hands tightened on his shoulders. ''Thank you.''

He gazed down at her for several moments that seemed to Genevieve as if they were crackling with electricity. Like the world before a thunderstorm. Like heat lightning in the summertime. Like—oh, saints above—like love.

''Thank *you*,'' he said at last, and he looked away. Genevieve sagged with relief when the electric moment ended.

With a sigh, Tobias dropped his arms. ''Well,'' he said, and to Genevieve it sounded as if he were straining to make his voice light, ''let's consider this problem.''

Although she wasn't entirely certain whether what she was feeling leaned more toward relief than disappointment or the other way around, Genevieve knew she should be grateful that Tobias hadn't tried to take advantage of her. If he had, she knew she wouldn't have tried to stop him. Ha! More than likely she'd have climbed all over him. She'd never experienced lust before she met him, but lust was her constant companion these days.

She told herself to stop thinking about it. ''Yes. I've been trying to find a spot on the wall that sounds hollow.'' Grabbing for all she was worth at the sense of fun she used to have when she and Benton went exploring together, she shot him a twinkling glance. "Want to tap while I listen, or would you rather listen while I tap?"

His grin told her how much he appreciated her endeavoring to lighten what had become a frankly provocative atmosphere in the attic room. "Either way's all right with me."

She decided to take the decision out of his hands and began tapping on the walls again. "Of course, if we find where the room is, we'll have to decide how to get into it."

"Maybe there's a trick passageway or something. You know, like they used to build into old English castles."

"You mean like a priest's hole or something?"

"Yes. Maybe you have to press a panel and a bookcase will creak open."

She laughed. "Except that there aren't any bookcases in this room."

"Details, details. Don't spoil my fun, Genevieve."

Warmth flooded her heart. When she'd first met him, wounded and bitter as he was, she'd never imagined he would, after so little time, sound so young and playful. "I wouldn't dream of it. Failing a bookcase, I'm sure we'll discover a secret trapdoor or something."

"Good. Now you're thinking."

"Undoubtedly guarded by a spring rigged to shoot poisoned darts at interlopers."

"Good Lord, you're really good at this." He laughed, sounding genuinely appreciative.

She gave him a conspiratorial wink. "I've had practice."

Their lighthearted banter continued as they tapped and listened, tapped and listened, tapped and listened. Genevieve had begun to think they were destined for disappointment when she tapped on a panel and heard, even without her ear pressed to it as was Tobias's, a distinctly hollow sound. Both of them straightened and looked at each other, plainly astonished. Then they turned back to the panel and Genevieve tapped it again. Again a hollow sound greeted her tap. Tobias tapped then, harder. Still hollow.

"My God," he said. "I think this must be it."

Genevieve shook her head. "I don't think I ever honestly believed it was here, you know. I was just having fun."

He grinned at her. "You're going to have to teach me how to do that."

"What? Have fun?"

"Exactly."

"I'll be more than happy to." She meant it, too. "But now we have to figure out how to get into this room. Do you want to search for a secret button or something?" She looked around doubtfully. All the paneling looked alike to her, and she didn't see so much as a knothole that might be a secret button in disguise. When she glanced at Tobias again, he was looking at her more mischievously than she'd believed possible.

"If I make a suggestion, will you think I'm a spoilsport?" he asked in a teasing tone.

She adopted an expression of dubious consideration. "That depends on what the suggestion is. We don't want to break any rules, you know."

"Rules? You mean there are rules for this sort of thing?"

She put her fists on her hips and tilted her head. "Didn't you read *Tom Sawyer* when you were a boy? Of course there are rules for this sort of thing!"

"No, I'm afraid my father didn't approve of novels. Obviously, I missed an important part of my education."

"You certainly did." Genevieve scowled at the paneling. "I hate to say it, Tobias, but I'm beginning to think your father was a terrible old poop."

He burst out laughing. Although Genevieve was a little embarrassed about having spoken her opinion aloud—after all, Tobias's father was a respected member of the Bittersweet community—she didn't really regret it when she saw how much her frank declaration tickled Tobias.

"You're right, you know. He is a terrible old poop. Always was, even before he got old."

She sighed. "I'm sorry about that. It must have been difficult for a child with imagination and a sense of humor to grow up with a parent who didn't possess either."

He looked at her oddly. "It was difficult. And you, my dear, are a very perceptive young lady."

The look in his eyes was so warm, Genevieve feared she might blush, so she turned to consider the paneling again. "Thank you, but what do you suggest we do about this paneling?"

He heaved a sigh. When Genevieve glanced over her shoulder at him, he looked like he wasn't entirely pleased to have his attention drawn back to the wall. Nevertheless, after tapping on it one more time, he said simply, "Break it down."

She blinked up at him, believing she hadn't heard him right. "I beg your pardon?"

"Break it down." He shrugged.

"Break it down?"

"Why not?" His grin was a work of art. "Is that against the rules?"

After a moment of surprise, Genevieve said, "I'm sure it must be, but—You really don't mind if we break the wall down?"

"No. Why should I?"

"Well, but it would make a big hole in the wall."

"So what?" He shrugged again. "It's not as if this is the grand ballroom or anything. It's an attic. And that wall may well have hundred-year-old secrets hidden behind it."

"But—but—" Genevieve had never imagined that he might enter into her treasure hunt with such enthusiasm.

"If it will make you feel any better, I'll set Old William Pickstaff to rebuilding the paneling after we take the ax to it." His face went grim for a second. "That'll not only take care of repairing the wall, but it will keep him occupied and unable to try to kill me for a day or two."

She winced at his frank words. "So you do believe it's him?"

He shook his head, as if he were tired of thinking about it. "I don't know. I can't think of anyone else who might want to do me in. Of course, I don't know why the Pickstaffs would want to, either." Grinning again, he said, "So let's not think about that. If you believe breaking the wall down is too simple, I suppose we can continue searching for a way in, but it'll take a lot longer. Or is that one of the rules?''

It looked to Genevieve as if he were honestly trying not to break any childhood codes, which she thought was incredibly endearing. ''I think we can dispense with further searching, actually. I don't recall a specific rule about how one is supposed to gain admittance to a treasure trove.''

''Good.'' He expelled a huge, mock breath of relief. ''I'm awfully glad to hear it. Let's go fetch the ax then, shall we?''

''Aye-aye, captain.'' Genevieve saluted smartly.

Tobias shook his head. ''I'm an army man, Genevieve. You're supposed to say, 'Yes, sir.' ''

She laughed. ''Yes, sir.''

It only took them another half hour or so to go down to the room off the pantry where the tools were kept, select an ax, broom, and dustpan—Genevieve said she intended to tidy up after they'd broken the wall down—and head back up to the attic. Then Genevieve stood aside while Tobias prepared to attack the wall.

He removed his jacket and rolled up his shirtsleeves first. She gaped at the way his muscles bulged under the fine cotton of his shirt. The man's body was a work of art. She almost wished she hadn't noticed. Then, when Tobias reared back with his ax and slammed the blade into the paneling, she ceased thinking and covered her ears.

It wasn't long at all before a gaping hole appeared in the wall. Tobias stepped back, and Genevieve ran over to him. They both stood still and stared for several moments at what his violence had revealed. Genevieve's mouth dropped open.

Tobias said, ''Um, that doesn't look much like a buried treasure to me.'' He glanced down at her and grinned. ''What does the rule book say about discovering a secret office?''

Chapter Fourteen

"Actually," Genevieve said, her voice sounding strange in the now-silent attic, "I don't think there are any specific rules covering this possibility."

Tobias's grin widened. She was such a darling. He wondered how he'd survived this long without someone like Genevieve Crowfoot in his life. "No? Perhaps I should widen the hole, then, and we can just step in and see what it's all about."

She nodded and saluted again. "Good idea, sir."

So he battered at the paneling for another few minutes, expanding the ragged hole until it was large enough for them to fit through. He and Genevieve then pulled debris away from the wall and stepped inside the small, formerly hidden room. Genevieve sneezed immediately.

"You all right?" He took her arm.

"Yes. It's just all this dust." She looked around with distaste.

"I suppose a room can accumulate a lot of dust in a hundred years."

"Yes, I suppose you're right. It's actually been more like a hundred and twenty-five years."

"True. It probably dates from right before the Revolution.

Genevieve glanced around dubiously. "What a mess."

It actually wasn't messy. It was merely dusty and full of cobwebs—and perhaps rats, mice, and spiders. And it was dark as a pit.

Tobias wrinkled his nose. "I think we'd be better off if we went downstairs again before we tackle this place. I'll fetch a lantern, and, if you don't mind, you could grab a couple of dust rags. Then maybe we can search through here without getting our clothes filthy."

"That's an excellent idea."

So they went downstairs once more, fetched the items in question, and climbed back to the attic. Several members of the household staff, including the dour Mrs. Watkins, looked at them oddly, but Tobias merely smiled at them, feeling intensely happy and pleased with life, as well as rather like a boy who'd discovered a secret cave with his best friend and now aimed to explore it without interference from nosy adults. Genevieve, too, seemed impervious to outside scrutiny. Bless her.

The room was quite little. It didn't take up more than ten square feet, by Tobias's estimation. Genevieve set to work with her dust rag and he with a feather duster, and they had soon dislodged enough filth to begin their search without fear of being smothered by drifting dust.

"This looks like a regular old office to me." Genevieve sounded disappointed.

"I'm not sure about that. If old Charles had nothing of a sensitive nature in mind when he worked here, why did he go to the trouble of concealing it?"

She glanced at him appreciatively, her eyes lighting up like stars. "What an excellent point, Tobias. You're truly catching the spirit of adventure. Let's investigate."

Her enthusiasm infected him, and they both set to work, digging around in desk drawers and shuffling through papers. Tobias, enjoying himself immensely, resolved a question that had kept him occupied for the last day and night. To hell with everything; he was going to ask Genevieve Crowfoot to marry him.

The idea of marriage, an idea Tobias had avoided contemplating for years now, had first struck him several weeks ago when he noticed the regiment of children Genevieve had set to working in the gardens. At first he'd sort of sneaked up on the notion obliquely, squinting at its edges, not wanting to pay much attention to it for fear it would scare him off. After he'd conquered the worst of his apprehension, he'd tackled the concept from a practical angle, still not caring to involve his emotions. He'd been carried away by emotion when he was a youth, proved himself to be a fool and his emotions to be unreliable, and once a fool was enough for anybody.

But, honestly, he did think that as long as he owned this huge old monstrosity of a castle, he might as well fill it up with children. They added a nice touch to the place. Cheered the old pile up some. And really, when he came right down to it, why shouldn't they be children of his own? No sense in importing the little rascals if he could provide the genuine article.

Of course, he himself knew as little about parenting as he did about flying to the moon, so he needed to select a female who'd be a good mother—if he decided to carry through with the astonishing concept. He didn't want any children of his to have cold, uncaring parents. If he ever did marry and have children, he aimed to break that particular Rakes family tradition once and for all.

It was only in the last day or two that he'd begun to realize his mind had conveniently skipped over the person who'd provided the initial prod to these strange wanderings: Genevieve Crowfoot. In fact, he hadn't realized until yesterday evening that if he'd never met Genevieve, he'd never have considered fathering children in the first place.

Genevieve would be a splendid mother; Tobias knew it in his soul. He watched her now as she pored over a musty old ledger, written in an old-fashioned florid script. She had a sense of fun and a sense of adventure. She was good-natured and kind-hearted, and Tobias knew, without knowing how he knew it, that she'd never treat a child—any child—coldly, as his father had treated him. Genevieve Crowfoot would never advocate the stern Yankee detachment that Tobias's father so prided himself in. No way in hell would Genevieve ever forbid a child of hers to mourn over a lost parent.

Damn. Tobias wrenched his gaze away from Genevieve, his thoughts having led him back to his dead mother's bedside, making his heart ache. He would never in a million years understand how his father—his mother's husband, for the love of God—could have chided Tobias for weeping over his own beloved mother's body. A mother who would never again rise to kiss him, or let him plant flowers with her, or read to him. What kind of perverted parenting was that?

"Have you ever considered children, Genevieve?"

The question popped out of his mouth as if from out of the blue. Tobias cursed himself as an ass.

Her head jerked up from the ledger, and she stared at him. Small wonder, Tobias thought grimly. "Children? What about children?"

Great. He'd not only asked a stupid question, but he hadn't even asked the question he'd meant to ask. "Er, I mean, have you ever considered having children of your own?"

She gazed at him as if he'd lost his mind, which he might well have done. "Well, unless I married, of course, I wouldn't want them."

Her expression seemed mischievous to Tobias, although he could be reading something into it that wasn't there. "Of course, I meant after you were married. Of course I did."

She laughed slightly and relented. "Oh, yes, I'd love to have children, although I fear I never will. Why do you ask?"

Truly embarrassed, Tobias mumbled, "Oh, nothing. Just thinking about old Charles Crowfoot and Granny Crowfoot, I guess." Liar. He was a damned liar, and he knew it. Still and all, while he might be harboring odd fancies in his mind, he wasn't altogether sure he wanted to invite Genevieve to share them until he'd come to grips with all their implications.

Her expression turned contemplative, and she gazed off into space—or at least at the wall across from the desk. "Yes. I've thought about Charles and Granny Crowfoot quite often lately. She seems to have loved and respected him a good deal. I guess he wasn't such an awful old crook if his daughter loved him so.''

Tobias nodded and decided to pursue the line she'd handed him. ''I expect you're right. But what makes you think he was an awful old crook?''

She shrugged and turned to grin at him some more. ''I don't know. I guess because of all this.'' She waved her arm in a gesture meant to encompass the castle and grounds. ''I mean, he must have been awfully wealthy.''

''True. But don't forget that back then, the country was brand new. I expect an enterprising merchant might have been able to make a fortune and keep it without tramping his fellow citizens under his feet too badly.''

She eyed him doubtfully. ''I'm not so sure about that. I have a feeling that people who love money are the same, no matter what century they live in.''

Another laugh ended in a sneeze. Tobias pinched his nose to stop the tickling. ''You're undoubtedly right.''

Genevieve went back to her ledger. Tobias sighed and decided to plow through a leather satchel he'd found propped up against a leg of the desk. The old thing was cracked with age, but he could detect the remains of fine tooling on the flap. It must have been an impressive piece of workmanship a hundred and twenty-five years ago. The flap broke when he lifted it. Tobias held the broken-off piece in his hand and was sorry he hadn't been more careful, although he wasn't sure even great care could have prevented such an event. Leather needed to be cared for if one wanted to keep it soft and supple.

Soft and supple. He glanced up from the satchel and gazed at Genevieve for a moment, his thoughts turning wistful. She was soft and supple. And funny and friendly. She was just about everything that Tobias's life had lacked these past thirty years. Well, the past twenty years, anyway—since his mother's death.

He told himself sharply to keep his mind on the business at hand. Speaking of hands . . . Tobias wasn't sure what kinds of arachnids liked to live in old leather satchels, but he took the thing over to the desk and gently shook out the papers that were inside it. He wasn't about to stick his naked fingers in there and meet up with a black widow spider or something. He was pleased when nothing but old papers slid onto the desk, and he picked them up, eager to find out what mysteries they held. Tobias surveyed the room, looking for a place to sit. The room only contained three chairs, one of which was occupied by Genevieve's bottom at the moment. Her soft, supple bottom.

With another heavy sigh, Tobias sat on a second chair and started to read. The words he read captured his attention, and he squinted at them hard. He soon forgot all about Genevieve's softness. And her bottom.

"Good God."

Genevieve looked up from her ledger. "What is it? Have you found something interesting?"

"I'm not sure." He glanced up once, shook his head, and resumed reading. After another minute or two, he whispered, "I don't believe this."

"What?"

He waved at her to be quiet for another little while. He heard her huff and didn't really blame her—after all, this had been her idea in the first place—but he was too absorbed in what he was reading to interrupt himself just yet. "Good Lord."

"What?"

"Just a minute." He turned the page and continued to read. "This is incredible."

"*What?*"

Genevieve's question was so piercing that it made Tobias jump in his chair. His head snapped up.

She had a fierce scowl on her face. "What is it, Tobias? You keep making comments, but you're not telling me what you're reading. That's not fair, you know. It's totally against the rules."

Tobias took note of her expression. She really did look peeved. He was sorry for having teased her, however inadvertently. He held up the paper in his hand. "I think our family feud may be based upon a faulty foundation."

Genevieve blinked at him as if she hadn't understood him properly. "I beg your pardon?"

Tobias bent his head and read another sentence or two. "Not only that, but I think our resident ghost is in for a very unpleasant shock." He smiled. "The shock of her death, as it were."

"All right, that's enough. What are you talking about?" Genevieve slapped the ledger shut and jumped up from her chair. She stomped over to him.

Tobias looked up at her, grinned, and handed her the two pages he'd already read. As she started perusing them, he continued reading from the stack in his lap. He wasn't surprised when, after fifteen seconds or so, Genevieve gasped. He peered up at her. "Surprised?"

She gazed down at him, wide-eyed. "Flabbergasted."

Nodding, he said, "Read on. Your flabber will be further gasted in a minute."

She did. After several seconds, she murmured, "I can't believe this."

"I can."

"Why, the miserable old goat!"

"Got to that part, did you?" Tobias laughed softly.

"I should say I did." Genevieve, on the other hand, sounded truly indignant. "Why, the scandalous old reprobate!"

"Better not say so in front of his daughter. She might leave off haunting me and take you on."

Holding the papers in both of her hands, Genevieve thrust them down flat against her skirt. Her cheeks had gone pink with indignation, and her eyes were flashing.

"This is the most incredible thing I've ever read! And imagine! Our families have been at each other's throats for more than a hundred years! And for what? For this!" She rattled the papers.

"It is pretty amazing, isn't it?"

"*Amazing?* It's—it's astonishing! Incredible! Appalling! Outrageous!"

For a moment, she stared at him, furious. Then, in a heartbeat, her expression changed, she threw back her head, and she burst out laughing. Tobias, whose grin felt as though it might split his cheeks, experienced a strange, bubbling sensation in his chest. He only realized it was mirth—an emotion with which he had very little acquaintance—when he, too, broke out into gales of laughter.

He didn't know how long they laughed in that attic room. Genevieve laughed so long and so hard that she eventually had to draw up another chair or fall down from weakness. Tobias laughed until tears streamed from his eyes and he had to draw out a handkerchief and wipe them away. Genevieve, too, clutched a hankie to her leaking eyes.

For at least five minutes, hilarity held them captive. Even then, they only gradually brought their amusement under control enough so that they could speak to each other. Tobias, not surprisingly, since he had so much less practice in laughing than Genevieve, was the first to speak, "I suppose we ought to find your family ghost and break the news to her." The notion of telling Granny Crowfoot what they'd discovered sent Tobias off into another roar of laughter.

It had the same effect on Genevieve, who whooped and covered her face with her hands. "Oh, my dear good gracious. She'll be furious. If she were alive, she'd die."

The idea of Granny Crowfoot in one of her apoplectic fits tickled Tobias's newly discovered funny bone once more, and it was a long time before he could speak again. "We—we'd better make sure we break it to her in a room with no lightweight, breakable objects in it."

Genevieve whooped again. "Oh, Lord, you're right. Maybe we should pad one especially for the purpose."

The notion of a ghost in a padded cell made them both lose what little control they'd gained over their giggles. Tobias slapped his knee hard several times, trying in that way to shock his senses out of their merriment.

"This is too rich," Genevieve gasped. "Too funny."

It was that, all right. And Tobias was ever so pleased that it had been he who'd found the punch line to the joke. It seemed to him that in that moment, his entire bleak life had been repaired.

Almost. There was one other thing he needed to do in

order to ensure that his life would never be bleak again. He reached out and took Genevieve's hand. She glanced at him, laughing too hard to be surprised.

"You know the next thing we have to do, once we tell Granny Crowfoot that her father was a scoundrel and in cahoots with my great-great-great-grandfather?"

She shook her head and wiped her eyes with her fingers. "No. What?"

Before he could think about it and frighten himself, Tobias blurted out, "We need to get married."

Genevieve's mouth was open, the better to expel more laughter, but no more laughter came out. Her eyes, wet from tears of amusement, went as round as blueberries and as big as platters. "Wh-what?"

Tobias took a deep breath and rushed on, "I'm asking you to marry me, Genevieve. To become my wife. To populate this old pile of stones with our children. They'd be happy children. I'm sure of it."

"You—you want to marry me?" She sounded breathless. Tobias wondered if it was merely because she'd laughed herself silly, or if his proposal had taken the wind out of her.

"I want to marry you more than I've ever wanted to do anything in my life, Genevieve. I love you." There. The truth was out. His confession seemed to him to hang in the air, as if waiting for Genevieve's answer to swat it down or gather it to her heart. He held his breath.

"Oh, Tobias." Her whisper feathered over his senses, and Tobias felt a very tiny iota of hope. "Do you really?"

"I wouldn't have said it if I didn't." That didn't sound very loverlike, but he'd had no practice in the art of courtship.

Slowly, a smile began to spread across Genevieve's face. Tobias, who didn't dare hope too hard, began to feel ever so slightly more optimistic. He licked his lips. "So, it being that this family feud has gone on for at least a hundred and twenty-five years longer than it ever should have in the first place, don't you think that a marriage between the last of the Crowfoots and the last of the Rakeses would put the capper on it rather splendidly?"

Her smile was so luminous, it nearly incinerated him. "Oh, Tobias!"

It wasn't exactly a yes, but it definitely wasn't a no. Tobias lifted his left eyebrow. "Well? What do you say, Genevieve? Could you stand being married to a sour-tempered cripple?"

"Oh, Tobias!" she said yet a third time. Then she cried, "Yes! Yes, yes, yes! I've loved you for the longest time!" And she hurled herself into his arms.

Tobias was very glad his leg had healed enough to bear her weight, because the feeling of holding her in his arms and knowing she was his was indescribably wonderful. He barely had a moment to register that thought before Genevieve's soft, sweet lips devoured his.

After quite a long time, Genevieve reluctantly came up for air. Tobias couldn't recall another time in his life when he'd felt so good. He felt happy. Content with things. Optimistic. He couldn't recall ever feeling optimistic before. But with Genevieve at his side, he knew in his guts that his life could never be miserable again.

Her soft hand caressed his cheek. "I do love you, Tobias. I don't know when it happened. I think it was gradual."

"Really?" Tobias wasn't sure when he'd realized he loved Genevieve, either, but he had a feeling it hadn't been especially gradual. The first time he met her, he'd felt as if a light had been lit in his soul.

She nodded. "The first time I met you, I thought you were cold and hard and unhappy."

Astute female, Genevieve. Tobias chuckled. "And you were right."

"Oh, no. You're not cold and hard at all. And I know you were unhappy, but you had good reason to be."

"I suppose so."

"I know so." She kissed him again.

Tobias wasn't sure how much more of this he could take without bursting his trouser buttons. Genevieve was too precious a cargo; she was too lush and passionate, and his gentlemanliness, which hadn't been cultivated in recent years, was about to snap. He was healthy enough by this time to have none but moral barriers in the way of his lust. "Er, perhaps we should go find Granny Crowfoot, Genevieve. I—ah—this is getting difficult for me.''

Genevieve hopped off of his lap, a horrified expression on her face. She slapped her hands to her cheeks. ''Oh, Tobias! Did I hurt your leg?''

Tobias shook his head and laughed. She was the most darling woman he'd ever met. ''It's not my leg, Genevieve. It's my base male instincts.''

Her cheeks, already rosy, went scarlet. ''Tobias! Do you mean—''

He rose from the chair. ''I mean we'd better go look for your blasted ghost, or I'm not sure I can be trusted.''

For no more than a second or two, Tobias feared Genevieve might slap his face. He'd never taken her for a particularly prudish woman, but one never could tell about these things. Then an expression of pure mischief entered her eyes.

No, wait. It wasn't pure. Not at all. Mingled in with the mischief was something else that Tobias recognized because he'd felt it himself. A lot. Especially lately. It was lust. Oh, Lord. If neither one of them could be trusted to hold back, what would become of them. ''Ah—Genevieve?''

''Tobias?''

''Why are you looking at me like that?''

Oh, Lordy, it was getting worse. She was positively devilish now. Not trusting himself, Tobias slid behind the chair and held on to the back of it to keep his hands occupied. They wanted to take Genevieve up on her invitation, but Tobias knew that would be wrong.

Wouldn't it?

She licked her lips. Tobias shut his eyes and prayed for strength.

''Um, I don't think it would be a sin for people who are engaged to be married to kiss a little, Tobias.''

He sucked in a huge breath and held it until he nearly turned blue. ''I don't just want to kiss a little, Genevieve.'' His voice was so tight it squeaked.

''Neither do I.''

Oh, Lord. ''Um, you don't?''

She shook her head. "I've never been in love before, Tobias. I want to experience the whole thing."

"But—but we aren't married yet."

"I know that. But I'm getting such a late start at this sort of thing, don't you see. It would be cruel to wait any longer."

This sort of thing? "Er, I'm not sure I know what you mean." He wasn't sure he wanted to know. He was fairly certain, however, that if he *did* know, his state of acute frustration might be on its way to being assuaged.

No, no, no. That was the wrong way to think. That was his wild, frontier side talking; trying to make him misbehave. He shut his eyes and tried to get in touch with his civilized, Eastern side, and discovered to his dismay that the civilized part of him was napping at the moment. "Oh, Lord." The words were whispered, and they were a nominal prayer.

His eyes were still shut when he felt Genevieve's hand on his shoulder. "I want to make love with you, Tobias."

Oh, Lord.

"I want you to teach me what it's like when a man loves a woman."

"But, we aren't married yet." The words crawled from his throat, clawing their way out.

"We will be." Her voice, on the other hand, was low and musical, and throbbed with promise.

"But—but—"

"I've been longing to feel your bare flesh, Tobias. And to feel your hands on my bare flesh. Is that shocking?"

Shocking? It was—it was— Oh, Lord. "Um—"

"Don't you want to make love to me, Tobias?"

Didn't he *want* to? He was about to die if he didn't, was all. Unable to form a coherent sentence, Tobias moaned softly.

Genevieve's arms slid around his neck. Her words came out hot against his neck. "Tobias? Tobias, are you all right?"

All right? Hell, yes, he was all right. With a growl of pure animal passion, Tobias gave up the struggle. He grabbed Genevieve so suddenly and so hard that it was she who squeaked this time. "I give up, Genevieve. I tried to be a gentleman, but I can't stand it any longer."

"Oh, good. I'm so glad." She sighed and seemed to melt against him.

"But I'm not about to make love to you in Charles Crowfoot's musty old office. Come downstairs to bed."

"Gladly."

She took his hand and charged to the door. Tobias, scarcely able to think at all by this time, chuckled as he stumbled after her. She made it into a game, peeking around corners so as to avoid any of the household staff. By the time they'd come to his bedroom door, Tobias felt as if he were on a secret mission. Which he was.

Genevieve pushed the door open, shoved him inside, closed the door, and locked it. Then she stood there with her back against the door, watching him, her eyes twinkling like diamonds. "Oh, Tobias, I'm so excited about all of this."

"Yeah. Me, too." That was putting it mildly. He was going to explode if he didn't get her clothes off pretty soon. Getting into the spirit of the thing, he began stalking toward her like a panther on the prowl. "All right, Genevieve. Are you sure you're sure about this?"

He could tell her heart was beating almost as fast as his. Her cheeks were flushed, her bosom rose and fell invitingly, and she nodded. Her smile was a pure marvel. "Oh, yes, I'm quite sure I'm sure."

With a lunge, he had her in his arms. "Good. Then let's get started."

She threw her arms around him with precious enthusiasm. Tobias's heart was so full of amazement, love, and happiness that he wasn't sure he'd survive.

"Oh, Tobias, I'm so happy!"

"So am I." And he was, too.

He'd have liked to pick her up and carry her to the bed but, even though she was small and slender, he didn't dare do it in case his leg gave out. He didn't think it would make a very good impression if he dropped her, even if the rugs were thick in here. So he guided her, kissing her all the way, to the tall bed. Then, in a fit of daring, he scooped her up and placed her on the bed. His leg didn't so much as twinge in disapproval, which he considered an excellent sign.

"Shall I undress?" she asked, not at all shyly, considering she was a twenty-five-year-old virgin.

Tobias said, "Let me help you."

"Gladly." She gave him another one of her devilish smiles; the ones that went in through his eyes, swooped around inside of him for several seconds, and then shot down to lodge in his sex.

Glad at once for his blisters—otherwise he'd have those damned riding boots on—Tobias joined her on the bed and immediately reached for her bodice buttons. As glad as he was that he no longer wore his boots, still more glad was he that Genevieve favored a plain style of dress. Today she was clad in a simple white shirtwaist and skirt, and he made short shrift of the shirtwaist buttons. He'd been dreaming about this for weeks now. Months, even.

"I wish ladies didn't have to wear so many undergarments," Genevieve whispered when Tobias thrust the shirtwaist open and stared ravenously at her generous bosom. It was still hidden from his eyes by layers of lawn and lace, but he was closer to it now than he'd ever been. His heart almost stopped when she lifted her hands and, with trembling fingers, began working at the laces of her corset.

His throat was too tight to respond, but his fingers didn't tremble as much as hers when he reached to help her. She sighed deeply when the whaleboned monstrosity released its hold on her waist and tumbled to the bed. "Oh, my." Inadequate. But Tobias was beyond words. He watched greedily as Genevieve slipped the straps of her camisole down and he watched her beautiful breasts reveal themselves to him.

"Am—am I pretty in your eyes, Tobias?"

Tobias realized with a jolt of astonishment that the question was genuine, that Genevieve honestly wondered about the merit of her feminine appeal. He jerked his attention away from her gorgeous, rosy-nubbed breasts and stared into her eyes. For the first time he read some doubt there.

"You're the most wonderful woman I've ever met, Genevieve. I've never been so—so—" What was a man supposed to say now? That he'd never lusted after a female the way he lusted after Genevieve? Tobias wasn't sure Genevieve would necessarily consider that a compliment, even though he meant it as such.

She smiled shyly and finished his sentence for him. "Aroused?"

His mouth was dry as cotton fluff, and he could only nod.

"Oh, I'm so glad!" And she threw herself at him. Again. Tobias wondered if he'd died and gone to heaven.

Chapter
Fifteen

Genevieve supposed that what she and Tobias were doing might be considered shocking by some people. Even sinful.

She knew better. It was no sin to love, and the expression of love, if carried out with commitment and honor, was no sin, either. She and Tobias were going to marry, and she'd never felt so excited and elated—and cherished—in her life.

"You've made me so happy, Tobias."

He had unfastened the button on her skirt. She wriggled out of it and the single petticoat she wore, and now lay before him, nearly naked, and writhing under the tender assault of his hands.

"You're making me pretty happy, too." He chuckled and dove toward her belly, which he'd only just uncovered, and dropped kisses all over it.

Laughing out loud, Genevieve lifted her hips so that he could slide her drawers down. He made quite a production of it, and she was squirming by the time he was through. She'd never realized exactly how many places on the human body could evoke sensations of an erotic nature, if approached in the proper—or improper—manner. She was more delighted than she could express to have found out.

And to think that Tobias actually wanted to marry her! She could scarcely believe it.

"Would you like to assist me now, ma'am?"

Tobias's voice had gone low and gravelly, and Genevieve knew he was having trouble controlling himself. But he was being gentle with her because this was their first time together, and they weren't married yet, and she was a virgin, and Genevieve thought that if she loved him any more, she'd burst with it.

"I'd love to."

So she did. First to go were his collar and cuffs. Genevieve, who used to think it was a fun treat to button her father's collar and cuffs, decided it was even more fun to unbutton those items on Tobias's shirt. After those accessories hit the floor, she made short work of the buttons down the front of his shirt. He shrugged it and his undershirt off. Then Genevieve, naked and oddly unembarrassed about it, was left with the prospect of revealing his amazingly hard masculinity.

She couldn't wait, but reached for his trouser buttons as if she were starving for what was concealed there. Tobias groaned and closed his eyes when she managed to unfasten the last button. It was a difficult task with his sex so large and pressing so tightly against the buttons.

Then she was suddenly stricken by a bout of nervousness. She dropped her hands and looked at him. They were both kneeling on the bed. The expression on Tobias's face told of the strain he was under. She licked her lips. He groaned again.

She said, "Um, perhaps you should take it from here, since you know what to do and I don't."

He nodded. Genevieve wasn't sure he could still speak. He ripped his drawers off in a split second, and she was left to stare in astonishment. Good heavens, he was so extremely large. She began to have some doubts about this whole process. She lifted her head and looked him in the eye, knowing her own eyes reflected her uncertainty.

His smile was tenderness itself. "Don't be afraid, Genevieve. People have been doing this since the beginning of time. If they hadn't—or if one sex didn't enjoy it—no doubt the human race would have died out long before this."

She smiled, too. "You're right, of course. It's only that—that . . ." Since she didn't know how to express herself, she decided not to.

Tobias understood. She might have known he would.

"It's only that it's all new to you. But I'll be as gentle as I know how to be. We're going to have years to refine this, you know, so don't worry too much if we're not perfect the first time."

"You mean you'll forgive me?"

"Forgive you? For what? For being innocent? Don't be a goose, darling."

Darling. He'd called her darling. And he was smiling at her so sweetly. Tears filled Genevieve's eyes and she felt foolish.

Tobias read those tears in entirely the wrong way. "What is it, love?" He reached out and nudged her chin up. "Are you too frightened? If you're too frightened, we can wait." He gritted his teeth and looked like he might not survive, but Genevieve knew he meant it, and she loved him all the more for it.

She shook her head. "No, Tobias. I want to. It's only that you're so kind, and I'm a little bit nervous. I know you'll take care of me."

"I will. You can be sure of it. For the rest of my life. Taking care of you—and our children, should we be fortunate enough to have any—will be my chief aim in life."

"I love you."

"And I you."

And, since she'd been doing it all day long and figured she might as well continue a successful practice, Genevieve threw herself into his arms again. Laughing, Tobias fell backward on the bed and held her tightly. Then he rolled over so that his body almost covered hers, and kissed her hard. Genevieve knew there was no going back now. She didn't want to go back. She was entering a new and exciting phase in her life, and she was eager to begin.

His hands were skillful, and they played her body as if she were a rare and precious instrument. She responded like one, too. In fact, it seemed to her that he was making magic with her body. New and wonderful sensations danced within and without, nearly dazzling her.

She'd had no idea how many places on one's body could be kissed, but Tobias didn't spare an inch of hers that day. He kissed every rounded millimeter of her flesh, murmuring words of love and passion the whole time. Genevieve, who tried very hard to keep her wits about her because she didn't want to miss anything, soon discovered that things were moving too fast. Every time she paused to relish one sensation, he created another one somewhere else. It wasn't long before she gave up even trying to savor any one individual marvel, because the whole experience overwhelmed her senses.

When he finally lay beside her and took her in his arms, her brain had been rendered useless. Her body was reacting on instinct by that time. She moaned softly when his skillful hands gently stroked the inside of her thigh. When he cupped the curls hiding her femininity, she gasped with pleasure. Her pleasure only increased when he gently probed her moistness.

"Tobias!" she cried when one of his fingers dipped inside her.

"Does that feel good, darling?" He had found the erect nubbin of her pleasure, and Genevieve hissed with astonishment and delight.

"Good?" she gasped. "What a ridiculous question, Tobias."

He gave out with one of his low, dark chuckles that feathered over Genevieve's senses like velvet. She sank back against the pillows, and gave herself up to whatever it was he was doing to her. It was exquisite. She'd been taught that a proper young lady never even looked at her naked flesh, much less touched it, and for years and years she'd believed it. She'd even wondered, from time to time, if there were something wrong with her when she felt certain intimate cravings. Now she knew exactly what those cravings meant and that there was nothing wrong with her at all.

She also understood what all the tittle-tattle was about.

This was what the old cats, piling euphemism upon euphemism, had been warning against. *This* was the great, titillating secret married ladies whispered about behind fans and cupped hands.

Well, Genevieve thought, as the pressure inside her built up until she feared she might explode, perhaps they were right. This was too great a phenomenon to take lightly. She felt privileged to be sharing it with the man she loved.

Then, out of the blue, her climax came. Genevieve's thoughts scattered to the winds, and she convulsed under Tobias's gentle touch.

"Beautiful," he murmured. "Beautiful." And he kissed her while she tried to recover her senses. It took a while.

"Oh, Tobias."

"Yes?"

"That was—that was—" It was what? Spectacular? Splendid? Incredible? All of those things and more. "That was wonderful." Inadequate, but Genevieve felt unequal to the task of describing it satisfactorily. Her eyelids fluttered open, and she found Tobias watching her, a gorgeous smile playing on his lips. "Thank you."

"Thank *you,* love." And he kissed her again.

This time he didn't stop, but lifted himself over her until he was poised on his knees above her. She suspected what was going to happen next, and she wasn't disappointed. With gentle force, he entered her, stretching her tight passage with his sex. Genevieve, feeling full of love and a heightened sense of adventure, lifted her hips to help him along.

With a feral groan, Tobias gave up on gentleness and thrust home, plunging past her maidenhood and filling her completely. Genevieve sighed. She'd heard women whisper about the duties of the marriage bed, often with distaste, and she was pleased to learn that she would never be one of those old biddies. This was a pure pleasure. She also knew, because she was a bright girl who paid attention to things, that it would only hurt this first time. And, in truth, it didn't hurt much.

"Are you all right?" Tobias's voice was ragged.

"Oh, yes." Genevieve hoped her own voice conveyed her absolute happiness.

"Thank God." He sank down on her for a moment, then lifted himself again.

Genevieve noticed, not for the first time, but from an entirely different perspective, that the arms propping up his hard, muscular body were hard and muscular, too. His body thrilled her, and she ran her hands over his biceps, marveling at the sculpted beauty of him. Then he moved, and she gasped again, this time from a renewal of that pleasure he'd lately stroked to fulfillment in her.

Merciful heavens! Was it possible to experience such a thing twice in one bedding? Her eyes popped wide open and she found Tobias grinning down at her. She thought that a god on Mount Olympus might have that same wickedly sensual expression on his face when he cavorted with a nymph. She liked thinking of herself as a nymph. She liked thinking of Tobias as a god. In fact, she discovered, she liked everything about this experience.

Tobias seemed to have gone past some barrier of control by this time. His strokes, slow at first, became faster. Genevieve met his every thrust with a lift of her hips, her own sensation of pleasure building every time their bodies met. The heat was intense. They were both dewy with perspiration. The pure animal nature of lovemaking was arousing to Genevieve, and she gloried in it.

And then it happened again. Tobias drove her to a pinnacle where she feared she would either come to completion or die, and then he drove her over the edge into ecstasy. She was so surprised this time that she cried out.

With a growl of primitive male lust, Tobias's own release came. Genevieve felt his seed spill into her, and she knew true fulfillment. She was his now, and always would be. The sensation was so incredible that, in spite of herself, she burst into tears.

Tobias was panting like a racehorse when he collapsed at Genevieve's side. He'd not been particularly celibate in his active life, but he'd never, not once, ever, experienced sex quite like what he'd just had with Genevieve. She was magnificent. She was superlative. She was stunning. She was spectacular.

Hell's bells, she was crying.

"Genevieve! Genevieve, what's wrong? Oh, Lord, darling, please don't cry. Did I hurt you?"

"Oh, Tobias!"

And, for what seemed like the thousandth time that day, she flung herself at him. Tobias grunted. He was so weak from his recent sexual escapade that he couldn't stop himself from rolling over onto his back, Genevieve propelling him. She splayed her breathtaking body on his like butter on a hot biscuit, and he couldn't help it; he laughed. For what was probably the first time in his entire life, he laughed with pure, absolute joy. Lord, he loved this woman!

"Oh, Tobias, that was so wonderful. I never expected it to be so wonderful."

He had to kiss her for that, so he did, holding her sweet face in his hands, and kissing her with all the love in his heart. She was his precious jewel. His wonderful one. The one woman in the world who was right for him. He hadn't believed she existed on earth—and to think she'd been here in Bittersweet all the time. She was even here when he was going through the first follies of youth and antagonizing his blasted Yankee father.

Of course, back then, he wouldn't have noticed her if she'd suddenly stripped naked and danced in front of him, because he'd been so besotted with Madeline Riley. Life was a strange bird, he guessed, and things happened when they were supposed to happen.

Thank God Genevieve had happened into his scope when he needed her the most. His life had sunk into a well of darkness and depression, and she'd bounded in and lit it up. Like a skyrocket, was Genevieve Crowfoot. Soon to be Genevieve Rakes.

Because he was the man and supposed to be the experienced one in this activity, he rolled her onto her back and continued kissing her until they both had to come up for air.

"I love you, Tobias." She stroked his cheek as if he were precious to her.

Damn. If she kept doing that, he might just cry himself. Because he wouldn't allow himself to do anything so embarrassing, he turned his head and kissed her hand. "And I love you, Genevieve. More than I ever thought it was possible to love someone." Should he have said that? Well, no matter. He'd said it, and that was that. It was also the truth.

She sighed. It sounded like an extremely satisfied sigh. Tobias considered all the physical problems he'd experienced in the last year and was really quite pleased with himself. He could still make a woman happy, anyway. And he'd never wanted to make any woman happier than he wanted to make Genevieve.

His leg, however, was about to give out on him. Believing it would be more to his credit to cease putting pressure on it than to collapse onto Genevieve—although such a prospect held a certain undeniable appeal—he lowered himself to her side again. "When do you want to get married, Genevieve? I vote for sooner rather than later." He turned his head and grinned wickedly. "Especially now."

She blushed. What a darling she was. "I'd like that, Tobias."

"I suppose we'll have to break the news to the resident ghost, too. Should we do it at the same time we tell her the bad news about her father, do you think?"

"That might be too cruel for one telling." She giggled, and Tobias actually felt a stirring in his groin. Good grief; the woman was amazing. "Perhaps we should split the news in half."

"You're probably right." Her body was gorgeous. Tobias supposed it wasn't any more gorgeous than a couple of others he'd had to do with in his life, but he loved it, and that made it special. This was Genevieve's body, and it was now his, too. As his body was hers to do with whatever she pleased. Tobias had a jolly feeling that she'd probably be pleased to do all sorts of things once he'd taught them to her.

His groin stirred more forcefully. He supposed he'd better stop thinking those thoughts. Although he was game for just about anything—hell, he'd just as soon spend the rest of the month in bed with Genevieve—this had been her first time, and she was probably feeling tender.

She heaved a big sigh that lifted her perfect breasts. Tobias was fascinated. "Well, I suppose we should get dressed and go find her. We ought to get at least one difficult task out of the way today, don't you think?"

He sighed, too. "I suppose so."

"I vote for telling her about her father first. Then the news about our marriage won't be so shocking to her."

"You think not, do you?" He lifted his left eyebrow.

She giggled again, and Tobias couldn't help but laugh. "I suppose that's merely wishful thinking on my part, but I do believe we ought to tell her about her father first. After all, she deserves to know."

"She deserves to know, all right. I'm almost looking forward to telling her, she's made our lives so uncomfortable."

"She's done that, all right."

"Maybe she'll be so upset, she'll go away and leave us alone."

"Maybe." She didn't sound very hopeful. Tobias wasn't very hopeful, either. Granny Crowfoot was too cantankerous to be that nice.

He didn't want to get up. He wanted to put his arms around Genevieve and sleep for a while, then wake up and make slow, lazy love. He wondered if she'd be shocked if he showed her some of the other things one could do with one's mouth, and decided perhaps he should wait until they were married. After all, she was a total innocent—had been a total innocent, at any rate—and although she seemed to have taken to sex with remarkable enthusiasm, he didn't want to shock her. With a smile, he realized there would be years and years to teach her things. Hell, after a while, she'd probably be teaching him things. She was a clever girl, his Genevieve.

When he turned his head to look at her again, she was watching him with an expression on her face that he wished he could have an artist render on canvas. "Are there any good artists in New York at the moment? Is Whistler here, or is he still in Europe?"

She blinked. "I don't know. What an odd question to ask at a time like this." She laughed out loud.

Her laugh was infectious, and he laughed, too. "It's not odd at all," he said when he could. "I want the best artist in the world to paint you, Genevieve. Then I'm going to put your portrait up in the entryway for everyone to see."

"Oh, Tobias, what a sweet thing to say."

"It's the truth."

"All right, but I think you ought to get our portraits painted together. As a family—sort of."

He thought about it and nodded. "I like that idea. Then, after the children start coming, we'll have other portraits painted, like those English aristocrats do. Hell, we can hang family portraits all over the place. Lord knows, it's big enough for a hundred portraits. And pets. We'll have to get the kids pets. Dogs and cats and things. I never had a pet. My father didn't allow dogs in the house."

"The monster!"

He thought she was serious until he glanced at her again. He grinned, answering her teasing grin. "Well, he was a hard old cuss."

"Yes, so I've heard." She heaved a big sigh and pushed herself to a seated position. "I need to wash up."

He sighed, too. He didn't want her to wash up. He wanted her to lie back down and sleep with him. Maybe tonight. He pushed himself up and sat next to her. "I suppose I should, too. The servants will start to talk if we don't show up again soon, I guess."

"I guess."

"Then I suppose we ought to go searching for Granny Crowfoot and get that over with."

"I suppose so."

So they did. Tobias helped Genevieve to her feet and hovered over her until he was sure she was all right. She washed up first, and he helped her back into her clothes.

As he buttoned up her bodice in front—enjoying the task almost as much as he'd enjoyed unbuttoning it—he said, "You'd better sneak out first. I'll meet you in the entryway, and we can go off in search of our resident hobgoblin."

"All right." When her bodice was buttoned, she looked at herself in Tobias's dressing-table mirror. "Good heavens, what did you do to my hair?"

"Not as much as I'd like to do with it."

She laughed. Little did she know. He watched while she brushed it out and wrapped it up in a bun again, contemplating the many ways he'd like to see her hair. Most of them included its being spread out on his pillow, although he decided he'd like to see it pouring over her shoulder and over her breasts, too. Then she stepped up to him, deposited a little kiss on his cheek, and took off before he could grab her back again. She blew him a kiss from the door and left. He felt bereft.

His leg was a little sore, but Tobias didn't dwell too much on the matter. It had held him up during the important parts, and that's what counted. As he poured more water into the porcelain basin, he grinned and wondered how long it would take his leg to get back into shape now that Genevieve was helping his cause along. He didn't anticipate it taking very long at all.

He didn't linger over his ablutions. Nor did he linger over dressing, although his feet objected to being shoved into shoes because of his blisters. It wasn't until he felt those blisters, in fact, that he recalled that someone had attempted to kill him earlier in the day.

"Damn." Life had seemed very sweet there for an hour or two, in Genevieve's arms. He should have known it wouldn't last.

He made up the bed, thanking his stars for his military training, and wished he hadn't remembered the blasted gunshot. Although nothing could completely drive away his happiness, Tobias felt somewhat subdued when he left his room. He cast one wistful glance back at the bed, thinking how nice life would be when he and Genevieve didn't have to hide the evidence of their love from the servants. Then he set out for the great flagged entryway in search of Genevieve.

She was there already. Tobias paused on the landing to watch her arranging a bouquet of roses in a crystal vase. His heart filled with amazement that she had agreed to marry

him. It didn't seem possible that someone as priceless as
Genevieve Crowfoot could want him. Yet she did. He knew
she did, or she'd never have made love with him.

Phenomenal. The whole thing was phenomenal. All in all,
when Tobias thought about it as he watched her, he decided
that Genevieve Crowfoot loving him was even more astonishing than meeting Granny Crowfoot. Hell, lots of people
claimed to have seen ghosts. There was only one man in the
entire world who could have Genevieve—and he was the
one. Until this minute, he'd never considered himself a particularly lucky man.

He looked around and saw no one else in the entryway,
so he clumped down the rest of the stairs. "Those roses are
almost as pretty as you are."

She turned and smiled at him. He was about to throw
caution to the wind and catch her in his arms when the
knocker sounded on the front door. Genevieve, who obviously hadn't expected it any more than Tobias had, jumped
and spun around, pressing a hand to her heart.

"Good heavens!"

Tobias didn't blame her for being startled. The damned
thing sounded like a bomb blast in the echoey old hallway.
However, it wouldn't echo so much once he had portraits of
his wife and children hung up all over the walls. With that
happy thought in his mind, he said, "I'll get it." And he
did.

He swung the huge oaken door open, revealing Wesley
Armitage, who looked almost as startled as Genevieve had.
His mouth fell open and he blinked at Tobias for several
seconds. Although Tobias wasn't thrilled to see him—it
seemed to him that Armitage almost lived at the castle these
days—he smiled. He wondered why Armitage looked so surprised, but didn't ask. Armitage was an odd duck, and that's
all there was to it.

"Tobias!" The lawyer sounded as astonished as he
looked.

"You were expecting someone else?" Tobias stepped
back and gestured for Armitage to enter the castle.

"Someone else? Oh! Oh, no. No. Of course not. I—I—

er—was only surprised to find you opening your own door,
is all."

"I'm sorry, sir."

This was a new voice, and it sounded almost as nervous
as Armitage's. When Tobias turned, he saw poor Godfrey
standing behind him, wringing his hands.

"I didn't know you were here, sir. You shouldn't have to
open your own door, sir. I'm sorry I didn't run faster, sir."

Good Lord, the poor boy was a wreck. Tobias shook his
head. "It's all right, Godfrey. You can't be everywhere at
once, and I was standing right here when Mr. Armitage
knocked. It's truly no trouble for me to open my own door.
Really, it isn't."

Genevieve uttered a strangled giggle. Tobias glanced at
her, and got such a significant look back that he almost giggled himself.

"Thank you, sir."

Now Godfrey looked like he might cry with relief. Tobias
sighed. His staff was really something. Someday he'd ask
Genevieve why she'd selected them. He turned to Armitage.
"Well, come in, Wes. No sense standing out there with your
mouth hanging open just because a man decided to open the
door to his own house. Come in, come in. You brought by
some papers earlier, didn't you?"

Armitage jerked, as if Tobias's words had called him back
to the here and now, and made a lurching step into the hallway. Tobias and Genevieve exchanged another look behind
the lawyer's back.

"Papers?" Armitage sucked in a deep breath. Tobias wondered if the man had been frightened in his mother's womb,
or if he'd developed his nervous disposition after birth.
Maybe his mother was an Amazon like Mrs. Watkins. That
might explain it. "Oh, yes, the papers." He looked at Godfrey, withdrew a handkerchief from his breast pocket, and
wiped his forehead. "Did you set those papers aside as I
asked you to, Godfrey?"

The butler, too, was as fidgety as a spooked cat. Tobias
guessed life in the civilized East didn't sufficiently prepare
folks for real problems, so they had to make do with little,

inconsequential ones. He couldn't recall ever being as temperamental as these two men. Then again, he'd been dodging arrows for several years, and that experience rather took the excitement out of a normal life filled with papers and butlers.

"Yes, sir. Yes, I did. Yes, I set them aside when you asked me to, sir. Mr. Armitage. Sir. And Miss Crowfoot took them to the library."

Tobias again glanced at Genevieve, who grinned back and shrugged her shoulders as if to say she didn't understand it, either. "When you're free, Mr. Rakes," she said, "perhaps we can discuss that other matter we need to talk about."

The matter in question being, of course, Granny Crowfoot. Tobias realized she was right; there would be no searching out the old ghost now. He'd have to deal with Armitage first. "Thank you, Miss Crowfoot. I don't believe my business with Wes will take very long. Perhaps you can visit me in the library in—forty-five minutes?" He lifted his left eyebrow at Armitage, who jumped again. Tobias sighed.

"Oh! Oh, certainly. Forty-five minutes should be quite sufficient." Armitage bobbed his head at Tobias and bowed at Genevieve. She smiled at him and sailed off to do whatever wonderful thing she needed to do.

Tobias watched her go, and wished Armitage possessed better timing. However, that was neither here nor there. He smiled at his attorney. "Well, Wes, let's go to the library and take care of—what are we taking care of today?"

"Ah, I brought those papers earlier."

"Of course," Tobias murmured. "How could I forget the papers?"

"One of them needs to be signed."

"I see."

So he led the way to his library, Armitage following him like a tame puppy. A skittish tame puppy. Which reminded him that he needed to discuss with Genevieve what kinds of dogs she liked. Tobias had always favored hounds, but he'd be happy to get Genevieve a different kind of dog if she wanted one. Hell, he'd even buy her a French poodle or one of those silly looking Pomeranian things—even a pug—if that's what she wanted. Or even a cat. Since Tobias had never cared much for cats, he figured love was warping his brain. And he didn't mind one little bit. He gestured Armitage into a chair, and he sat in the one behind his desk.

"All right, Wes. What do I have to sign today?"

"Let me get it out here, Tobias. It's just a check to Golden's Livestock and Seed Store for horse fodder."

"Very well." Tobias read the paper over, picked up his pen, dipped it in the inkwell, and signed on the line Armitage indicated. As he handed the paper back, he decided he might as well tell the lawyer his good news. After all, if he was going to take on the responsibilities of a family man, he imagined he'd have to do things. Write a will. Start a college fund. Things like that. The notion of a family gave him a soft, gooey feeling in his middle. Since he'd never considered marriage before he met Genevieve—well, not since his idiotic elopement with Madeline Riley—he hadn't anticipated that feeling. It made him smile.

Armitage evidently noticed his smile—and it must have been a particularly sappy one—because the lawyer eyed him oddly. "Are you all right, Tobias? Is everything well with you?"

"Everything's wonderful, Wes." Except for someone trying to kill him—but he didn't want to think about that now. "Everything's better than it's ever been, in fact." The lawyer's smile appeared tentative. But then, everything about Armitage struck Tobias as relatively tentative.

"I'm glad to hear it. How's your leg?"

"My leg is almost as good as new now, thank you, Wes." And it had performed manfully today. Tobias's whole insides smiled, thinking about his delicious afternoon in Genevieve's arms.

"Good. Good. I'm glad to hear it." Armitage began tapping papers together into a neat stack. He stuffed them into the leather satchel he always carried.

"I do, however, have some news that you need to know, Wes. It's going to change everything."

Armitage stopped tapping and stuffing and looked up, his eyes wide. "Oh?"

"Indeed." Tobias grinned the widest grin he had in him. "Genevieve Crowfoot has agreed to marry me."

Armitage dropped his satchel.

Chapter
Sixteen

After Wesley Armitage left the castle—tottering like an old man and looking like he might faint dead away, according to a puzzled Tobias—he and Genevieve searched the castle high and low. They called as loudly as they dared—they didn't fancy being thought mad by the household staff—but they couldn't find Granny Crowfoot anywhere.

Genevieve decided it was just like the contrary old crone to hide when they needed her. Yet they searched from attic to cellar, and nary a sign of the troublesome ghost did they see. Genevieve batted a cobweb away from her face. She hadn't been in the castle cellar since before Tobias had moved in, and she wasn't altogether pleased by the state of it.

"I know this place is only used for storage, but I really do think Mrs. Watkins could get a girl to sweep the cobwebs down, don't you?"

Tobias grabbed her by the waist and swung her around and into his arms. "I love the cobwebs, darling. They give the place atmosphere."

He kissed her deeply, his tongue tasting how wonderfully sweet she was. If the cellar had been a shade less cobwebby, Genevieve might have succumbed to another bout of lovemaking then and there. As she wasn't eager to get filthy, however, she didn't allow the kiss to go too far.

When she came up for air, Genevieve frowned and grumbled, "I suspect the 'atmosphere,' as you call it, is why no one comes down here with a broom. They're all afraid of the ghost. Which is silly, of course. We're the only ones who've seen her, as far as I know, and we're not afraid of her."

Tobias chuckled. "I don't blame them. It's easier to be frightened of something you only suspect than of something you've seen and argued with."

"I'm not sure about that," she muttered, thinking of that gunshot earlier in the day. Since she didn't want to worry him, she didn't mention it.

He ran his finger over a bottle of wine that looked as if it might have been bottled and tucked away down here in Charles Crowfoot's day. His finger came away coated with dust, and he brushed his hands together to get it off. "Whew."

Genevieve pondered what they should do now. They really did need to break the news about old Charles Crowfoot to Granny Crowfoot, but it was probably more important to tell the world that the Crowfoot-Rakes feud was about to come to a spectacular—as well as permanent and peaceful—conclusion. Perhaps that might make whoever was perpetrating the assaults on Tobias cease and desist. She made a decision.

"Tobias, I think we should give up looking for Granny Crowfoot today. She's obviously still in a temper and is hiding from us. I think we should go to town and begin spreading the news of our engagement."

He smiled as if she'd just offered him the moon. "What a splendid idea. I think I'll take out an ad in the *Bittersweet Journal.*" He spread his hands out, as if to show her a display. "Tobias Rakes redeemed at last."

She smacked him lightly on the arm. "Don't be silly. What do you have to be redeemed from?"

"Life. It's been rough on me, Genevieve. You're the first good thing to happen to me in twenty years or more."

"Oh, Tobias!" If he wasn't the sweetest thing in the

world, she didn't know what was. She had to kiss him for it. When she'd done a thorough enough job, she stepped away from him. He looked disappointed. "However, I think we should begin with Aunt Delilah. She's my only relative in Bittersweet, and it will save us a good deal of time."

"How so?"

Obviously, Tobias hadn't lived in Bittersweet long enough to know that Delilah and her friend Mildred Hotchkiss were the two most fervent gossips in town. "Just trust me, Tobias. If we tell Delilah first, not only will we be adhering to polite convention, but it will save us a lot of announcing."

"Ah. I see." He nodded and gestured her toward the staircase. "I'll have Small William hitch the horse to the surrey."

"I don't mind walking."

"You may not mind walking, but I've had my fill of walking today, thank you. My blisters would prefer a ride."

She laughed. "I'd forgotten all about your blisters. It seems so long ago." Recalling how he'd come by those blisters sobered her. "Oh, Tobias, I hope this will put an end to those awful attacks."

"I do, too."

So, while Tobias went outside to get the surrey ready, Genevieve trotted upstairs, donned a fresh, day dress, popped a pretty flowered hat on her head, and joined Tobias on the massive front porch of the castle.

The summer sun gave the bricks a warm, golden patina that appealed to something deep in Genevieve's soul. She took Tobias by the arm and he helped her into the surrey. Then she gazed at the castle. The full implications of her marrying Tobias hit her, and she grew misty-eyed for a moment.

Crowfoot Castle was going to remain in the family. And the feud that had smoldered for over a hundred years would finally be rendered extinct. She couldn't recall another time in her life when she'd been this happy. If only Tobias and his father could be reconciled, Genevieve thought her life might be complete. Well, and if Delilah would forget about being afraid of ghosts and actually enter the castle again.

Delilah was a sweet woman with a good heart, and Genevieve missed her companionship.

"I'm taking you to the jeweler in Bittersweet, Genevieve my love. We're going to pick out wedding rings—if they have such items available."

She beamed at him as he clucked to the horse and they set off down the drive. "What a wonderful idea, Tobias. I do believe we should give all of our business to Bittersweet merchants. And invite the whole town to the wedding."

He lifted that eyebrow of his. Genevieve wanted to hug him, but didn't, since he was driving.

"The whole town?" He didn't sound exactly elated by her suggestion.

Because she knew her neighbors, she nodded. "The more you associate with them, the more they're liable to forget about the feud."

He heaved a sigh that Genevieve judged wasn't entirely in jest. "I suppose you're right. I'm glad you know everyone so well, my love, because I'd forgotten about how things are carried on back here."

She sat up straight and folded her hands in her lap. "I'll be more than happy to teach you, Tobias. We can perpetrate an exchange of information."

"Oh?" His eyebrow lifted higher. "Tit for tat?"

He didn't know how right he was. Because she'd been reared to be a proper lady, although she was eager to learn how not to be one under certain circumstances, she lifted her own eyebrow at him. Then she waggled it suggestively and had the satisfaction of watching understanding strike. His right eyebrow rose to mimic the left, and his eyes opened wide. Then he grinned a grin Lewis Carroll's Cheshire cat would have been proud of. "What a brilliant idea, my love. Why didn't I think of that?"

"I have no idea."

"It will be my great pleasure to exchange knowledge with you, Genevieve. My *very* great pleasure. In fact, I can hardly wait to begin."

She could tell he was speaking the truth, because she saw the bulge growing in his trousers. Never having been so bold before, she blushed, and Tobias laughed. She thought the day couldn't get much brighter.

Delilah dropped the knitting she had been holding since she had stood up to greet Tobias and Genevieve and pressed her hands to her cheeks. "*Married?* You're really going to be *married?* Oh, my goodness." As if her knees couldn't hold her up under the weight of her astonishment, Delilah collapsed onto her favorite sofa and repeated, "Oh, my goodness. My goodness gracious sakes alive."

Genevieve wasn't sure she appreciated this reaction in her favorite aunt. She'd expected surprise, but she'd hoped for a little joy, too. Perhaps even a jot of excitement. "Yes, Aunt Delilah. Mr. Rakes asked me to marry him, I accepted, and we're going to be married as soon as may be. Aren't you happy for us?"

Delilah looked up at her niece with eyes that couldn't have gotten any wider if they'd tried. "Happy? Why—why—why—of course I'm happy for you, dear."

She wasn't either, and Genevieve could tell. Genevieve didn't appreciate her aunt's reaction a whit. Shooting a troubled frown at Tobias, she went to sit beside her aunt. She took up one of her aunt's hands and didn't like it that Delilah appeared apprehensive. "All right, Delilah, why do you not think Tobias and I should wed? If you mention that wretched feud, I believe I'll scream."

Tobias sat in a chair set beside the sofa. Delilah had plastered all the furniture with her hand-crocheted antimacassars. Genevieve hoped her aunt wouldn't crochet any for her and Tobias, but didn't hold out much hope. She gazed at Delilah, hoping to receive an answer to her question any year now.

Tobias said, "Don't pester your aunt, darling. I'm sure it will take lots of folks some time to adjust. After all, the Rakeses and the Crowfoots are supposed to hate each other, don't forget." He gave her a smile that made her glad she was already seated, because her own knees went watery.

"That's very true, Mr. Rakes." Delilah nodded vigorously. "Why, I was telling Mildred Hotchkiss this very day about how worried I am to have you living in that awful place, Genevieve."

Genevieve gritted her teeth. "It's not an awful place, Aunt Delilah. It's a beautiful castle, and Mr. Rakes is turning it into a splendid showcase of a house." Because she didn't want to give the impression that she cared more for splendor than domestic tranquility, she added, "An extremely comfortable and homey splendid showcase."

"I'm sure that's true, dear. Although—" Delilah cast an apprehensive glance at Tobias. "Although I'm sure I could never be tranquil knowing that horrible ghost is haunting the place."

"Granny Crowfoot doesn't bother us, Aunt."

"Well . . ."

Genevieve shot Tobias a look, and he didn't continue, although from the twinkle in his beautiful eyes, Genevieve didn't trust him to remain silent for long. "She doesn't." She thought of a brilliant addendum. "In truth, she can't."

"What do you mean, she can't?" Delilah gazed slantwise at Genevieve, as if she suspected her niece of prevaricating for some fell purpose—probably because she'd been possessed by a wicked ghost, Genevieve presumed.

She sighed, fearing this was going to be impossible, but knowing she had to try. After all, when she and Tobias began having children, a prospect that filled her with delight, she wanted them to know their great-aunt Delilah. "The ghost told us so herself, Delilah. She can't harm people. She can only make noises and pilfer things that aren't too heavy for her to lift."

From the skeptical look in her aunt's blue eyes, Genevieve knew she still didn't believe.

Tobias stuck his oar into the muddied waters. Genevieve blessed him for it. "It's the truth, Miss Crowfoot. The old ghost is a considerable bother, but she's never tried to hurt any of us. Not even me, whom she seems to regard with particular disfavor, although she doesn't seem to be very fond of anyone."

"Of course she wouldn't like you," Delilah said. "You're a Rakes."

Genevieve huffed. "That's another thing, Aunt Delilah. The family feud that has kept Bittersweet amused for over a hundred years is based upon a foundation of sand."

"I beg your pardon, dear?" Delilah blinked at Genevieve.

Genevieve wished she'd kept her mouth shut about that part. She and Tobias had already decided that the fair thing to do would be to tell Granny Crowfoot about her father's treachery before they broke the news to anyone else. The poor old ghost was liable to suffer a spasm, if ghosts did such things, and they felt it was only honorable that she be the first to know. Or the third, if one counted Genevieve and Tobias. "I'll tell you all about it later, Aunt Delilah. Tobias and I are going into town now, to visit Mr. Hanks."

"The jeweler?"

"Yes, indeed."

"Your niece and I are going to select wedding bands, Miss Crowfoot."

"Oh!" This time Delilah blinked at Tobias.

"I offered to buy her a diamond in New York City, but Genevieve wants me to spend my money in Bittersweet. She's a wise woman, Miss Crowfoot. You should be very proud of her."

"Oh, I am," Delilah assured him, although Genevieve noticed that her eyes appeared slightly unfocused.

"I'm sure you had a lot to do with turning her into the lovely woman she is today," Tobias continued. "She's extremely special, Miss Crowfoot."

"Oh, my, yes."

Genevieve hoped Tobias wouldn't lay it on too thick, or perhaps even Delilah might notice—although, it must be admitted, she thought it was awfully sweet of him to say such things about her. It was also unlikely that Delilah, who seldom looked beyond the surface of anything, would suspect Genevieve and Tobias of trying to persuade her. Genevieve was pleased to note that her aunt's expression seemed a trifle less unsettled.

She had another brilliant idea. "Would you like to come with us, dear? Your taste is so exquisite." She hoped Tobias wouldn't mind, but it was true about Delilah's taste. The woman had a knack for style. She also loved to shop. If anything could reconcile Delilah to her niece marrying a Rakes, Genevieve suspected shopping would be it. She looked hopefully at Tobias, who grinned at her, so that was all right. She did love him very much.

"Oh, but, Genevieve, I'm sure you want to be alone with your young man."

"Nonsense," Tobias said briskly. "We'd love to have you come along. The more we all appear in public together, the sooner people will become accustomed to the idea that they're going to have to find something other than the Crowfoot-Rakes feud to chatter about."

"How astute of you, Tobias." Genevieve nodded her approval, and got another one of his beautiful grins for her effort. Her heart sped up, and she hoped she wouldn't swoon. "Don't you think so, Aunt?"

Obviously, Delilah did not think so. She cast such a worried glance at Tobias that Genevieve wondered if the poor old soul feared he might try to overturn the surrey just to rid the world of another Crowfoot or two. Shaking her head, Genevieve began to despair of ever easing her aunt's mind about her upcoming nuptials.

Because she wanted to get started, she decided that if delicate persuasion didn't work, she'd try an ounce of blackmail and see what happened. She took Delilah's other hand in hers and stared deeply into her eyes. "Please come with us, Aunt Delilah. I'd feel so much better if you were to participate in my wedding plans. I always hoped you would, you know, since Mother and Father are no longer with us. You're my only relation in Bittersweet, after all." Although she feared it might be too much, she took out a handkerchief and delicately held it to her eyes. She drooped a bit on the sofa, trying her best to appear disconsolate. She'd softened more than one punishment meted out to Benton and herself by such tactics.

It worked. Although Tobias eyed her as if he suspected her of losing her mind, Delilah's own dear eyes filled with tears.

"Oh, Genevieve, please don't be sad. I didn't mean that

I'm not happy for you, dear. Of course I'll come with you. Just let me fetch my hat and shawl.''

Delilah popped up from the sofa and scurried off to do exactly that. Immediately Genevieve straightened and shot Tobias a look of triumph, only to find him shaking his head.

"I had no idea I was marrying an actress, Genevieve Crowfoot. You're good at that.''

"I know I am.'' She preened, got up, and walked over to the love of her life. He took the hand she held out to him and gently drew her down to sit on his lap.

"How will I know when you're telling me the truth, though? Will I always have to wonder if you really love me?''

Horrified, Genevieve threw her arms around his neck. "Tobias! How can you even ask me such a thing?''

He laughed and kissed her. Hard. They were still kissing when Delilah came back into the room. They wouldn't even have known she was there except that she let out a short, shocked "Oh!''

Genevieve jumped up from Tobias's lap at once, and Tobias surged to his feet. "I beg your pardon, Miss Crowfoot.''

Still looking scandalized, Delilah worked her mouth several times, but didn't speak.

Genevieve hung her head. "It's my fault, Aunt Delilah. I attacked him.''

Delilah gasped.

"Well,'' Genevieve expounded. "I didn't exactly attack him, but I did go over and sit on his lap.''

Delilah's lips pinched tightly together for a moment. After she'd stared at Genevieve and Tobias in extreme disapproval for several more seconds, she said, "I can only hope that you'll behave with more propriety in public, Genevieve Crowfoot. Your dear mother and father taught you manners. I trust association with a Rakes—I beg your pardon, Mr. Rakes, but I can't help but worry about these things—isn't going to ruin your character.''

"No such thing, Aunt Delilah. It's quite the other way around, I can assure you.''

Delilah was still thinking about that when Tobias handed

her into the surrey. It was a tight fit, but fit they did, and Genevieve felt as if she'd won a major battle when Tobias clicked to the horse, and they set off for town.

By the time they'd concluded their business in Bittersweet, Genevieve knew that reports of her upcoming marriage to a Rakes would soon be common knowledge in the small community. She also had come to the conclusion that, no matter how vague she sometimes was, and no matter how worried she was about Genevieve marrying a Rakes, Delilah Crowfoot was a brick.

The first person they encountered when Tobias drew the surrey up to the railing in front of Clarence T. Hanks, Fine Jewelers, was Mildred Hotchkiss. Mrs. Hotchkiss looked startled to see two Crowfoots and a Rakes sharing the same vehicle. The trio disembarked.

Her back as straight as a lance, Delilah looked her best friend in the eye and smiled as if she hadn't a qualm in the world about what she aimed to say. "Mildred, the most marvelous thing has happened. Genevieve and Mr. Rakes are going to marry!"

Mrs. Hotchkiss clapped her hands to her cheeks, much as Delilah had done not twenty minutes earlier. "Marry? They're going to *marry*?" She apparently realized she had an audience—and who the audience was—because she then turned beet red.

Genevieve took the arm Tobias crooked for her. "Indeed we are, Mrs. Hotchkiss. Isn't that splendid news?" Again drawing on her years of experience with Benton, she gave the old biddy a beaming smile that held not a trace of her own apprehension about how this news was going to be received.

"Mercy," Mrs. Hotchkiss said faintly.

"Mercy, my foot," Delilah said stoutly, sending a spurt of love and admiration through Genevieve. "This is the finest thing that could have happened, Mildred Hotchkiss, and you know it."

"I do?" Mrs. Hotchkiss stuck a hand out to grasp the hitching rail as if she needed its support or would faint dead away on the street.

"Of course you do." Delilah nodded firmly. "This alliance will lay to rest all the tittle-tattle once and for all."

"The tittle-tattle?"

"Yes. The tittle-tattle. Now we must be on about our business, Mildred. Genevieve and her dear young man are going to select wedding rings at Mr. Hanks's establishment." With one more decisive nod, Delilah marched onward, using her parasol as a cane and looking to Genevieve as if she aimed to skewer anyone who dared offer an objection to their purpose in visiting town that day.

Genevieve smiled kindly at Mrs. Hotchkiss. Tobias gave her an amiable nod and tipped his hat, and they sailed after Delilah, leaving Mrs. Hotchkiss to totter over to Mrs. Carvahal's bake shop. Genevieve trusted that she would have a cup of tea and a sweet to calm her nerves, and then begin to gossip.

She was happy to see that her trust seemed to be justified when they set out toward home again after having spent an hour in Mr. Hanks's shop selecting two lovely rings. Every single person they passed stared after them as if they'd been handed the juiciest bit of gossip the town had ever heard. Which might well be a fact. And at least this piece of gossip was the truth, unlike the hundred-year-old dollop that had started the wretched family feud.

"Won't you please reconsider dining at the castle this evening, Aunt Delilah? It's true that Molly Gratchett isn't the finest cook in the world, but Tobias and I would love to have you."

"That's the truth, Miss Crowfoot. We would both be honored if you'd join us for the evening's meal."

Genevieve thought Tobias was being awfully noble about this whole thing. When they were in town, she could tell he wasn't much of a shopper. And she knew good and well that he'd just as soon dine alone with Genevieve, because she felt the same way about him. But Delilah was Genevieve's closest surviving relation, and she wanted to celebrate with her family. She wished her mother and father could be there.

"Oh, dear." Delilah looked guilty. "I'm sorry, dear, but— but I just can't. I—I can't."

Disappointed, Genevieve asked, "You will come to our wedding, though, won't you, Aunt?" She couldn't stand the notion of not having any close family members at her wedding.

"Of course I'll come to your wedding. What do you take me for, Genevieve Crowfoot?"

"Even if we decide to hold the ceremony in the castle chapel?"

Delilah's indignation evaporated in a flurry of apprehension. "The castle chapel? Why ever would you do something like that? You're going to hold the ceremony at the church, aren't you?"

Neither Genevieve nor Tobias said anything.

"Aren't you?" Delilah began chewing on her lip. "Oh, but you must, Genevieve. It's—it's family tradition."

"Is it?" Genevieve eyed her aunt slantwise. "I'd never heard that."

"Oh, but of course it is."

Genevieve chuffed impatiently, wishing her aunt would overcome her aversion to Granny Crowfoot. Although, it must be admitted, Granny Crowfoot did take some getting used to. "Even if we do hold the ceremony in the church, we'll have the reception at the castle, and you *have* to attend the reception, Aunt Delilah. In fact, I want you to be my maid of honor."

Delilah perked up immediately. "Why, how sweet you are, my dear. I'll be proud to be your maid of honor, and of course I'll attend the reception. As long as I don't have to go inside that place."

Tobias chuckled as he drew the horse up to the cottage door and Genevieve gave up trying to convince Aunt Delilah for the time being.

The two lovers made one last search for the recalcitrant spirit of Crowfoot Castle before they took dinner that evening. No Granny Crowfoot.

"You know," Tobias told Genevieve, "life really is rather

pleasant without that old ghost constantly popping up and annoying one.''

Genevieve shot a glance around the dining room, hoping none of the servants were there to hear. None were. ''I must agree with you, although I wish she would show up this time.''

With a chuckle, Tobias raised his wine glass. ''I'm sure she's hiding because she knows we want to talk to her. If she thought we didn't want to see her, she'd be here in a flash.''

Recalling the way Granny Crowfoot seemed to flash around when she was peeved, Genevieve couldn't fault Tobias for his wording.

They slept together that night. Genevieve knew such behavior was shocking—perhaps even the tiniest bit immoral—but she had a hard time caring when Tobias crept into her room after the rest of the castle was asleep. She loved him so much, and he loved her so much, that what they did didn't seem sinful at all.

''I shouldn't be doing this, you know.'' He was standing at the foot of her bed, holding a brass candlestick and looking anxious, as if he expected a contingent of morally outraged Bittersweet citizens to burst into Genevieve's room any second.

''Nonsense. We shall be married soon. Besides, no one except Mrs. Watkins and Godfrey and us sleep in the castle.''

His expression lightened considerably. ''Good point.'' He set the candle down and dove into the bed, where he proceeded to make Genevieve feel even better than he had that afternoon. The physical expression of love truly was quite thrilling. And here she'd believed she could live without it. Silly Genevieve.

''I hadn't expected making love to feel so good, Tobias. I'm awfully glad you've taught me better.''

Tobias looked pleased with himself, and Genevieve was interested to note that even the most wonderful man in the world could suffer from an attack of pride occasionally. She

stroked his damp chest, loving the feel of his soft thatch of
hair. He stroked her damp chest as well, and she got the
distinct impression he was as delighted with her as she was
with him.

Sated and happy, Genevieve was just drifting off to sleep
when she felt a cold blast of air, like an icy winter wind—
or perhaps an icy winter hurricane—shoot through the bedroom. She sat up with a start, covering her naked bosom
with the sheet.

Next to her, Tobias grunted sleepily. "What's that?"

Genevieve was about to answer him when Granny Crowfoot spared her the effort.

"*I am what* that *is, you young scoundrel. And what exactly
are you doing in my great-great-great-niece's bed?*"

Tobias sat up with a start, blinked at the ghost, then sank
back against the pillows and groaned.

Chapter
Seventeen

"I have never been so scandalized in my life!"

Granny Crowfoot had stopped rocketing around Genevieve's bedroom, although she still looked stormy. Tobias had risen from the bed and put his robe back on. He was very tired of the ghost's theatrical displays. Not only did he consider such nonsense undignified, but when Granny Crowfoot shot through his body, it was uncomfortable and felt like a sharp, icy arrow. He snapped, "You're not alive."

"Don't nitpick with me, you beastly lout. Your behavior is outrageous."

"Don't call Tobias a lout, Granny Crowfoot. It's not nice."

The ghost snorted with what sounded like utter contempt.

"Besides, we're going to be married soon." Genevieve held out a hand in a placating gesture. Granny Crowfoot looked at her hand as if it were something loathsome and slimy.

"I can't believe a relative of mine could behave in such a vulgar, wicked way. Never has a Crowfoot female fallen so low, Genevieve Crowfoot. Never! First you deign to work for this horrible Rakes villain, and then you succumb to his

vicious lures. Shocking! The licentiousness of modern-day youth is perfectly sordid!''

Genevieve cast a beseeching glance at Tobias, who shrugged to let her know that he didn't know what to say, either. If the old crone wouldn't accept the fact that they loved each other and were going to be married soon—and had elected not to wait until after the vows were said in order to get things started—there wasn't much either of them could do about it now.

Except, perhaps, to divert the old bat's mind, if the transparent mass of cheese between her ears could be called a mind. He cleared his throat. "Miss Crowfoot, Genevieve and I have something of vital importance to discuss with you."

Genevieve sagged with relief and shot him a glance that told him so. "Oh, yes, that's right. Er, perhaps you should try to calm yourself, Granny Crowfoot. I fear the news will come as a great shock."

The ghost puffed herself up until she filled the room from the bed to the fireplace. Tobias had to jump out of her way or be subsumed by her freezing vapor. Lord, he hoped the ghost would go away soon. He was really tired of this sort of thing.

"If there is anything more shocking than discovering the two of you sharing a bed, I'd like to know what it is.''

"Good," Tobias said sourly. "Because we're going to tell you now."

Genevieve, who had been trying unsuccessfully to hide under the covers, said, "Do you think we should do it here, Tobias?" She cast a significant glance at the Chinese vase filled with roses sitting on her dressing table. A framed photograph of her parents resided there, too, as well as Genevieve's brush and comb and a pretty, enameled hand mirror. Tobias understood. She didn't want the ghost to go on another rampage and start hurling those items around.

"Ah, yes." He thought, frowning, for a moment, then decided that even if the demented old thing threw a fit of monumental proportions, she'd only be damaging papers if she did it in her father's secret office. He had a pretty good notion she'd demand to see proof, too, and it was all up there.

"Perhaps we should go upstairs." He lifted his eyebrow at Genevieve, who nodded.

"Good idea." She looked disconcerted for a moment. Then she blushed. "Er, I have to get something on."

"*Scandalous!*" the ghost cried.

Tobias didn't consider Genevieve's nudity scandalous; he considered it wonderful. He deemed it prudent not to say so aloud with Granny Crowfoot nearby. He did, however, mutter, "Nuts." He walked to the bed, plucking Genevieve's silk robe from the back of her dressing chair on the way, and handed it to her.

She murmured, "Thank you," and wiggled herself into the robe while still under the covers.

Tobias longed for the day when he could watch her climb out of bed, buck naked, and wrap that robe around herself. Or, better yet, not wrap it around herself at all. Genevieve gave him a pleasant glimpse of her shapely legs when she finally shoved the covers aside and climbed out of the bed. All too soon, the robe fell down to conceal those legs again. He sighed.

"All right, I'm ready now." Genevieve pulled her pretty hair away from her face and flung it back with her hands. "Let me tie my hair up first."

Tobias didn't want her to do that, either, but he didn't object. He'd delighted in tonight's romp in her bed. The sight of her hair spread out against her virginal white pillowcase had been a very arousing one, and it was one he hoped to see again soon. And often.

The ghost hovered around them as they ascended the staircase to the castle attic, muttering and complaining and scolding all the way. Tobias led the way, carrying a kerosene lantern. "I'll be glad when we get gas and electricity hooked up in this old tomb, so we can have some decent light in here."

"*This is my home, young man, and it is assuredly not an old tomb.*" Granny Crowfoot sniffed with disdain.

"No? It certainly seems to be your tomb. Ow!" He frowned at Genevieve, who'd smacked him smartly on the arm. "Well, it does."

"Don't be absurd, you loathsome, heathen Rakes. My tomb is alongside that of my parents in the Crowfoot family cemetery, and you know it."

"I wish you'd stayed there." Tobias yanked his arm out of Genevieve's range before she could smack him again.

"My bones are there, young man. It is only my spirit that wanders. All the Crowfoots are buried there in the family plot." Granny Crowfoot lifted her head and struck a noble pose.

Tobias had the fleeting wish that she were only a shade more solid. He'd delight in knocking her off her pedestal. "Personally, I think it's way past time your spirit and your bones got back together again."

Granny Crowfoot sniffed disdainfully. *"Gas piping is a ridiculous modern invention."*

"A lot you know about it. Anyway, you ought to love gas since you're so full of it."

"How dare you!"

Since her target had moved and she couldn't whack his arm anymore, Genevieve tried to change the subject. "Families aren't permitted to bury their deceased in family plots any longer, Granny Crowfoot. The health authorities don't like it."

The ghost stopped so suddenly, Tobias walked through her. Damn, she was cold. "I wish you wouldn't do that," he growled.

Granny Crowfoot ignored him. *"What do you mean, families are no longer allowed to bury their dead in family plots? I've never heard anything so ridiculous in my life."* She glared at Tobias. *"Or my death. Don't you dare say anything, you young whippersnapper."*

"Wouldn't dream of it."

"They had a service for Hubert here."

"Yes," said Genevieve, "but his body is buried in Bittersweet Cemetery."

Genevieve elbowed past Tobias and stood between him and the ghost. Tobias got the impression she was attempting to placate both of them, and he felt a little guilty, but not much.

She continued, "Apparently, it is considered more healthful to bury everyone in a common cemetery nowadays, Granny Crowfoot. I think it has something to do with the control of infectious epidemics or something like that."

"I never heard of such a thing. Why, it's preposterous. Imagine the government daring to come between families that way."

"They did it for the public good, I believe," Genevieve said in a conciliatory tone.

"I've still never heard of such a thing. Such nonsense wouldn't have happened in my father's day, let me tell you. Why, he'd never have permitted it. It sounds like the country hasn't improved a jot since that wretched madman King George had the running of it. My father would be appalled, since he struggled so hard against oppression."

Tobias caught the look Genevieve shot him, and returned it. They were almost to the attic, and he decided it was time to stop arguing with Granny Crowfoot and try to prepare her for what lay ahead. He couldn't find it in his heart to feel sorry for the old bag, but he knew Genevieve would expect him to be gentle. "Ah, you seem awfully certain about your father's sentiments regarding the colonists versus the British, Miss Crowfoot. Do you—ah—remember him speaking of such matters?"

Ahead of him, Genevieve pushed the door open. The ghost swooped through it, and Tobias brought up the rear.

"Of course I'm certain about my dear father's sentiments. Charles Crowfoot was a patriot. A hero of the Revolution. Or at least he would have been if your wretched ancestor hadn't murdered him before it started, the despicable cad."

"Hmm. Not even I have the temerity to call my own father a despicable cad, Miss Crowfoot. I'm surprised at you."

Tobias regretted his sarcasm when Genevieve shot him a black look. Granny Crowfoot stared at him for a moment or two before she untangled his meaning.

"How dare you? You wretched boy! You know exactly who I meant when I called him a despicable cad, and it was most assuredly not my sainted father. It doesn't take a being as perspicacious as I to see that the beastly propensities of

the Rakeses have carried down to this present generation. Why, I ought to—''

She left off scolding Tobias when she glanced at the hole in the attic wall. *"What in the world have you been doing to my father's home, you devil? What is that hole doing in the wall?''*

"That's partly why we asked you to come up here with us this evening," Tobias said, trying to soften the rancor in his voice.

"You wanted to show me that you're destroying my father's home? I might have known."

"I'm not destroying it," Tobias said testily.

"Actually, I'm the one responsible for the hole in the wall, Granny Crowfoot," Genevieve said.

"You? Why on earth would you want to hack holes in your family's ancestral abode?'' She looked more closely through the hole in the paneling. *"What is this place? I've never seen it before."*

"We believe this was your father's secret office," Tobias told her. "It's where he carried out some clandestine business."

"Ah. No doubt something related to the glorious cause of colonial independence." Granny Crowfoot both looked and sounded smug.

"Not exactly," Tobias muttered.

He and Genevieve exchanged another look. He nodded at her, hoping she'd take it from here, since he expected Granny Crowfoot would accept the bad news better from a Crowfoot than from a Rakes. Actually, he didn't expect the volatile old ghost to accept it well at all, no matter who told it to her, but he could always hope.

Genevieve understood. "Granny Crowfoot, are you able to sit down?" she asked politely. Tobias stifled a grin.

The ghost glared at Genevieve. *"Of course I can sit down. You've seen me sit down. What a nonsensical question."*

"That's right. Now I remember seeing you sit before."

"Association with that Rakes fiend is softening your brain, child."

Genevieve ignored the jibe and gave her deceased ancestor

what Tobias expected was one of the sweetest smiles in her repertoire. "Perhaps you should sit now. We have some rather—ah—unexpected news."

Looking far from happy to oblige, Granny Crowfoot flounced over to her father's desk chair and sat. *"Unexpected news? What unexpected news? What are you talking about?"*

Genevieve sat across from the ghost and looked at her earnestly. "Granny Crowfoot, I fear we have some information that may surprise and sadden you. It concerns your father and his activities just prior to the Revolution."

The ghost's forehead furrowed. *"What do you mean, sad and surprising information? What information? Spit it out, girl."*

Tobias wished Genevieve would spit it out. Maybe the blasted ghost would choke on it.

Genevieve took a deep breath. "Your father wasn't a patriot of the Revolution, Granny Crowfoot. He was a spy for the British, and working hand in glove with Gerald Rakes and Ivor Pickstaff to pass information regarding the colonists' plans and activities to the British government."

The ghost burst up from her chair as if she'd been shot from a cannon. Tobias and Genevieve both ducked. Granny Crowfoot blasted around the room several times before she calmed down enough to sit once more. *"Rubbish! Vile calumnies! Wicked lies! Slander! How dare you try to besmirch my sainted father's name in this outrageous way?"*

Genevieve heaved a large sigh and straightened in her chair. Tobias moved over to stand behind her, ready to protect her if the ghost were to lash out at her.

"I fear they aren't vile calumnies and rubbish, Granny Crowfoot. We have proof."

The ghost's eyes went as round as billiard balls and turned blood-red. Spikes of lightning flashed in the air, and her hair stood on end. A misty aura surrounded her. The effect was eerie. Tobias didn't appreciate it, but he felt impelled to get everything out now, while they had a chance. "It's the truth. Charles Crowfoot, Gerald Rakes, and Ivor Pickstaff were in league together. They were passing information to the En-

glish government and amassing a horde of money to aid in
the British cause.'' He took a deep breath, knowing that what
he next aimed to impart might be the cruelest blow of all.
''That's not all. Charles also had a mistress, and was planning to leave your mother and run off to Europe with her.''

''Tobias,'' Genevieve muttered, obviously wishing he'd
couched his revelation more euphemistically.

The ghost wasn't pleased, either. With the spookiest shriek
Tobias had yet heard her utter, she shot up and careened
around the room for another little while. He crouched down,
wishing she didn't love these damned ghostly displays so
much. They were unnerving. Since Genevieve had slid out
of her chair and was crouched right next to him, he whispered, ''I'm sorry, but we had to tell her.''

''Yes, but not like that.''

Tobias hated to admit it, but he agreed with her. He should
have left it to Genevieve to break the news, as she was infinitely more diplomatic than he.

*''I've never heard such slanders! Never! I don't believe
it! It's not true! You're a vicious, lying beast! You're a*
Rakes! *I can say no worse of* anyone!''

''Comprehensive,'' Tobias grumbled, wondering if he was
going to have to listen to the ghost abuse him and his family
for the rest of his days. Maybe buying Crowfoot Castle
hadn't been such a good idea after all, even if it was guar-
anteed to infuriate his father. The feel of Genevieve under
him—he was trying to cover her body with his in case the
ghost got any mean ideas—disabused him of the fleeting
notion. If he hadn't bought the castle, he'd never have met
Genevieve. Genevieve was worth any number of crazy old
ghosts.

''Er, Granny Crowfoot,'' Genevieve ventured, lifting her
head—bravely, to Tobias's way of thinking. ''There are papers that prove Tobias's allegations. He didn't make any of
this up, unfortunately.''

*''I don't believe it. You're lying to me! You're under the
spell of that wretched Rakes devil, and he's turned your
mind.''*

"Good Lord." Tobias was getting really sick of being vilified by that dratted ghost.

"He's not a wretched Rakes devil, and he hasn't turned my mind." Genevieve herself sounded as if she were getting peeved. Tobias thought it was about time.

"Utter nonsense! Malicious falsehoods."

"They are not!"

Even though Tobias tried to hold her back, Genevieve scrambled up from the floor and, disregarding Granny Crowfoot's bristling hair, her misty aura, the sparkles of lightning, and her blood-red eyes, she grabbed the old cracked leather satchel from Charles Crowfoot's desk, reached inside, and came out with a fist full of papers. "You stop calling us names right this instant, you miserable old ghost! Read *this* if you don't believe us!"

She slammed a paper down on the desk. "Proof! Charles Crowfoot, Gerald Rakes, and Ivor Pickstaff each signed this oath of allegiance to each other and to the Crown of England!"

Granny Crowfoot hovered over the desk, moaning ghostishly.

"And if *that's* not enough, here!" Genevieve smacked a small leather-bound volume down beside the old yellowed paper. "A diary in which Charles Crowfoot—your own beloved father—documents the disagreements he, Rakes, and Pickstaff had been having for several weeks. Evidently the other two didn't trust your *sainted* father—and for good reason! Here!" Another paper smacked onto the desk, propelled by Genevieve's flat palm. "His mistress!"

"Aaaaaaauuuuugggh! Noooooo! Eeeeeeek!"

"Yes! His mistress! Right here in this diary"—she shook the diary at her—"in Charles Crowfoot's own hand, he tells of his plan to steal the money he, Rakes, and Pickstaff had been salting away for use by the British government. He was going to steal that money and run off to France with his mistress! You tell me how noble *that* is, you ghost you!"

"Noooooo!"

Tobias covered his ears. The old ghoul really had a wail on her when she got wound up.

"Oh, hush up!" Genevieve stood back from the desk and glowered up at the ghost, who still hung in the air, an agitated bundle of ghastly plasma. Tobias decided it was safe for him to get up from the floor as well, so he did. Because he didn't trust Granny Crowfoot any more than he trusted a band of Sioux warriors on the warpath, he stood behind Genevieve and rested his hands on her shoulders, primed to rescue her if the ghost tried anything. Anything at all.

"You might as well face facts, Granny Crowfoot," Genevieve continued, not giving an inch. Tobias was proud of her. "Your father, Tobias's ancestor, and the original Pickstaff were all beastly, conniving blackguards. They were also traitors to the Revolution. They wanted Britain to retain control of the colonies, because the Crown aimed to reward them with vast fortunes and property in payment for their help against the colonists. They were all scoundrels! This means, of course, that the feud between our families was based on faulty premises, and people have been fighting for more than a hundred years over nothing but a pack of lies!"

"Noooooo! It can't be true!"

"It is true, so hush up. We're all tired of your constant disturbances."

"No. No, no, no! It isn't true. It can't *be true!"*

"Oh, but it is true. And it's about time you faced facts. This nonsense has gone on for at least a century too long already, and I want it stopped immediately. Now! It's over! Do you hear me?"

"But—but the murder!"

"There was no murder!"

"But—but—"

The ghost stared at Genevieve for several seconds before drifting to the attic floor like a popped balloon. Tobias might have felt sorry for her if he didn't know her to be such a miserable old coot.

"It can't be true," Granny Crowfoot repeated in something that sounded awfully like a sob.

"It is true." Genevieve, on the other hand, pitched her voice to sound firm and severe. "And I want you to read it for yourself."

"I don't want to read anything." The ghost turned her head away, like a troublesome child refusing to take her medicine.

"I don't care whether you want to read it or not, you're going to. You've pestered poor Mr. Rakes abominably since he bought the castle and began fixing it up, and you're not going to get away with sulking like a spoiled brat. He deserves it of you. *I* deserve it of you. Read this!"

"No." Granny Crowfoot was pouting in earnest now, but Genevieve, whom Tobias hadn't known could be so adamant, wouldn't let her get away with it.

"Oh, yes, you will! You read this piece of paper right now. If you don't, you're no better than a rank coward."

"What?" The ghost's shriek almost split Tobias's eardrums. Evidently it had the same effect on Genevieve, because she clapped her hands over her ears. Tobias could tell she was mad as a wet hen.

"Stop that hideous screeching right this instant!"

She stormed over to the desk, darting this way and that in order to stay in Granny Crowfoot's line of sight, because the ghost kept flitting around. She wasn't going to let the old ghost get away with any more of her shenanigans. Tobias hadn't thought he could love her any more than he already did, but he discovered he'd been mistaken. She was nervy, his Genevieve; a true heroine.

"No! You can't make me!"

"You're right. I can't make you read these things, but if you don't, you'll be proving yourself to be a craven coward, and I'll broadcast the contents of this satchel to the entire world! Or at least to Bittersweet. Everyone will know what kind of a man your father was. *Everyone!*"

The ghost paled. Tobias hadn't realized ghosts could do that. *"You wouldn't!"*

"Try me!" With her lips pinched into a straight line, Genevieve began grabbing the papers from the desk and stuffing them back into the leather satchel. "I'm going to march these things down to the *Bittersweet Journal* first thing in the morning. I'm going to talk to the editor and have him print the whole story. Then everyone in the entire town will know the truth. Why, I'll even send copies to *The New York Times!*''

''No! You can't!''

''I can if you continue to avoid reading these papers. You've annoyed and bullied and threatened people for entirely too long—and for what? For a lie! I'm not going to let you get away with it another second longer. If you don't read these documents right this minute, I'm going to paper the castle walls with copies of the *Bittersweet Journal* when they write the true story of Charles Crowfoot! Just you wait!''

With a swirl, Genevieve turned to leave the office. Tobias was right behind her, wanting to applaud.

''No! No, wait.'' Granny Crowfoot sounded desperate.

Genevieve turned, but she didn't let go of the satchel. She squinted at the ghost, resolution radiating from her entire bearing. ''Are you going to play fair?''

The ghost sniffled miserably. *''You aren't giving me a choice, apparently.''*

If the spirit was hoping to soften Genevieve by trying to sound pitiful, she wasn't succeeding. If anything, Genevieve seemed to become even more irritated by Granny Crowfoot's pathetic mien.

''You're right,'' she said. ''I'm not. You either read these papers here and now, or you'll be reading them when I've plastered them inside every room in the castle.''

''I don't believe you'd do such a thing.''

''Try me.''

Tobias believed her, by damn. He hoped the ghost would, because he truly didn't fancy having newsprint wallpaper in his home—especially not newsprint broadcasting the demise of the Crowfoot-Rakes feud. By this time he was so sick of the blasted feud, he never wanted to hear it spoken of again.

''I can't believe my father was a traitor.'' Granny Crowfoot sniffled again, and wiped a tear away from her transparent cheek. If Tobias hadn't seen it with his own eyes, he'd never have believed the old ghost had a tear in her.

''Well,'' Genevieve said judiciously. ''I don't suppose one can truly call him a traitor, since the colonies were technically the property of England at the time, but if one looks at his deeds from a modern-day perspective—well, yes. He was a traitor.''

"No. Oh, no!"

"Oh, yes. In fact, if anything, Charles Crowfoot—and don't forget that he was my relative as well as yours—was worse than a traitor. He not only betrayed his country, but he betrayed his friends and family as well.''

"Impossible." The ghost had taken to whispering now.

"It's not impossible. Read these papers. Now. I'm giving you one last chance. You won't get another.''

Granny Crowfoot heaved a dispirited sigh. *"Oh, very well. I'll read the papers. I still don't believe it."*

"You will.''

She did. The three of them trooped back to Charles Crowfoot's desk, and Genevieve—making sure not to let the ghost have full possession of any one paper because she didn't trust her not to run off with it—showed her the proof of Charles Crowfoot's perfidy.

The experience devastated the ghost. Tobias observed the proceedings with his elbows propped on the desk, alternately watching the ghost read and eyeing Genevieve's beautiful body, covered only by her silk robe. Her breasts were clearly delineated, the silk falling deliciously over her curves. Tobias itched to follow the shiny smoothness of the fabric with his hands, but he contented himself with watching and appreciating. There would be time for all of that later. He'd have the rest of his life, in fact.

"There," Genevieve said, after Granny Crowfoot had read the first paper, which documented the oath of allegiance entered into by Charles Crowfoot, Gerald Rakes, and Ivor Pickstaff. "You see? All three men signed here at the bottom. They were in cahoots." She tapped the paper with her forefinger so the ghost couldn't escape the evidence.

"I see it," Granny Crowfoot muttered, sounding very crabby.

Genevieve didn't let her ancestor's crankiness stop her. She shoved the oath of allegiance back into the satchel and drew out Charles Crowfoot's diary. "Here. Let me show you this passage—the one in which he says that he aims to take the money he and his cronies had been amassing for the Crown and use it for his own despicable purposes. He wrote right here—'' She flipped through several old, yellowed pages. ''Ah, yes, here it is. He says clearly here that he has a mistress and that he aims to grab the money and run away to France with her.''

''Louise D'Aullaire. I remember her.'' Granny Crowfoot's voice had sunk to a whisper. *''She was quite pretty, but . . . I had no idea. Oh!''* She pointed her ghostly finger at another page, her expression transforming into one of outrage. *''Why, look at this! He calls my mother an overbearing hag!''*

''A trait she passed on to her daughter, evidently,'' Tobias muttered. Genevieve frowned at him, and he mouthed an apology. She grinned, so he guessed she forgave him.

''I can't believe it.''

Tobias knew the words were said more out of shock than of true disbelief, because he'd read those papers himself. He and Genevieve had pored over them, in fact.

''Tobias and I believe that your father died in an accident, Granny Crowfoot. He was on his way to pick up Miss D'Aullaire when it happened. I don't know why the authorities decided Gerald Rakes had anything to do with it but, of course, since no one ever went into Charles Crowfoot's office after his death, they wouldn't have had access to Charles's secrets. They couldn't. No one knew the office was here.''

''No. I didn't even know this room was here.'' The ghost sniffled again.

''So you see,'' Genevieve said. ''The feud that's kept the citizens of Bittersweet amused and irate for over a hundred years was based on a whole pile of false assumptions.''

''Yes.'' The ghost buried her face in her hands.

Tobias and Genevieve exchanged a glance, and Tobias reached for her hand. Genevieve seemed glad to let him hold it.

''I am sorry that you had to learn of your father's—ah—problems this way, Granny Crowfoot, but you must admit that you've behaved in rather a beastly way to poor Tobias.''

When she lifted her head again, Tobias could tell the ghost wasn't about to admit anything of the sort. He shook his head. "Don't push it, Genevieve. The old bat's suffered a shock."

"Don't call me an old bat."

"Why not?" Tobias sat up straight in his chair. "The good Lord knows, you've called me names enough since I moved in here. And for what reason? All I've done is fall in love with your great-great-great-niece and try to fix the place up some. I should think you'd be grateful."

"Grateful? But you're a Rakes!"

"You're damned right I'm a Rakes. And you're a Crowfoot. And between the two families, there's not enough goodness to float a canoe. Face it, Granny Crowfoot—my ancestor and your father were two of a kind, and they were both bad men. You might as well come to grips with it, because it's the truth."

"Don't be too brutal, Tobias," Genevieve said gently. "I'm sure this has been a great shock to her."

"Yeah. Well, she's been quite a shock to me more than once." Tobias knew he shouldn't grumble at Genevieve, but all the abuse the damned ghost had heaped on him weighed heavily at the moment.

"That's true." Genevieve looked at the ghost. "He's right, you know. I think you owe Tobias an apology, Granny Crowfoot."

"Apologize? To a Rakes?"

"There's no sense in hating him because he's a Rakes, you know," Genevieve said reasonably. "I shall be a Rakes soon myself. Besides, Charles Crowfoot and Gerald Rakes were in cahoots until Charles betrayed his friends."

Genevieve's plain speaking was seemingly more than the ghost could bear. With one wild shriek, she swooped out of the room, rocketed around the attic for a minute or two, and vanished up the chimney, leaving behind one of her smoky vapor trails.

Tobias sighed. So did Genevieve. Then they went back downstairs and crawled into Genevieve's bed, where they slept the sleep of the innocent.

Chapter
Eighteen

Tobias and Genevieve were in Tobias's library the following morning, sorting through Charles Crowfoot's old papers, when Wesley Armitage came to call. Tobias looked up and stifled a sigh. He really did like Armitage, but the man always seemed to be at the castle. Sometimes Tobias wondered if Armitage had any other clients.

He smiled and stood. "Good morning, Wes. Have you had breakfast? There's probably some kippers and eggs left, if you can stand eating Molly's cooking."

"Tobias!"

Tobias grinned at his lovely, lively wife-to-be. "I don't mind, darling. I think it's charming to have such an inept household staff."

Genevieve humphed, but Tobias could tell she didn't mind his teasing by the rosy blush in her cheeks. Lordy, he loved her. He hadn't believed he'd ever fall in love again; after the Madeline Riley debacle, he'd believed himself to be immune to such nonsense. Only it wasn't nonsense. He'd been basing his perception of love on his long-ago, miserable, doomed-from-the-first obsession with Madeline. He'd been a boy then. Now he was a man, and he knew what it was to love a woman.

"Besides," he continued, laughing, "if I didn't employ them, they'd all probably starve to death because no one else in this town would hire them."

"Tobias!" But Genevieve laughed, too, and Tobias realized for perhaps the millionth time that he was the luckiest man in the world.

It was then he noticed that Wesley Armitage held a gun in his hand. And that it was pointed straight at his heart. Perhaps not straight. The gun wavered in Armitage's hands as if the poor fellow had a palsy.

"What are you up to, Wes?" Tobias still smiled. He had a vague notion that Armitage must have discovered another trap someone had set to do Tobias in. "Where'd you find that?"

Genevieve stopped smiling. She stared at the gun in Armitage's hand and blinked, plainly startled. "My goodness, Mr. Armitage. I don't believe it's wise to point a gun at Tobias. It might go off."

"Oh, it will go off, all right." Armitage wet his lips. "It will go off at least twice, because I'm afraid I now will have to get rid of both of you."

"What?" Genevieve's question came out in a little gasp.

"What the hell are you talking about, Wes?" Tobias, on the other hand, began to get a sinking feeling in his gut. Perhaps it wasn't a Pickstaff who'd been behind all the deadly incidents that had plagued him since he'd moved into the castle.

Armitage nodded slowly, looking more nervous than ever. Tobias wished he'd hold his gun hand steady. The man was a wreck and looked like he might snap any second.

"You understand now, don't you, Tobias?" Armitage's voice wobbled as badly as his gun hand.

Shaking his head, Tobias said, "I don't understand anything, Wes. What reason do you have for getting rid of me?"

"You honestly don't know, do you?" The bitterness in Armitage's voice surprised Tobias.

"What don't I know?" Holding his hands up so that Armitage wouldn't suspect him of anything, Tobias walked out from behind his desk and went to Genevieve's side. She clutched his arm tightly, although her fear didn't show in any other way.

"What are you two talking about?" she asked softly.

"Neither of you understands why I have to kill you," Armitage said.

"Kill us?" Genevieve turned to give Tobias a startled glance. "He's going to kill us?"

Tobias put his arm around her waist and gave her a quick squeeze. He got the feeling the poor fellow had gone off the deep end. This wasn't the first time Tobias had faced a person who wanted to kill him, but before he'd at least known why. He hoped he'd be able to keep Armitage talking for a while, so he could think of some clever plan to disarm him.

"No, I don't understand why you have to kill me. Tell me, Wes."

Armitage gave a short, biting bark of laughter. "You don't even know we're related, do you, Tobias? No. Of course you don't. You don't know that our mutual great-grandfather disowned my grandmother when she eloped to New York City with my grandfather. He never acknowledged the relationship again. Had her name stricken from the family Bible." Armitage's grin was as twisted as any Tobias had ever seen. "That's Yankee Christianity for you. He wouldn't allow her name to be spoken in his household."

Tobias squinted at Armitage, not believing his ears. "What are you talking about? You mean we're related? On whose side? Which grandfather? I don't understand."

"Your father's side, of course. Evidently all the Rakes men have been bastards—in the literary sense of the word. Our great-grandfather never forgave my grandmother for not marrying money. That's the only thing the Rakeses have ever cared about, money. I don't expect there's a soul living in Bittersweet who even remembers the story of my grandmother any longer. People's memories are short."

"Yours doesn't seem to be," Tobias remarked.

Armitage gave a ghastly approximation of a laugh. "No. My memory is fine. Although I wouldn't have known about our relationship if I hadn't found some papers after my mother died.''

''Good heavens,'' Genevieve whispered. She pressed her fingers to her mouth. ''Can this be true?''

''It's true all right.'' Armitage pointed the gun at her for a second before he transferred his aim back to Tobias. ''I moved to Bittersweet several years ago, knowing that one day I'd figure out how to rejoin the moneyed side of the family. I didn't expect to have to do it this way.''

Tobias shook his head. ''I had no idea, Wes. Do you mean you're the one who's been behind all the attempts on my life?''

Another grim laugh and a nod issued from Wesley Armitage. ''Yes. I'm not very good at killing, am I? But I have to get it over with, and there's no use wasting any more time.''

Tobias furrowed his brow. ''But, Wes, I inherited my money from my maternal grandmother. We aren't related on that side.''

An expression of fury entered Armitage's face, and Tobias wished he'd kept his logic to himself. ''Don't quibble. Your damned father aims to give you all of his money, or didn't you know that?''

Tobias blinked. ''No. I didn't know that.'' Such a possibility had never crossed his mind, in fact.

''It's true. Your father hired me, you know.''

''What?'' Tobias stared at him, astonished.

''Oh, yes. He hired me.''

''He hired you to murder me?'' Tobias had no great love for his father, but he couldn't envision the old man going this far.

''No, not to kill you. Far from it. He wanted me to get close to you and persuade you to forgive him. The bastard was too proud to apologize for himself. Another family tradition, I suppose.''

Tobias discovered he was speechless. His father had hired this villain. To lure him back into the family. All in all, he was less surprised than he figured he should be. It sounded like something the old man would do.

"He didn't know how much I hated the Rakeses. He didn't even know I was one of them, or he might have been more cautious. I didn't tell him, either. He thought he was being benevolent, giving me his business. But I used the opportunity to my advantage. You didn't know, either, did you?"

"That you hated us? No, I had no idea."

Armitage's smile froze Tobias's blood. "Of course not. I'm accustomed to hiding my true feelings. One has to be when one has been thrust aside and left to fend for oneself."

After a moment, Tobias nodded. He understood that.

"At first I thought I'd work my way into your good graces. Perhaps be so useful that you'd hire me to work for you here at the castle."

"I'd have been happy to hire you, Wes."

Armitage let out another bitter laugh. "Oh, yes. The altruistic Tobias Rakes. Ha!"

Tobias shrugged helplessly. Genevieve shuddered, and he held her more tightly.

"Then I decided I wanted it all. Why should you have everything?"

Why indeed? Since he had no answer, Tobias didn't respond.

"But I blundered badly. I'm not adept at killing, you see." Another harsh laugh made Genevieve release a small gasp. "Why, I understand I even killed a cat once. It's because you wouldn't drink those blasted powders, damn you."

"A cat?" Tobias didn't know what he was talking about.

"Oh!" Genevieve's hand flew to cover her mouth. "Gray Baby."

"Was that the animal's name?" Armitage looked uninterested. "I had to throw the poisoned water out. I assume the cat got into the garbage."

"Oh, my," Genevieve whispered.

Tobias said, "I see."

"And then, of course, you, Miss Crowfoot, drank another dose I'd intended for Tobias."

Tobias stiffened, wishing he dared lunge at the vile bastard. He might have if he'd been alone, but he'd die before he jeopardized Genevieve.

"Then, when you told me you were going to marry Miss Crowfoot, I realized I'd missed my opportunity to do it surreptitiously. Unlike you, I have no experience with these things, and I'm afraid I bungled it."

"Unlike me?" Tobias didn't know whether to be offended or to laugh. "How much experience do you think I have with murder?"

Armitage shook his head hard. "No. Not murder. With killing. You spent your whole life killing Indians, Tobias."

"That was war." Tobias ground the words out. He had been of two minds about the Indian situation for years now, but he didn't aim to argue with Armitage about it now. "I've never killed anyone in cold blood."

"Cold blood? Ha! That's a rich one." Armitage's sneer conveyed pure malice. "Cold blood runs in the family. Don't you know that by this time, Tobias? If you don't believe me, consider your father. And our great-grandfather."

Slowly Tobias nodded. "You're right. It takes cold blood to cast off a daughter or a son, and our great-grandfather and my father did just that. But you don't have to carry on with family tradition, you know, Wes. You can break it off now. If it's money you want—"

"Money! Yes, Tobias. I want money. I want all of it. I want all the money my family was denied for so many years. I want all the advantages you had and I didn't have because, for money, your grandmother married a man she didn't love and my grandmother didn't."

Tobias didn't know anything about who his grandmother had loved, but he did know that Wes had things mixed up. "Advantages? What advantages do you think I had, Wes? I had a mother who died when I was ten and a father who didn't care if I lived or died. Still doesn't, for that matter. Obviously."

Armitage's crazy smile widened. "Good. Then he won't mourn your passing."

Genevieve cried, "Mr. Armitage!"

Armitage turned his beady stare on her. Genevieve shrank against Tobias, who squeezed her again.

"I suppose your muddle-headed aunt will mourn for you,

Miss Crowfoot, but I can't help that. I couldn't take the chance that you and Tobias wouldn't jump the gun. If you were to be with child, for instance, before you married, you might be able to claim the child as Tobias's and get a portion of the inheritance. If I allowed the two of you to marry, I know the money would be willed to you. In fact, Tobias and I spoke about making out his will just yesterday.''

"Damn it, Wes, don't talk to her like that.''

Armitage's head swung toward Tobias again. For the first time since he'd met him, Tobias recognized in Armitage's expression the rage he usually kept so carefully contained.

"It doesn't matter how I talk to her, Tobias. The both of you will be dead in a very few minutes. I'm not sure . . .'' His gaze darted around the room. He appeared displeased. "No. Not in here. In the cellar. That's where I'll do it. No one will hear the shots there. Even if they do, no one will investigate. They're all afraid of the ghost.'' He laughed, a grating sound that made Tobias's nerves jump.

"The ghost does exist, you know,'' Genevieve said, her voice a whisper.

"Right. And the tooth fairy does, too, I'm sure. Don't be ridiculous, Miss Crowfoot. I always took you for a sensible woman. Don't spoil my image of you now.''

"Listen, Wes,'' Tobias pleaded. "Why don't you put that gun away. I'm sure we can work something out. If I'd known we were related before now, I'd have made arrangements. You know that. I don't hold with the way my father—and our great-grandfather—treated their children. You already know that. Don't do this. You'll never get away with it.''

"Like hell I won't. I'll shoot you down there, and cart your corpses away at night. Everyone will be looking for you. No one will ever know what happened to you. It will be a mystery—the capper on the Rakes-Crowfoot feud. I like it, don't you?''

This time when Armitage laughed, Tobias sensed an edge to the sound—an edge of desperation or insanity, or a combination. The notion gave him no comfort at all.

"But it's likely that someone will find out someday, Wes. Murder is a difficult crime to cover up. Then you'll be tried

for murder, and they might send you to the electric chair.
You don't want that. Why don't we talk about it, and work
something out. I'm not a greedy man. I'll be happy to share
the inheritance with you. You deserve it, after all.''

"I deserve it! I *do* deserve it! I deserve it more than you
ever did. I didn't run off with a married woman, like the
damned fool you were! I didn't leave home and sail the seven
seas, or go exploring in Africa, or head west to fight Indians.
No! I moved to Bittersweet. I stayed in Bittersweet. Where
I belonged—where *you* belonged. I did everything that was
required of me. And what did I get for it? Nothing! Nothing!
Well, I'm through with nothing. I'm taking it all. All!''

Tobias heard Genevieve whisper, "I think he's gone
mad.''

He nodded gloomily, fearing she was right. For the first
time since he realized the ghost of Granny Crowfoot existed,
he wished she'd appear. But, of course, she was off sulking
somewhere. Even if she weren't, Tobias doubted that she'd
exert herself to rescue a Rakes. Or a Crowfoot who intended
to marry a Rakes.

Armitage stopped laughing abruptly and made a quick gesture with his gun. "Walk ahead of me. If you so much as
think about trying something, I'll shoot you. Don't think I
won't. I've gone this far. I'm not about to back down now.''

"Where to?" Tobias tried to picture the cellar in his
mind's eye. Overall, he guessed he'd as soon tackle Armitage
there as anywhere. The cellar stairs were steep, and there
were places to hide down there, where it was dark. He had
to protect Genevieve. More than anything else in the world,
he had to protect Genevieve.

"Don't trifle with me, Tobias. You know where the cellar
is,'' Armitage said gruffly. "Go there.'' He gestured again
with the gun. "You first.'' He spoke the latter to Genevieve.
"If you try to run, your lover here will get a bullet in the
back.''

Tobias felt her shudder at the threat. He whispered,
"Don't worry, darling. I'll think of something.''

"Stop that!'' Armitage poked Tobias in the back with the
gun. Damn, it hurt. "Don't whisper! Don't say a word.''

"The servants are going to do something when they see you have a gun to Tobias's back," Genevieve said, her voice tart.

"They won't see me. You've managed to hire the most incompetent people in Bittersweet." Armitage laughed again. "You certainly did me a big favor when you hired that lot, Miss Crowfoot."

Genevieve snorted. Tobias might have thought it was funny if he weren't worried about their lives. He nudged her gently to let her know she should obey Armitage. He didn't want her doing anything that might get her shot. The idea of living the rest of his life without Genevieve at his side gave him a sick feeling in his gut.

"You take the candle, Miss Crowfoot," Armitage demanded. "Walk next to your lover here, and don't try to be smart. It won't work, and I have the gun."

"I don't think I could forget that, Mr. Armitage." Genevieve sounded like a schoolmarm scolding a child.

Unfortunately, Armitage proved to be right about the staff. While there probably should have been a couple of housemaids dusting the hall tables or polishing the picture frames, there wasn't a soul in sight. Tobias decided he was going to have to have a chat with the staff—if he survived the day.

The cellar stairs looked even more steep than usual when Tobias opened the door and peeked down. He hesitated, wondering if Armitage had it in mind to shoot them as they descended.

"She goes first," their captor growled. "If she tries anything, I'll shoot you and then get her. I don't trust you." Again he poked the barrel of the gun in Tobias's back. Tobias wished he would stop doing that. It hurt like the devil to have a cylinder of metal thrust against one's spine. He gently guided Genevieve in front of him and gave her a look that he hoped conveyed the great love he had for her. From the look she gave him back, he guessed it had. Just before she put her foot on the first step, she turned, lifted her head, and kissed him on the lips. Armitage growled and hit her across the arm with the gun. She stepped away from Tobias and, rubbing her arm, began slowly to walk down the cellar stairs, clutching the banister rail.

"That was unnecessary, Wes," Tobias said sharply. "There's no need to hurt Genevieve."

"Keep your mouth shut, Tobias. I'm not interested in anything you have to say. Get moving."

Armitage shoved the gun in his back once more, and Tobias started after Genevieve. Lord, it was dark in the cellar. Genevieve's candle flickered feebly, doing its best to light the place, but it was as dark and dank as a tomb down there. Tobias wished he hadn't thought of it as a tomb. It might be entirely too appropriate a metaphor in this case.

The staff, he noticed, still hadn't taken any dust rags to the place. The single banister running on one side of the stairs had a layer of dust a quarter inch thick on it. It felt unpleasant under his hands, so he didn't grip it when he'd gone past the first stair.

"All right," Armitage said at his back. "I'm coming now. Don't try anything."

Annoyed by Armitage's constant reminders that they not try anything, Tobias grunted, "Don't worry. We're not trying a thing, Wes."

He was almost right. Genevieve had made it to the cellar floor by this time, and she stood to one side as Tobias descended. Tobias smiled at her, hoping in that way to give her courage. He should have known better. If there was one commodity Genevieve Crowfoot had never lacked, it was courage. He hadn't even taken his foot from the final step, when she almost gave him a heart attack by lunging forward. He didn't know what she was doing until he heard Armitage yell.

"Grab the gun, Tobias!" she shrieked.

It was then Tobias realized what she'd done. Damned if she hadn't pushed Armitage right off the cellar steps, sideways, because there was no railing to stop his fall. Flailing wildly, Armitage screamed as he fell. He pulled the trigger, either by mistake or design—Tobias couldn't see a blasted thing. The bullet went wild, and Armitage hit the floor on his side.

Immediately, Tobias jumped on top of the fallen villain, grabbing for Armitage's gun hand. The candle had gone out in the melee and he couldn't see. In the furious struggle that followed, the gun flew out of Armitage's grasp. Tobias lost sight of it in the dark, and both men scrambled after it.

Genevieve yelled something Tobias didn't catch, although it sounded as though she were calling for Granny Crowfoot. Tobias would have been happy to see the old hag, but he didn't believe she'd come to anyone's rescue. The ghost was far too self-involved, by his way of thinking, to care about the fate of anyone else.

Armitage seemed to be hollering, too. Tobias made out, "You bastard! You bastard!" as they scrabbled for the gun. The fellow was stronger than he looked, unfortunately, and Tobias wasn't in as good shape as he used to be since he'd been laid up for several months, recuperating from his injury. Genevieve's life, as well as his own, hung in the balance, however, and he fought like a tiger.

The struggle seemed to take hours. Tobias knew it wasn't really a long time, but the darkness, the gravity of the situation, and Armitage's crazy determination all combined to make it seem like an eternity passed as he and Armitage wrestled on the cellar floor. He felt a chill breeze an instant or two before he realized what this atmospheric sensation presaged, and his heart soared.

Lord, Lord, was the old bat really going to take a hand in this? Was she really going to help him? He didn't dare believe it.

He did, however, allow himself to be distracted for a moment and Armitage took advantage of that one tiny second to wriggle his finger to the trigger of the gun. Tobias realized what his enemy had done an instant before the gun, sounding like a cannon blast in the confines of the dark cellar, went off.

A hot, searing pain ripped into his chest. Tobias cried out, "Genevieve!" And then he knew nothing.

"Tobias!" Genevieve heard the gunshot, heard Tobias's voice, and knew what had happened. She screamed once for someone—anyone—to come and help them, and raced over

to where she'd heard him call to her. It was a foolish thing to do—afterward, she realized it—but at that moment, she could do nothing else. Her love had been shot.

Suddenly a bright light filled the cellar. Genevieve didn't halt her pell-mell dash toward Tobias, lying deadly still on the cellar floor, but she saw the startled look on Wesley Armitage's face. She also saw that he was rumpled and battered. Tobias had put up a good fight. Then she saw Granny Crowfoot, shrieking like a banshee and putting on the best show of her death, swoop down on Armitage.

Screaming wildly, Armitage lifted the gun and shot at the streaking ghost. Genevieve threw herself on the floor beside Tobias and tried to stay out of the way. From the floor, she watched Granny Crowfoot's spirit shoot straight through Armitage's body. Genevieve hoped it hurt. She suspected it did when Armitage doubled over, clutching at his stomach. He cried out again, and it sounded like a cry of pain. Good.

"No!" the lawyer shouted. "No! What is it? What are you?"

"*I am the ghost of Crowfoot Castle!*" Granny Crowfoot cried out in her most spectacularly sepulchral tone. "*And I won't tolerate behavior of this sort in my home, young man! Not from you or from anyone else. How dare you?*"

Trust Granny Crowfoot, Genevieve thought, grimly amused by the ghost's words. She saw her carom against the far wall and make another swoop toward Wesley Armitage. The lawyer hollered, "No! No! Not again!"

His words, naturally, had no effect on the ghost, who shot straight through him again, this time penetrating his arms as well. It must have hurt a good deal, because his arms went limp and the gun dropped from his fingers. He fell to his knees and tried to clutch at his stomach again, but his arms didn't seem to be working anymore. Genevieve figured Granny Crowfoot must have put a little extra oomph on her trajectory, because the man truly did seem to be in a good deal of pain. She hoped so.

As soon as the gun hit the cellar floor, Genevieve made a lunge for it. Her hands trembling with fear for Tobias's life and with pure hatred for the man who'd shot him, she pointed the weapon at Wesley Armitage.

"Stand up, you wretched coward!"

"*Eeeeeeeee!*" cried Granny Crowfoot, preparing for another flight through Armitage's middle. "*Aaaaaaaargh!*"

Armitage looked wildly from the gun in Genevieve's hand to the rocketing ghost and shouted, "No!" Then he covered his head with his arms—Genevieve was disappointed that he seemed to be able to use them again—and flung himself to the cellar floor. Such shenanigans didn't deter the ghost, of course. She shot straight down through his back, causing him to scream in pain and terror.

Genevieve didn't care. She gave one glance at Tobias, still as motionless as a dead man—which he might be, for all she knew, and a coldness permeated her body, as if she'd been invaded by something from beyond the grave. She'd never felt so cold. Nor had she ever felt such a pitiless desire to avenge anyone. She aimed the gun. Her hands no longer shook. She took three steps forward, until she stood directly above Wesley Armitage, and pointed the gun straight at his skull.

Armitage lifted his head. Tears streamed down his face, and he whimpered pathetically. "No. No, please, don't shoot me."

"You foul monster. You shot Tobias. You were going to kill the both of us. And I should have pity on you? Don't make me laugh." She laughed. It was a sound the likes of which she'd never heard come from her throat. She sounded evil in that moment, and knew that hate propelled her—and she didn't care. "I'm going to treat you the way you treated Tobias, you awful pig."

"*Shoot him! Shoot him!*" Granny Crowfoot cried in what could only be described as glee. "*Kill the bastard!*"

Genevieve pulled the hammer back on the gun. It sounded like a crack of thunder. Armitage whimpered and covered his head again.

"Genevieve! Genevieve, no! Don't do it."

At the croaking command, Genevieve's heart almost

stopped. She jerked her head. "Tobias! Tobias! You're alive!"

"Don't shoot him, darling. He's not worth it." Tobias struggled to his hands and knees, pleading with her. "Don't do it. You'll have him on your conscience forever."

"My conscience? He *shot* you!"

"Please don't kill me." Armitage sounded truly wretched.

The ice in Genevieve's heart, which had begun to melt when she realized Tobias still lived—for however little time he might have—solidified again. "You miserable excuse for a thing," she said, her words falling like chunks of ice. "You don't deserve to call yourself a man." And she pointed the gun at his head again.

Tobias lunged at her legs, and she pulled the trigger as he hit. The shot went wild, she went down hard, and Tobias fell on top of her.

"Tobias!"

But he was unconscious. He'd used his last ounce of strength to prevent Genevieve from killing Wesley Armitage. Genevieve burst into tears and struggled to a sitting position, where she cradled Tobias on her lap.

The cellar door crashed open, and several pairs of footsteps sounded on the steps. Genevieve looked toward the light streaming from the doorway—Granny Crowfoot had vanished by this time and taken her eerie light with her—and whispered, "Thank God."

Almost immediately, she regained control of herself. She had to, for Tobias's sake. "Godfrey?"

"Yes, ma'am. What happened? What was that terrible noise?"

"Send someone to fetch Dr. Johnson, Godfrey. If your mother is there, please have her come down here. Mr. Rakes has been hurt, and he needs immediate attention. You go for the sheriff, but not until you've bound Mr. Armitage up. He tried to kill Mr. Rakes."

Genevieve later considered the ensuing several minutes in the light of a miracle. For the first time since the staff of Crowfoot Castle had been hired, they worked efficiently and as a unit. She'd never seen them operate with such precision.

Mrs. Watkins didn't bother running back upstairs to fetch bandages. She ripped her own petticoat off and tore it into strips. Genevieve hurriedly took Tobias's coat and shirt off. She gasped when she saw the hole in his side, bleeding sluggishly. He'd lost a good deal of blood.

Then, while Genevieve bathed Tobias's head with water offered by Molly Gratchett, Mrs. Watkins pressed a wad of ripped petticoat strips over the wound to stanch the bleeding, and wrapped it tightly with the remaining pieces.

While this was being done, several housemaids, Godfrey, and Small William Pickstaff, who had heard the racket and run to see what was happening, bound a weeping Wesley Armitage hand and foot. Small William, who seemed to enjoy the duty, then bullied him up the stairs where he and his father, Old William, tied him to a chair in the kitchen. Old William stood guard over the bound man while Small William ran for the constable.

Meanwhile Godfrey dispatched another housemaid to fetch Dr. Johnson. Then he himself, without any prompting from his mother or anyone else, removed the hinges from one of the kitchen doors, and he and another servant took the door down to the cellar.

"Do you want us to carry him upstairs, ma'am, or should we wait for the doctor to get here?"

Unable to fight her tears, Genevieve silently blessed Godfrey Watkins. He was a good boy, and a positive hero in an emergency. "It's so dark and dusty down here, Godfrey. If we can be gentle, I think it would be best to carry him upstairs to the parlor."

So they did. Genevieve, wringing her hands and speaking softly to Tobias all the while, accompanied the makeshift stretcher upstairs. They laid him on the sofa and Genevieve elected to stay with Tobias while Mrs. Watkins bustled to the kitchen to boil water and prepare more linen strips.

Tobias was in the parlor, pale as marble and motionless as a statue, when Dr. Johnson, driving like a madman, pulled his buggy up outside the castle. Dr. Johnson didn't even have to ask Small William to take care of the horse. The boy was out of the house and at the horse's head before the doctor alit. A regiment of household servants led him to the parlor.

Genevieve looked up from her position on the floor next to the sofa. She'd been holding Tobias's cold hand and whispering her love to him for what seemed like hours. "Thank God you've come."

"What the devil happened?" Dr. Johnson didn't wait for Genevieve's answer, but immediately went to Tobias's side.

"Wesley Armitage shot him."

The doctor gave her a look of pure incredulity, but he didn't pause to ask any questions. With his usual brisk efficiency, he set to work.

Genevieve and Mrs. Watkins assisted as the doctor drew the bullet out of Tobias's side, cleaned the wound with water and antiseptic, and bound it again. When the operation was finished, he stood up, wiped his hands on a wet towel, and frowned down at his patient. Mrs. Watkins began tidying up the operating theater and setting the parlor to order.

"He's lost a lot of blood." Dr. Johnson sounded very grim.

Genevieve could only nod. Her heart ached, and she couldn't stand to see Tobias lying there so still and cold. He looked dead, and she couldn't stand the thought. If he died, Genevieve wasn't sure she wouldn't die, too, because she couldn't imagine going on without him. Oh, Lord, he couldn't die!

"But he's a strong man."

Although she wasn't sure she wanted to know the answer, Genevieve dared to ask, "Will he recover, Dr. Johnson?"

He looked her straight in the eye. Genevieve knew he wasn't a man to mince words, and she braced herself.

"I don't know, Genevieve. The bullet missed his heart and lungs, but it's a bad wound, and I won't deny it. As I said, he's a strong man, but he's been through a good deal in these past few months. It might have weakened him."

Genevieve held her breath because she feared she might cry out in grief.

The doctor shook his head. "Whatever possessed Wesley Armitage to shoot Tobias Rakes?"

Trying valiantly not to break down, Genevieve endeavored to explain. The doctor scowled.

"So he's a Rakes is he? He was driven mad for the money, I suppose," he said with a growl. "It's always been money with the Rakeses and the Crowfoots."

Unable to say another word, Genevieve only nodded, sure the doctor didn't know how right he was.

Chapter Nineteen

Genevieve didn't even try to rest. She didn't want to leave Tobias's sickbed for so much as a second. Reluctantly, however, she agreed to go upstairs and change clothes, because Tobias's blood had soaked her gown and petticoats. She came downstairs again as soon as she'd cleaned herself up. Mrs. Watkins hadn't left Tobias's side in the interim. She probably didn't dare, for fear of what Genevieve would do to her if she stirred so much as a foot in either direction away from the patient.

Hurrying, her heart hammering, praying that no further evil had befallen the man she loved during the six minutes she'd been away from him, Genevieve pushed the parlor door open. The room was dark, the curtains drawn. The atmosphere in the normally cheerful room seemed stark and grim, even though the same comfortable furniture graced the place. Tobias hadn't decorated the castle in a formal manner. Rather, he'd seemed to crave hominess and comfort, explaining to Genevieve that his own life had always lacked such pleasant qualities.

As she glanced around the room where he lay close to death, Genevieve's entire being felt heavy. This wasn't fair. Tobias would never have withheld from Wesley Armitage the money denied him by a temperamental quirk of their mutual great-grandfather's tyrannical vindictiveness. Armitage plainly had never even considered that Tobias's uncomfortable life might have given him a more generous outlook on mankind's foibles than his own Rakes ancestors harbored.

She shook her head, chiding herself. Of course not. The Rakes legacy was one of bitterness and expulsion. It had taken a strong, good man—a better man than his forebears—to break from that heritage and bring lightness, understanding, and generosity to the Rakes line.

She didn't even want to consider her own family's history. She actually felt rather guilty about it, since it had been her ancestor's avarice, licentiousness, and betrayal—of his unborn country, his business partners, and his family—that had spawned the feud in the first place.

And now Tobias lay near death in the home that Charles Crowfoot had built. The home Charles Crowfoot had been deserting when he met his own death. How horrible that Gerald Rakes had been hanged for Charles's death. Genevieve had heard people say that life isn't fair. She knew exactly what those people meant by that saying. There was nothing fair about life—not only had she lost her parents and Benton, but now she might lose Tobias as well.

She tiptoed to the sofa and peered down at him. He looked simply awful. He looked dead, in fact, and Genevieve's heart ached as if it were being gripped by pincers. "Has he stirred at all, Mrs. Watkins?"

The gruff old lady shook her head. "No. But he's still breathing. That's the important thing, Miss Crowfoot, and don't you go forgetting it. Strong prayers and a strong woman by his side are what he needs now."

Startled by the crusty Mrs. Watkins's words, which might almost be considered sentimental, Genevieve left off staring down at Tobias and glanced at the housekeeper. Good heavens, her eyes were red-rimmed and puffy, and she looked as if she'd been crying, too. Genevieve had never thought about Mrs. Watkins as having a woman's sensibilities, but obviously she did. It took a crisis to bring out her softness. She reached out and gripped the older woman's work-worn hand.

"Thank you so much for your help, Mrs. Watkins. I'll watch over him now. I have Dr. Johnson's instructions, and if he should wake, I'll send for tea."

Mrs. Watkins nodded grimly. "I'll brew up some beef tea, too, Miss. Beef tea will buck him up when he's strong enough to take it."

"Thank you."

"And you can be sure I won't leave Molly Gratchett to the feeding of him, either. He's a good man, Mr. Rakes, and I'm not going to allow that girl to poison him."

Poison. Oh, dear. Genevieve had forgotten all about the poison. She wondered if Wesley Armitage had set any more sneaky traps around the castle. She decided she'd better send a note to the constable, requesting that he pose the question to Armitage. She supposed he'd tell, unless he was so maddened by avarice and hatred that he still wished for Tobias's death. The thought sent a shudder through her.

Unaware of the motivation for Genevieve's shudder, Mrs. Watkins gave her a quick hug. "He's a fighter, Miss Crowfoot. If he hadn't been a fighter, his dratted father would have broken his spirit years ago."

Foolish tears sprang to Genevieve's eyes. She hadn't expected tenderness from Mrs. Watkins, and it unnerved her. She whispered, "Thank you."

Mrs. Watkins marched to the door. Just before she reached it, the two women heard a soft knock. The older woman snatched the door open and scowled. Small William Pickstaff, after taking a quick leap backward as if startled by the abrupt opening of the door, stood there, twisting his hat in his hands.

"What do you want, boy?" Mrs. Watkins asked harshly.

The poor lad looked scared, and Genevieve took pity on him. "Come in, Small William," she called softly from her station beside the sofa. "Are you here to ask after Mr. Rakes?"

The boy nodded and skirted around Mrs. Watkins, hurrying as if he expected her to whack him one on the head. The housekeeper watched him as if she expected him to steal the silver candlesticks from the mantelpiece, but at a nod from Genevieve, she left the room.

Small William slowed considerably as approached the sofa. Genevieve got the feeling he was afraid to look. She smiled at him. "Mr. Rakes is still very poorly, Small William."

He nodded again. "My ma says I'm to ask what I can do for you, ma'am. She says we owe Mr. Rakes, and we don't want nothing bad to happen to him."

"Yes, I can understand that. Your mother is a very kind woman."

Small William stared at her, his eyes big and scared. "Mr. Rakes gave us all jobs," he said simply.

Indeed, he had given them all jobs. Tobias Rakes had given jobs to a number of people in Bittersweet—many of them who weren't particularly qualified for any sort of work. After heaving a heavy sigh, Genevieve tried to smile at Small William, who shuffled and looked as if he were getting antsier by the second. He obviously didn't feel comfortable near sickness. Genevieve couldn't find it in her heart to fault him for his reluctance. She did, however, have what she considered a brilliant notion.

"Small William, if you'd like to be useful, there is something you can do for me. And for Mr. Rakes. It will mean taking a short ride."

The boy seemed relieved, as if he'd feared she'd ask him to share nursing duties. "Yes, ma'am," he said with more enthusiasm than she'd heard in his voice before.

"I believe we should notify Mr. Rakes's father. He should know that his son has been hurt." And might die. She couldn't say those words aloud.

"You want I should tell him?" Small William was back to looking scared again. There wasn't a soul in Bittersweet who didn't know of the animosity between the elder and the younger Rakes.

"You needn't tell him, Small William." Genevieve gave him an understanding smile. "I'll write him a note. All you need do is hand it to him."

The boy's relief was so obvious, Genevieve's heart almost

worked itself up to a laugh. Because she didn't want to leave Tobias's side even for a moment, she asked Small William to fetch paper and a pen from the small writing desk in her bedroom. The boy didn't appear awfully happy about venturing into a lady's bedroom, but he set out to do it, bless his heart.

"You can ask Mary to help you," Genevieve told him, mentioning the kindest of the troop of housemaids Tobias employed. Small William shot her a smile of appreciation and vanished.

No more than five minutes later he was back, several sheets of notepaper in one hand, and a pen and a bottle of ink in the other. Genevieve smiled her thanks. She didn't move from Tobias's side, but used the table at the end of the sofa upon which to compose her note. It took a while, because she'd never met the elder Mr. Rakes. The Crowfoots and the Rakeses hadn't shared more than common civilities—a nod in passing, for instance—with each other for more than a hundred years. Hostilities between the two families had cooled over the years until they now no longer tried to shoot each other from behind hedges, but relations had never been exactly cordial.

Several attempts and a few crumpled pieces of paper later, Genevieve decided she might as well give up and tell the truth in a simple, straightforward manner. If Mr. Rakes cared enough about his son to visit what might yet become Tobias's deathbed, Genevieve would welcome him gladly. If he didn't, so be it. However, she decided not to tell him about her engagement to Tobias. He may already have heard about it from village gossips, but if he hadn't, she reckoned one shock at a time was enough for any man.

"Here, Small William. I believe it would be best if you were to hand this to Mr. Rakes personally. If you can manage it, please don't give the note to a servant, but give it directly to Mr. Rakes yourself."

"Yes'm."

Small William had no sooner shut the door behind himself when Granny Crowfoot appeared, hovering over Tobias like the ghost she was. Genevieve sighed forlornly, hoping the volatile spirit wasn't there to make trouble.

"Is he badly hurt?"

Genevieve squinted at her deceased relative. The old ghost didn't sound sarcastic—or even happy—to see Tobias in this plight. "Yes. He's very badly hurt. Mr. Armitage shot him in the chest."

"Good heavens. The base villain!"

"Yes, he is that, all right."

"Why didn't you shoot him when you had the chance?"

Frowning, Genevieve muttered, "I wanted to. Tobias stopped me."

"Harrumph. The more fool he."

Suspicious of the ghost's motives, Genevieve eyed her sternly. "Don't you dare try any of your tricks, Granny Crowfoot. Tobias Rakes is a good man, and he's been grievously injured. If you disturb him in any way, I'll—I'll—" Since she didn't know what she'd do—after all, how could one hurt a ghost?—her threat stuttered out.

Granny Crowfoot waved an ethereal hand at her. *"I shan't do anything to cause trouble."*

She sounded more gloomy than Genevieve had ever heard her sound. The old ghoul had come to their rescue in the cellar, and Genevieve supposed she ought to thank her, even though she didn't honestly believe she'd done it out of any sort of humanitarian motives. Feeling somewhat reluctant because she didn't want to give the ghost more credit than she deserved, she said, "You might have saved Mr. Rakes's life when you appeared to us in the cellar, Granny Crowfoot. You scared the daylights out of Mr. Armitage, which distracted him and caused him to drop the gun. Thank you for showing up when you did."

"You're welcome."

Genevieve waited, expecting her to continue with some sort of diatribe against Tobias Rakes, the Rakes family in general, or the perfidy of a Crowfoot female daring to ally herself with a Rakes scoundrel.

Silence permeated the parlor like a fog. Granny Crowfoot didn't say a word more, but only remained there, suspended above Tobias's inert form like a storm cloud. Genevieve peered up at her warily. Because her nerves were about to explode in anticipation of the mischief she felt sure the ghost had in store, she said sharply, "Don't you dare do anything to disturb him, Granny Crowfoot."

The ghost frowned down at her. *"Do anything? What do you expect me to do?"*

"I don't know, but I'm sure you've got something up your sleeve."

"I don't even have a sleeve," Granny Crowfoot said snappishly, waving her arm. Sure enough, the ghost wore a sleeveless robe today. It made her appear even more amorphous than usual. *"I'm not planning anything, and I think you're being unconscionably vicious to me."*

"Vicious?" Genevieve could scarcely believe her ears. "Why, you've done nothing but cause trouble for Tobias ever since he moved in here." She realized her voice had risen and, not wanting to disturb the patient, lowered it. "You're probably only here to drop something on him."

"Nonsense! I'm here because—because—" Her agitation was evident in the flutteriness of her transparent form.

Genevieve had never seen her thus. Her eyes thinned. She still didn't trust her. "Because what? Why are you here? You make the room awfully cold, you know. I'm sure a draft isn't good for Tobias in his condition."

"Oh, bother!"

Nevertheless, Granny Crowfoot quit hovering and made a swoop down to sit in the chair opposite the low stool Genevieve occupied. Because she feared for Tobias's life and loved him madly, Genevieve picked up one of his hands and stroked it tenderly—one never knew about these things. Perhaps he might be aware of the ghost's presence, even if he didn't seem to be conscious, and Genevieve didn't want him to worry. She didn't take her gaze from Granny Crowfoot.

"Why are you here?" she asked again. Something occurred to her. "Is there something you, as a spirit, can do for him?" She tried not to sound too optimistic, since she knew Granny Crowfoot quite well by this time.

The ghost shook her head. *"I'm powerless to meddle in*

the affairs of living men.'' She sounded a trifle self-righteous.

She was also lying through her transparent teeth. "That's a fib, and you know it," Genevieve said bitterly. "You've done nothing but interfere with poor Tobias since he bought the castle. You've been horrid to him, and you know it. And why? All he ever wanted to do was fix the place up some.'' Because she feared she might begin to cry again, Genevieve shut her mouth. Oh, but she was angry at this ridiculous ghost!

"That's not true.'' Granny Crowfoot looked a little angry herself. She lifted her chin obstinately and glared at Genevieve. *"I probably saved the lout's life! You said so yourself.''*

Genevieve couldn't deny it. "But you also probably did it in spite of yourself and not because you meant to. And don't call Tobias a lout.''

"That's not fair. I knew exactly what I was doing. I wasn't about to let another blasted Rakes—and one who didn't have the decency to respect his own family—take over the running of the castle.'' She sniffed indignantly.

Eyeing her askance, not entirely believing her, Genevieve muttered, "Well, I do appreciate your interference in that instance. You probably saved both our lives, if it comes to that.''

"Exactly.'' The ghost raised her chin some more and looked to be preening.

Genevieve shook her head and didn't speak. Because she wanted to be doing something—anything—for Tobias, she smoothed his hair back from his pallid forehead and decided to lay a cool, damp cloth across it. Couldn't hurt, and Dr. Johnson had told her it might help.

Granny Crowfoot watched her as she dipped the cloth in a basin of water and wrung it out. *"That creature told me cupping is no longer considered an efficacious treatment for illness.''*

Cupping? Genevieve glanced at the ghost and decided to ignore her reference to Tobias as a creature. "Er, no, it isn't. Nor is bleeding a patient. Medical science has determined that people need all the blood they can get. Tobias has lost too much of his already.''

The ghost nodded, evidently interested in the miracle of modern medicine. *''In my day, no one called a doctor unless the situation was considered hopeless.''*

With a small shudder, Genevieve said, ''I can understand that, if they did hateful things like stick leeches on you.'' She wished the ghost would go away. She wanted to kiss Tobias's forehead where she'd wiped it with the cloth. Then she decided she didn't care if Granny Crowfoot became offended or not, and kissed him anyway. She thought she felt a faint fluttering of his eyelids, but wasn't sure. She knew she felt his breath on her cheek, though, and that was the important thing. If he'd only stay alive and give his body a chance to rest, he might heal.

Granny Crowfoot glared her disapproval. *''Modern customs are not universally admired, young lady. Such displays as that were kept to the bedroom, where they belonged, in my day.''*

''Such displays as what?'' asked Genevieve, nettled. ''Tobias and I love each other. We're going to be married as soon as he recovers.'' If he recovered. The knowledge that he might not made her voice catch. She resolutely choked down her fears. ''Besides, we're supposed to be alone in here. You're not generally held to exist, in case you didn't know it. It's not *my* fault you butted in to Tobias's sickroom this way.''

''Butted in? Why, I like that! Lest you forget, young woman, I am not merely your elder by a good century and more, but I recently saved your life and that of your wretched lover there.'' She jabbed a ghostly finger in Tobias's direction.

''He's not my 'wretched lover.' '' He was a brilliant lover, in fact. Genevieve didn't say so.

Silence prevailed once more. Genevieve gently smoothed the cloth over Tobias's forehead. Then she took his pulse. It seemed so faint to her. He wasn't feverish. She supposed that was a good sign. But his skin felt clammy, and he looked so—so—dead. She shook her head hard and commanded herself not to think like that. She had to believe he would recover. She *had* to.

Granny Crowfoot cleared her throat. Genevieve had almost forgotten her presence, and glanced up at her.

"And besides," the ghost said, her voice carrying a tone Genevieve had never heard in it before, *"I suppose I was wrong all those years."* She turned her head away, as if she didn't want to witness Genevieve's reaction to her admission.

Genevieve hardly reacted at all. "You were wrong about what? You've been wrong about so many things, as nearly as I can tell, that I don't know which one you mean. Which one are you talking about?"

The ghost's head whipped around again, and she scowled at Genevieve. Genevieve was used to Granny Crowfoot's scowls by this time, and didn't so much as blink.

Granny Crowfoot muttered something under her breath that Genevieve didn't catch. "I can't hear you."

The ghost expelled a huge breath. Genevieve still didn't know how and why she did such things. She couldn't possibly need to breathe, could she?

"I said I was wrong about my father." The ghoul sucked in another breath. *"I apologize for pestering Mr. Rakes. I suppose there wasn't really any reason to dislike the Rakes family so vehemently."*

Genevieve stared at her for a moment, then shook her head. "It's about time," she grumbled. "Imagine, carrying on a silly feud for over a hundred years. What an idiotic waste of time and energy."

The ghost stuck her stubborn chin out once more. *"It didn't seem like it at the time. You, young lady, have no compassion in your heart. How would you like it if some horrid man killed your father?"*

"He'd have a difficult time trying, since my father has been dead for quite a while. Besides, nobody killed your father. He died while he was trying to run away with his mistress." Genevieve didn't feel like giving an inch to this beastly ghost who had made Tobias's life so difficult in the past months.

"You needn't be cruel, young lady. You know very well what I mean."

Genevieve heaved a sigh of her own. "Yes. I know what you mean." Although she didn't much want to, she added, "I appreciate your apology."

Granny Crowfoot nodded graciously, for all the world like a proper lady and not the troublesome hoyden who'd been creating havoc in the castle for so long.

Because she was annoyed with the specter, Genevieve ground out, "And I expect you to offer Tobias an apology, too, when he recovers enough to hear it. You've been perfectly horrid to him, for no good reason, and he deserves to hear you admit it."

The ghost frowned and looked defiant. Genevieve could tell she didn't like her dictum one little bit. Too bad. Genevieve wasn't going to let her get away without apologizing to Tobias—providing Tobias ever woke up.

"Oh, very well," Granny Crowfoot said at last, obviously hating the necessity of apologizing to a Rakes.

Genevieve didn't say anything more, but concentrated on Tobias. Granny Crowfoot remained in the room but, for the first time since Genevieve met her, being still and not causing any trouble. She hoped this new, chastened demeanor would last, although she didn't expect it to.

It seemed like hours passed. Genevieve gave up swabbing Tobias's forehead, checked his pulse again, kissed him—on the lips this time—felt his breath, and sat in the chair next to the stool she'd been using. She had a crick in her back from stooping for so long. Granny Crowfoot sat in her own chair and watched Tobias, an enigmatic expression on her face. Genevieve didn't quite trust her yet, but at least the ghost didn't seem to be in any hurry to disturb Tobias.

Although she wouldn't have believed such a thing possible before it happened, Genevieve dozed. She didn't know how long she'd been sleeping when a sound made her sit bolt upright in her chair. Blinking, she lurched out of the chair and knelt beside the sofa. She heard it again.

"Genevieve?"

Faint, very faint—but it was there. She hadn't dreamed it.

"Tobias?" Tears started in her eyes. She gripped his hand. "Tobias?"

"Genevieve?"

"Tobias!" Weeping openly now, she kissed him on the lips. When, fearing for his health, she jerked away from him, he was smiling. She wiped her tears away and smiled, too. Tremulously.

"I like it when you do that," he whispered. His eyelids fluttered and opened.

Genevieve's heart soared. "Oh, Tobias! We were all so worried about you."

"I hurt like hell," he said, still smiling. "Where'd he hit me? My whole body feels like it's been scraped raw."

"Your chest. Dr. Johnson said the bullet didn't hit your heart or your lungs, but—but—" Genevieve swallowed a sob. "But you were grievously injured, Tobias. You have to rest. Don't move a muscle. Don't talk. You aren't supposed to do anything but rest."

Tobias shut his eyes and chuckled weakly. "I don't think I could do anything but rest if I tried."

For another moment or two, Genevieve thought he'd gone back to sleep, but he was evidently only resting because he opened his eyes again. "What happened to Wes?"

Genevieve shot a look at the ghost and smiled. "Granny Crowfoot showed up and scared him almost to death."

Tobias's eyes went wide. "You're joking."

She shook her head. "I'm not. Granny Crowfoot saved the day."

"I don't remember any of that."

"It happened, though. Thank God."

"Good Lord."

"What do you mean, good Lord, you young whippersnapper? I did save the day!"

Tobias caught Genevieve's eye. She understood his unspoken question and nodded. "Yes," she said, smiling. "I fear she's here."

Tobias sighed. "I might have known."

"Harrumph. Young people these days have no manners at all."

Tobias didn't even groan. He merely closed his eyes again and looked sick. Genevieve said softly, "She claims she isn't up to any mischief, Tobias. And I must admit she's behaved herself since she showed up."

"Mmmmm."

Genevieve laughed. A soft knock at the door startled her and made Tobias open his eyes again. She gazed at him lovingly. "It's probably Mrs. Watkins, Tobias. Be prepared. She's not a nurse to trifle with, and you can expect to be force-fed beef tea and all sorts of strengthening elixirs before you're well again."

He let out with a soft grunt. Genevieve giggled, got up, and went to the door. She was prepared with a happy greeting for Mrs. Watkins, but the words died on her tongue when she saw who stood there, looking ill at ease and worried.

"Mr. Rakes!"

Granny Crowfoot vanished.

Ernest Rakes, who probably had been the spitting image of Tobias in his youth, nodded. He held a spiffy derby hat in his hands and twiddled it between nervous fingers. "Yes, Miss Crowfoot. It is I. And I thank you for sending this young man to tell me of my son's accident." He nodded at Small William.

Accident! The tale of Wesley Armitage's perfidy almost tripped over itself in its haste to leave Genevieve's mouth, but she resolutely denied herself the pleasure of venting. Oh, but she wanted to demand how this awful old man could have sent such a villain as Wesley Armitage into his own son's house—how he could have disowned Tobias in the first place. But Genevieve held her tongue, knowing this wasn't the time or the place.

She could not, however, keep a certain coldness from her manner when she stepped aside and gestured Ernest Rakes into the parlor. At a look from Small William, Genevieve nodded, and the boy took off, evidently not caring to witness the ensuing scene between father and son. Genevieve almost wished she could join him.

Watching Ernest Rakes narrowly—she didn't know whether to trust him or not—she said, "He's on the sofa,

Mr. Rakes. Dr. Johnson didn't want to take the chance of carrying him to his bed. It was difficult enough getting him out of the cellar.''

Tobias's voice reached her, soft and pained. "Who is it, love?''

Ernest Rakes shot a startled glance at Genevieve. She nodded. "Yes, Mr. Rakes. Tobias and I plan to marry as soon as he's well enough.'' To Tobias, she called, "A moment, darling. I'll be there in a moment.''

The elder Rakes stared at her for another second or two and nodded, apparently not wishing to say anything—anything at all—that might cause further dissension between himself and Tobias. He licked his lips. "May I see my son?''

Genevieve eyed him for another moment, unsure what to do. She wasn't certain Tobias wanted to see this old man who'd caused him so much grief. On the other hand, Ernest Rakes had come, and he was Tobias's father. If he truly begrudged Tobias his name and held the past against him, she supposed he'd have let his son die without stirring from his family home. Therefore, she nodded. "Over here. Please don't try to talk to him. He's terribly weak.''

Again, Ernest Rakes nodded, and he walked behind Genevieve without a word, evidently willing to follow her commands if he was allowed to see his son.

Tobias had closed his eyes again and seemed to be dozing. Genevieve knelt beside him and felt his cheek and forehead. He still didn't seem feverish, and she hoped that condition would continue.

Mr. Rakes said, "He looks terrible.'' His voice broke.

She looked up at him and nodded. "He's been badly wounded.''

"And Wesley Armitage did this to him?''

Again she nodded.

"My God.'' The two words came out in a miserable whisper. Ernest Rakes didn't seem to know what to do with himself now, and repeated, "My God.''

Tobias slowly opened his eyes. "I thought I heard . . .'' His voice trailed off.

Genevieve said, "Yes, darling, your father has come to call."

Ernest Rakes gave his son a shaky smile.

Tobias squinted at his father. Then he moaned piteously and closed his eyes again.

Chapter
Twenty

Damn it, why did the old man have to show up now, when he was incapacitated? Hundreds of times in the past seventeen years, Tobias had envisioned meeting his father again. Sometimes his mind's eye pictured Ernest Rakes groveling and Tobias gracious. At other times, the imaginary Ernest and Tobias remained cold and hostile to each other.

Not once, in all those seventeen years, had Tobias featured himself laid out flat on a sofa with a bullet hole in his side, shot by a man hired by his father to lure him back into the family fold. He didn't know what to say. Since that was the case, it was perhaps fortunate that he was too weak to say anything at all.

Obviously, however, Ernest had no idea what to say either. He stared down at Tobias, mute as a statue. Tobias peeked up at him through slitted eyelids, figuring that since he was the wounded party, he could be forgiven for his own silence.

Genevieve—God bless her—took the initiative from both men.

"Tobias," she repeated in her soft, lovely voice. "Your father has come to call."

There was no help for it. Tobias guessed he'd have to open his eyes all the way and acknowledge his parent's presence.

So he did. He even managed to whisper, "Sir." It was formal and cold, but Tobias had never known his father to be anything but formal and cold.

"Tobias." The older man's voice quavered.

Genevieve, still standing close, asked quietly, "Would you like me to leave you alone with your father for a moment, Tobias?"

Tobias jerked his head sideways and, using all the strength in his body, croaked, "No!" Good God, if there was one thing he didn't want even more than he didn't want to be laid up again, it was to be alone with his father.

Genevieve clearly understood. She nodded and said, "I'll sit over here."

Blast it, she moved out of his range of vision. Tobias felt abandoned, although he figured he was being silly. He frowned up at his father. Summoning all of his waning strength once more, he said, "Sit down, sir." He hated having the old man looming over him like that. Reminded him of his childhood.

Ernest Rakes did as Tobias commanded. He did so without voicing an objection, or taking Tobias to task for being impolite. He did not, however, sit far enough away for Tobias to lose sight of him, blast it. He considered asking his father and Genevieve to trade places, but was too weak to voice his suggestion. This wasn't fair.

Since he'd been shot and was in no fit condition to initiate a conversation, he decided to let his father do it. If the old man didn't want to talk, so be it. Tobias felt too rotten to indulge in chitchat anyway.

His father cleared his throat. It was a start. It might have been the finish as well, but right before Tobias drifted into unconsciousness, Ernest Rakes spoke.

"I'm sorry, son."

Tobias could hardly credit his ears. He managed to pry his eyelids up so he could squint at the old man. He was an old man, too. He looked ever so much older than Tobias remembered. Almost too feeble to speak, Tobias gazed at him for a moment or two, trying to figure out what he was supposed to say now. In a way, he wasn't altogether sure he even cared if the old fool was sorry or not.

His father, nervous in the face of Tobias's silence, spoke before Tobias could summon the energy and the wit to say a word.

"I believe I was unfair to you all those years ago, son."

Son, again. When was the last time the old man had called him son? Tobias, whose mind seemed unwilling to do much work, couldn't recall. He still didn't speak.

"I never meant for us to be estranged for so many years."

Fine time to think about that. Fortunately, Tobias was too exhausted to say so. He did manage to utter a small, pained grunt. Fat lot of good that did anyone.

He heard a sob, and his eyes popped open. That sob didn't sound like one of Genevieve's.

Good God, it was his father's! Tobias saw Ernest Rakes, his face buried in his hands, crying. He wondered if he was delirious. When he'd been wounded by that arrow, he'd been delirious for several days. He might well be delirious now.

He squinted harder. No. He was pretty sure he wasn't seeing things that weren't there, because Genevieve was now standing next to Ernest, handing him a handkerchief. The old man was taking it, too, and wiping his eyes with it.

Good God. Tobias almost wished he'd pass out again.

After several good sniffles, his father continued speaking. "I know I was too hard on you, son. I wrote you a letter when they told me you'd moved back to Bittersweet. Perhaps I phrased my request for a reconciliation too harshly."

Perhaps? Tobias would have snorted if he'd been able.

"But I didn't mean to, Tobias. I—I—" He sniffled again. "It's difficult for an old man to change his ways, I suppose. I hope you'll be able to forgive me. I never meant to sever the ties between us."

Interesting. Tobias wasn't sure whether he believed him or not. Fortunately his father didn't seem to expect an immediate answer—probably thought Tobias was about to croak—so Tobias remained silent.

"I've met your young woman, son. She seems like a lovely woman, even if she is a Crowfoot."

Tobias's squint thinned. He could scarcely believe the old goat had said that.

"Honestly!"

That from Genevieve. Although too sick to laugh out loud, Tobias laughed inside. He hoped Genevieve would clue the old man in on a few things. Since she still stood at Ernest's side, he managed to catch her eye. She understood, and nodded. Tobias's insides, which hurt like fire, lit up a very little bit.

"Don't try to speak, son," Ernest continued. "I only want you to know that I forgive you."

He forgave *Tobias?* If he'd felt better, Tobias would have sent the awful man away. Since he couldn't, he was pleased when Genevieve took up the battle on his behalf.

"I beg your pardon for interrupting this tender scene, Mr. Rakes," she said in the most sarcastic tone Tobias had ever heard issue from her marvelous lips. "But I don't believe your son has done anything for which to be forgiven. *You* are the one whose coldness sent him off into the arms of a conniving harpy all those years ago, don't forget. And *you* are the one who sent a murderer into our midst. If you'd exhibited even an iota of human kindness and understanding, you wouldn't have been estranged from your only son for so many years."

Through slitted eyelids, Tobias watched as his father's face went through a variety of emotions, from surprise to anger to resignation. The old man wasn't used to people standing up to him, more's the pity, or for reminding him what a miserable skinflint he was. With an internal grin, Tobias figured the old man had better get used to it, since neither Tobias himself nor Genevieve, God bless her, was a shrinking violet.

"Not only that," Genevieve went on, "but I think it's unconscionable for a father to disown his son. I think it's you who should be asking Tobias's forgiveness, rather than the other way around." She flounced out of Tobias's sight, and he sighed, sorry to see her go. He peered at his father to see what the bastard would do in the face of such a scolding.

Ernest Rakes, head bowed, whispered, ''I'm sorry. You're right. Please forgive me, son.''

The shock of the old man's words sent Tobias reeling off into unconsciousness once more.

The relationship between Ernest and Tobias Rakes was not repaired in an instant. Too many years and too much heartache had gone by to make a reconciliation easy.

Nevertheless, Genevieve was happy that Tobias did not bar his father from his home. If he wasn't precisely cordial, he at least let him visit. Often during the weeks of Tobias's convalescence, Ernest Rakes came to call on a warm summer afternoon when Genevieve read to Tobias as he rested in the sunken garden. Delilah was often there, too—though she still refused to go inside the castle—and the older Rakes and the older Crowfoot seemed to become friendly to each other, after an initial period of suspicion and mistrust.

Of course, their mutual mistrust suffered a severe bludgeoning when Genevieve and Tobias told them the truth about the origins of the family feud. It was difficult to tell which one of the older folks was more shocked by the news.

Delilah paled. ''I don't believe it!''

Ernest didn't look so hearty himself. He frowned—an expression Genevieve imagined Tobias remembered well from his boyhood, poor man. Genevieve was sure she'd be a different person today if she'd grown up under such severe, constant disapproval. ''You say Charles Crowfoot was a traitor?''

But Genevieve wasn't about to let him get away with that one. ''He and Gerald Rakes, both, were traitors, Mr. Rakes. It's not a one-sided treachery, unfortunately. Charles Crowfoot, Gerald Rakes, and Ivor Pickstaff were all scoundrels.''

Genevieve could tell that Ernest didn't like such plain speaking. He did not, however, take her to task, probably because he knew Tobias would have him booted from the castle grounds if he did.

''Hmmm,'' Ernest mumbled eventually.

Genevieve could tell he was unhappy to have the truth of

the feud's origins cleared up. She sniffed, astonished by how stubbornly people could cling to their misconceptions rather than accept an unpleasant truth.

"I don't want to talk about the damned feud." Tobias shared his frown between Delilah and his father.

Genevieve patted his hand, understanding how cranky he was to be laid up and in pain. But he was recovering, and that was the important thing. "You're right, Tobias dear," she said in a voice she expected she'd be using on her children one of these days. "It's an unpleasant topic and it has caused all three families too much grief already over the years."

His frown visited her for a moment before it softened, as his frowns always did in her presence. He turned his hand over and caught hers, then lifted it to his lips and kissed it. Genevieve was delighted.

Delilah blushed.

Ernest Rakes grimaced and looked away.

Silly people. Genevieve leaned over to return Tobias's chaste kiss—only she kissed him right on the lips. Let Delilah and Ernest disapprove if they wanted. Genevieve didn't give two hoots.

That night, in Tobias's bed, Genevieve was very careful when they made love. Tobias had taught her an important lesson in lovemaking: The man didn't always have to be on top.

Naked as a jay and totally uninhibited in the presence of Tobias's loving approval, Genevieve rode him as if she were riding a stallion. Which, in a way, she was. Her release came in a wild, convulsive rush. Tobias, with a roar, joined her in completion.

Sated, she sank to his side so as not to put any pressure on his healing chest wound. "Oh, my," she whispered.

"I love you more than I ever expected to love anyone, Genevieve Crowfoot—soon to be Genevieve Rakes."

She sighed and smiled. "Doesn't that sound nice. We ought to name our children Ivor, Gerald, and Charles, you know."

He chuckled weakly. "What if they're girls?"

Genevieve thought for a minute. "Ivory, Geraldine, and Charlotte?"

"Good God. Why don't we forget the instigators of the feud entirely, love, and name them Jane and Peter."

"Wonderful idea." Genevieve turned on her side and kissed him so thoroughly that she had to climb back on for another ride in a very few minutes.

Granny Crowfoot remained blessedly absent from their lives during the several weeks of Tobias's convalescence. Genevieve and Tobias sometimes wondered if the spirit had finally laid herself to rest, although neither of them dared to hope too hard.

Wesley Armitage was arraigned in the Bittersweet courthouse on charges of attempted murder. During the third week of his confinement in the courthouse's only cell, he ripped a bed sheet into strips, tied the strips together, and hanged himself from an overhead fixture. Since the town was too small to have a guard on duty twenty-four hours a day, no one was accused of negligence.

"If a fellow tries to kill somebody and then decides to kill himself instead, I don't suppose it's anyone's lookout but his own," Old William Pickstaff said in an uncharacteristic burst of eloquence.

Although much head-shaking ensued, the majority of Bittersweet citizens agreed with Old William.

Tobias had Wesley Armitage buried in the Rakes vault. As he told Genevieve, rather sadly, poor Wes had cared more about the family name than Tobias ever did.

Genevieve and Tobias were wed in the Crowfoot Castle chapel on October 23, 1895. Tobias's wound, which had been sustained on August 3, was fairly well healed by that time. It was at least healed enough so that Genevieve no longer had to do all the work when they made love, which they both considered a blessing. Not that they didn't enjoy making love no matter how they did it.

After much pleading, Genevieve persuaded Delilah to enter the chapel and serve as her maid of honor. Pale and shaky, Delilah performed her duty. She had even begun to enjoy the reception, held in the castle's huge flagged entryway, until Granny Crowfoot put in an appearance in a gown that would have looked at home in George III's court.

Genevieve saw the ghost first, and tugged her husband's sleeve. Tobias, grinning down at her, saw her expression and his grin faded as he realized what had happened. "Please tell me it's not true," he whispered, only half joking.

"I fear it is," Genevieve whispered back.

Delilah, standing next to Genevieve, said, "What's true, dear?"

Genevieve, hoping to prepare her aunt, said gently, "Ah, I think our family ghost has come to enjoy the festivities, Aunt Delilah."

"*What?*" Delilah dropped the cup she'd been filling into the punchbowl and shot a frantic look around the hallway.

Genevieve took hold of her arm, hoping to forestall blind panic on her aunt's part. Her gesture was of no avail. As soon as Delilah caught sight of the ghost, hovering just above the landing where the grand staircase separated into its two sweeping arcs, she let out with a shriek that caused every one of the guests to freeze. Then she headed for the double doors of the castle at a dead run, as if all the demons in hell pursued her.

Ernest Rakes, who had been chatting nearby—he lately seemed to hover around Delilah much as Granny Crowfoot now hovered over the staircase—shot Genevieve and Tobias a look that as much as accused them of pinching Delilah out of malice.

Tobias held Genevieve's arm as she tried to race after Delilah. When she glance at him over her shoulder, he nodded in the direction of the front door. Genevieve looked—and relaxed. She now saw what Tobias had seen: Ernest Rakes hurrying after Delilah. Then she saw Delilah respond to Ernest's call, turn, and rush back to him. Ernest caught her in his arms and held her tight.

Genevieve murmured, "My goodness."

Tobias said, "Indeed."

And they both laughed.

Granny Crowfoot swooped down to scowl at them both. Right before she vanished in a puff of smoke that left the rest of the guests blinking with wonder, she hissed, *"Another Crowfoot-Rakes alliance? I can't stand it."*

She did stand it, though. She stood it for decades. And, although she fussed and prattled about the horror of it all, and set up the occasional noisy haunt when one of the children annoyed her, she even allowed Genevieve and Tobias's progeny to introduce her to their childhood chums occasionally. They especially enjoyed doing so on All Hallow's Eve.

"You'd think I was a household pet or something," Granny Crowfoot grumbled one early November night as Genevieve cradled newborn baby Deborah on her lap. Tobias had been reading to her by the light of the brand-new Tiffany electrical lamp. The rest of their children—Philip, Andrew, Jane, and Paul—slept upstairs.

Tobias laughed. Genevieve, grinning, said, "They love you, Granny Crowfoot. They even begged Tobias and me to name Deborah after you." Genevieve and Tobias had been living in the castle for ten years before Granny Crowfoot admitted that she had been christened Deborah.

The ghost humphed. This evening she was clad in a high-waisted, empire-style gown that would have looked right at home in George IV's day. Granny Crowfoot preferred fashions of an older era, claiming modern garb was both shocking and ugly. Genevieve never argued with her.

"Besides, you know you love all the attention," Tobias said. He'd taken to ribbing the ghost whenever he could. He figured she deserved it.

"Love it?" Granny Crowfoot gave one of her patented snorts.

"It's true, you know," Genevieve said, smiling at her husband. "And they love it, too. You're their favorite. I'm sure they enjoy you more than they do Aunt Delilah or Grandpa Ernest."

The ghost snorted again. *"Who wouldn't like me better than either of those old sticks? That ridiculous aunt of yours is forever screeching about something, and your father, young man, is the horridest old curmudgeon I've ever met."*

"I'm not going to argue with you about that one," Tobias muttered.

Genevieve laughed once more. "Well, if you'd stop trying to frighten Delilah every time she sets foot on the castle grounds, she might stop screeching."

"Nonsense. She's a ridiculous old woman. Imagine being afraid of ghosts."

Genevieve and Tobias exchanged a look. Tobias stuck a marker in the book and laid it aside. "Is the baby asleep yet?"

"Almost."

"Let me see that child," Granny Crowfoot said. She swooped over to observe her namesake. Even she, the crankiest of a cranky race, couldn't repress a rush of tenderness in the presence of so sweet a bundle of innocence. She even touched the child's cheek, producing a babyish smile and a bubble on Deborah's pink lips. *"She's the loveliest of the lot,"* the ghost declared proudly. *"Good thing, too. I wouldn't want my name bestowed on an ugly duckling."*

"All of our children are lovely," Genevieve reminded her stoutly.

"Except for the boys," Tobias temporized. "They're handsome."

"As handsome as their father." Genevieve gave her husband a loving look, which he returned with warmth.

"And I," Tobias continued, "believe it's time we went upstairs and started working on more beautiful children."

"What a splendid idea."

Genevieve laughed when Granny Crowfoot rolled her eyes and muttered, *"God give me patience."*

She didn't mean it, though. She loved her family, even if it had been commingled with the seed of the demon Rakeses. She scowled after Genevieve and Tobias as they left to take Deborah to her crib.

As soon as the door closed behind the happy couple and their latest treasure, however, the ghost hugged herself and did a little swooping dance around the parlor. For the first time in her life and death, she was truly happy.

Turn the page for a preview of

JILL MARIE LANDIS'S

latest novel

Blue Moon

Coming in July
from Jove Books

Prologue

She would be nineteen tomorrow. If she lived. In the center of a faint deer trail on a ribbon of dry land running through a dense swamp, a young woman crouched like a cornered animal. The weak, gray light from a dull, overcast sky barely penetrated the bald-cypress forest as she wrapped her arms around herself and shivered, trying to catch her breath. She wore nothing to protect her from the elements but a tattered rough, homespun dress and an ill-fitting pair of leather shoes that had worn blisters on her heels.

The primeval path was nearly obliterated by lichen and fern that grew over deep drifts of dried twigs and leaves. Here and there the ground was littered with the larger rotting fallen limbs of trees. The fecund scent of decay clung to the air, pressed down on her, stoked her fear, and gave it life.

Breathe. Breathe.

The young woman's breath came fast and hard. She squinted through her tangled black hair, shoved it back, her fingers streaked with mud. Her hands shook. Terror born of being lost was heightened by the knowledge that night was going to fall before she found her way out of the swamp.

Not only did the encroaching darkness frighten her, but so did the murky silent water along both sides of the trail. She realized would she soon be surrounded by both night and water. Behind her, from somewhere deep amid the cypress trees wrapped in rust colored bark, came the sound of a splash as some unseen creature dropped into the watery ooze.

She rose, spun around, and scanned the surface of the swamp. Frogs and fish, venomous copperheads and turtles, big as frying pans, thrived beneath the lacy emerald carpet of duckweed that floated upon the water. As she knelt there wondering whether she should continue on in the same direction or turn back, she watched a small knot of fur float toward her over the surface of the water.

A soaking wet muskrat lost its grace as soon as it made land and lumbered up the bank in her direction. Amused, yet wary, she scrambled back a few inches. The creature froze and stared with dark beady eyes before it turned tail, hit the water, and disappeared.

Getting to her feet, the girl kept her eyes trained on the narrow footpath, gingerly stepping through piles of damp, decayed leaves. Again she paused, lifted her head, listened for the sound of a human voice and the pounding footsteps that meant someone was in pursuit of her along the trail.

When all she heard was the distant knock of a woodpecker, she let out a sigh of relief. Determined to keep moving, she trudged on, ever vigilant, hoping that the edge of the swamp lay just ahead.

Suddenly, the sharp, shrill scream of a bobcat set her heart pounding. A strangled cry escaped from her lips. With a fist pressed against her mouth, she squeezed her eyes closed and froze, afraid to move, afraid to even breathe. The cat screamed again and the cry echoed across the haunting silence of the swamp until it seemed to stir the very air around her.

She glanced up at dishwater-gray patches of weak afternoon light nearly obliterated by the cypress trees that grew so close together in some places that not even a small child could pass between them. The thought that a wildcat might be looming somewhere above her in the tangled limbs, crouched and ready to pounce, sent her running down the narrow, winding trail.

She had not gone a hundred steps when the toe of her shoe caught beneath an exposed tree root. Thrown forward, she began to fall and cried out.

As the forest floor rushed up to meet her, she put out her hands to break the fall. A shock of pain shot through her wrist an instant before her head hit a log.

And then her world went black.

One

Noah LeCroix walked to the edge of the wide wooden porch surrounding the one-room cabin he had built high in the sheltering arms of an ancient bald cypress tree and looked out over the swamp. Twilight gathered, thickening the shadows that shrouded the trees. The moon had already risen, a bright silver crescent riding atop a faded blue sphere. He loved the magic of the night, loved watching the moon and stars appear in the sky almost as much as he loved the swamp. The wetlands pulsed with life all night long. The darkness coupled with the still, watery landscape settled a protective blanket of solitude around him. In the dense, liquid world beneath him and the forest around his home, all manner of life coexisted in a delicate balance. He likened the swamp's dance of life and death of the way good and evil existed together in the world of men beyond its boundaries.

This shadowy place was his universe, his sanctuary. He savored its peace, was used to it after having grown up in almost complete isolation with his mother, a reclusive Cherokee woman who had left her people behind when she chose to settle in far-off Kentucky with his father, a French Canadian fur trapper named Gerard LeCroix.

Living alone served Noah's purpose now more than ever. He had no desire to dwell among "civilized men," especially

now that so many white settlers were moving in droves
across the Ohio into the new state of Illinois.

Noah turned away from the smooth log railing that bor-
dered the wide, covered porch cantilevered out over the
swamp. He was about to step into the cabin where a single
oil lamp cast its circle of light when he heard a bobcat
scream. He would not have given the sound a second thought
if not for the fact that a few seconds later the sound was
followed by a high-pitched shriek, one that sounded human
enough to stop him in his tracks. He paused on the threshold
and listened intently. A chill ran down his spine.

It had been so long since he had heard the sound of another human voice that he could not really be certain, but he
thought he had just heard a woman's cry.

Noah shook off the ridiculous, unsettling notion and
walked into the cabin. The walls were covered with water
the tanned hides of mink, bobcat, otter, beaver, fox, white-
tailed deer, and bear. His few other possessions—a bone-
handled hunting knife with a distinctive wolf's head carved
on it, various traps, some odd pieces of clothing, a few pots
and a skillet, four wooden trenchers and mugs, and a rifle—
were all neatly stored inside. They were all he owned and
needed in the world, save the dugout canoe secured outside
near the base of the tree.

Sparse but comfortable, even the sight of the familiar surroundings could not help him shake the feeling that something unsettling was about to happen, that all was not right
in his world.

Pulling a crock off a high shelf, Noah poured a splash of
whiskey in a cup and drank it down, his concentration intent
on the deepening gloaming and the sounds of the swamp.
An unnatural stillness lingered in the air after the puzzling
scream, almost as if, like him, the wild inhabitants of Heron
Pond were collectively waiting for something to happen. Unable to deny his curiosity any longer, Noah sighed in resignation and walked back to the door.

He lingered there for a moment, staring out at the growing
shadows. Something was wrong. *Someone* was out there. He
reached for the primed and loaded Hawken rifle that stood

just inside the door and stepped out into the gathering dusk.

He climbed down the crude ladder of wooden strips nailed to the trunk of one of the four prehistoric cypress that supported his home, stepped into the dugout *pirogue*, tied to a cypress knee that poked out of the water. Noah paddled the shallow wooden craft toward a spot where the land met the deep dark water with its camouflage net of duckweed, a natural boundary all but invisible to anyone unfamiliar with the swamp.

He reached a rise of land which supported a trail, carefully stepped out of the *pirogue*, and secured it to a low-hanging tree branch. Walking through thickening shadows, Noah breathed in his surroundings, aware of every subtle nuance of change, every depression on the path that might really be a footprint on the trail, every tree and stand of switchcane.

The sound he thought he'd heard had come from the southeast. Noah headed in that direction, head down, staring at the trail although it was almost too dark to pick up any sign. A few hundred yards from where he left the *pirogue*, he paused, raised his head, sniffed the air, and listened to the silence.

Instinctively, he swung his gaze in the direction of a thicket of slender cane stalks and found himself staring across ten yards of low undergrowth into the eyes of a female bobcat on the prowl. Slowly he raised his rifle to his shoulder and waited to see what the big cat would do. The animal stared back at him, its eyes intense in the gathering gloaming. Finally, she blinked and with muscles bunching beneath her fine, shiny coat, the cat turned and padded away.

Noah lowered the rifle and shook his head. He decided the sound he heard earlier must have been the bobcat's cry and nothing more. But just as he stepped back in the direction of the *pirogue*, he caught a glimpse of ivory on the trail ahead that stood out against the dark tableau. His leather moccasins did not make even a whisper of sound on the soft earth. He closed the distance and quickly realized what he was seeing was a body lying across the path.

His heart was pounding as hard as Chickasaw drums when he knelt beside the young woman stretched out upon the ground. Laying his rifle aside, he stared at the unconscious female, then looked up and glanced around in every direction. The nearest white settlement was beyond the swamp to the northeast. There was no sign of a companion or fellow traveler nearby, something he found more than curious.

Noah took a deep breath, let go a ragged sigh and looked at the girl again. She lay on her side, as peacefully as if she were napping. She was so very still that the only evidence that she was alive was the slow, steady rise and fall of her breasts. Although there was no visible sign of injury, she lay on the forest floor with her head beside a fallen log. One of her arms was outstretched, the other tucked beneath her. What he could see of her face was filthy. So were her hands; they were beautifully shaped, her fingers long and tapered. Her dress, nothing but a rag with sleeves, was hiked up to her thighs. Her shapely legs showed stark ivory against the decayed leaves and brush beneath her.

He tentatively reached out to touch her, noticed his hand shook, and balled it into a fist. He clenched it tight, then opened his hand and gently touched the tangled, black hair that hid the side of her face. She did not stir when he moved the silken skein, nor when he brushed it back and looped it over her ear.

Her face was streaked with mud. Her lashes were long and dark, her full lips tinged pink. The sight of her beauty took his breath away. Noah leaned forward and gently reached beneath her. Rolling her onto her back, he straightened her arms and noted her injuries. Her wrist appeared to be swollen. She had an angry lump on her forehead near her hairline. She moaned as he lightly probed her injured wrist; he realized he was holding his breath. Noah expected her eyelids to flutter open, but they did not.

He scanned the forest once again. With night fast closing in, he saw no alternative except to take her home with him. If he was going to get her back to the tree house before dark, he would have to hurry. He cradled her gently in his arms, reached for his rifle, and then straightened. Even then the girl did not awaken, although she did whimper and turn her face against his buckskin jacket, burrowing against him. It felt strange carrying a woman in his arms, but he had no time to dwell on that as he quickly carried her back to the *pirogue*, set her inside, and untied the craft. He climbed in behind her, holding her upright, then gently drew her back until she leaned against his chest.

As the paddle cut silently through water black as pitch, he tried to concentrate on guiding the dugout canoe home, but was distracted by the way the girl felt pressed against him, the way she warmed him. As his body responded to a need he had long tried to deny, he felt ashamed at his lack of control. What kind of a man was he, to become aroused by a helpless, unconscious female?

Overhead, the sky was tinted deep violet, an early canvas for the night's first stars. During the last few yards of the journey, the swamp grew so dark that he had only the yellow glow of lamplight shining from his home high above the water to guide him.

Run. Keep running.

The dream was so real that Olivia Bond could feel the leaf-littered ground beneath her feet and the faded chill of winter that lingered on the damp April air. She suffered, haunted by memories of the past year, some still so vivid they turned her dreams into nightmares. Even now, as she lay tossing in her sleep, she could feel the faint sway of the flatboat as it moved down river long ago. In her sleep the fear welled up inside her.

Her dreaming mind began to taunt her with palpable memories of new sights and scents and dangers.

Run. Run. Run, Olivia. You're almost home.

Her legs thrashed, startling her awake. She sat straight up, felt a searing pain in her right wrist and a pounding in her head that forced her to quickly lie back down. She kept her eyes closed until the stars stopped dancing behind them, then she slowly opened them and looked around.

The red glow of embers burning in a fireplace illuminated the ceiling above her. She lay staring up at even log beams that ran across a wide planked ceiling, trying to ignore the pounding in her head, fighting to stay calm and let her memory come rushing back. Slowly she realized she was no longer lost on the forest trail. She had not become a bobcat's dinner, but was indoors, in a cabin, on a bed.

She spread her fingers and pressed her hands palms down against a rough, woven sheet drawn over her. The mattress was filled with something soft that gave off a tangy scent. A pillow cradled her head.

Slowly Olivia turned her aching head, afraid of who or what she might find beside her, but when she discovered she was in bed alone, she thanked God for small favors.

Refusing to panic, she thought back to her last lucid memory: a wildcat's scream. She recalled tearing through the cypress swamp, trying to make out the trail in the dim light before she tripped. She lifted her hand to her forehead and felt swelling. After testing it gingerly, she was thankful that she had not gashed her head open and bled to death.

She tried to lift her head again but intense pain forced her to lie still. Olivia closed her eyes and sighed. A moment later, an unsettling feeling came over her. She knew by the way her skin tingled, the way her nerve endings danced, that someone was nearby. Someone was watching her. An instinctive, intuitive sensation warned her that the *someone* was a man.

At first she peered through her lashes, but all she could make out was a tall, shadowy figure standing in the open doorway across the room. Her heart began to pound so hard she was certain the sound would give her consciousness away.

The man walked into the room and she bit her lips together to hold back a cry. She watched him move about purposefully. Instead of coming directly to the bed, he walked over to a small square table. She heard him strike a piece of flint, smelled lamp oil as it flared to life.

His back was to her as he stood at the table; Olivia opened her eyes wider and watched. He was tall, taller than most men, strongly built, dressed in buckskin pants topped by a buff shirt with billowing sleeves. Despite the coolness of the evening, he wore no coat, no jacket. Indian moccasins, not shoes, covered his feet. His hair was deep black, cut straight, and worn long enough to hang just over his collar. She watched his bronzed, well-tapered hands turn up the lamp wick and set the glass chimney in place.

Olivia sensed he was about to turn and look at her. She wanted to close her eyes and pretend to be unconscious, thinking that might be safer than letting him catch her staring at him, but as he slowly turned toward the bed, she knew she had to see him. She had to know what she was up against.

Her gaze swept his body, taking in his great height, the length of his arms, the width and breadth of his shoulders, before she dared even look at his face.

When she did, she gasped.

Noah stood frozen beside the table, shame and anger welling up from deep inside. He was unable to move, unable to breathe as the telling sound of the girl's shock upon seeing his face died on the air. He watched her flinch and scoot back into the corner, press close to the wall. He knew her head pained her, but obviously not enough to keep her from showing her revulsion or from trying to scramble as far away as she could.

He had the urge to walk out, to turn around and leave. Instead, he stared back and let her look all she wanted. It had been three years since he had lost an eye to a flatboat accident on the Mississippi. Three years since another woman had laughed in his face. Three years since he moved to southern Illinois to put the past behind him.

When her breathing slowed and she calmed, he held his hands up to show her that they were empty, hoping to put her a little more at ease.

"I'm sorry," he said as gently as he could. "I don't mean you any harm."

She stared up at him as if she did not understand a blessed word.

Louder this time, he spoke slowly. "Do-you-speak-English?"

The girl clutched the sheet against the filthy bodice of her dress and nodded. She licked her lips, cleared her throat. Her mouth opened and closed like a fish out of water, but no sound came out.

"Yes," she finally croaked. "Yes, I do." And then, "Who are you?"

"My name is Noah. Noah LeCroix. This is my home. Who are you?"

The lamplight gilded her skin. She looked to be all eyes, soft green eyes, long black hair, and fear. She favored her injured wrist, held it cradled against her midriff. From the way she carefully moved her head, he knew she was fighting one hell of a headache, too.

Ignoring his question, she asked one of her own. "How did I get here?" Her tone was wary. Her gaze kept flitting over to the door and then back to him.

"I heard a scream. Went out and found you in the swamp. Brought you here—"

"The wildcat?"

"Wasn't very hungry." Noah tried to put her at ease, then he shrugged, stared down at his moccasins. Could she tell how nervous he was? Could she see his awkwardness, know how strange it was for him to be alone with a woman? He had no idea what to say or do. When he looked over at her again, she was staring at the ruined side of his face.

"How long have I been asleep?" Her voice was so low that he had to strain to hear her. She looked like she expected him to leap on her and attack her any moment, as if he might be coveting her scalp.

"Around two hours. You must have hit your head really hard."

She reached up, felt the bump on her head. "I guess I did."

He decided not to get any closer, not with her acting like she was going to jump out of her skin. He backed up, pulled a stool out from under the table, and sat down.

"You going to tell me your name?" he asked.

The girl hesitated, glanced toward the door, then looked back at him. "Where am I?"

"Heron Pond."

Her attention shifted to the door once again; recollection

dawned. She whispered, "The swamp." Her eyes widened as if she expected a bobcat or a cottonmouth to come slithering in.

"You're fairly safe here. I built this cabin over the water."

"Fairly?" She looked as if she was going to try to stand up again. "Did you say—"

"Built on cypress trunks. About fifteen feet above the water."

"How do I get down?"

"There are wooden planks nailed to a trunk."

"Am I anywhere near Illinois?"

"You're in it."

She appeared a bit relieved. Obviously she wasn't going to tell him her name until she was good and ready, so he did not bother to ask again. Instead he tried, "Are you hungry? I figure anybody with as little meat on her bones as you ought to be hungry."

What happened next surprised the hell out of him. It was a little thing, one that another man might not have even noticed, but he had lived alone so long he was used to concentrating on the very smallest of details, the way an iridescent dragonfly looked with its wings backlit by the sun, the sound of cypress needles whispering on the wind.

Someone else might have missed the smile that hovered at the corners of her lips when he had said she had little meat on her bones, but he did not. How could he, when that slight, almost-smile damn had him holding his breath?

"I got some jerked venison and some potatoes around here someplace." He started to smile back until he felt the pull of the scar at the left corner of his mouth and stopped. He stood up, turned his back on the girl, and headed for the long wide plank tacked to the far wall where he stored his larder.

He kept his back to her while he found what he was looking for, dug some strips of dried meat from a hide bag, unwrapped a checkered rag with four potatoes inside, and set one on the plank where he did all his stand-up work. Then he took a trencher and a wooden mug off a smaller shelf high on the wall, and turned it over to knock any unwanted creatures out. He was headed for the door, intent on filling the cook pot with water from a small barrel he kept out on the porch, when the sound of her voice stopped him cold.

"Perhaps an eye patch," she whispered.

"What?"

"I'm sorry. I was thinking out loud."

She looked so terrified he wanted to put her at ease.

"It's all right. What were you thinking?"

Instead of looking at him when she spoke, she looked down at her hands. "I was just thinking . . ."

Noah had to strain to hear her.

"With some kind of an eye patch, you wouldn't look half bad."

His feet rooted themselves to the threshold. He stared at her for a heartbeat before he closed his good eye and shook his head. He had no idea what in the hell he looked like anymore. He had had no reason to care.

He turned his back on her and stepped out onto the porch, welcoming the darkness.